Alfred Duggan was born in Argentina in 1903, of partly American descent: his
Hinds, was born in Illin
grandmother (born in A
appointed Consul Gene
England at the age of
College and Balliol Co
British Natural History
the age of twenty-one he
St George, from England via Madeira, Trinidad and Panama to the Galapagos Islands, pursuing his job for the museum. In later years he travelled extensively in Greece and Turkey, studying Byzantine monuments, and in 1935 helped to excavate Constantine's Palace, Istanbul, under the auspices of the University of St Andrews. From 1938 to 1941, when he was discharged as medically unfit, he served in the London Irish Rifles (TA) and saw active service in Norway. For the rest of World War II he worked in an aircraft factory.

A prolific writer, Duggan turned out more than one book a year. His first was *Knight with Armour*, written in 1946 and published in 1950. Next came his novels *The Conscience of the King* and *The Little Emperors*, the latter dealing in lively fashion with the decline and fall of the western Roman Empire as it impinged upon the life of a British civil servant. 'As one novel follows another in pleasant succession', wrote Thomas Caldecot Chubb in the *New York Times*, 'it dawns upon this constant reader of historical fiction that in Alfred Duggan he has found an extremely gifted writer who can move into an unknown period and give it life and immediacy.' 'A specialist in decline and fall', in *Lady for Ransom* he dealt with one of the great crises of Byzantine politics. 'Mr Duggan's characters are sharply drawn', wrote Chubb, 'and, as always, he keeps his eye on the flow of history'. His 'cheerful cynicism' and satirical view of men and politics 'have introduced a refreshing new element into current historical fiction'. Orville Prescott wrote in the *New York Times*, 'Mr Duggan looks upon the past with a connoisseur's relish of villainy and violence'.

Alfred Duggan died in 1964.

By Alfred Duggan

Winter Quarters
God and My Right
Leopards and Lilies
Knight with Armour
Conscience of the King
The Little Emperors
The Lady for Ransom
Lord Geoffrey's Fancy
Thomas Becket of Canterbury
Three's Company
The Cunning of the Dove
Elephants and Castles
Founding Fathers
Count Bohemond
Sword of Pleasure
Devil's Brood
Besieger of Cities
Family Favourites
He Died Old

LORD GEOFFREY'S FANCY

Alfred Duggan

PHOENIX

A PHOENIX PAPERBACK

First published in Great Britain in 1962
by Faber & Faber Ltd
This paperback edition published in 2006
by Phoenix,
an imprint of Orion Books Ltd,
Orion House, 5 Upper St Martin's Lane,
London WC2H 9EA

1 3 5 7 9 10 8 6 4 2

Copyright © Alfred Duggan 1962

The right of Alfred Duggan to be identified as the author
of this work has been asserted by him in accordance with
the Copyright, Designs and Patents Act 1988.

A CIP catalogue record for this book
is available from the British Library.

ISBN-13 978-0-3043-6647-7
ISBN-10 0-3043-6647-1

Typeset by Deltatype Ltd,
Birkenhead, Merseyside

Printed and bound in Great Britain by
Clays Ltd, St Ives plc

The Orion Publishing Group's policy is to use papers
that are natural, renewable and recyclable products and
made from wood grown in sustainable forests. The logging
and manufacturing processes are expected to conform to
the environmental regulations of the country of origin.

www.orionbooks.co.uk

CONTENTS

. Prologue   1

1   La Cremonie   6

2   The Lady Isabel   21

3   War in Negripont   36

4   War in Satines   52

5   Sir Geoffrey Stands Trial   68

6   The Grifons of Wallachia   84

7   Pelagonie   105

8   The Grifons   125

9   The Parliament of Ladies   146

10   Jeanne de Catabas   162

11   A Pilgrimage to Rome   184

12   The Grifon Invasion   203

13   Turks and Grifons   220

14   The Return of Sir Geoffrey   239

15   Conclusion   260

   Author's Note   264

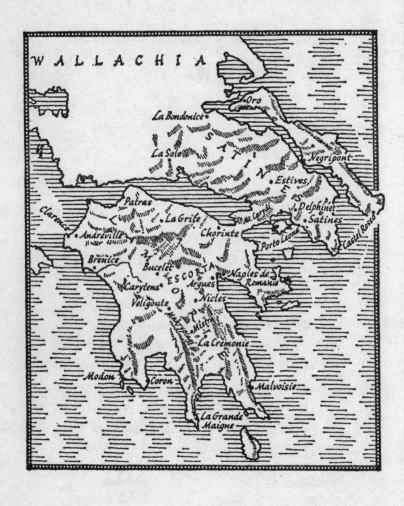

GLOSSARY OF PLACE NAMES

Andreville:	Andravida
Argues:	Argos
Brenice:	Prinitza
Mount Caride:	Carydi
Castel Rosso:	Carystos
Channel of St George:	Dardanelles
River Charbon:	Alpheus
Chorinte:	Corinth
Clarence:	Glarentza
Dalphinet:	Daphni
Estives:	Thebes
La Bondonice:	Boudonitza
La Cremonie:	Sparta (Lacedemon)
La Grande Maigne:	Maina
La Grite:	Calavryta
La Sole:	Salona
Lambasse:	Lampsacus
Lamorie:	the Morea
Malvoisie:	Monemvasia
Naples de Romanie:	Nauplia
Negripont:	Euboea
Nicles:	Nikli
Oro:	Oreus
Porto Leone:	Piraeus
Satines:	Athens
Veligoute:	Veligosti
Wallachia:	Thessaly and Epirus

PROLOGUE

Yesterday I overheard one of my grandchildren boasting that his grandmother, my wife, had been a cannibal heathen Turk until she married me. So I have decided to write down the adventures of my youth; partly to inform my descendants of their noble, Christian and civilised ancestry; but partly as some little memorial to the hero I followed in my youth, the best knight in all Romanie, my lord Geoffrey de Bruyere.

I myself was born into one of the great families of England, the Briwerrs. But my father was the younger son of a younger son, holding only a single fee from the Bohuns of the Welsh March; and in the very year of my birth, 1233, the greatness of the Briwerrs vanished with the death of Sir William Briwerr of Devon. He had been one of the foremost barons of England, a stubborn old-fashioned King's Man who told Archbishop Langton to his face that Magna Carta did not bind King Henry, for it had been extorted from his father by force. Yes, while he was alive the Briwerrs mattered. But he left no male heir, and his lands were divided among women. Nowadays there is no great magnate to look after country knights of the house of Briwerr.

Our fee will support only one knight, and I was the third son. Richard would stay at home, and in due time succeed; Henry became a clerk in the family of the Bishop of Hereford, for we all had a sound education; but I told my father, as soon I was old enough to decide, that I had no vocation for the celibate life. In our old-fashioned family we believed that rules are made to be kept, so I could not be a clerk. Since a Briwerr cannot go into trade I must fight for my bread. At twelve years of age I went to learn the profession of arms as a page in Ludlow Castle.

Then my father won a good ransom, and very generously used it to fit me out with sound mail and a destrier. When I was twenty years old, and properly equipped, Lacy of Ludlow dubbed me knight. I came home for a few days, to take leave of my parents before I went out into the world with their blessing.

My mother was interested chiefly in my private life.

'Never seduce a virgin,' she said most earnestly. 'You'll hear men boast of it, but it's a felon's trick. Half an hour's fun for the man, and the girl ruined for life. Don't rape peasants, either, even if you are ravaging the land of their lord. That's not even fun, for a fastidious gentleman. Marry a nice girl as soon as you can support a wife; and remember that nice girls don't make the first advances. In the meantime, if you please some pretty married lady there's no harm in making her happy so long as you are discreet about it. No harm in this life, I mean; you know your catechism. But chastity is too much to expect from a man, though most men take it for granted in their womanfolk. For the rest, say your prayers night and morning, try not to get excommunicated, and remember that by now your grandmother is probably out of Purgatory and can see from Heaven everything you do. Don't make her ashamed of you.'

My father was more practical.

'Choose a good lord and stick to him. Take a ransom if it's offered, and remember that there's no point in killing even a penniless foe after the fighting is over. But if you are going to kill a prisoner, tell him. Let him see a priest if one is handy; then cut his throat and get it over. King John used to lock up his captives and let them starve, not knowing whether they were meant to live or die. That's a beastly trick; no knight should ever do it. That's why you must make sure you serve a good lord. Take wages at the beginning, without giving your fealty; then you can leave without dishonour if you don't like your lord's habits.'

He shook a finger in warning.

'Some lords will try to pay you with empty titles, so don't do homage for a fee until you have seizin of it. Grand Babylon would make a very nice barony; but if you are offered it in lieu of wages point out that the infidels hold it and you are not strong enough to dislodge them. Oh, and by the way,' he added, 'remember that you come from what has been a great family. Our ancestors came here from France in King William's time, but they may have left brothers behind them. If you meet a Briwerr anywhere overseas you may claim kinship with him.'

I rode southward from the March into the King's England, with a single servant to lead my packhorse and clean my mail. At Portsmouth they were recruiting for the mesnie of the Earl of Leicester, governor of Gascony, and I enlisted at a wage without any oath of fealty. But one season in Gascony was enough for me, though Earl Simon was an honest lord. The Gascons hated him, King Henry did not trust him, and he was always short of money; I would never get rich while I followed his banner. So early in 1254 I rode eastward into Toulouse, and then on through Provence towards Lombardy. I could have found employment in Toulouse, but it would have meant serving the King of France, who is usually at war with the King of England. That might have brought trouble to my father. But on the far side of the Rhône, and even more on the far side of the Alps, no one either helped or hindered our unfortunate King Henry.

In Lombardy there were wars on every hand; but they were private fights between Guelfs and Ghibellines which were really hereditary blood feuds, and a stranger from England would never be trusted. King Manfred of Sicily was recruiting troops and had the reputation of an honest paymaster; but there were a great many Saracens in his army and all his followers were under the special excommunication of the Pope. I felt that my mother would not like me to join him. There were also papal forces, who enjoyed great spiritual benefits; but there was no money to pay them, and in my twenty-first year I needed money more urgently than a safe conduct through Purgatory. I

3

wandered uneasily through Tuscany to the lawless Abruzzi, where any castellan would give me hospitality if I fought for him in the next skirmish; but they were all treacherous brigands, and I had no desire to stay with them.

Then one evening at supper in a little mountain castle I sat beside a French knight on his way home from Acre, where King Louis had discharged him as too sick for further warfare. It was pleasant to talk proper French again after the barbarous jargon of the Italians, and we quickly became friends. When I had told him my story he gave me sound advice.

'You should try Outremer,' he said. 'Can you pay for your journey?'

'I can pay for a sea voyage,' I answered. 'A few days ago a knight was killed who had a gold chain round his neck, and I was first to reach the body. But what is there for me in Outremer? I want to marry, so the Temple and the Hospital are no good. A man of my birth can't open a shop in Acre. The barons of the land have no fees to spare for strangers. I suppose King Louis would hire my sword, but they say he won't be staying out there much longer.'

'Outremer is more than the Kingdom of Jerusalem,' said the Frenchman. 'There is all Romanie to choose from. Constantinople is a dead end, with schismatic Grifons raiding right up to the walls. But in Lamorie there are wealthy French barons, eager to enlist good knights. The lord of Satines is a de la Roche from Burgundy, and the Prince of Lamorie a Villehardouin from Champagne. He has recently conquered fresh cities and castles from the Grifons, and he will have vacant fees. Over there we are all Franks together, you know, even those who come from England. The Grifons, who have never forgotten Charlemagne, call everyone a Frank who hears Mass in Latin. To them even Germans and Italians are Franks.'

'Though of course they cannot compare with genuine north Frenchmen,' I took him up. 'It seems to be the right place for a penniless knight. Who is the overlord of these princes and barons?'

'That's the beauty of it,' he said with a smile, 'they haven't one. At the conquest, fifty years ago, it was arranged that they should owe service to the King of Salonique. But Montferrat of Salonique was killed by the Bulgars, and his kingdom died with him. So the Franks of Lamorie and Satines acknowledge no overlord at all, and they get on very well without one.'

'It sounds a place that would suit me,' I answered. 'Tell me how I get there.' We talked far into the night.

CHAPTER ONE

La Cremonie

I left my Italian servant in his own country, for across the water I would need a man who spoke the local language. At Bari I took passage in a Venetian ship. The Venetians stood neutral in the quarrel between Guelf and Ghibellines, and their ships traded to any harbour except those held by Pisa or Genoa, their mortal enemies. After coasting down a mountainous shore we reached Clarence in Lamorie. There I landed, and rode a few miles to the little town of Andreville, where the Princes of Lamorie have their lawcourt and their family tomb. But recently Prince William had fixed his chief residence in the town of La Cremonie farther to the south-east, which he had newly conquered from the Grifons. I was told that the road was safe and peaceful, as were in that happy time all the roads of Lamorie. So I set off to visit the court, with only my new servant for company.

In those days Lamorie was the most prosperous land in the world, as well as the fairest. It is nearly an island, joined to the lordship of Satines only by a narrow isthmus; the whole of it was under the rule of Prince William who kept good peace. On the seas round about the only shipping was Italian; and the Venetians, though they fought the Genoese wherever they met them, kept down pirates. Neither infidel nor Grifon dared sail so far to the west. By every mountain pass there were great castles, but many towns were unwalled. I met merchants from Florence and Siena, journeying to buy the currants of Patras or the silk of Estives. They rode without escort for they carried no money; in any market they might cash their sealed letters of credit.

It is hard to describe to a northerner the beauty of that land. Great mountains shut in every horizon, but between them stretch level plains, well cultivated. The mountains are taller and steeper than anything you will see in Wales, and the narrow roads that climb them are most frightening; though they were paved and embanked by the mighty men of old. Stone bridges cross every stream, and in the plains stand huge buildings of solid marble, intricately carved. You see something of the sort in Italy, but the old Italian idol-houses were built of brick under a marble facing, and as a rule someone has stolen the marble veneer. In Lamorie the solid marble keeps its dignity, even after the roof has gone. Orderly plantations of olives and mulberries make the plains seem like a pleasure garden, and wherever the hillside is not too steep thrifty Grifons sow their grain. Whitewashed churches stand at every crossroad, even in open country; they are roofed with domes, such as I had seen in Italy. But in Italy a dome is something special, reserved for an important building; here you saw them everywhere.

But the beauty of Lamorie does not reside in any particular building or mountain. Something in the quality of the light would make a lazar-house look beautiful. Except in mid-winter the sun shines all day from a flawless sky, and at night the stars burn close at hand. The sea is a level plain of purple; rock-shadows move over the violet mountains; a knight glows in the plain tinctures of heraldry, until when I first came home even the golden leopards of Anjou seemed dull and dingy. Remember that in this land of the silkworm every respectable man or woman dresses in brilliant silk. White houses, honey-coloured marble, purple mountains, red ploughland, blue sea and blue sky – Lamorie is the fairest land in the world, and to breathe its air makes a man feel young and brave.

The villages on my way were thickly inhabited, with industrious Grifon peasants who were more than a match for a Frank when I bargained for a jug of wine or a night's lodging.

As a rule my servant could cope with them. Theodore was a young Gasmule, son of a Grifon mother and a Frank father, who had attached himself to me when I landed at Clarence. He spoke the French of Champagne with a slight accent, and Greek like a native. He cheated me in moderation whenever I spent a penny, but he did his best to stop my being cheated by others. I suppose he was a coward, since he chose to hang about Clarence and prey on strangers, though Gasmules are welcome in both Frankish and Grifon armies; but since I never put his courage to the test I cannot be sure.

Theodore told me that the peasants were in general content under Frankish rule. The taxes were lower than in the days of their Emperor, and our justice is fairer and very much cheaper; he added with a grin that we are more easily deceived than the Grifon officials who used to keep them in order. What they really wanted more than anything else was freedom to practise the schismatic rites of their church, and this Prince William permitted. Of course he could not openly countenance heresy and schism, but he allowed Grifon priests to serve their parish churches after their own fashion on condition they swore obedience to Latin bishops. For centuries these peasants had been downtrodden taxpayers, supporting the splendour of the imperial court and getting absolutely nothing in return for their money. They were men of peace, and it would be useless to call them out even in the *arriere-ban*; but they would obey Frankish lords, as they would obey anyone who held the castles looming over their villages.

I have said that Prince William ruled all Lamorie, but this was not wholly accurate. On the last day of my journey to La Cremonie a great range of mountains filled the horizon on our left, and Theodore glanced nervously at the peaks. He explained that among the glens of these mountains live the Esclavons of Escorta, wild mountaineers who acknowledge no lord. Their warriors come to battle on foot, so they cannot meet Franks in the field. But they skip over their mountains by paths no stranger can follow; and since they are too ignorant to plough they come down whenever they feel hungry to plunder in the lowland villages.

'But on the plain we shall be safe from them,' he added. 'They fear even one man on horseback. And to get here from their mountains they must pass the castle of Carytena, which was built to keep them in. They prefer to raid northwards. I am glad the Prince is at La Cremonie and not at Chorinte, which lies at the end of that dangerous northern road.'

In the afternoon we came in sight of the low unimpressive walls of La Cremonie, which lies in a rich valley between two jagged mountains. The walls still showed the scars of Prince William's capture a few years ago. For nowadays La Cremonie depends for protection on the mighty castle of Mistra which the Prince has built on a spur of the mountain above it. Whoever holds Mistra holds La Cremonie. All that valley is very good land, with fine grazing for oxen; a precious thing in Lamorie, where sheep range on every hill but horned cattle are few.

We entered the town just before sunset, and went straight to the Prince's hall. This was a long building set in a huddle of houses, with no open space before it and without fortification; but it was roofed with a vault of masonry, like a basilica, which made it look imposing though it was only a single storey high.

At the door stood a sentry, who called a French-speaking under-steward when he saw I was a gentleman of quality from the west. The steward, an Italian of the kind who pretends to knighthood and passes his spare time selling groceries, made me welcome in the most gratifying way. Before I entered the hall I saw Theodore and the horses bedded down in dry straw; though the steward in his burgess fashion thought it unfitting that a knight should look to the welfare of his following before he found a place for himself.

The Italian did not recognise the arms of Briwerr on my shield, though he took in the label of cadency which marked me as a younger son. His manner was a little patronising as he asked me why I sought audience with Prince William of Lamorie.

'You are welcome,' he said smugly, 'but it would be

convenient if you will tell me on what errand you have come. Have you left home to escape the gallows, to win fame as a knight-errant, or merely to earn a livelihood? By what name shall I announce you?'

'I am Sir William de Briwerr, from England,' I answered with some stiffness. 'No gallows waits for me at home, and I never expect to be famous. If the Prince will hire me I shall be glad to serve him, but if he already has swords enough I shall go on to Constantinople.'

'Constantinople today is no place for a knight,' he said with a smirk, 'unless you are willing to be paid in holy bones. That's all the Emperor has to offer, now that he has sold the lead off his palace roof. But our Prince will always find room for another good western sword.'

He led me into the long hall, where hundreds of knights and ladies sat drinking on the benches. On the dais at the far end was a table of state with no less than twelve chairs behind it, and I recalled that this must be about the time of the Michaelmas parliament when vassals visit their lords; for on my journey I had lost count of the calendar.

The Prince received me graciously, urging me to be his guest for the few days of the parliament until his marshal had time to talk business with me. He was a tall knight of about forty, with long fair hair and a rabbit mouth, very splendidly dressed; his French had a faint Levantine accent.

A servant showed me to a vacant place at one of the lower tables. As I drew my knife to cut off a piece of meat I had the first of many surprises in this strange world of Romanie. A page leaned over my shoulder and placed a metal eating-prong before me.

In Italy I had heard rumours of this dirty Grifon habit, current in Constantinople because Grifons can't be bothered to wash their hands properly between the courses; but I had not expected to meet it in a decent Frankish court. However, I saw that all my neighbours were using these bone-handled eating-prongs; so I felt mine cautiously to make sure that the points were not sharp enough to damage my mouth and then stuck it into my lump of beef. Then I looked about the hall, to see what other novelties might be waiting for me in this foreign land.

The surcoat and tunic I had bought in Milan were cut correctly, but the fine woollen cloth seemed clumsy and provincial when so many of my neighbours wore silk. Every man kept his long hair tidy under a white linen coif, tied with strings below the chin; even the youths wore beards, curled and combed as carefully as their hair. The dresses of the ladies were very elaborate, but I shall not attempt to describe them. I saw that my cropped head and shaven chin were definitely wrong; but they could easily be put right.

Everyone spoke in French or Italian, which was a relief; but Grifon words popped up here and there, and they would break off to speak in Grifon to a servant without any fumbling, showing that they were at home in both languages. I was certainly in a foreign land. I kept my eyes on my food and said nothing, for fear of making some social blunder. My neighbours were not interested in yet another stranger, and in peace I ate very good food and drank very fine wine.

Presently servants began to remove the tables, and most of the company went off to sleep in their own apartments somewhere in the town; it seems that in Romanie halls are not used for sleeping as in the west. I shared the straw of the stable with my destrier and my servant. In that warm climate it was as comfortable as a bed.

On the next morning, after a solemn High Mass very badly sung by a scratch collection of clerks (for Romanie gets only the leavings of the Latin church), the parliament of Lamorie tried several cases of disputed inheritance. I kept away, for fear of being expelled with ignomiy as a landless stranger. But this was the last day of the Michaelmas parliament, and by dinner-time I was told that the marshal was at liberty and ready for business. In the shade of a church porch I found Sir John de Neuilly, marshal of Lamorie, leaning against a pillar.

'Ah, Sir William,' he said in a friendly voice, 'you have come to help defend Romanie from infidels and schismatics. That entitles you to the privilege of a Crusader, you know, if you are in trouble at home. But the steward tells me you have not so far committed any capital crime. We shall be very glad to employ you, as a household knight at the usual daily wage. But I am afraid we can't offer you a fee until we conquer more land from the Grifons, and even then there is a long waiting list.'

'I understand, my lord. I should like a fee of my own, and before I die I hope to get one. But in the meantime service for wages will suit me very well.'

'Have you in mind any particular lord? Prince William pays wages to more than eight hundred knights, and his mesnie is already as big as his wealth will support. It would suit us better if you chose to serve one of his barons, though of course we don't want to lose you. The Prince will employ you rather than see you go home. No, we mustn't lose you, Sir William – er – I forget your family name?'

'Briwerr, my lord, from the March of Wales beyond the Kingdom of England. Of course my family is French by origin, like most of the knighthood of England.'

'Bri-werr, Bri-werr,' he muttered, pronouncing it in different ways as he turned it over on his tongue. 'A French name all right, a bit altered by barbarous northern speech. That gives me an idea. You would do better in a smaller mesnie than the Prince's and the lord I suggest is certainly worthy to command you. Come with me and meet Sir Geoffrey.'

He bustled me along through narrow streets, shaded by tall houses whose tiled eaves left only a narrow ribbon of sky. In Italy I had met this habit of walking about a town; but it still seemed strange to go on foot with a lord of his distinction. I was careful not to damage my spurs on the cobbles; Sir John wore high soft Grifon boots without spurs.

We came to an inn, where escutcheons hanging from the windows marked the quarters of noble guests. 'One wolf's-head, you see, and on your surcoat are three. But there's nothing strange in that, since you come from another kingdom.'

One of the painted escutcheons bore a single wolf's-head, in the Briwerr tinctures. 'Will you wait below a minute?'

I heard him inquire for the lord Geoffrey de Bruyère, and understood the scheme in his mind. It seemed to me a good one. This lord of Outremer might or might not be my cousin; if he were, our common ancestor must have lived about two hundred years ago. But a tie of kinship between lord and knight, even imaginary kinship, is stronger than the mere bond of wages.

Presently Sir John came downstairs with a young lord, very magnificently dressed. But before I had time to take in more than the general effect the young man gathered me up in the formal embrace usually exchanged between equals, and then stepped back with a dazzling smile to take a look at me.

'Welcome to Romanie, cousin William,' he said, grinning. 'Will you join my mesnie? There aren't half enough of us Bruyeres in Lamorie, in fact until you arrived I was the only one. I'm very glad to have a new cousin, even though we can't trace our exact degree of kinship.' Here he winked, to show that he knew as well as I did that the relationship probably existed only in Sir John's ingenious mind.

'There will be another Bruyere next year, God willing,' said the marshal with a smirk.

'Tut tut, Sir John, I am still an innocent bachelor. He means, cousin, that when this parliament is over I go to Estives to fetch my affianced bride. I want to take a good mesnie to the wedding, naturally, and another genuine western knight will add to my splendour. Now this evening I must attend the Prince's council, so you will have to dine with the general company in hall. Tomorrow you show your horse and arms to my constable, Sir John de Catabas. Only a formality, of course, but old John might take offence if we skipped it. He will fix up your rate of pay and all the other tiresome details, and you can arrange with him whether you serve me for a weekly wage or whether you take oath to be my man until I can find you a fee. It wouldn't be fair to ask you to decide now, in my presence. You may be hating the sight of me, and too polite to say so. Then a couple more days in La Cremonie, giving uncle the benefit of my sage advice. After that we all go back to Carytena to put on our best clothes, and on to Estives for a gay and gorgeous wedding. That's a pleasant prospect, isn't it? Aren't you grateful to the marshal of Lamorie for bringing us together? I am. Now I must see my steward, or I shan't have any money when I bring my bride home.' With a wave of the hand and another dazzling smile he hurried off.

After thanking the marshal I went to look over my mail and horse in readiness for the next day.

I was eager to serve Sir Geoffrey. I have repeated his words, which I shall never forget; but I cannot describe the charm of his manner. He was about twenty-five years of age, still half a boy but a few years older than myself, as it was right that my leader should be. He was not very tall; but he moved with a graceful swagger, broad shouldered, slim waisted. His golden hair brushed his shoulders, and he sported an absurd little wisp of golden beard. His hands were very clean and well tended (which was common enough in Romanie) and his long silken surcoat fitted him perfectly. His smile was the most delightful I have ever seen; he looked on every stranger as a friend and on the world as a queer but amusing place. From the coif which controlled his curls to the golden spurs which never got in his way as he walked, he was the image of a knight who would have won fame at King Arthur's Round Table.

I had found a good lord, rich and noble and willing to call me cousin. For the rest of the day I walked on air.

In the evening I drifted into the Prince's hall, where there would be food and drink for any well-born Frank at any hour until bedtime. A servant recognised me, and explained that Sir Geoffrey had left word that I was to dine among his retainers. That was cheering evidence that my lord looked after his followers, and I was anxious to see my future companions. I was shown to a long table in a corner, where among the household of Bruyere I sat down modestly just above the salt.

A servant immediately brought me cold mutton and a jug of local wine, which tastes of resin but is otherwise wholesome. Since I was very late for dinner this was generous treatment. Once I knew I would be fed I looked round at my neighbours, who had dined and were passing the time with drink and conversation.

In my modesty I had taken the last place above the salt. On my right was a gap, and then an elderly Grifon who looked like a huntsman; he was talking busily in his own tongue and I did not care to interrupt him. On my left, I saw with some annoyance, sat a pretty young woman.

On the wages of a household knight I could not afford to marry; so that social intercourse with ladies of my own class, the tail-end of the gentry, was a waste of time. A great lady might take me as her lover, if I tried hard enough; and my spurs would win me the favours of any servant-girl if I chose to condescend. But with a poor lady it is marriage or nothing; and poor ladies want to marry land, not wages. If I tried to be pleasant to this chance companion I ran the risk of a snub.

But the young lady herself turned to me, with the easy manners that are more common in Romanie than in the west. 'You must be the new Frankish knight,' she said with an encouraging smile, 'the long-lost cousin who turned up just in time for the wedding. Tell me, how does it feel to find an unexpected cousin? If you are really his cousin, that is. And what do you think of Prince William's hall in La Cremonie? If you find any of our customs strange perhaps I can explain them to you.'

The lady smiled happily. She was about seventeen, with a pleasant expression; though her language was not quite the French of France.

'I felt honoured that the lord Geoffrey should recognise me as a cousin,' I said carefully, determined not to give offence in this strange company. 'There is no record of our relationship, but two hundred years ago my ancestors certainly lived in France. Until recently the Briwerrs were great lords in England, though now their barony has been divided among heiresses; and in any case I am a landless younger son from a cadet branch. All the same, it is not impossible that I am kin to the lord Geoffrey, as the marshal of Lamorie suggested before the idea had entered my head.'

I wanted to make it clear that I had not turned up as a poor relation; Sir John de Neuilly had seen the possibility without any prompting from me.

'I expect you are cousins, then,' she said carelessly. 'All the poor gentry have cousins among the great. I myself am a cousin of the King of France; though there is a bastardy in the line, naturally. My mother's father was a Branas, son of Theodore Branas and the lady Agnes, daughter of the King of France and widow of the Greek Emperor. Of course he wasn't married to my grandmother. My parents served in the household of the Frankish Emperors, until they came to Lamorie in the train of the other lady Agnes, the daughter of the Frankish Emperor who married Prince Geoffrey. He was the elder brother of our present Prince William. I was born in the great city, though I have lived most of my life in Lamorie. My mother has just found me a place in the household of Bruyere, since our new lady from Satines will need attendants who know the country.'

'Then you are not entirely French, madam?' I said politely, overwhelmed by this cataract of information about descents unknown to me.

'Well done, sir knight, you didn't ask if I was a Gasmule. That is a rude word. Never use it unless you mean to give offence. No, I suppose I am more Roman than Frank. That's another stumbling block, by the way. Grifon is an insult, and Greek, though clerks use it when they try to be correct, is not much better. The people who lived here before the conquest are the Romans of New Rome. Sir Geoffrey is careful always to call the native gentry Romans; that's one reason why they are so fond of him. I am more of a Roman than anything else, with a little Frankish blood. My name is Melisande Melissena. But my parents lived all their lives among Franks, and I think of myself as a Frank, or a follower of the Franks.'

'Thank you, demoiselle. I am ignorant of the customs of Romanie. There's nothing more annoying than to give offence when you don't mean to, though it's useful to know a few local expressions that are definitely insulting. Now please tell me more about Romanie and Lamorie. Start with my new cousin, Sir Geoffrey. Is he really a very great lord hereabouts?'

'Indeed he is. Noble blood, strong castles, and a rich fee. He is one of the twelve Barons of the Conquest, the peers of Lamorie. Prince William is himself a Baron of the Conquest. His father took the Principality from the Champlittes, but he was only a baron to start with. A complicated story, too complicated to tell in mixed company. Hugh de Bruyere, the conqueror, married the sister of Prince William, the lady Elizabeth who is the mother of Sir Geoffrey. You may not meet her; she hates Carytena and lives in her own dower lands. So Sir Geoffrey is the nephew of his lord, and high in his favour. He is also a gallant knight, the most gallant of all the young Franks born out here. You see, his barony of Escorta is really a border fee, though it's right in the middle of the Principality. The savages in the hills want to raid the lowlands and Sir Geoffrey holds them in check. They say he can get his horse over mountains where even the wild Esclavons must climb with their hands. You couldn't have chosen a better lord. Even the peasants love him.'

'Thank you, madam. And the bride he will marry shortly? Is she worthy of him?'

'I have never seen her, but she ought to be. Her father is the Megaskyr of Satines. That's a Greek title, meaning Great Lord; because Satines is more than an ordinary lordship. He holds it direct from God, too, with no other overlord. But he is the vassal of Prince William for some castles in the south, whereas Prince William owes homage to no man. Satines is only a village with a strong castle; but with it goes the rich town of Estives, where they weave the best silk in the world. The de la

Roches are great lords indeed, as I believe they were great lords in Burgundy. It is an honour for a Bruyere to marry their daughter, but I suppose they are pleased at the alliance with Prince William.'

The lady Melisande chattered eagerly about pedigrees. I wondered cynically how well she really knew these great men and the nuances of their social position. I thought of a test question, which had been told me in Italy.

'Tell me, demoiselle,' I asked innocently, 'is the Church here truly at peace, or is there strife between Latins and natives?'

'That I would hardly know, sir,' she answered with a blank face; but there was a mischievous twinkle in her eye. 'I hear the Latin Mass only, and never worship in schismatic churches. In general you will find that true of everyone in Romanie who sits, as we do, above the salt.' She gazed at the narrow gap between my seat and the great silver salt-cellar. It was a fair point; if she was barely among the gentry I sat even lower.

'But I'll tell you one thing,' she went on with more animation. 'The pictures in the native churches, icons they call them, have greater power in Romanie than our Latin statues. If you are in trouble and you want a saint to help you, offer silver to an icon, don't burn candles before a statue. Even the Archbishop of Patras did that when his best hawk flew away; and what's more, the bird came back. This country belongs to the icons. Never be rude to them.'

So the lady was more than a ready retailer of pedigrees. She could take a point in conversation, and throw back the ball. I looked forward to further talks with her when we were both in the Bruyere castle high among the hostile mountains.

Sir John de Catabas, constable of the barony of Escorta, was a middle-aged knight who moved stiffly and complained of rheumatism. But he knew his business, and made up his mind quickly. We soon agreed on a wage, which seemed to me very generous; but in those days Lamorie was full of gold and silver, and prices were high. On his advice I got rid of my rogue of a servant, who went back to Clarence to pick up another innocent foreigner. Until we were in the castle of Carytena the Bruyere grooms would look after my horse, and then I could engage a native of the barony. I was content with my employment. In the last two summers I had seen many great households, in Gascony and Italy. There was no lack of money in Sir Geoffrey's mesnie, and a comforting air of efficiency about the military arrangements. My wages would be paid punctually, and in war I would probably be on the winning side. No stipendiary knight can ask for more.

I liked my comrades also, and in particular the lady Melisande Melissena. Luckily she seemed to like me too, in spite of hot competition from other bachelor knights; for at this parliament there was a shortage of ladies.

The Princess of Lamorie lay sick in Andreville, and Sir Geoffrey was unmarried, as were several of the other great barons. Among the elderly were numerous widowers, for Franks find Romanie unhealthy, and many ladies die of fever in their first years oversea. So do many lords, of course, but if they held land someone will come from the west to inherit it; a lord who has an heir will not always bother to marry again after his wife dies.

Before the gathering broke up there was a tournament, as is customary in most countries after a parliament; only in England, I think, is this diversion illegal. I watched, noting that the jousting was of very high standard, as good as one would see in France. But I did not take part. I was in no position to wager horse and mail on a single encounter; besides, like most English knights, I am a poor lance in single combat for lack of early practice. My lord, Sir Geoffrey, rode very skilfully at the ring; but he did not ride in the Round Table because he was known to be the best jouster in Romanie and no one would face him. He refused to ride in the mellay, which was a very tame affair with wooden swords. The Prince forbade anything more exciting, since Lamorie depends on its knights and he did not wish them to be injured. Sir Geoffrey thought such a scrimmage beneath his dignity.

But the barony of Escorta maintained its reputation. Our constable, Sir John de Catabas, won the prize in the Round Table. I was surprised to see it, for he was stiff and no longer young; but he rode as though part of his horse, which obeyed him as though they were one creature with two heads. The prize was a pair of scented gloves, and he looked rather absurd as he received it at the hands of a pretty little damsel who can't have been older than twelve. Sir John was no lady's man; he looked as awkward as he probably felt, stiffly kissing her hand before she could offer her cheek. But though he was shy of the ladies he was a gallant and debonair knight in the field, and he generously allowed the defeated to take back their horses and arms in exchange for a few gold pieces. Everyone liked Sir John, all the more because it was so easy to make jokes about him.

CHAPTER TWO

The Lady Isabel

To a Frank all the buildings of Romanie are strange, but the castle of Carytena is really astonishing. It overhangs a stupendous gorge, in which a swift stream rushes westward; this is all the more strange because the stream leaves a level plain to flow between high mountains, instead of the other way round as you might expect. On a crag above the gorge, joined to the northern range by a low saddle, stands the citadel of Carytena; but the outer bailey takes in the whole crag, so that as soon as you cross the river you face the lower gate. The fine masonry bridge, built by Sir Geoffrey at his own charges, is a famous landmark; for its pointed arch was a novelty to the peasants. On it stands a little chapel dedicated to St Christopher, where every traveller stops to say a prayer; for any journey through Escorta will be dangerous.

From the keep you look eastward to the Mesaree, the central plain of Lamorie, where Sir Geoffrey's peasants ploughed under his strong protection; on every side this plain is girdled by the steep mountains of the Esclavons. Westward lies the gloomy gorge, and to north and south mountains shut in the view. The path from the bridge to the inner gate zigzags up the slope, too steep for a more direct approach. It must be one of the strongest castles in the world, but as a home it is undoubtedly gloomy.

Much of the crowded summit is taken up with vaulted water cisterns; though below the donjon is a little spring, and in peacetime mules carry water from the river. Sir Geoffrey's fine hall was paved with white marble, as were the solar and chamber opening off it. The other buildings were cut up into many small rooms, after the fashion of those parts; for Grifons dislike living in a perpetual crowd as we do in the west. I myself had a corner of a little square room, which I shared with three other household knights, an Italian and two Frenchmen; when I served Earl Simon in Gascony I had bedded down among the sleepers in the hall.

Sir Geoffrey had seen the castle finished, not ten years ago. He thought it a splendid and commodious palace, for he had been born and bred in the mountains of Escorta. But as soon as his mother was widowed she went to live with her brother in level Andreville. The greatest inconvenience of Carytena was that horses had to pick their way down to the bridge before you could let them out into a trot, so that exercising them was tedious and difficult. But on top of that windy keep you certainly felt safe from your enemies.

At this time there were only four ladies in the castle: Melisande and two other young damsels, under the care of an elderly widow whose husband had been a vassal of Bruyere until the Esclavons caught him. Sir Geoffrey looked after his dependants, and had invented the post of lady-housekeeper to provide for poor madam Magdalen. All the household knights buzzed round the three damsels; but Melisande, as fresh to Carytena as I was, seemed pleased to poke about the strange place in my company.

'Perhaps it won't be so gloomy when the bride comes here with her gay young ladies,' she said hopefully. 'Poor madam Isabel! She is younger than I am, so they say. She will find this a great change from Estives in its grassy plain, and from Satines where you smell the thyme and the sea. She will miss the burgesses too. Burgesses are often more lively and intelligent than provincial knights. In Romanie we mingle with Franks of every class, since there are so few of us in the country. Most of the merchants of Estives are gay, fashionable Tuscans. This won't be a bit like the crowded de la Roche castles by the shore.

I hope she has a full nursery. Otherwise I don't know how she will fill her days.'

'Not even any hunting,' I added, 'unless she rides a mule. Have you ever seen anything like these roads? Yet they tell me we have to ride after the Esclavons. On foot you cannot catch them.'

'You will get used to it, Sir William. In Romanie we ride wherever a goat can find foothold. Ride a local nag, and keep your great war-horse for battles in the open plain. The ponies of these parts never put a foot wrong. Drop your reins, if need be shut your eyes, and a native pony will take you to the end of your journey.'

That sounded comforting, and later I discovered that it was more or less true. But during that autumn the Esclavons gave us no trouble, since Franks riding to La Cremonie had traversed every road in their land. Winter and spring are their favourite times for raiding, when snow blocks the passes and fords are flooded. During our short stay, before we set out for Satines, I did not put on my mail.

For the journey I wore mail, partly because we must ride northward through the heart of the mountains, partly because Sir Geoffrey wished to make a display of his power in the lands of his father-in-law. But in the baggage I brought a silk surcoat and a fine woollen tunic in the colours of Bruyere, an extra livery which Sir Geoffrey had given to all his household knights in honour of the wedding. We were a small army, all the warriors of Escorta except for the small permanent garrison of Carytena. We reached the isthmus without incident, though some of the roads we travelled seemed to me at first sight impassable.

We hurried, to have time to finish the festivities before Advent, which is taken more seriously in Romanie than in the west. Estives is the chief town of the Megaskyr, as even Franks then called Sir Guy de la Roche; but the wedding was to be celebrated in Satines, which was his favourite residence and graced with a famous church. I was warned that this church would surprise me when I saw it, but the reality surpassed my expectation.

Satines is a little unwalled village, so near the sea that no one bothers to build fine houses because pirates often land to burn it. But all around are the great marble ruins of the ancient; long ago it must have been an important place. As you come to it from the west you see first a tall pointed hill, very steep, with a little church on it. That is where you would expect to find the castle. Instead the citadel crowns a lower, flat-topped hill, which does not look nearly so strong. Then as you get nearer you see that the sides of this hill have been built up with masonry into sheer vertical walls. The flat summit has room for many fine buildings of pale marble; but the glory of it is the great many-columned cathedral of Our Lady.

In Italy there are more spacious cathedrals; in parts of France they nowadays build higher into the sky. But there is no church more beautiful, more delightful, more satisfying than Our Lady of Satines. All is of smooth honey-coloured marble, exquisitely joined; and on the outer wall, within the colonnade, is carved a great procession bringing offerings to Our Lady in glory. Round the roof there are smaller carvings of saints warring against very queer devils, but no one could tell me what legends they illustrate. The whole thing was built by St Denys the Areopagite, a native of these parts, to the designs of St Luke.

You enter the citadel by an imposing stair. The marble gatehouse above has been made into a small but luxurious palace for the Megaskyr and his household.

In this wonderful setting the lady Isabel de la Roche, daughter of the Megaskyr of Satines, was married to Sir Geoffrey de Bruyere of Escorta, a baron of the conquest of Lamorie. Afterwards the whole company feasted at long tables in the open air, in the village below the citadel.

Naturally I was placed far from the high table, but in that clear air you see every detail. The de la Roches and their household seemed to be mostly jolly, red-cheeked Burgundians, rather coarser and more beefy than true Frenchmen; but the lady Isabel was beautiful.

She was sixteen, tall and slim, grey-eyed, with golden hair hanging to her waist in token of maidenhood. She held herself very straight, and looked remarkably calm during all the excitement. Her face was lightly freckled but the skin of her neck was quite white; her hands were delicate yet capable. We all thought Sir Geoffrey a very lucky man, to gain so much beauty with high birth and a rich dowry thrown in. He thought so too, from the way he gazed after his bride. She met his glance, and obviously liked what she saw.

The marriage was a dynastic alliance, and I believe the happy couple met for the first time at the altar. But they proceeded to fall in love at first sight. It was a love-match, as well as the outcome of cautious political bargaining.

On the second day of the feast, news reached us that the Princess Carintana of Lamorie, wife to Prince William, had died in Andreville. She had been Sir Geoffrey's aunt by marriage, and everyone was sorry that she had died young and childless; in Satines there was court mourning, and the tournament arranged for the next day was cancelled. We all prepared to go home, as soon as we could round up our baggage animals.

During the festivities I had seen nothing of Melisande, but on the journey home I rode beside her whenever the track was wide enough for two horses abreast. She was a stimulating companion. Thanks to her Frankish upbringing she could cope with the usual protestations of courtly love, the only manner of talking to a lady that I had been taught as a boy at Ludlow; but her eastern blood made her alive to little niceties of affection and enmity that a Frankish lady in her position would never have bothered to notice.

I began to see also that she was very beautiful, though her looks were not of the kind I had been brought up to admire. On the March we praise golden hair and a skin as white as snow; but Melisande's glowing black eyes and olive skin seemed better suited to the translucent air of Romanie.

'It's very lucky that Sir Geoffrey and his bride should be in love with one another,' she said as our horses ambled side by side. 'This match was meant to bind together Lamorie and Satines, and if they had quarrelled all the Franks of Romanie might have to choose sides in a dangerous civil war. You see, William, the Megaskyr is in an awkward position. In theory he is the peer of the Prince of Lamorie, neither owing homage to any lord except a non-existent King of Salonique. But the Megaskyr also holds two fees in the south, Argues and Naples de Romanie; and for them he owes homage to the Prince. Naturally, he has never performed his homage; something has always turned up to keep him at home when he ought to be kneeling to a lord who is in most ways his equal. But one day Lamorie will go to war, and Sir Guy de la Roche will be summoned to lead the knight service of Argues and Naples under the banner of Villehardouin. Then he can send his son-in-law to serve in his stead, a son-in-law who would have to serve Prince William anyway. No danger of a great lord having to take orders from a lord no greater than he. And perhaps one day, if Isabel has children and the young de la Roches continue to die in their cradles, Lamorie and Satines will be united into one great Frankish principality.'

'No need to explain, my lady,' I answered cheerfully. 'Any knight born in England has heard of these problems since he was breeched. Our King owes the homage of Gascony to the King of France, and never performs it. The King of Scots owes the homage of Huntingdon to our King Henry, and never performs it. It's all great nonsense anyway. Little knights like me must be true to our lords, or no one will employ us. A great baron or a prince may fight on whichever side he likes; he is never reproached for felony to his lord.'

'But you see how important it is that this marriage should be a success? Isn't it lucky that Isabel loves her lord? Don't you think her beautiful?'

This was twice that Melisande had referred to her lady as Isabel, with no more formal title. I hugged myself with delight.

She must think of me as a very close friend, with whom she could speak her thoughts in complete confidence.

'Do you attend my lady when she dresses?' I asked, to keep the conversation going. 'Is it easy to get on with her?'

'She's quite charming. I waited on her this morning, when we had to make such an early start. Getting up at dawn in riding clothes is a test of anyone's temper. But dear Isabel enjoys long rides, she told me so. She is wonderfully happy, and we all like waiting on her. She never forgets that we are ladies. My mother warned me that some young brides treat their ladies like common servants, because they don't know any other way of enforcing their authority.'

'There's great courtesy in Romanie,' I agreed. 'I like it here. I can't think why more landless knights don't come out from the west.'

'No hope of further conquest, that's why,' said Melisande at once. 'Jerusalem lost, and the inland of Syria. The Emperor afraid to venture beyond the walls of Constantinople. France full of returned Crusaders whose castles have fallen to the infidel. In the west they see us as tottering to disaster. And so we are, in all the lands of Outremer except Lamorie and Satines.'

'You may be right, though fear of defeat should never keep a good knight at home when there is wealth to be won from schismatics and infidels. Here at least we are safe. I have never seen such mighty castles.' I nodded towards the great flat-topped citadel of Chorinte, looming above us as we rode through the isthmus.

When we reached Carytena bad news awaited poor Melisande. Her mother had died suddenly of some obscure fever, in the great hall at Andreville where she served the lady Agnes, widow of the late Prince of Lamorie. Franks often die suddenly in these hot foreign lands, where the air and water do not suit us; it is the sole disadvantage of Outremer.

Melisande was now completely orphaned, for her father had died of the plague a few years ago. No marriage had been arranged for her, and she had no dowry. Her future looked bleak. While she was young and strong she might continue as a waiting lady in some great household, dining above the salt and clothed at the Christmas livery. But her wages were only four golden hyperpers a year, with occasional presents when her lady felt generous; and to maintain her dignity she must from time to time tip the common servants. If she lived to grow old she would end as an unwanted pensioner, sitting all day by someone else's fire, grubby and fusty for lack of soap and clean linen, hated by servants as an encumbrance, avoided as a bore by the younger ladies, idle, neglected, miserable. At Ludlow there had been an old lady of that kind, only survivor of a massacre. I had heard her regret that the Welsh spared her when they killed her father and three brothers; it would have been better if she had died young and fair and full of hope.

For a whole day I was sorry for Melisande; until at last I understood that I was more than sorry, I loved her. When I thought over the matter I was surprised to see that there was no reason why we should not marry: that is, if she would have me. Except among the peasantry I had never heard of a marriage of this kind; every married knight I knew had taken the bride chosen for him by his parents, chosen for her dowry rather than her charm. But there is no law forbidding the gentry to marry for love, if they choose to. In some ways the world would be a better place if it happened more often; instead of all this tedious convention of courteous love, with knights moaning in every corner over an unattainable mistress while they neglect their own wedded wives.

It is easier to behave unconventionally in a foreign land where no one knows your family; a proof of this is that the first person to whom I broached my new idea was Melisande herself. I found her alone on a tower, catching a last glimpse of the midday sun before it went behind the southern mountains. With deliberation I knelt down on one knee to make my formal declaration. Then, seeing that she was confused by the novel form of the proposal, I stood up again and outlined its practical advantages.

'With no parents to negotiate on your behalf, and no dowry to offer, you will never marry a stranger in the normal manner of the gentry. I am no worse than the sort of man your poor mother would have chosen for you. I come of a noble house, as you do; and like you I am a cadet of a very minor branch of it. I am twenty-one years old, with the right number of arms and legs and so on. At present I hold no land, but perhaps one day Sir Geoffrey will give me a fee. Certainly I shall fight to gain one, and if the Grifons kill me you will be no worse off as a young widow than you are now as a dowerless maid. It may be bad manners to approach you so directly. I should have opened the matter through a third party; but the other fellow might have been indiscreet, and I didn't want gossip all over the castle. Will you be the landless Dame de Briwerr?'

I had a lot more to say, for I had composed this speech very carefully beforehand. I stopped because Melisande exploded with laughter.

'Dear William,' she gasped, 'you were prudent not to open the matter through a third party. As you say, there might have been gossip. But need you make this romantic declaration as if you were the third party? Yes, I will marry you. Not because you are Sir William de Briwerr, of noble birth and no prospects, with the right number of arms and legs, very much the kind of man my dear mother would have found for me if she had lived. But because you are dear William, who sounds pompous when he is embarrassed. And besides, I happen to like the way your hair stands on end at this minute. There now, we shall be married. That is settled. Now we must arrange time and place, and how we break the news to Sir Geoffrey and my lady. And . . .'

This was one of the few occasions when my dear wife was unable to finish what she wished to say.

We agreed that I should tell Sir Geoffrey. He was himself newly married, and very happy about it. So he ought to approve, though if he didn't I should have to look for another lord. A landless married couple, lodging permanently in their lord's castle, take up valuable space which ought to be free for important guests.

That very evening I went to Sir Geoffrey. He took the news very well.

'I suppose I am the lady's guardian, in so far as she has one at all,' he said with a chuckle. 'At any rate, she lives under my roof in the service of my wife, though she has never taken oath to me. You are her peer in blood, and a knight; there can be no question of disparagement. You both live here already, so I can't complain that you bring a stranger into my castle. Most suitable in every way. I thoroughly approve.'

'Thank you, my lord,' I said with relief.

'You must put up with cramped quarters,' he went on. 'Carytena fills the summit of this rock, and I can't enlarge it. I can give you the top room in the north tower, which ought to be enough for any couple. But if little cousins of mine come along every year, as I hope they will, we shall have to make other arrangements; especially as by that time I hope the place will be overrun with little Bruyeres.

'Now about money,' he continued. 'I can't increase your wages, I'm afraid. Of course madam Melisande will be paid so long as she waits on my lady. After that you must manage on your pay alone. Perhaps we shall have a good war soon, and you can pick up plunder or a ransom. The Esclavons round here have nothing worth taking. When do you want to be married? Advent is coming, and we shall keep Christmas at Estives with my lady's family. So the wedding must be soon unless you wait for the New Year. Which suits you best? I will warn the chaplain.'

'There's nothing to wait for, my lord,' I said gratefully. 'We will be married as soon as the chaplain can manage it. My kin would not come to the wedding if we gave them a year's warning, and though there are Melisseni all over Romanie none of them are close cousins of my lady. All our friends are already gathered under this roof.'

'And a cousin of yours, Sir William, don't forget that. We may or may not be connected in blood; but I feel like a cousin to you, and that's what matters, isn't it? I shall provide the wedding feast for my cousin who marries in a strange land. You

30

may call it my wedding gift, if you like. Don't thank me. I enjoy parties, and this is an excuse for a really good one.'

My lord could be generous without being patronising, a difficult feat. He was not only the best knight in Romanie; he was the most courteous and honest gentleman.

'There's one thing you should bear in mind, cousin, when you are married,' he continued after I had expressed my gratitude. 'They tell me that in the west courteous love and troubadours and wearing a lady's favour in the joust and that sort of thing are going out of fashion. In Lamorie we are always a bit behind the times, and there are not very many of us. All my household knights are sighing with hopeless love for the lady Melisande, as you know as well as I do. After the wedding they will go on sighing, and serve her with the usual declarations of devotion. I won't say it doesn't mean a thing; you never can tell. But remember that it *may* not mean a thing. Don't spoil the fun that your wife is used to, and don't go killing good Frankish knights because you see them wearing her favours. There's a point where honour demands that any husband must go out and slay. Don't take offence before that point is reached. I am sure you know what I mean.'

I did, and after I had taken my leave I was glad he had reminded me of it. I found Melisande playing cat's cradle with a handsome young Lombard. He gazed into her eyes with rapt devotion, taking every opportunity to touch her fingers. But tomorrow he would be off on his journey to Negripont. I felt that even the most handsome young stranger could not cut me out in less than two days.

My lord practised what he preached. The lady Isabel, a happy bride, was the most beautiful young woman in Carytena, as many gallant knights told her to her face. She was delighted with everything she saw in the barony which would be her home, and went about telling everyone how pleasant it was. Carytena can be pleasant in autumn. There was plenty of fuel for the numerous fireplaces, the window-shutters fitted closely, and the overhanging mountains kept off the worst of the north wind. When snow drifts before a gale outside you feel very snug in a thick-walled tower. It is summer, when you long to ride in open country and must struggle down that frightful path, that you feel imprisoned.

Sir Geoffrey watched the lady Isabel play backgammon with gay young men, or dance in the hall after supper; and smiled to see her happy, without any display of jealous ownership. He was courteous, and he trusted the vassals who loved him.

Melisande and I were married in the castle chapel, in a ceremony which was sufficiently canonical though irregular from start to finish. It was irregular because the chapel was a private oratory and not a public church, because the chaplain had been suspended by his bishop, and because many of the congregation were excommunicate. There was nothing odd about that in the Romanie of those days. Ever since the conquest there had been a standing feud with the Archbishop of Patras, whose palace had been demolished to make a castle for Sir William Aleman; gradually the quarrel had grown, until all over the country bishops were at feud with barons. But the priest who married us was only suspended, not schismatic; Melisande and I have always been faithful children of the Roman pontiff, though from time to time we have been driven to disagree with some of his inferior ministers.

The wedding feast was a very jolly affair. Melisande and I sat in the place of honour. Sir Geoffrey and the lady Isabel ceremonially handed us the first dish; after that they sat beside us. There was good food and plenty to drink, and I managed to dodge making a speech. Among the guests were several Grifons in long silk robes, their ladies with remarkably painted faces under fantastic headdresses. Of course Melisande rebuked me for calling them Grifons, and I promised to say Roman in future if I could remember to do so. She explained that these Gri – *Romans* were gentry, holding land by knight service with all the privileges of their rank. The richer among them came to the muster on good horses, carrying an iron mace instead of a lance; the rest served as mounted sergeants. She told me that in general they were loyal to their Frankish lords, who took much less from them in taxes than they used to pay to their Emperor; and that the vassals of Sir Geoffrey were exceptionally faithful, because he was a good lord who understood their customs and gave them justice.

In all the Frankish lands beyond the sea you find a scattering of these Roman gentry. They can be trusted against Bulgars and Esclavons and other enemies of all civilised men; but when it is a question of making war on other Grifons you never know whether the bond of a common religion will prove stronger than the memory of rapacious Grifon tax-gatherers. In any case, their short weapons and timid tactics unfit them for a place in a squadron of real knights. It seemed to me a mistake to leave them in occupation of fertile land that might otherwise support proper warriors. But when Sir Geoffrey's father had conquered the land he had guaranteed their rights; and Sir Geoffrey, a gentleman of honour, held himself bound by his father's promise.

Presently the hall was cleared for dancing. After a few bawdy jokes I was able to slip away with my bride. And so began the married life which still continues as I write, and which I have never regretted since first we met in that far-off enchanted land.

At the beginning of Advent I rode in my first foray against the wild Esclavons. These miserable creatures wander on foot in twos and threes, with no weapons save axe and dagger. If you catch them you can kill them without trouble; but they are very hard to catch, since they skip over the crags like goats. Our aim was to prove that even in their mountains they were not safe from us. For lack of a worthier foe the knights displayed their prowess by riding over ground which seemed too steep for anything on four legs. But if a horse has been reared among the mountains it is astonishing what it can do. To begin with I was very frightened, but later I found I was reasonably safe if I left the reins alone and used my legs to keep the beast pointing more or less in the right direction. The Grifons who used to rule in these parts take no pride in risking their necks in bravado, and the Esclavons had thought themselves safe on any rocky spur. But a good knight, if other good knights are looking

33

on, will try anything. We rode up to some Esclavon hamlets, chasing their women and children out into the weather; though the wretched huts had been built in places that a man on foot could reach only with difficulty.

We did not kill any Esclavons; but we showed them that there was no peak within the barony of Escorta where they might store their plunder in safety. They must raid somewhere, since their steep mountains will not yield them a livelihood; this year they would raid northwards into Sir Geoffrey de Tournay's barony of La Grite, and leave the lands of Bruyere in peace.

Ten days before Christmas we all rode over the isthmus to keep the feast in the Megaskyr's hall at Estives. The lady Isabel brought all her train, so that my Melisande could come too. She had been looking forward to the visit to the gayest and most thriving town of Frankish Romanie, and after hearing her stories I also was anxious to see it.

Estives is indeed a delightful town, inhabited by rich and contented Grifons who tend silkworms and weave silk and pay their taxes punctually. Italian merchants come every summer; there is even a prosperous community of unbelieving Jews, the ultimate proof of wealth in any market.

There are Frankish burgesses also, and the town supports two noble families. The Megaskyr holds a castle on a flat-topped hill, not so beautiful as his other castle as Satines but more roomy and just as strong. Sir Bela de St Omer, a Fleming in spite of the name given him by his Hungarian mother, holds half the town in fee from his brother-in-law the Megaskyr. He also has a castle within the walls, a strong tower such as you see in Italian cities; his young and handsome family gave parties as splendid as those of their overlord.

In this gay round of visiting and dancing and music the lady Isabel flourished. I have never seen anyone so vital and energetic; her statuesque beauty as a great and remote lady had been changed into the prettiness of a merry young bride. She was always in a crowd of young men, naturally; but other girls, especially the St Omers, were just as eager for her company. It was a kind of life that you see more often in Romanie than in the west – a group of young people, equal in social rank, chattering together and planning their own amusement; instead of a single family living isolated in a castle, and meeting other families three or four times a year at parliaments and tourneys.

Sir Geoffrey threw himself into this new mode of life. He had always been popular with knights, and he could dance and gossip well enough to charm the young ladies. I suppose it was something like being at the court of a very great King, in France or England; but not at all the kind of thing you would find in an ordinary baronial castle of the west, or indeed in mountain-girt Carytena.

My Melisande enjoyed herself, chattering French and Italian and Grifon all at once, while I stumbled behind in the old-fashioned north-French of the Welsh March. These Franks had picked up some of the volatile wit of their Grifon neighbours; naturally enough, since they had been reared by Grifon nurses and most of them had Grifon blood somewhere in their pedigrees.

Best of all, we could enjoy ourselves out of doors even in midwinter. Estives lies in a fertile plain, though unfortunately during the anarchy of the conquest fifty years before the local peasants had exterminated all the deer. But the hawking was really very good, with wildfowl flighting from the marshes at dawn and sunset; and at that season you might ride after your hawk in any direction without damaging the crops. In Romanie the winter days are longer than in England, and though it can be cold the sun often shines. The St Omers kept a very good mews, and I have never enjoyed better falconry.

Too soon the time came to return to rock Carytena, where ladies may not venture out alone for fear of the Esclavons and the hills are so steep that you cannot ride after a hawk. Though Melisande always tells me that I am slow in noticing these things, even I could see that the lady Isabel might be discontented in her new home.

CHAPTER THREE

War in Negripont

❦

Sir Geoffrey led his mesnie to the spring parliament of 1255 in La Cremonie. But this time we brought no ladies with us, for the lady Isabel was with child and the doctors would not let her ride. Lamorie is a bad country for babies, at least Frankish babies; many are still-born, and of the rest more die in infancy than grow up. I don't know why this should be, since the peasants have the usual large peasant families. Of course the food and the climate are not what we are used to.

My Melisande was also expecting a baby, so I was glad of the excuse to leave her quietly at home. No harm would come to her while Carytena was commanded by Sir John de Catabas, who had been appointed castellan because his rheumatism made riding painful.

But when we reached La Cremonie I regretted that Melisande had not come with us, in a litter if there was no other way for her to travel. For the parliament was faced with a complicated question of inheritance, which I am sure she would have made clear to me in a few words. Only a native of Romanie could understand the rights of it, since the roots of the quarrel lay deep in the past.

On the face of it the question seemed simple enough. The Princess Carintana of Lamorie had died childless, and by the custom of the whole civilised world her husband should succeed to her possessions. At her death she had been seized of a barony in the island of Negripont, and Prince William now called on the other barons of the island to grant him peaceful seizin of his wife's fees. I was so astonished to hear that they were making difficulties about it that I went privately to my lord and asked him for an explanation.

Sir Geoffrey was in the solar of his lodging, a comfortable little room with a balcony looking down the green valley. All the houses in Romanie are more comfortable, and divided into many more small rooms, than our halls in England; you must bear that in mind throughout this story. Sir Geoffrey smiled when he heard my question, and motioned me to sit on a stool beside his chair. He was always willing to talk with any household knight as though they were his equals.

'Landholding in Romanie is more complicated than it seems, cousin William,' he said with one of his charming grins. 'It's the fault of our fathers, who divided the land so carelessly that they left two claimants to nearly every fee. You see, this country was really divided twice. After the Crusaders had won Constantinople they held a meeting to elect an Emperor, and at the same time allotted the unconquered provinces. But it so happened that the lords who at Constantinople were granted these provinces were not the lords who later conquered them from the Grifons. So afterwards there were various compromises . . .'

I began to see. This was more tangled even than questions of inheritance in Wales.

'There has never been another claimant to Escorta,' he went on, 'which my father won from the Grifons with his own sword. But in Negripont the question of right is unusually difficult. At the conquest of Constantinople it was granted to the Venetians, who took no steps to occupy it. Then the dalle Carceri, nobles from Lombardy, invaded overland from Satines and divided the island into three baronies. By the way, we must call it an island; but it is so near the mainland that it is joined to it by a bridge. By treaty the Lombard conquerors gave Venice the town of Negripont itself, with the usual civic rights. Then these dalle Carceri began to quarrel among themselves, as Italians will if they have no foreign enemies to fight; until there were two claimants for each of the three baronies. So they asked the

Venetian bailey to arbitrate, and he decided that each barony should be divided, making six fees in all. But that was to last only one lifetime. On the death of any baron the two halves of his barony should be reunited under the surviving claimant. The Princess Carintana, God rest her soul, holds one-sixth of the island. Now do you see?'

'Of course I see, my lord. That Venetian left the makings of a very pretty quarrel. But though the kinsman of the Princess may expect to inherit, our Prince has the right of it. A private arbitration before a foreigner cannot override the God-given right of hereditary succession, on which all Christendom rests. Prince William must hold the land of his late wife, or we might as well be savages living by stealing acorns from one another.'

'A sound view, cousin William, and cogently expressed. Say that again in parliament, if you can make yourself heard above the hubbub of those Lombards. But the latest news is that they may not come to the parliament at all. In that case the Prince intends to summon them to attend his court, the court he will hold as overlord of the whole island of Negripont. There he is on much more shaky ground. I doubt whether he is truly overlord of Negripont. I don't see how he can be overlord of the Venetian town by the bridge; when by a treaty with Venice his father, my grandfather, became a burgess of Venice and bought a house there. You can't be overlord of the town in which you are a burgess. But then uncle William is a little inclined to see himself as overlord of all the Franks in Romanie.'

'Is the Megaskyr also his vassal?' I asked in surprise. 'They told me in Satines that these two lords are peers and equals.'

'They are, of course; with no superior except the King of Salonique, and there isn't one. But uncle William won't rest until he has made my father-in-law do homage for the lordship of Satines, as already he owes homage for Argues and Naples. By the same token, the Megaskyr won't like having uncle William on both sides of him, in Negripont as well as the isthmus. Tiresome, these jealousies among Franks, who should be united to oppose the Grifons. But you and I have no problem, my dear cousin. The Prince is our only lord, and if he leads us against the dalle Carceri our only duty is to follow him. No one else holds my homage.'

In the west a landless knight would not be allowed to attend parliament, but in Romanie the Frankish minority cling together. I had a chance to add my voice when the parliament of La Cremonie clamoured for war against the felons of Negripont who detained the rightful inheritance of our Prince.

Prince William, however, was determined to proceed with all the formality of the law, since the law was on his side. When the parliament ended he allowed his vassals to go home while he himself, with only his own mesnie, rode to Rupo on the strait between Negripont and the mainland to summon once again the dalle Carceri.

At Carytena we prepared for a brisk and pleasant war, a war against men of our own kind, who would take ransom from prisoners and grant mercy to the wounded. Nothing very much was at stake, only a small barony in a remote island. No one would be beggared, or driven from his home; unless you count the unlucky peasants, who must be getting used to that sort of thing after enduring it nearly every year since Adam left Eden. Although no one would be fighting very hard many great powers would be taking part in the war. Venice openly backed the dalle Carceri, her vassals; which meant that sooner or later Genoa would come in on our side. For fifty years there has not been a battle fought east of the Adriatic in which these two cities have not opposed one another, no matter what the ostensible cause of the conflict.

Sir Geoffrey had one private worry which did not afflict his comrades. He might find himself charging with couched lance against his father-in-law. So far the Megaskyr stood neutral, but it was no secret that his sympathies lay with the dalle Carceri.

We saw to the shoes of our horses and gave them extra corn. The armourers were busy. Sir John de Catabas, the constable, inspected us frequently, and made us joust at the quintain. For a long day the whole mesnie of Carytena practised wheeling and charging as a squadron, to make sure that our horses would gallop in close ranks without fighting their neighbours. Perhaps we should have practised this more often; but near the castle there was no ground level enough, so that for that single drill we must ride many miles.

Then we heard the news of the colloquy at Rupo, which made war inevitable. I did not like what had been done, though most people saw nothing wrong in it. After all, the law is the law; if right is on your side you should take every advantage of it. But taking advantage of the letter of the law is an old Villehardouin custom which does not appeal to me.

Prince William had summoned the two leading dalle Carceri barons. Most astonishingly, they obeyed the summons. They had just concluded an alliance with Venice, which probably gave them courage to face the Prince. Besides, they may have expected, as most people expected, that he would argue for a few months more before proceeding to extremes. But the two dalle Carceri barons were loaded with fetters as soon as they defied the Prince, and sent across the lordship of Satines to lie in gaol in Andreville.

So we were summoned to muster under the Villehardouin banner at the bridge of Negripont. We also must ride across the lordship of Satines, which might be about to join our enemies; so we could not start until the whole knight-service of Lamorie was ready to ride with us. Meanwhile we heard that Prince William, with only his own mesnie, had captured the town of Negripont and most of the island. But as we were passing the isthmus news came that the Venetian bailey, a man of great energy, had collected sergeants from the dalle Carceri castle and thrown back the Prince across the strait.

The knight-service of all Lamorie made up a good army, though we were not at full strength. No one came from Argues or Naples, the fees held by the Megaskyr as vassal to the Prince; it was even more serious that no one came from Veligoute, one of the twelve baronies of the conquest. That barony had come by marriage to Sir William de la Roche, younger brother of the Megaskyr, so that its allegiance was always doubtful. Now Sir William had openly turned felon, as a party to the treaty between Venice and dalle Carceri.

But we had Sir Geoffrey de Bruyere to lead us, the best knight in all Romanie; we would soon make short work of Lombard city-nobles and bow-legged Venetian horse-marines. When we reached the narrow strait we could see the island beyond, open country where Franks might charge and over-throw their enemies.

This was the first time I had been so far to the eastward, and the geography was puzzling until I grasped that a great many different places are all called Negripont. This was originally the name of the strait between the island and the mainland, a strait so narrow that it is often called a river though its water is salt. At the narrowest point of the strait is a bridge; half-way along the bridge is a little rock, on which is perched the castle of Negripont. At the far end of the bridge lies the town of Negripont, at that time in Venetian hands. Stretching for a long way north and south, and for a short way to the east, is the island of Negripont. I hope this description is clear to the reader; it was a long time before it became clear to me.

Our first task was to capture the castle, and then the town behind it. This looked to be a very dangerous assault. Like any other knight, I hate to leave my horse and fight on foot; but no one can ride up a scaling ladder. However, the war was still in its half-hearted beginning, and no one's blood was up. The Venetians had no ships in these parts, and so could not harass us as we defiled across the bridge. At sight of our great army their courage failed, and they withdrew from the castle without fighting.

The town is encircled by sound masonry walls, but these fortifications are badly planned. At the far end of the bridge a rocky foreshore leaves room for attackers to deploy in line. Of course the wall ought to rise sheer from the water, but it was laid out by Grifons at a time when their Emperor had undisputed command of the sea. His engineers thought it more important to provide shelter for his fleet than to close the gap at the bridgehead.

We had to fight for the town, but not very desperately. After a night in the castle we rode to the end of the bridge. Sir Geoffrey had been given command of the van, so his mesnie came first in the host. Somehow we got off the bridge, our horses stumbling over the seaweed-covered rocks. Then a party of Grifon foot brought up some kind of machine with which they broke down the gate. Grifons are clever at making siege-engines; the trouble is to persuade them to get close enough to the enemy to use them.

When the great oaken gates fell inwards the Venetians withdrew from the walls. Sir Geoffrey led us at a gallop into the town, though I flinched under my shield as we passed through the archway; we were sitting targets for anyone above with a cauldron of boiling pitch and his wits about him. But Italian burgesses don't like facing knights in full career, and we got through unhurt. At the end of the street stood a group of cross-bowmen, but they were only keeping an eye on us. We drew up to see what they would do, for no one wants to ride a good war-horse against crossbows at short range. When they saw the town gate firmly in our hands they very sensibly dodged round the street corner.

Technically, the town had fallen by assault. But there had been so little fighting that Sir Geoffrey was able to persuade us to forgo our right of pillage. This was still a friendly war, between two groups of Franks who saw themselves as exiles in foreign Romanie; we had no blood to avenge, except for a few Grifons shot down while working their machines. We did not want to sack the shops of harmless Italian merchants.

Prince William took formal possession of the town of Negripont, and then went home to defend Lamorie from seaborne raids. Sir Geoffrey was left in command, with instructions to reduce as much as he could of the island before winter. For a few days we were quartered in the castle, where we lived very well; the leading merchants had collected a good ransom, grateful that we had spared them from sack. Sir Geoffrey distributed it honestly, and my share was three golden hyperpers.

Negripont is more than a hundred miles long, though you can ride across it in half a day. Our mission was to hold the open country for the Prince; a large undertaking, but made easier because the land is flat and more suitable for cavalry than most of the mainland. Besides, we had allies on the spot, for not every baron of those parts upheld the shocking breach of the laws of inheritance which had been procured by the Venetian bailey; in the far south Castel Rosso was held for the Prince by Sir Otho de Cicon, a Burgundian who did not like Italians. But the disputed barony of the Princess Carintana lay round the castle of Oro in the north; perhaps the most northerly of all the castles of the Franks, looking across a strait to the hills of Wallachia. After a few days of rest Sir Geoffrey led us northward.

It was a scrambling little campaign, amusing and not very dangerous. Lombard knights at the head of their Grifon peasants disputed our advance, but nowhere were they strong enough to challenge us to battle. To conquer as much land as we could we split into small groups; every day there would be a joust with a few Lombards or a skirmish with local archers.

I was among the dozen knights who rode always behind Sir Geoffrey; and I saw why he had won his reputation as the best knight in all Romanie. He was a very fine jouster; that is a thing that can be measured, and there was no doubt of it. Whenever a Lombard challenged us he would ride out alone, at a trot, his horse playing with the bit under perfect control. Not until the last few yards would he set it galloping, but then he bounded along, his legs seeming rooted to the saddle. The distance was judged so accurately that he always seemed to jump into his opponent, with a crack of steel lancepoint on wooden shield that could be heard far off. Usually his opponent shot out of the saddle; but if he met a good horseman then both horse and rider would be overthrown together.

But skill in jousting is not much more than a social accomplishment, a trick to win smiles from ladies and prizes in peaceful tourneys. In a genuine battle you can only joust once, in the opening charge; and some good jousters are notoriously little use on a stricken field. What made Sir Geoffrey a good knight was his skill in foraging, his management of his mesnie, his eye for country. At the end of the day he always led us to a small but prosperous village, where there was enough to eat and we could not be ambushed among crowded houses; he saw to it that our horses had full mangers, and that we ate a proper dinner of mutton and bread. Then we slept all together on clean straw in some weather-tight barn, with sentries posted. He would not allow us to rape, or burn houses, or plunder the church. In the morning we would ride on, having taken from the peasants no more than they were accustomed to give to peaceful travellers. Except that we did not pay for our food and lodging, we behaved as though we were stopping at an inn.

Word of our conduct went before us. Peasants did not flee from their villages at our approach. As a result we lived in comfort. Of course this method of waging war gave us no chance to grow rich, and there was some grumbling. Sir Geoffrey answered that we were not ravaging the lands of our enemies but taking over a fee which belonged by right to the Prince our lord, and that it was our duty to hand it over in good condition. Besides, in a strange country to have the peasants friendly is a great advantage.

We never rode into an ambush. Sir Geoffrey could spot from the movement of sheep or the behaviour of birds where armed men might be hiding; and he kept a good look-out without ever relaxing. He could see, from the layout of the farms, where there must be a ford or a pass through the hills, so that we never wasted time in a blind alley. He made us ride in close order, shield on arm; so that even if his precautions should fail a sudden onset would not do us much harm. Every morning he inspected our horses, and the duty of keeping watch at night was fairly apportioned.

We were as safe as men at war can ever be, we were well fed, and we seemed to be on the winning side. Sir Geoffrey was the perfect leader for a campaign of this kind. Every man in his mesnie would have followed him anywhere, or risked his life to get his leader out of a tight place.

After ten days of this pleasant excursion we reached the castle of Oro, a strong place and the centre of Princess Carintana's barony. The small Lombard garrison was not provisioned for a siege and not very fervently attached to the unrighteous cause of dalle Carceri. Sir Geoffrey offered to let them go free, with horse and arms and baggage, on condition they yielded the castle undamaged. They accepted gladly. As far as the mesnie of Escorta was concerned the war was over, for we had won it.

Until autumn we remained in the castle of Oro, collecting the harvest on behalf of Prince William. The peasants gave us no trouble. They are a peaceful, cowardly race, for many generations oppressed by pirates; sheeplike compared to their cousins on the rocky mainland. They were not truly loyal, as were the peasants of Escorta; for they could see across the water the Wallachian hills, where the schismatic church of their allegiance flourishes in freedom. But they were glad to see Oro garrisoned by competent warriors who could keep the pirates at a distance.

Shortly before Advent Sir Geoffrey received permission to go home. The whole island of Negripont was safely in Villehardouin hands. But the Venetians had not admitted defeat and the war would begin again in the spring, so we left a strong garrison in Oro. I was one of the lucky majority who went home to keep Christmas at Carytena.

That was a good Christmas. My dear Melisande had given birth to a son. My lord was his godfather, so we named him Geoffrey. We hired a peasant-woman as nurse, since I had brought home a little plunder; and lived in great content in our warm snug room at the top of the tower.

But Sir Geoffrey still lacked an heir, for the lady Isabel had miscarried. All that winter she was ill and discontented, blaming her misfortune on the cold water and mountain air of Escorta.

She went about telling anyone who would listen that she would never bear healthy children in such an unhealthy place; if Sir Geoffrey wanted sons to come after him he must bring back his wife to breezy lowland Estives.

Another of her grievances was the lack of company. She had married a neighbour, she would explain, because she had counted on frequent visits from the brothers and cousins who had been the companions of her childhood. That year no one travelled the isthmus road. So far the Megaskyr had taken no part in the war, though the lord of Veligoute had openly adhered to the enemies of his lord; but everyone knew that the house of la Roche favoured dalle Carceri and Venice. Sir Geoffrey, the champion of Lamorie, was not invited to pass Christmas at Estives. For the first time in her life, as she frequently reminded us, the lady Isabel must celebrate the feast of the family without her kindred.

Melisande and I, and little Geoffrey Briwerr, passed a happy Christmas. We were together, and soon I must leave to continue the campaign; so we wanted no outside company. Carytena as a whole was not a happy place, and Sir Geoffrey went about with a hangdog air. It was hard to believe that the best knight in all Romanie was bullied by his wife; but very courteous knights are peculiarly open to feminine blackmail.

Meanwhile the war, which we thought we had won, spread on all sides. During the winter it caused grave inconvenience throughout Lamorie. As usual, the Venetians were at the bottom of the trouble. They had been taken by surprise, with their eastern fleet at Constantinople to help the Emperor or at Acre to carry on their eternal feud with Genoa; that was why we had been able to drive them from the castle and town of Negripont. Now reinforcements came from the Adriatic, Venice sent only three galleys, but Prince William had no warships whatever. The Venetian ships held the River of Negripont, so that castle and town were closely besieged. But we supposed that the ships could not stay there for long, since there was no harbour nearby where they could take in fresh water and rest the rowers.

As a counter, Prince William blockaded Coron, the Venetian harbour on the south coast of Lamorie. The investment was very strict, so that the merchants of the town could not deal with their customers inland. But we could not harm the Venetians behind their walls. They just treated Coron as an island, like the many other islands they hold in these seas; and sent in stores and reinforcements by ship.

Prince William tried again. Since he had no ships of his own he called in the Genoese, who are always willing to fight the Venetians anywhere. We hoped that the Genoese squadron would attack Coron from the sea. But our allies were looking for plunder, not for hard knocks; instead of attacking where their enemies would fight back they sailed out from Malvoisie, the harbour the Prince had placed at their disposal, to prey on unarmed Venetian merchantmen sailing to the Black Sea.

The Venetians besieging Negripont found a harbour nearer than Coron. The Megaskyr allowed them to use his port of Naples, which he held in fee from Prince William. He still pretended to neutrality, and made the Venetians pay cash for their fresh water and provisions; but even neutrality was felonious after his lord had summoned him to war. On the other hand, though Naples was a fee of Lamorie he had never done homage for it, so there was something to be said for him. There are few wars in which one party is wholly in the wrong.

In the south our peasants passed a very disturbed winter; for the Venetians from Coron and Naples, and even our Genoese allies from Malvoisie, preyed on coastal villages when more valuable quarry was scarce. In these conditions few merchants dared to cross the Adriatic, and the trade of Andreville and Estives declined. Even the Pope took a hand in the affair, though I cannot see that it was in any way his business. Papal letters commanded Prince William to cease attacking his fellow-Christians, and to set free the dalle Carceri barons whom he had imprisoned at the beginning of the war. Of course we

47

were all of us faithful sons of Holy Church; that was our justification for taking the lands of schismatic Grifons. But Prince William decided that the Pope was misinformed about the affairs of Romanie and his letters mistaken. It was all the easier to defy the Curia because King Manfred and his Ghibellines held the greater part of Italy. Unless Romanie was to be cut off from the west we must keep on good terms with the King of Sicily, even if he happened to be excommunicate; and so far as we took any interest in the troubles of Italy we were more Ghibelline than Guelf.

The prisoners remained in their dungeon and the war continued.

In the spring of 1257 the mesnie of Escorta once more rode out to war. But this year we must defend the lands we had won in the last campaign; and defence is never so interesting, or so remunerative, as the overrunning of enemy territory. Sir Geoffrey went first to the open country of Negripont, where his mesnie must ride hard to repel Venetian raids. By seaborne descents the Venetians and Lombards had won a few castles on the coast, and the whole island was exposed to raiding at every hour of the day and night. It was like being watchmen in a riotous city; no proper rest, hurried riding in mail, and neither glory nor plunder to be won if we did catch up with the enemy.

In midsummer we were fetched back from Negripont to guard the southern shore of Lamorie. That was an even worse occupation. The Grifons of those parts are the most desperate ruffians, especially those who inhabit the mountains of La Grande Maigne. They are not notably loyal to their schismatic church; in fact their neighbours will tell you that they are not Christians at all, even of the wrong kind. But they cut the throats of any Franks they can catch, because they don't want foreigners in their native land and they do want Frankish mail without paying for it.

The mountains were very hard on our horses. We could not see why we should risk our lives to protect these nasty people from pirates who were probably more civilised than they.

In early autumn, before the normal end of the campaigning season, Sir Geoffrey led his mesnie back to Carytena. The official excuse, sent to Prince William, was that the Esclavons were giving trouble, emboldened by the long absence of the natural defenders of the peasantry. In fact Sir Geoffrey cut short the campaign because he feared his sergeants would desert if he kept them much longer on this pointless, plunderless, mountain patrol.

Since several of the Prince's vassals were going home without permission he saved his dignity by summoning them all to a parliament at Nicles. This is a strong town in the centre of Lamorie, where several roads meet. It is a good place for a business parliament, though the amenities of La Cremonie are lacking. Sir Geoffrey turned aside to attend the parliament, sending on his household knights to Carytena.

When he caught up with us two days later he was in a very bad temper. News of what had been done at the parliament of Nicles reached us independently, but the version I heard from my lord's own lips puts the position very clearly. I happened to be riding near him, and he was so mad angry that he had to tell it all to someone.

'You are English, cousin William,' he said to me. 'You must have heard about what happened to your King John, in the days when our fathers were young. Isn't it true that loyal knights may turn against a lord who shows himself a tyrant?'

'Perhaps, my lord,' I answered cautiously, 'though that is not exactly what happened in England. Our Archbishop raised a sedition against the King, but many of the lesser knights remained loyal. My own house of Briwerr was distinguished for its loyalty; my cousin the lord William Briwerr denounced to his dying day that extorted Charter.'

'I seem to have consulted the wrong cousin,' my lord answered with a smile. 'All the same, you will admit that it is possible for a lord to be a tyrant. Listen to what our Prince has done in this parliament. He has proclaimed publicly, before all the world, that the Megaskyr and the barons of Negripont are

49

rightfully his vassals, and felons because they refuse him homage.'

'That is surely a new claim, my lord? What foundation has the Prince for it?'

'He says that the Emperor in Constantinople has given him suzerainty over all the Franks in these parts. Though which Emperor, and on what occasion, was not made clear to us.'

'That raises two points. Is it true that an Emperor granted this franchise? And if he did, was he granting what it was in his power to grant?'

'Exactly, and both points are doubtful. My uncle probably has a grant from some Emperor. If he hasn't got it now he can buy it tomorrow, and very cheap. Poor Baldwin would be glad of the money. He can't sell any more relics, because the market is glutted. Constantinople can hold out for ever, of course; the strongest walls in the world, manned by Frankish knights and Venetian sailors. But the Empire ends at the suburbs. So Baldwin would sell the homage of Satines and Negripont as readily as he sold Our Lord's Crown of Thorns. Personally I don't think he has the right to dispose of them.'

'Forgive me, my lord, if this sounds stupid, but I am a stranger from England and I really want to know,' I answered. 'Who in fact holds the homage of Lamorie, and for that matter the homage of Satines? Those fees must have an overlord; that is shown by the titles of their rulers. The Prince of Wales holds of the King of England, the Prince of Orange holds of the Emperor. If he had no overlord Prince William would be styled King. One would expect Satines to have an overlord also, though Megaskyr is a title without parallel in Christendom. There must be an overlord somewhere. A fee without an overlord is against nature.'

'At the time of the conquest there was an overlord, the King of Salonique. The Bulgarians overthrew him, and now Salonique is held by Grifons.'

'But surely the King of Salonique held of the Emperor?' I persisted.

'Perhaps, but I don't think so. He was the famous Marquis of Montferrat, you know, and he was given his crown as a consolation prize when he did not get the Empire. Probably he had no overlord. So my uncle and my father-in-law are genuinely equal, and my uncle is trying to encroach. I remember my father used to say that all the Villehardouins are crafty quibblers, who know more about the law than an honest knight should. He warned me to watch them, for all that he himself had married one. In my opinion uncle William has been greedy. But if all his barons tell him to pull up he may drop this silly quarrel with de la Roche.'

Sir Geoffrey's rage had dwindled. Nothing is more soothing to the nerves than a detailed discussion of homage and lordship; and I have noticed that though every knight begins by explaining that he is not one of these pettifogging lawyers, every knight prides himself on getting to the heart of a complicated question of homage.

Sir Geoffrey closed the subject. 'What we all ought to do is to choose King Manfred for lord. We have to be friends with the ruler of southern Italy anyway; and since he is the vassal of the Pope for his kingdom of Sicily neither Guelf nor Ghibelline could object.'

In those days the excommunicate King Manfred was the Pope's most deadly foe; so I understood that my lord was joking, though Melisande tells me that I am slow to recognise a joke.

We rode on to Carytena, stopping at every village to hear an address of welcome from the schismatic priest, in Romanie the usual representative of his parishioners. We had passed the summer in protecting Lamorie from pirates, which these peasants see as the chief duty of their lords. Besides, Sir Geoffrey, born in the country and speaking the language, was genuinely loved by villagers who remembered the oppressive rule of their native lords before the conquest.

CHAPTER FOUR

War in Satines

I found Melisande with another baby, a girl whom she had named Sophie. Such a name is more common among Grifons than among Franks, and if I had been consulted I would have suggested Margaret; but Melisande told me that by the custom of the country daughters are named by the mother. I suppose I was lucky; she might have chosen Eudocia.

The lady Isabel was still childless; or rather, the son born to her had died on the same day. That is a sorrow many women must face, and most of them get over it; but the lady Isabel took it very hard. She wandered about the castle, white-faced and thin-lipped, telling anyone who would listen that these barren mountains were fatal to Frankish babies, who did well enough in the milder air of Satines.

She had another grievance, which she mentioned nearly as often as the unhealthiness of her new home. She was cut off from her family. As yet there was no fighting, but Satines and Lamorie were obviously on the brink of war; no traffic crossed the isthmus. One day in early spring, when she had found me alone in a sunny corner of the bailey, she poured out all her troubles.

'I love my brothers and sisters. We are a very united family. When I was a child I begged my father not to marry me to some stranger on the other side of the world. One of my sisters is married in Syria, the other in France. I might have been a Countess in peaceful and civilised Italy, where they make lovely jewellery and fine gowns. Instead I persuaded my father to choose me a husband in Romanie, so that I could often come home to see my family. I married Sir Geoffrey, and I love him. But I married him especially because his castle is within a few days' ride of Estives. And what comes of it? I lose my babies because this godforsaken rock is too much for any new-born child; and at Christmas I shall be as solitary as if my kin were a thousand miles away. Don't you think it unfair, Sir William? What ought I to do? Must I endure without complaint?'

'Not without complaint, madam,' I answered. 'That is too much to ask of any lady. But are your complaints well founded? Carytena is not always fatal to baby Franks, as you can see from the crowd in my little tower room. Your third time may be lucky, and indeed the whole barony is praying for an heir for Sir Geoffrey. Your real sorrow is that you are separated from your brothers, and that is not a matter completely beyond your control. As yet we are not at open war with Satines. Can't you persuade my lord to invite the de la Roches over here? Or before the campaigning season opens you might cross the isthmus and visit them. In short, don't recite your wrongs, try persuasion. It is the natural weapon of every lady.'

I did not sympathise greatly with her troubles; my own kin were very far away. I spoke in the hope of making life easier for Sir Geoffrey. His unhappy wife was making him unhappy; if she tried to coax him she must put on a smiling face.

The lady Isabel took my advice; or else she saw of her own accord that she must win over her husband instead of nagging him. She became cheerful and friendly; Sir Geoffrey, who loved her as deeply as she loved him, found his life running smoothly.

That was a very open autumn; right up to Christmas we could ride out with our hawks, and even in December there were picnics in the open air. With the mesnie on a war footing the castle was crowded. It was nothing like the gay life of Estives, where St Omers went visiting de la Roches and Italian merchants brought the latest fashions and gossip; but it was much more cheerful than Carytena in a normal winter when the Esclavons are on the prowl and the snow lies deep. But with the

New Year the weather changed; by Epiphany 1258 the track down to the bridge was so icy that no horse could face it. We were cooped up in the cold gloom, huddled round the fire in the hall or lying in bed with all our clothes on.

The news of public affairs was depressing. The castle of Negripont, blockaded by those confounded Venetian galleys, was likely to yield unless relieved in the spring. For fear of pirates the currant fleet had remained in Patras harbour, and all Lamorie was short of money in consequence. On the isthmus there were raids and counter-raids, so that by spring we should be at open war with Satines. The Emperor in Constantinople, hard-pressed by the Grifons, sent urgent appeals all over the west; but no help came, because intending Crusaders found it easier and cheaper to fight for the Pope against the Ghibellines of Italy.

Those who had at heart the welfare of Frankish Romanie deplored the prospect of war between the only two Frankish states not beset by Grifons; but such people were few, for Franks do not settle in Romanie out of public spirit. Among those who took a narrower view there was a good deal of sympathy with the Megaskyr. Perhaps he owed homage for Satines to the powerless Emperor; but that was not the same as doing homage to an equal and neighbour who might be in a position to give him definite orders. As for Naples and Argues, many great lords owe homage for outlying fees to some other great lord; no one blamed Sir Guy de la Roche for holding his castles against the Prince, any more than our King Edward is blamed for holding Bordeaux against the King of France.

Sir Geoffrey was worried about his personal position. He took me aside for another discussion. Nowadays, thanks to our famous Charter, any Englishman is regarded as an expert on the ethics of rebellion.

'Uncle William is not to be trusted, that's the long and the short of it,' he began. 'I suppose you have heard the old story: how the first Villehardouin, my grandfather, got Lamorie from Champlitte by a trick? The original conquering Champlitte was dead, and the law lays down that an heir coming from France must take possession within a year and a day. Young Champlitte arrived with a few days in hand; but old Sir Geoffrey de Ville-hardouin kept parliament on the move, a day's ride ahead of him, until time had run out and the fee lacked a lord. Then, of course, the barons chose Geoffrey himself to rule over them. Well, I feel that uncle William is another Geoffrey. Yet I am his man, and I have done homage to him. Must I follow him through thick and thin?'

'I don't see what else you can do,' I answered at once. 'Lawyers imagine cases which would justify a breach of homage; but you can see how binding it is, from the extraordinary cases they have to think up. Prince William has not become an infidel, for example? Or set up a new religion of his own? His only troubles with the Church, I believe, are the usual money-squabbles. He isn't even excommunicate, unless he has incurred the ban by friendship with King Manfred. On that point, remember that the barons of Acre chose the Emperor Frederick for Lord, though he was truly an enemy of God and excommunicate in the strongest way. Yet they remain Cru-saders, with all Crusading privileges. No one suggests that their vassals ought to desert them.'

'You know too much law, Sir William,' he said moodily. 'If I wanted legal advice I would consult a learned clerk. What I want to know is how an honourable knight thinks I ought to behave.'

'You know that already, my lord, since you are yourself an honourable knight. The answer is certain. Homage binds more strongly than anything else in the world.'

'All the same, Sir Guy is in the right and uncle William in the wrong. I wish I could see my way.'

'You must find your own way,' I said shortly. On such a great matter he ought not to ask the advice of a landless household knight. 'You are the sole guardian of your honour. No one else can carry that burden for you.'

'Quite so. At your knighting, did you swear to defend the right?'

I couldn't answer that one. In silence I shrugged my shoulders.

Early in Lent the Prince sent a message commanding Sir Geoffrey to bring all his power to Nicles in the week after Easter. Prince William intended to finish the war by a full-scale invasion of Satines. Unless the Megaskyr yielded in face of this threat there must be a decisive battle in the open field.

As we sat in the hall after supper Sir Geoffrey made a speech to us, a regular rhetorical exercise. Standing on the dais he looked very imposing; the arms of Bruyere glowed on the breast of his white surcoat, his Sword of Justice (for he held high justice in his barony) rested against the banner of Bruyere behind him.

'Gentlemen, I have searched my heart, and I have decided not to follow the Prince of Lamorie. Consider how this land was conquered. It was not conquered by Villehardouin, nor even by Champlitte; it was conquered by Crusaders, coming of their own free will from every corner of France and the Empire. My barony of Escorta is a barony of the conquest. My father won it by the sword, and I inherit his rights and duties. I hold Escorta from God alone, not from any human lord. I am free to choose. And I choose to lead my followers to help my father-in-law, Sir Guy, in the great battle which will decide the sovereignty of Romanie.'

He paused, as a sigh rose from his audience. Though whether the sigh meant agreement, or disagreement, or merely relief that the question had been settled at last, I cannot say.

'But you gentlemen took oath to serve a vassal of Prince William,' he went on. 'You may wish to reconsider your plans. Anyone unwilling to follow me should come up to the dais and diffidate now, in sight of the whole homage of Escorta. No harm will come to him, though of course he loses any land he holds of me, or must hold it by the sword against my power. Is anyone going to diffidate? Don't keep us waiting.'

56

In the solemn hush no one moved. Sir Geoffrey spoke again, but now there was more levity in his manner.

'Well, boys, I mustn't rush you. Anyone who is still thinking it over may come to me later this evening. Understand, this isn't a grave question of principle, on which a knight should seek the advice of his confessor. I have chosen my father-in-law because I like him better than my uncle, and to please my wife. If you think the Megaskyr will win, come with me. If you think Prince William the stronger, stick to him. I don't suppose any knight of the mesnie of Bruyere wants to miss the great battle that is coming, so I don't suggest you should stay quietly at home. This is a war to decide who shall rule the Franks of Romanie. I think my uncle was stretching the truth when he claimed the homage of Satines; but I dare say the Megaskyr also exaggerates sometimes. Don't worry over it, seeing it as a conflict between right and wrong. It's a straight struggle for mastery. Back the side you like best.'

That made it easier. Perhaps Sir Geoffrey had seen my frowning face as I tried to choose the more honourable course. Now I left the chattering crowd in the hall and climbed to our snug tower to consult Melisande, who knew more than I did of the confusing politics of Romanie.

She was nursing Sophie, while for once little Geoffrey slept quietly. She heard my news without excitement.

'So the lady Isabel has won. I thought she would. Let that be a lesson to you, William. In politics husbands are guided by their wives, and that is true even of the best knight in all Romanie. Poor Isabel, she has been miserable here all summer, with her baby dead and her husband away on campaign. I know the kind of life she came from. You can't expect her to be happy in Carytena, where the sun disappears behind the mountains at midday and the neighbours can't come visiting for fear of savage Esclavons. She wants to get back to her family, even if her lord has to fight his way through an army to get there.'

'The lady Isabel is much to be pitied,' I answered. 'But her husband proposes to desert his lord. May I follow him, or would that be dishonourable?'

'Dishonourable? Sir Geoffrey will ride openly, won't he? That is not like changing sides in the middle of a battle, or hiring someone to poison Prince William. A baron of the conquest holds his land by the sword. In a war between Franks he may choose his side; though perhaps it would be dishonourable to help Romans against his own people.'

'But his homage to Prince William?' I persisted.

'Oh, homage. That's a lot of nonsense, a boy's game played by grown men. Out here no one takes it seriously. Do you remember that Prince William is a burgess of Venice, owning a house in the city? Did that stop him making war on the Venetians in Negripont?'

'That's important, my dear.' I snatched eagerly at the straw. 'If Prince William is himself a felon it cannot be felony to desert him. I must follow Sir Geoffrey anyway, since he holds my oath. Now I may follow him with a clear conscience.'

'There's nothing to worry about. We all approve your choice, even little Sophie. See how she smiles, though it may be only wind. Women have a better notion of these things, for we are not blinded by fantastic ideas of honour. Together Sir Geoffrey and the Megaskyr will beat the Prince, and then there will be land to be given in fee. Soon we may be living on our own lordship.'

That had been in my mind also, though I tried not to think of it lest it tempt me to dishonour. A man without land is only half a man.

There were no defections from the mesnie of Escorta; though Sir John de Catabas asked to be left behind in Carytena, where he might suppress the Esclavons without drawing his sword on fellow-Christians. Sir John was a stickler, who took seriously the Crusading vow that had brought his father to Romanie. Even he did not think Sir Geoffrey did wrong, it was just that he was vowed to fight only schismatics and infidels.

We made no secret of our intentions, though Sir Geoffrey forgot to send the Prince a formal message of defiance. In that he may have been at fault; though the fault was caused by carelessness, not by double-dealing. It happened that news of our change of sides did not reach Prince William, who was busy organising the great muster at Nicles. When we set out from Carytena he thought we were riding to join him, and made no effort to stop us. Thus we passed the isthmus without trouble, though it could have been barred against us.

The lady Isabel rode with her lord, since she was the true leader of this expedition. Melisande attended her, leaving our children in Carytena with their Grifon nurse. But I made her promise not to ride with the mesnie to battle. Women can be a nuisance on campaign, though of course it is hard on them to make them miss the excitement of the main business of life.

After a peaceful journey we reached the army which was being mustered at Estives, and a very fine army it was. The knights of that more level country are better mounted than the knights of Lamorie, and with the silk of Estives at their disposal they dress very splendidly. No one at that time wore a silken surcoat over his mail, though sometimes you see fops with them nowadays; but some of the gay young men had ordered their arms to be embroidered in silk thread on the linen. The azure chequers of la Roche stood out on a banner woven of gold thread, which was heraldically correct since the other chequers of the coat are *or*; but it was an extravagant thing to carry into battle. The banner streamed from a pole covered with blue and yellow silk, topped with a silver image of Our Lady of Satines.

That was our main banner, but the army contained other mesnies besides the vassals of Satines. Some dalle Carceri came from Negripont, leaderless because their leaders had been treacherously imprisoned; which made them the more eager for revenge. There was the mesnie of Veligoute, who fought as flagrantly against the lord who held their homage as did the mesnie of Escorta. From the northern march came two great lords, peers of the vanished kingdom of Salonique: Sir Hubert

Pallavicini of La Bondonice, and Sir Thomas de Stromoncourt of La Sole, whose castles restrain the Grifons of Wallachia. There was a company of Italian crossbowmen, lent by the commander of the Venetian galleys; though we left them behind to garrison Estives, because they had come ashore without horses and could not ride with us. There were of course a great number of Grifons and Gasmules, who rode ponies or mules on the march but fought on foot if they were called upon to fight; though they were rather the grooms and servants of their Frankish lords than a serious military reinforcement.

This was to be a short campaign, fought in summer barely two or three marches from our comfortable base at Estives. So every knight wore his best surcoat and mail. I have never seen a more glorious army. My own white surcoat had been freshly painted with the arms of Briwerr under the correct label of cadency. My shield also gleamed fresh and unscarred, for the armourer at Carytena had covered it with new leather. On my head I wore a plain steel cap, for in that climate fresh air is more valuable than protection for nose and cheeks; but the great lords carried at their saddle-bows closed helms, the barrel-shaped affairs that nowadays you see only at tournaments. Such helms are very heavy, and you get very hot inside them. But their tall crests of stamped and painted leather, lions, eagles, bears, in battle served as rallying points for the steel-capped household knights and sergeants who rode behind them.

A few ladies came with us: Isabel de Bruyere of course, since her persuasion had brought Escorta to the army; and the ladies of Satines and La Sole. These last were nieces of Prince William; it was said that they came with us to make sure that their uncle's life would be spared after their husbands had overthrown him. Every great lady must be used to watching battles in which her kinsmen are engaged on both sides.

Before we started the Archbishop of Satines gave us his solemn blessings as warriors fighting righteously in defence of their fatherland (though this could not apply to the mesnie of Escorta). Nothing like that ever happened in Lamorie, where the Prince was on bad terms with the church because of his support of King Manfred and the Ghibellines. The blessing gave me a comforting sense that I was back again in civilisation. On the March English and Welsh clerks always bless their own side before an important fight. A good blessing, with plenty of holy water and if possible a first-class relic, adds to the dignity of any battle.

Hitherto I have said nothing about my horses, because in the mountains I usually rode a hackney from the Carytena stables. It would be rash to risk the legs of a good war-horse on those rocky paths. But for the coming battle, in which I would joust against real Frankish knights, I rode a proper western war-horse. He was a light, showy chestnut, with good shoulders and good quarters but a middle like a greyhound; in fact the two ends of a good horse poorly joined together. I had him off a Sienese as the result of a complicated exchange. This Sienese, though he passed as a baptised Christian, charged me interest on the unpaid balance of the purchase price; so I called the horse Banker, in memory of the disgraceful transaction.

In fine spring weather we set forth from Estives to meet the invader. From a blue sky the sun shone on the flat clear colours of heraldry, on enamelled horse-trappings, broadswords of Spanish steel and chased daggers from Damascus. On white mules the ladies sat enthroned on velvet saddles, their long skirts flaunting the bright silks of Estives. Every knight displayed his arms thrice repeated, on the back and front of his surcoat and on his shield. In addition the horses of great lords were covered by emblazoned housings. I have never seen a more beautiful army; though any well-fed army marching to battle is a beautiful sight.

We must have been about five hundred knights; a great array to be led by barons only, without a king. Of these, thirty followed the wolf's-head banner of Escorta; and as soon as the march had begun Sir Geoffrey came back from his place beside his father-in-law to lead us. It was that kind of thing that made him so beloved by his followers. Most barons would have continued to ride beside the commander, where they could hear the latest news and perhaps wheedle some private advantage. Sir Geoffrey knew that his knights wanted and deserved his company.

We were arguing among ourselves about the banner of Escorta. On the march it is carried by a sergeant, for it is a cumbersome thing to have in the hand all day. In the charge it should be borne by the constable; but the scruples of Sir John de Catabas had kept him at home. Most of the household knights were newcomers from the west; we told some pretty tall stories about the nobility of our birth and the grandeur of our kin, each trying to prove himself worthy to carry the banner. Sir Geoffrey deftly silenced a boasting-match which might have ended in a quarrel.

'You are all very fine fellows, I'm sure,' he said, 'but you are foreigners, if you don't mind my saying so. The banner of Escorta must be carried by one born under it. Sir Stephen Sophianos, would you like to take it? Your house has lived in Escorta a great deal longer than mine. Remember, you ride behind me, let there be no mistake about that. You mustn't get in front to shame me in the eyes of the ladies.'

Sir Stephen was a Grifon, a cadet of a family which used to rule in Malvoisie in the old days. The small fee he held in Escorta had been held by his ancestors for centuries. The honour paid to a Grifon pleased his fellow-countrymen and roused no jealousy among the Franks; for no Frank supposes that a Grifon can really surpass him in anything.

Although I was now twenty-five years of age and had been on various campaigns since I was seventeen, this would be my first great battle. They are rare in modern warfare, where everyone concentrates on the capture or defence of important castles. So next day I was understandably nervous when we came over a shoulder of Mount Caride and saw waiting for us a great host, marshalled under the anchored cross of Villehardouin.

We had eaten a good campaigning breakfast, salt pork and biscuit and plenty of wine; the sun shone, the turf underfoot was firm and level, my horse was fit. But as I gave a last tug at the girths before slipping my arm through the shield-strap I felt my stomach fill with wind and my mouth with evil-tasting saliva. I was not especially afraid of death, no more afraid of it than when I had ridden in the little bickering skirmishes of Italy or clattered about the precipices of Escorta; but I was terribly afraid of disgracing myself before the eyes of nearly fifteen hundred veterans. For the army of Lamorie, as we could see from the banners and pennons waving above it, outnumbered us by nearly two to one.

Sir Geoffrey had been riding with his father-in-law among a little cluster of great lords. Now he cantered up to give final instructions to his mesnie before he put on his great helm.

'The plan is quite easy and straightforward,' he said with a reassuring grin, 'the routine counter when you bump into an army bigger than yours. We charge the centre and forget about the wings. If we break their line and overthrow the Prince the men on the flanks will run away. So it's just a matter of one good charge. Now remember, this is a friendly fight. No bad blood in it, nothing but a dispute about homage and lordship. Knock these people off their horses, and get rich on their ransoms. Don't kill anyone if you can avoid it, and especially don't do any serious damage to my uncle. There's nothing wrong with him except greed, and he wouldn't be a Villehardouin if he wasn't grasping and covetous.'

His head disappeared within the barrel of his helm. His voice boomed strangely from below the tall wolf's-head crest.

'Everybody ready? Girths tight? Stirrups level? Helms straight? Then get into line, as close as you can. When the chequers of la Roche move forward my banner also will advance, and we race the others to reach the Villehardouin banner before them. Oh, and by the way, our cry today is "Satines, Our Lady of Satines". Don't get confused and cry "Passavant, Get Forra'd". That's last season's war-cry, quite out of fashion. If you shout it today you may find both sides fighting you.'

Of course I was in the front rank, in virtue of my knighthood. There were good men on either side of me, and a second rank of sergeants and Grifons. My position was as safe as any place can be in battle. The only bother was that everyone was trying to get immediately behind the banner of Escorta, and in the jostling there was a danger of being kicked by a bad-tempered stallion. My Banker played up, trying to bite other horses. So I got off to rather a bad start.

Once we were on the move my nervousness left me. The trampling, the war-cries, the rush of air against my face, even the bumps I got from my neighbours before Banker settled down, all combined to make me feel godlike and invincible. There is nothing like a fast gallop to instil courage. But the Prince's men also galloped to meet us, which of course made them feel as brave as we did.

We had set out with more than two hundred men in the front line, but each little mesnie was racing for the Villehardouin banner. Sir Geoffrey gained the lead, with his household close behind him; we were going so fast that I must squeeze Banker to keep up. Behind us the line shortened to a wedge, with the chequered banner of la Roche on the heels of the sergeants of Escorta. The enemy kept their formation. Their thin array stretched far on either flank, and I could hear the familiar war-cry of Passavant rolling for hundreds of yards to right and left. Then we met, with a staggering shock.

No one jousted against me personally. At the last moment the enemy on our front bunched together, as knights recognised the crest of Bruyere and turned aside for the honour of encountering Sir Geoffrey. The knight before me swerved until he presented to me his right, unshielded side. He was a decent man whom I had met once or twice, and I did not wish to kill him; I raised my lance which otherwise would have struck him in the neck, and held Banker straight so that we crashed head-on into his right leg. Horse and man went down together, as though they were made of paper. Jumping over them, Banker slid with all four feet together into a sergeant of the Prince's second rank.

I dropped my useless lance to draw my sword. That is one reason why I dislike set battles; whether you win or get beaten you are sure to lose an expensive lance. The sergeant swung his sword at my head, but I ducked under my shield and took no harm. Then I swung at him and he parried, and the swirl of horses swept us apart.

I had time for a quick look round. We had very nearly pierced the Villehardouin line; but not quite, and a miss was as good as a mile. I waited in apprehension for the counter-stroke that must be coming.

If we had broken the hostile line there was a good chance that the two separated wings would have ridden in dismay from the field. That had been our plan, the best plan for an outnumbered army; and it had very nearly succeeded. Now the knights on the wings were free to attack us as soon as they got their horses under control. Luckily the attack would probably come in on my shielded left side.

It didn't. Or rather, it came from all directions at once. Some of the Prince's men, who must have been well in hand, rode over to reinforce the few champions who had stopped us; others charged in from the flanks, as I had expected. But a squadron galloped right round us and came in from the rear. Their attack caught us off balance, and our enemies also; in a few minutes the whole mellay was moving fast in the direction of the isthmus, with the army of Satines completely surrounded.

One of our sergeants pushed up beside me, shouting: 'Let's get to Hell out of here!' When I heard that cry I knew all was lost. Warriors *will* shout it in a tight place, I suppose because they think it sounds manly and defiant. You can be certain that the man who does so will be running like a hare in a minute.

Then the knight on my left pushed into me, until I had to lean on him with my shield to avoid being knocked over. Beyond him I could see the crest of an enemy baron.

Sir Geoffrey's voice reached us. 'Come on, gentlemen. One more push and we are through. In the open we can re-form and come back to the charge.' It was nearly the same as the sergeant's cry which had disheartened me; but the tone was very different. I took a fresh grip of my sword and touched Banker with my spurs.

I had to kill a good war-horse, though I hate doing it. He reared over me to box with his forefeet, and he would have had me down if I had not run my sword deep into his throat. Banker lurched over the struggling carcass, and for a second there was no enemy on my front. Then 'Satines' rang in my ears, and Sir Geoffrey shot past. Throughout the mellay he had kept his lance; now I saw it shiver on an enemy shield. The stricken knight hurtled from his saddle, leaving his horse standing. In such a narrow space it was an amazing joust. A gap appeared in the hostile line. It widened, and the mesnie of Escorta galloped out behind Sir Geoffrey.

We were the first to win clear of the trap; but all the army of Satines struggled to follow us, their war-horses stampeding like cattle.

Sir Geoffrey swung right, over a gentle ridge with a sharp drop on the far side. Sophianos with the wolf's-head banner was still half a length behind him, doing his duty better than I had expected of a Grifon. A ledge of jagged granite barred our way, but Sir Geoffrey spotted a gap and twisted through it at full gallop. The tall banner was a beacon to us; we shook out and galloped two abreast through the gap.

Behind us galloped the remainder of the army of Satines, with behind them and on both sides the army of Lamorie. Every horseman on the field pounded after the banner of Bruyere. The ledge of rock stopped those who could still control their horses, and some good knights of the Megaskyr's own mesnie faced about to hold the narrow passage against our pursuers. Our men filtered through, like wine poured from a narrow-necked jar. The enemy were slow to find another gap, so that more than half our army got clear from that doleful field of Mount Caride.

Now we were headed for the safety of Estives. All over the plain before us I could see scattered puffs of dust, as ladies and clerks who had ridden out to see the battle sought refuge before the enemy could catch them. I wondered which dust-cloud was the lady Isabel. Thank God she was not with child that summer, as far as I knew; she could ride as well as most men, and with any luck she would reach the castle before her lord. But still we must hurry. The enemy pressed us close.

Sir Geoffrey's eye for country took us swiftly over this unknown plain, as new to him as to me. I wondered whether presently we would turn and make a stand; until as we checked to ford a little stream Sir Geoffrey unlaced his helm and hung it from his saddle. His face streamed with sweat, for those close helms are ghastly things to wear for any length of time; but it was also calm and composed, almost cheerful, as though the thrill of crushing defeat was the next best thing to the exhilaration of victory.

The afternoon sun was very hot. The trampling of our horses filled the air with the fine marble-dust of those parts. But as a horse-master Sir Geoffrey was beyond compare, and he kept us moving at just the right pace. My narrow-gutted Banker was very distressed, but his good shoulders kept him on his feet. Few horses foundered completely, though for the rest of their days most of them showed the effect of that hurried flight. Every man who lagged behind the column, or dismounted from a beaten horse, must fall into the hands of our pursuers.

Presently the chequers of la Roche showed us on our right rear; Pallavicini and Stromoncourt, who had charged at the rear of our wedge, joined us before evening, having fought their way free of encirclement by another gap. As the sun was setting the first of our knights clattered under the gateway of the castle of Estives; looking back as I climbed the rock I saw the anchored cross of Villehardouin less than half a mile away. It had been a very near thing, but we were safe.

CHAPTER FIVE

Sir Geoffrey Stands Trial

The lady Isabel was waiting for us in the inner bailey, quite calm. When Sir Geoffrey dismounted and kissed her hand she said to him: 'My lord, forgive me. My advice has brought you to ruin.'

'Nonsense, my dear,' he answered briskly. 'In the first place, your father is a nicer man than my uncle and I followed him of my own free will. In the second, we are not yet beaten. This castle is as strong as Carytena, and much roomier. We shall sit here and make faces at uncle William until he tires of the siege and goes away.'

Then he stood on the mounting block to address us. 'We shall hold this castle. We can hold it for as long as we like. But first we must get organised. We are the Megaskyr's guests. So long as you are in his castle you will obey his commands, as soon as he gives them, without arguing or referring the question to me. But I know you are sensible men, who would do that anyway. Now straightaway I want you all to go with the steward and find your sleeping quarters. All the men of Escorta will sleep together, so that we can fight as a unit. Disarm by your bed-places, and then do what you can for your horses. I shall propose to the Megaskyr that tonight his men guard the castle, since they know it and won't lose their way in the dark. I shall also inquire about the prospects of supper. If I get my way you will rest tonight, after caring for your horses. But you will be on guard in the morning. Now be off. I shall tell you the news, in the stables, as soon as I have seen the Megaskyr.'

Of course all our baggage had been lost in the rout, stolen by our servants or captured by the enemy. Our servants and grooms were also missing, except for those few who had stayed behind in the castle. We would live rough for at least the next few days. But the greatest of my worries was quickly set at rest; while I was disarming Melisande came to me.

She had clung to the corner allotted to us in the gatehouse before the army rode out. Our bedding was intact, and my little bag of money. She herself was not so frightened as I had expected, though this would be her first siege. But the news she told me was depressing.

'The chief cook is tearing out his hair in handfuls,' she said with a rueful grin. 'Only three days ago he prepared a great feast to mark the opening of the campaign. He used up all the sugar and white flour and fresh meat in the castle. He thought there was plenty of time to get in more supplies. We all thought so. I suppose I knew we might be beaten, because that can always happen in war; but I never expected to see you all back defeated on the evening of the second day. Now the Megaskyr has ordered another great feast, to hearten Sir Geoffrey and Stromoncourt and Pallavicini and his other allies; and the cook has nothing but the salt meat and biscuit of the campaign stores.'

'Well, I can live on biscuit and salt meat, and so can anyone accustomed to war. But you won't like it, my darling.'

Then another thought struck me, a dismaying thought.

'The castle is pretty full, many more than the normal garrison. If there is any fresh food the allied lords and the great ladies will have first call on it, and none will reach us. I wonder what they have as a campaign reserve? They ought to have food for a year, especially in war-time. But a sensible castellan turns over his salt meat every year, before it goes putrid. I suppose we are not far off harvest? I can never get used to a harvest in June, instead of September. I bet our stores are very low, ready to be replenished. Say six months' supply for the garrison, and we are many more than a normal garrison. Look here, sweetheart. If anyone offers to sell you food, either a luxury or ordinary rations, you buy without haggling over the price. And don't bother if it's been stolen, either.'

Melisande stared straight into my eyes. 'Shall I slip over the wall? Remember, if I have to I can pass as a native. I might get back to Carytena on foot; if the countryside is unsafe I could take sanctuary in Our Lady of Satines, only two days' walking from here.'

I thought it over, and decided against the plan. 'It's brave of you to suggest it, but there are too many risks. If you carry money someone will probably steal it; if you go penniless you must beg your bread, and that would be unseemly. There is always the danger of rape. True knights should never rape ladies, even the ladies of their enemies. But it happens from time to time all the same.'

'Would you mind very much if I were raped?' she asked, in that irritating way women have of intruding personal matters into a serious discussion of military operations.

'Of course I would mind, though I would do my best never to mention it in your presence. Serious consequences would follow. I would be bound to wage war on Prince William for the rest of my life; and Sir Geoffrey, as a true lord, would be bound to maintain the quarrel of his man. There could never be peace between Escorta and Lamorie. And all to save you from the short commons of a siege.'

'If the castle falls by assault I may be raped anyway,' said Melisande with a shrug.

'That is so, and you are right to face the possibility. People of our birth must endure the chances of war; we are not peasants, to dodge the misfortunes that befall our lords. But if that should happen I would not be alive to see it, and I suppose you would be dead soon after. An assault of that kind leaves no survivors.'

'But of course there won't be an assault,' Melisande said cheerfully. 'The Prince doesn't want to kill his nephew, any more than he wants to start a bloodfeud with all the noble houses of Romanie. People don't go to that kind of extreme when nothing more is at stake than a disputed homage.'

'We'll hope so, anyway. There's nothing we can do about it. Perhaps I was wrong to bring you to this war, though my own conduct has been blameless. I did nothing but follow the lord who holds my fealty. But it may not be a long siege. The Megaskyr has been beaten, and he knows it. He is intelligent enough to climb down gracefully and fix up a peace.'

We need not have worried. Every Frank in Romanie was eager to fix up a peace; and they went about it with the supple readiness to compromise which babies breathe in with the air of that land.

After supper of biscuit and salt pork we passed an unpleasant night. Our horses were in a shocking state; my Banker was permanently broken down. Nearly half the knights of Escorta were missing, though it seemed likely they were prisoners, not dead; it is difficult to kill a mailed knight, unless you murder him deliberately after you have got him down.

By midnight our Venetian crossbows were exchanging arrows with the besiegers, who crept close to the wall. We had not tried to hold the flimsy rampart of the city. The castle, and the neighbouring tower of the St Omers, could shelter all the Franks in the place, and the Grifon burgesses were glad to stand neutral in this quarrel of their foreign lords. After making themselves snug in the town the Prince's men settled down to starve us out.

In the morning Sir Geoffrey took over a sector of the walls. We sheltered close behind the merlons, and did not try to shoot back. There was no point in killing a sergeant or two and making the Prince angry. But the walls must be manned day and night, or the castle might fall to a surprise escalade.

It was very dull sitting about in armour in the hot sun; but in any war there is more boredom than excitement. Then at midday things began to stir.

The besiegers blew trumpets for a parley. We stood up in the embrasures, hanging our shields over the wall to make a good show and prove that the castle was strongly defended. The Megaskyr called from a window that no envoy would be admitted; all negotiation must be conducted in shouts across the ditch. That is standard procedure at the opening of any parley, for fear the garrison will suspect they are being secretly betrayed.

But the envoy who appeared was the Archbishop of Satines, a vassal of the Megaskyr for his temporalities and in this war a cautious neutral. We could not bar the gate against the Archbishop of the province (though Estives has its own bishop, as does nearly every inhabited hamlet in Romanie). The Archbishop was allowed in, with two unarmed clerks; and all the leaders settled down to a conference in the solar.

The conference continued until sunset, with clerks scurrying to and fro through the gate with messages. We all felt more cheerful. If a conference lasts a long time it must end in peace; no one can keep on defying his enemies all day.

At sunset the Archbishop rode out, and sentries relieved us on the wall. We sat down to our supper, two biscuits each and a fragment of salt pork. As soon as we had gobbled it, for we were very hungry, Sir Geoffrey summoned the mesnie of Escorta to a private meeting in the mews. We squatted on the floor below the restless hooded falcons.

'We are all in this together,' he began, 'and I won't make peace without the consent of all of you. But I think we have got you pretty good terms, and I advise you to accept them. We lost the battle, so uncle William must have the homage of Satines and so on. That's only fair, and it would be silly to dispute it. But he is not angry with the lesser knights who follow their lords as they were sworn to do. All he wants from the knights of Escorts is two oaths: that you will never again bear arms against the Prince of Lamorie, and that you will serve loyally the baron of Escorta, whoever he may be.'

He paused to let this sink in.

'What about my fee of Crevecoeur? Do I keep it?' asked one of the greater vassals.

'You do, if you take oath as I said. That's the point of it. The household knights may garrison Carytena under the command of Sir John de Catabas until the baron of Escorta arrives to take charge. All the prisoners taken at Mount Caride will be freed on payment of a moderate ransom. The rest of you keep horse and arms, no worse off than you were before the battle. No one suffers, except the two or three unlucky knights who got themselves killed in the mellay; and that's a thing that might happen to anyone, in a tournament for example. Now, are you all willing to promise what uncle William demands of you?'

We all shouted at once, saying the same thing in different words. We would not swear a peace unless Sir Geoffrey were included in it; we would not abandon him to his enemies.

'That's very kind of you, and no more than I expected,' he said easily, holding up his hand for silence. 'As you have already noted, I am not included in this peace. All the same, by submitting to the Prince of Lamorie you will help me. It will put him in a good temper. I don't want to harp on it, but I must remind you again that he won the war. Uncle William must have what he fought for.

'And you can't defend me even if you wish to, because I haven't a leg to stand on,' he continued with a cheerful smile. 'There's no doubt that uncle William held my homage, and that I made war on my lord. At the time I thought it a good idea, and indeed my wife still thinks so. But it wasn't, as has been proved in the field. So I must stand my trial for felony, and I am willing to face it.'

There was another roar of disapproval. Sir Geoffrey waited for it to subside, and continued undismayed. 'That's not so bad as it sounds, you know. The Archbishop has been fixing things a little. No bishop likes uncle William, for one reason or another. This is what has been arranged. I am a felon. I must admit my guilt and plead for mercy. The Megaskyr is equally guilty, as has been proved on the field. Yet no one blames him very much.

73

We shall be tried together, that's been promised. And we shall be judged, not by an angry uncle William, but by our peers, the barons of Lamorie. The High Court of the Principality will not be hard on my father-in-law. If they let him off with a caution they can scarcely hang me for the same offence. The worst that can come to me is forfeiture of my lands. Then I shall go to Acre to fight for the Holy Sepulchre, and I dare say some of my friends will follow me. Uncle William can't keep you here if you want to go on Crusade. The Archbishop of Satines, and for that matter his own Archbishop of Patras, wouldn't stand for it. Now that I have explained everything will you take oath as I advise, and make peace with your lawful overlord?'

We were persuaded. We promised to take oath as soon as the Archbishop arrived with his relics and witnesses. When the meeting broke up I ran off to tell Melisande. She understood the implications of any political agreement more clearly than I could.

'It only shows that it never pays to rob a clerk,' she said as soon as she had heard the story. 'Prince William turned the Archbishop of Patras out of his palace, to make it into a castle. But the Megaskyr has always given God His due. When all the Frankish lords of Romanie are at war with one another of course the clergy must arbitrate; and they have given the Megaskyr the best of the deal. Already he owes homage for Naples and Argues; now he will owe homage for Satines also. Otherwise he loses nothing. Sir Geoffrey's life must be safe. He may lose his barony, but they won't hang him. He won't even be powerless when he comes up for trial. His followers go free, with horses and arms; and as I see it there's nothing to stop them attending the parliament. They will be sworn vassals of Lamorie, owing suit of court. It's a great deal better, isn't it, than what your King John did to defeated rebels?'

The oath-swearing took three days, during which the castle of Estives continued formally under siege. We swore on holy relics, in the presence of the Archbishop. Prince William stood by, but we did not place our hands in his to swear fealty; for we

74

were not his tenants in chief, but vassals of the future baron of Escorta. On the fourth day we marched out, with horse and arms and all our baggage. A garrison of the Prince's sergeants took over the castle of Estives.

After swearing fealty to the Prince the lords of Bondonice and La Sole rode off as free men to their own fees. The Megaskyr came out unarmed, to show he was a prisoner; but he was allowed to retire to his other castle of Satines until the parliament of Lamorie should be ready to judge him. All his knights went with him, armed; and so did the lady Isabel his daughter.

Sir Geoffrey alone was kept a close prisoner. He surrendered formally to his uncle, and was confined in the best guest-room in the castle of Estives. I feared that we might never see him again; the prisoners of King John used to die while awaiting trial. But Melisande told me not to be silly; all the barons of Lamorie were looking forward to this interesting suit, and if it did not come off they would rebel against Prince William.

We rode to Carytena, leaving our lord alone.

Our home had not changed. Sir John de Catabas had been genuinely neutral. The peasants paid their dues and the household knights drew their wages. The Esclavons gave us occupation, without being more than a nuisance.

Then it was time to ride to Nicles, for the parliament which would decide the fate of our barony. A small garrison of sergeants and Grifons remained in the castle, for no knight could bear to miss this crucial trial. We rode armed, but there were peaceful tunics and surcoats in our baggage. Sir John de Catabas warned us that to attend the parliament in mail might be considered provocative.

We brought our own food, and at Nicles slept in tents. But as lords came in from all over Frankish Romanie the place became very gay. On the outskirts the ground was level and open, which is rare in Lamorie. We could pass the time in jousting and hawking.

When the great day came Prince William rode in with a

powerful and splendid mesnie. Sir Geoffrey was with him, but I was unable to see my lord; for he was still under close arrest, though servants told me he had been well fed and adequately looked after. There was no sign of the Megaskyr, and the place was full of rumours that he would not appear.

The parliament met on horseback, as is often the custom of Romanie. The mesnie of Escorta attended completely unarmed, and mounted on quiet hackneys; which was as well for me, since Banker was dead of his exertions and I was without a war-horse. Most of the knights of the parliament carried shield and sword to show their quality, though they did not wear mail. Sir John led us to a quiet corner of the field, where if we all shouted together the Prince might hear us and heed our advice; though it was unlikely that he would change his opinions to please us.

Then out of the low morning sunrise came riding a most gorgeous procession; the Mekaskyr of Satines, in a silken surcoat of blue and gold chequers and a velvet cap of estate, mounted on a white hackney. He carried not even a dagger; but behind him rode all the knights of Satines in full mail, mounted on their war-horses.

There was a buzz of talk. Some said the Megaskyr would seize Prince William from the midst of his parliament before his knights could arm and dress their ranks. But such treachery is not the custom of la Roche; when I saw in his train a group of ladies, including his daughter Isabel, I knew that he came in peace. Then a trumpet sounded and a herald proclaimed that the high and mighty prince Sir Guy de la Roche had come to hear the judgement of the parliament of Lamorie. There was no mention of a trial, for he had already admitted his guilt.

Dismounting, the Megaskyr stood before Prince William. A clerk handed a scroll to the Prince, from which he read a long indictment. Then he turned to the nine barons of the conquest sitting their horses behind him, and asked them to pronounce their verdict. There are in all twelve baronies of the conquest; but the Prince himself held one, and two were held by accused felons, Sir Geoffrey de Bruyere and Sir William de la Roche. That left only nine peers to judge them.

What followed was exquisitely funny. It must have been planned in advance, with a good many people in the secret; but the secret had been well kept, and the Prince was taken by surprise as much as the rest of us.

For a long minute there was silence. Then Sir John de Neuilly, marshal of Lamorie and baron of Passavant, spoke for his fellows.

'We cannot judge the Great Lord of Satines, for we are not his peers. He is more than a baron of the conquest. Only a King or an Emperor may judge him.'

Prince William gaped in rage and astonishment. Among the lesser knights of the parliament the buzz of surprise soon gave way to chuckles of amusement. The Prince's most faithful vassals, who had ridden with him to the conquest of Satines, now openly avowed their disbelief in the justice of the cause to which their swords had brought victory! In Romanie Franks behave worse than they would at home, infected by the double-dealing of their Grifon neighbours; but this was an amazing display of barefaced duplicity.

'You won't judge him, eh, though he has pleaded guilty to felony?' the Prince spluttered as soon as his emotions were under control. 'Then I myself must judge him. Shall flagrant treason go unpunished, just because my barons stand in awe of the great name of la Roche?'

'I beg your pardon, my lord, but that's just what you can't do,' broke in the Archbishop of Satines, who sat a tall white mule in the front rank of the la Roche mesnie. 'I made the peace at Estives, and its terms are fresh in my memory. The Megaskyr is to be judged by the parliament of Lamorie, not by the Prince alone. On that understanding he surrendered his strong castle of Estives. You must observe the terms of your own treaty, or send Sir Guy back to his castle and begin the war again. Otherwise you will incur the ban of the Church.'

In his exasperation the Prince squeezed his horse, so that for a minute he was too busy controlling it to address his loyal barons. Then he snarled at them: 'You see? I can't judge him and you won't. Yet he admits felony, the disgraceful crime of making war on his lord. Must this traitor go free, so that your own vassals are encouraged to rebel against their rightful lords?'

That is an argument any baron understands. The nine whispered together, their horses shuffling and passaging as groups formed and dissolved. (These mounted parliaments can be a severe test of horsemanship. Our English custom of meeting indoors, on our feet, is less chivalrous but more practical.) At last they agreed, and moved their horses back into line. Once more the marshal of Lamorie was their spokesman.

'My lord,' he said formally, 'here is the advice of your parliament. We cannot judge the Great Lord of Satines, since we are not his peers. You may not judge him, for it is forbidden by the oath you swore to the Archbishop. Nevertheless the Great Lord is a felon, and should suffer judgement. Therefore he must seek judgement from some prince greater than himself, a true knight, a brave warrior, a just judge. Let him go in person, not by deputy, to lay his case before the King of France, binding himself by oath to pay the penalty demanded of him. King Louis will do right; and we, the barons of the conquest, agree in advance to enforce whatever judgement he may lay down.'

'And who will hold the lordship of Satines while its lord is oversea?' asked Prince William, at once putting his finger on the really important question. All Villehadouins are at home in the law.

'The Megaskyr may appoint a deputy, who will take oath to serve him loyally,' the marshal answered. So this was not a plot to cheat de la Roche of his fee, as one might have supposed.

The Prince frowned in disappointment, scanning the faces of his barons. He saw they were in earnest; and made up his mind to give way gracefully, since give way he must.

'I accept the advice of my parliament,' he said with a formal smile. 'Let the Megaskyr take oath to abide by the judgement of

King Louis; and let him set off as soon as may be for Paris, at his own charges. He may appoint a deputy to rule in his absence. That is the judgement of the Prince and High Court of Lamorie.'

There followed a few minutes of bustling about, as the Archbishop dismounted with his reliquary and the Megaskyr dismounted to take oath on it. He announced that his brother Sir Othon de la Roche would be his deputy in Satines until his return, and to this the parliament gave formal agreement. I wondered what would befall his other brother, Sir William of Veligoute, who had been as flagrant in rebellion as my own lord. But it so happened that he was lucky, as you will hear.

The mesnie of Satines were already preparing to depart. I noted with satisfaction that the Archbishop remained to hear the next case, that of Sir Geoffrey. An Archbishop does not as a rule plead for heavier punishment, unless the culprit owes him money; and my lord had not taken more of the old endowments of the Church than was customary among the Franks of Romanie.

Sir Geoffrey had been well advised, for he had friends in high places. He would never have humbled himself before his uncle if he had not been persuaded that it was his only chance to save himself. Now he appeared dramatically, the only man on foot in that crowded parliament. His legs were bare, his sole garment a linen shirt; round his neck was a short length of rope. Bareheaded he strode forward, to kneel before the hoofs of his lord's destrier.

Still kneeling, he spoke in a loud voice. His words were as humble as any wronged lord could desire. But for all his efforts he could not keep out of his voice a ringing note of challenge, the tone of a knight who risks his life and glories in the risking of it.

'My lord, I am guilty of felony. I betrayed my homage, and bore arms against you in the field. I deserve your justice. Nevertheless I beg the good knights here assembled to show mercy.'

The whole parliament craned forward to hear his words above the stamping of restless horses; but he had no more to say. It must have been one of the shortest speeches ever uttered in a court of law.

The Prince looked across at Sir John the marshal, who urged his horse over so that he might confer with his lord. The eight remaining barons stared into the sky, their faces expressionless; they knew that to smile at the prisoner would be to increase the anger of the Prince, but they could not bring themselves to frown on the gallant and charming Sir Geoffrey.

The marshal returned to his place among the barons of the conquest, and Prince William addressed them formally.

'My lords, I may not judge this cause, because of the oath I swore at Estives. It is for you to pronounce the penalty. I must remind you of the gravity of the offence admitted by the prisoner, and of the extreme penalty you have the right to inflict. In all civilised hands the punishment of felons is death and confiscation of goods. But no matter what you decree I, your lord, have the right of pardon, and I declare that my nephew shall not suffer in life or limb. Therefore I ask you to declare the escheat of the barony of Escorta, and of any other fees now held by Sir Geoffrey de Bruyere. Let him be stripped of all his goods and sent into exile. If he will go to Acre, to fight for the recovery of Jerusalem, I will give him horse and arms such as a knight should have.'

I had been waiting for what happened next, surprised that it was so long in coming. The dowager of Escorta, the Prince's sister, rode up to him on a little hackney to plead for her son. I suppose she knew her brother's character, and that it would be useless to ask for mercy until he had enjoyed himself by denouncing the wickedness of Sir Geoffrey in open court. The nine barons came too; until there was such a crowd that they dismounted to get nearer the Prince, a breach of the normal etiquette of parliament which showed they were deeply in earnest.

Meanwhile Sir Geoffrey stood on his bare feet, with the tail of his shirt fluttering against his knees. Luckily in that climate he did not shiver with cold; in fact he looked debonair and at his ease. Presently he caught sight of the mesnie of Escorta, and waved his hand cheerfully. Then he winked at the Archbishop of Satines, and ogled a pretty girl at the back of the crowd. He was safe from hanging or mutilation; he did not care whether when the court rose he would be a penniless knight errant or a great baron.

The Prince was arguing excitedly, and getting the worst of it. So much I could see from the set of his shoulders, as he leaned down from his horse to talk with the barons and clerks crowding round him. Presently he straightened himself with an angry shrug; his advisers hurried back to their horses. Something had been decided, something Prince William did not like; that promised well for my lord.

When everyone was ranged in due order Sir John de Neuilly spoke: 'Geoffrey de Bruyere,' he said sternly, 'by felony you have forfeited life, lands, even your knighthood. If you were hanged here and now there would be no injustice. But by the mercy of your uncle the Prince, and by the advice of the barons of the conquest who remember your former prowess, life and knighthood will not be taken from you. Your barony of Escorta escheats to the Prince, with any other fees you may hold in Lamorie. Sir Geoffrey, approach your lord and receive the Kiss of Peace, in token that you leave this parliament absolved of your crimes.'

Sir Geoffrey hesitated. Perhaps he wanted to jump on a horse and gallop away, a free man and a landless foe to all Lamorie; perhaps he just disliked the idea of kissing his uncle's bristly beard. But the marshal and the Archbishop signalled to him to come nearer. Suddenly he grinned as though he understood, and walked briskly forward.

A groom handed the Prince a clod of dry earth, so I also understood, and knew that the affair would have a happy ending after all.

The Prince leaned forward in the formal embrace, then held

aloft the clod of earth. Sir Geoffrey waited with his hands out-stretched to receive it. The Prince spoke in a loud voice.

'Sir Geoffrey de Bruyere, take seizin of my barony of Escorta, with its castles of Carytena and Bucelet and all that belongs to it. You will hold it by knight-service, and the heirs of your body after you . . . . Now do homage for it, nephew, and in future remember that you are my knight and my vassal.' He ended with quite a pleasant smile. Prince William could make friends with an air, if he knew that he had to make friends.

The parliament dispersed in a chatter of congratulations. Everyone was pleased. The best knight in Romanie was back under the Villehardouin banner, and all was as it had been before the civil war. The herald who proclaimed a great joust for next day could hardly make himself heard above the uproar. In this transport of universal good feeling no one remembered Sir William de la Roche of Veligoute, whose treason had been just as flagrant as Sir Geoffrey's. He went quietly back to his barony just south of us, and continued to enjoy all his rights and privileges. As I said earlier, he was a lucky man; though perhaps it was rather shameful to be forgotten because all minds were fixed on the fate of Sir Geoffrey de Bruyere, the best knight in all Romanie.

The tournament continued for three days, and was the gayest ever held at Nicles. In a fit of prudence Sir Geoffrey declined to ride in the mellay, where enemies can easily work off a secret grudge; but in the single jousting of the Round Table he overthrew several good knights, and increased his popularity by letting them keep horse and arms. His mother was proud of him, and they appeared to be excellent friends; but when the tournament was ended she rode back to Andreville and I think never saw her son again. Isabel was not the only lady who could not abide mountain-shadowed Carytena, though my Melisande never let it bother her.

We all rode back in high spirits to the mountains of Escorta. It seemed to me remarkable that a bitter war could end with nothing changed. I said as much as we rode along; but Sir John de Catabas overheard and corrected me.

'Sir William,' he said gruffly, 'I thought you understood the customs of chivalry, though perhaps they are different in your remote island. Sir Geoffrey has been punished heavily; punished in his dignity, which to a true knight is more painful than bloody wounds. He put a brave face on it, for he knew he was in the wrong and deserved what came to him; but every suitor at the parliament saw what had been done. Sir Geoffrey has been deprived of the barony his father conquered from the Grifons. It's true that the Prince gave back to him the land and castles, but not on the same terms. He is no longer a Baron of the Conquest, one of the twelve peers of Lamorie. You heard the Prince enfeoff him, and the heirs of his body. A Baron of the Conquest may dispose of his fee by will; if Sir Geoffrey dies childless Escorta escheats to the Prince. A Baron of the Conquest has High Justice; a vassal of the Prince must send his thieves to be hanged in Andreville. A tenant of Villehardouin is a very different man from a Baron of the Conquest.'

'But since Sir Geoffrey does not mind we need not mind either,' put in another knight. 'I shall be merry keeping Christmas in Carytena. A month ago it seemed that we would pass the winter starving on the walls of Estives. Sir Geoffrey has made a very good peace.'

'Sir Geoffrey has been lucky. Let us hope his luck holds,' said the constable, whose rheumatism inclined him to take a gloomy view of the future.

That Christmas of 1258 was indeed very merry; though the lady Isabel was absent. She had gone to a great gathering in Satines, where her uncle the regent feasted her sister who had come on a visit from Acre. But then the lady Isabel never pretended to like the mountains of Escorta.

CHAPTER SIX

The Grifons of Wallachia

In the spring the family of Bruyere was once again united, though the lady Isabel still avoided Carytena. She met her lord at Andreville, where all the nobility of Lamorie was gathered to feast at the third wedding of Prince William. Melisande and I were there also, in the suite of Sir Geoffrey.

In 1259 Andreville was not much of a place, a half-empty town with more clerks than merchants to be seen in its streets. But the archives of Lamorie were kept there, and in the big collegiate church of St James lay the two previous Frankish rulers, Geoffrey I and Geoffrey II, father and elder brother of our Prince William. As the family church of the Villehardouins it was the natural place for the Prince's wedding.

Fifty years earlier Andreville had been the centre of the new Frankish colony. Just inland from the west coast, it faces Italy and the seas dominated by Venetian and Genoese galleys. But for half a century the colony had been expanding, until the whole of Lamorie was in western hands. Prince William now looked eastward. The Grifon lords were at loggerheads and new opportunities opened for our swords. La Cremonie in the south-east faces towards Asia.

After burying two wives Prince William was still childless; so it was natural that he should marry again. But in fact this third marriage, which took his vassals by surprise, marked a daring change of outlook. As soon as Melisande heard of the alliance she began to talk foreign policy. As we rode down the gorge from Carytena she chattered incessantly, trying to 'put me in the picture' as she called it: a metaphor frequently used in the Grifon language.

'Quite soon there may be a fee for us,' she said hopefully. 'This is the wisest thing Prince William has ever done. An alliance with one Roman against the other Romans is much more sensible than trying to overcome all the natives of these parts with our own swords alone.'

'Is it?' I answered. 'There seem to be two grave objections. In the first place, Grifons won't honestly help us against fellow-Grifons. And if they did help us, so that we defeated our enemies, our allies would be certain to cheat us of the reward of victory. Whenever you do business with a Grifon you get the worst of it.'

'William, you're hopeless. I tell you again and again that the only polite name for these people is "Romans", but even when our Prince is about to marry one of their princesses you continue to call them Grifons. Why can't you remember to be courteous?'

'I'm sorry, my dear. It slips out. Everyone else calls them Grifons, even Sir Geoffrey the most courteous knight in these parts. Perhaps there is a limit to the improvements that can be effected in any husband, even though his wife works hard.'

'Oh, very well. I think in Greek, the language of the Gospels and of the wise men of old. I shall speak of Romans, which is correct. But I shall understand you when you call them Grifons, because you are only a poor ignorant Frank.'

'I admit my grave faults. But you were saying that there might be a fee for us, so perhaps I shan't be poor for ever; though of course I shall remain an ignorant barbarian. You must explain what you think our Prince is after. I know he is going to marry a lady from beyond our frontier, if that description is colourless enough to satisfy you. Can any lady from over the frontier bring us a valuable alliance?'

'This one can. She is Anna Angelina of Wallachia. Her father is a very great lord, who may one day become Emperor of the Romans.'

'Anyone might become Emperor of the Romans. They say that poor Baldwin is in a very bad way, and would abdicate if he could find another prince to take on his responsibilities. The Grifons have an Emperor already, I understand. Isn't that the title of the schismatic rebel who rules from Nice in Asia?'

'Let me explain. The Romans have always been ruled by an Emperor, and they can't be happy without one. But for the last fifty years there has been no recognised leader of all the Romans. After the capture of Constantinople the free Romans served any petty lord who would fight the Franks. Now only two of these lords are left, and one of them will soon be father-in-law to our Prince. That gives promise of a fee for little Geoffrey Briwerr.'

Melisande went on to explain at length the tangled history of the free Grifons after the Latin capture of Constantinople. Her father had been on the skirts of it, for all that he adhered to the Franks; among the Grifons the Melisseni are a great house. To her it was all vivid and important and breathlessly exciting; but I had never heard of any of these people and did not know where their castles lay, so that I found it hard to remember. When she came down to the present day, and said that the sister of this lady Anna had left home at the same time to marry King Manfred of Sicily, I realised that she was describing something important. In the end I had a coherent view of the Grifon world as it was in the year 1259; though I have never been able to remember the chain of treasons, blindings, poisonings, and other betrayals which got it into that condition. This is more or less how things were at that time.

Only two Grifon rulers mattered, the Emperor in Nice and the Despot of Wallachia. The Emperor's title had come to him more or less by accident, though it was recognised by every Grifon free to express his own opinion. When Constantinople fell the schismatic Patriarch got away to Nice, a city of Asia; in Nice there was now a schismatic Patriarch-in-exile, whose coronation of the lord who ruled him conferred, in Grifon eyes, the title of Emperor. But at this moment the lordship of Nice was in very low water. A child sat on the throne; an ambitious soldier, one Michael Palaeologue, had proclaimed himself colleague and guardian. It was unlikely that their joint rule would endure, but which faction would come out on top was still uncertain.

Wallachia, Melisande told me, was a very different matter. There they had solved the problem of succession in a typically Grifon manner. The lordship had been founded by a bastard of the great Angelus house, the family which had ruled in Constantinople before the Franks; and bastardy had become the distinguishing mark of his dynasty. That is to say, the lord of Wallachia married, but he kept concubines as well; and he chose as his successor the most promising of his sons, who so far had never been a son of his wife. The present lord, Michael Angelus, had married a Grifon lady of high birth and virtuous life, and it was with her daughters as brides that he was now seeking allies; but his favourite son and probable successor was as usual a bastard, one John Ducas.

Of the ancient Empire of Romanie the Franks held the city of Constantinople, the islands, and the mainland provinces of Satines and Lamorie. The rest of the mainland, from the Black Sea to the Adriatic, was divided between the Grifon lords of Nice and Wallachia. Nice had the lion's share, from the strip of Asia on the frontier of the Turks as far west as the great town of Salonique. Wallachia was a land of mountains and mountaineers, poor, war-like and savage. According to Melisande, Michael Angelus the Despot intended to alter all that with the aid of his Frankish sons-in-law.

'Every Roman knows what is coming,' she ended her exposition. 'The Wallachians and the Franks will drive the Nicenes back to Asia. Then the Despot Michael will proclaim himself Emperor, with his capital at Salonique; and Lamorie will be enlarged. Sir Geoffrey is sure to be given some part of our new province. That's where you must ask him for a Briwerr fee, which one day will come to our little Geoffrey.'

'It all sounds very hopeful,' I answered, still mildly puzzled.

'The geography is a bit beyond me. Where is Wallachia? And will any share of the conquered land go to our Emperor Baldwin?'

'Wallachia? North and east of Satines. You must have seen it from the castle of Oro in Negripont. It's called after the Wallachians who pasture their flocks there, but Romans live in it as well. As for the Emperor Baldwin, it's no use pretending he has a future. The Romans take it for granted that soon Constantinople will change hands. The only question is whether it will fall to Wallachia or to Nice.'

I was nettled. Why should these Grifons suppose that the famous trophy of the Fourth Crusade was about to fall into their hands?

'Grifons in Constantinople? What next? The strongest city in the world, and a garrison of Frankish knights and Venetian sailors. Can you imagine Grifons storming those walls?'

'I have seen the walls and you haven't, William, so don't get excited. I agree that they are very strong, and that it would be hard to storm them. Nobody hopes to turn out the Emperor by force. They expect he will go away of his own accord, because he has no land to enfeoff his knights and no money to pay them. One day the Venetians will get tired of keeping their ships in the Golden Horn with no chance of profit. The Romans of the city dislike Frankish rule. When the Frankish garrison leaves the Emperor must leave with them.'

I did not answer. Melisande sometimes complains that I cannot discuss public affairs without losing my temper, and I did not want to give her cause for legitimate complaint. The trouble is that we look at public affairs from different angles. I see Right battling against Wrong, and assume that Right must triumph in the end. She sees only strength and weakness, and assumes that the weak will be beaten. When I argue with her she will admit that God defends the Right sometimes, though not always. But she says that in questions of sovereignty and dominion there is no right or wrong, but only a struggle

88

between tyrants. She supports the Franks against the schismatics of the east; but merely because it is the cause of her husband and her dead parents, not because she holds it to be righteous.

By the time we reached Andreville I knew all about the politics of Romanie; in fact I knew too much, so that I saw subtleties and significant hints in every casual word. But that also is one of the customs of the country. A Grifon cannot hear a pedlar cry figs without wondering whether a hidden meaning is concealed in the message.

The wedding in the family church of the Villehardouins was an elaborate ceremony, a mixture of the ritual of east and west. A crown was held over the head of the bride, but the bridegroom stood bareheaded. The canon of the nuptial Mass was sung in Latin by the Bishop of Andreville, the Gospel and Epistle and the proper were intoned by priests of the Greek rite in their own tongue. The questions and answers of the marriage were repeated in both languages, so as to be binding everywhere.

All the same, the bride's relatives did not receive Communion. There might be Grifon priests on the altar. But those priests had sworn obedience to Rome; to any Grifon that is more disgusting than the Bulgarian heresy.

Afterwards there was a short breakfast at tables set up in the main square (for in Romanie you can count on fine weather). In the afternoon we all rode a few miles to the castle of Clarence. The decaying town of Andreville could not lodge such a large company.

The tournaments and feasting must have cost a mint of money, but the new Princess had brought a great dowry with her. Everyone was happy, even the bridal couple; which is not always the case when a middle-aged widower marries a pretty young girl.

The Princess Anna was an attractive girl, with some Frankish blood; her saintly mother had been born a Petralipha, descended from a knight named Petrus de Alpibus who had settled in the east long ago. But for two generations the family had followed the customs of Romanie, and in sentiment Anna was entirely Grifon. She wore the heavy shapeless robes of a Grifon lady, so that from a distance you could not tell whether she was male or female; but at close range the paint on her face made her look like a western whore. In eating she used a golden fork, with a great pearl in the handle. She used it gracefully, without dropping her food or missing her mouth, so that even the most hidebound Frank saw that the custom could be courteous in those who had been trained to it from childhood.

Prince William was delighted with her. She had been educated in the true spirit of royalty, to marry a stranger and please him so that in old age she might rule through her children; she was more than twenty years younger than her husband, and prepared to endure married life while awaiting the consolations of widowhood. Her manners were charming, a little more formal than the Frankish mode; she was one of those tender, shrinking, feminine wives who leave everything to the gentlemen, confident that the gentlemen will follow their advice.

In addition to her suite of ladies and clerks she brought a small bodyguard. On their first formal appearance, at the wedding feast, these guardsmen made a sensation. They were not a bit like the Grifons we were used to.

The vulgar legend that all Grifons are cowards is not believed by the Franks of Romanie; we know that when Grifons choose to fight in earnest they can be very tough customers. But it is true that they are slow to take up arms, swallowing slights and challenges that would have a true knight calling for his sword whatever the odds. In general Grifons want to die in their beds, not on the field of honour; and they value bodily prowess lower than cunning, provided the cunning leads to victory.

The attendants of Princess Anna were not at all that kind of man. They wore heavy Grifon robes and towering Grifon headdresses, so unlike our tight surcoats and flat coifs; their eyes and lips were improved by paint after the Grifon custom, which always startles a Frank when first he sees it. (But this custom is not really wicked. As Melisande pointed out to me, if it is right to alter the colour of your face by washing it, it cannot be wrong to improve the colour of your lips with red paint.) Their beards were plucked to a point and strongly scented. They must have taken a long time to get dressed for the wedding.

But in their long robes they moved easily; their boots of scented leather were apt for walking; their under-tunics were girdled with wide silken sashes, and in the sashes were three or four short swords or long daggers. These men were warriors, as much as any Frankish knight. There was something in the way they strode up the nave of St James that reminded me of the Esclavons; after four years in Romanie I could recognise a mountaineer, even when his legs were hidden under a long gown.

Seeing my interest, Melisande whispered to me. 'Those are the chieftains of Wallachia. Their fathers carried the Angelus banner into Salonique. Now do you see why I expect this alliance will give us new land for a Briwerr fee?'

At the feastings in Clarence the guardsmen attracted a good deal of attention. Of course some people were saying that our Prince disparaged himself by marrying the daughter of a savage hill-chieftain, but to that there was a crushing answer. If the lady Helen Angelina was good enough for King Manfred Hohenstaufen, then her sister must be good enough for Villehardouin of Champagne and Lamorie.

For a week there was jousting and hunting all day, and feasting in the evening. To live in such a crowd of strangers seemed odd, almost like living in a large army. It was like being in an army in another way also, for everyone you met talked of the coming war.

No war had been proclaimed; this was not a parliament, and Prince William had not even spoken publicly to his followers. But everyone knew that war was in the offing. A great lord does not marry a schismatic foreigner merely to have a foreign mother for his children.

Sir Geoffrey was delighted at the prospect of battle. Riding back from a hunt I had a long talk with him. One of his hounds had been injured by a boar, and I had volunteered to take it on my saddle back to the kennels; since I was riding a hackney borrowed from the Carytena stable this was more or less my duty. Sir Geoffrey rode with me because he wanted to oversee the dressing of the hound's injury.

'Next month we shall be riding destriers,' he said cheerfully, 'and properly dressed. I hate the feel of a riding boot against my stirrup, where there should be mail. That last battle at Mount Caride was no fun at all; just one joust and then a lot of galloping in the heat, and afterwards a tedious lonely imprisonment to pay for it. But after the next charge we shall be digging our hands to the elbows in caskets of rich Grifon jewels. Romanie is a wonderful land to plunder, and a most difficult land to defend. Thank Heaven next time we shall be on the attack.'

'Do you enjoy killing men, my lord?' I inquired. It may sound an odd question, but I was not trying to be impudent. Sir Geoffrey was by common consent the best knight in all Romanie; I myself wanted to be a good knight, and I was eager to know how a good knight felt about war.

Sir Geoffrey stared at me, but he took my point. He thought for a moment before answering.

'I don't look forward to killing men,' he said consideringly, 'though it comes easily enough and I sleep well afterwards. Besides, how often do you kill a knight? You knock him off his horse and leave him to take his chance on the ground. As to the common foot, there's seldom any need to hurt them. They will run, or surrender, as soon as their leaders are beaten. No, the real thrill of battle is seeing all that crowd of men eager to kill *you*, and not letting them do it. There's no finer sport in the world.'

'I don't think I have ever killed a man, unless you count Esclavons,' I went on, pursuing my own train of thought. 'I find killing horses rather horrible.'

'Who doesn't? Sometimes you can't avoid it. A pity no one can train a destrier to surrender when he has had enough. By the way, cousin William, how are you horsed for this campaign? Your last destrier broke down, didn't he, when we ran away so fast from Mount Caride? No offence meant, I ran faster than any of you. But you will need a good horse in the summer.'

'I have my eye on one, my lord. He's more or less half bought. We are still haggling over the price. An import from Italy, not a local nag. A gelding. But he may be safer than a stallion among those precipices.'

'I'll lend you the money for him, if that's the difficulty. But you must pay it back out of your future wages. I had to give a good many presents in connection with my trial, and at the moment I'm hard up. A gelding will carry you well enough, but one day you ought to try a local charger. Your horse wouldn't have been exported from Italy if the Italians had thought he was any good.'

'Perhaps I know better than the Italians,' I answered shortly. Anyone takes offence at a slur on his judgement of horseflesh.

'Perhaps you do, cousin William,' he said pleasantly. 'It won't be long before the matter is tested. We march at Pentecost, I believe.'

'We all look forward to it, my lord. But could you tell me whither we shall march, and whom we shall attack? Nothing has been said in public about this campaign, and today we are at peace with all the world. Perhaps it's a silly question, everyone else seems to know all about it. But I have been in Romanie for less than five years, and I find local politics most baffling.'

'It's quite simple, really. The big surprise is that uncle William has despaired of Frankish Constantinople. I dare say he is right. He thinks about these things and I don't. But if the Emperor Baldwin is chased out some Grifon will get the city. Two Grifons are in the running, the fellow in Nice who hates Franks, and the fellow in Wallachia who has a more open mind. So we all help the fellow in Wallachia against the fellow in Nice, and when our man has Constantinople he gives us some of the land he holds now, land he won't want then because to a Grifon Wallachia is not really civilised. It ought to work out very well. In fact it must be a sound scheme, because everyone backs it.'

'Everyone, my lord? Do you mean we have other allies?'

'Indeed yes. It's all fixed up. Michael Angelus leads his army to the eastward; you can see it's a good army from the bodyguard who came with the Princess. All the Franks of Romanie march with him; not only Lamorie but Satines and La Sole and La Bondonice, everyone who fought at Mount Caride on either side. But the big news is that King Manfred will join in. Some say he will come with all his power, but I think that's too good to be true. It's definite that he has promised to send three hundred knights to fight for his father-in-law, and Manfred is a man of his word.'

'That's news indeed. Why, it will be practically another Crusade!'

'You may *think* that, cousin William, but don't say it. You can't have a Crusade led by an excommunicate King. At least, it's been done, and by Manfred's own father, but it wasn't a success. Besides, talk about Crusading annoys our Grifon allies. We shall march to bring peace to the disordered Empire, and to thrust back the Turks. Grifon burgesses like that kind of language, so they won't defend their cities against us. But in these parts Crusaders have a bad name. Oh, and by the way, I've just remembered that all this is highly confidential. I heard it at the Prince's council, and he doesn't want it known. So don't tell anyone until William announces it officially.'

After a minute he added: 'But in Nice they will have known it since the marriage was proposed. Probably earlier, for that matter. Grifons know everything that a Frank plans to do.'

'That's true, my lord,' I agreed. 'But in this case advance knowledge won't help them. No Grifon lord can stand up to the power we shall bring against the east. May I tell my wife? I value her advice on local matters.'

'Don't bother to tell her – wait until she tells you. The lady Melisande has many friends among the Grifons. But that's enough about war and politics. Mind the hound doesn't fall. With a gash like that on his leg he'll never be sound again. But even though he can't hunt I want to breed from him.'

After a week of tournaments and feasting Prince William left Clarence for La Cremonie, and we went back to Carytena. There had still been no official summons to the coming war, but everyone in Lamorie knew it was to begin before Pentecost. It was a bad time to buy a destrier. I had to close the deal without further bargaining, and to borrow heavily from my lord's steward to make up the price. The horse I bought had some high-sounding Italian name, too grand for an animal not in the top class; I called him Tom, so that too much should not be expected from him. He was a big brown eight-year-old gelding, sure-footed and a good jumper and up to any weight, quiet in a crowd and willing to do what was asked of him. But his large body stood on short though sound legs, so that he was slow; and he leaned on the bit and bored whenever you made him hurry. A mule could have caught him on the flat; if I got into a tight place I must jump a wall.

The lady Isabel came with us to Carytena. She was to be castellan while we were on campaign, and it was rumoured that her uncle had advised her to live with her husband lest she lose him. This year she was not pregnant (in fact she never started another child), and in spring Carytena can be reasonably bright and cheerful. But she was not getting on well with my lord. He could not forget that her advice had persuaded him into the felony which lost him the rank of a baron of the conquest; she sometimes murmured, so Melisande told me, that the best knight in all Romanie should have taken over the defence of Estives and avoided a humiliating peace. They shared the state bed in the state chamber, but they were rarely together in the daytime.

When the formal summons came to muster at the isthmus everyone was prepared for war. It was an unusually fine spring, with birds singing in every tree; we all longed to be ravaging in hostile territory. There was a veteran sergeant who could remember the vanished kingdom of Salonique, destroyed by the Bulgarians before I was born; he told us that it was much better land than Lamorie, flat and full of hard-working and obedient peasants. Salonique was reputed to be the wealthiest city in Romanie after Constantinople; it had been sacked more than once in the last twenty years, but there should still be plenty left. If this campaign went according to plan it should make us all rich.

Melisande prophesied that it would not go according to plan. She turned down my suggestion that she should ride with the army, partly because she thought a third little Briwerr might be on the way, partly, as she frankly confessed, because she was frightened.

'Those Wallachs are not ordinary Romans,' she explained. 'In Constantinople they are regarded as treacherous savages. Michael Angelus himself is not an ordinary Roman. If he were a man of honour he would not have called in Frankish allies; no honourable Roman would lead foreigners against his own people. Franks never understand how Romans hate and fear them. And since he is not a man of honour he may very well betray his allies. Mind you stick in the middle of the mesnie. If Sir Geoffrey tries to send you off with a party of mountaineers make some excuse; they would murder any Frank who rode with them alone. The worst of it is that even if you beat the Nicenes you are sure to quarrel with your allies immediately afterwards.'

'That's going too far, my dear,' I said as soothingly as I could. 'We are setting off to plunder between Salonique and Constantinople, and in that rich land there will be enough for all.'

'That's the mistake all Franks make,' she answered with a sob. 'It isn't a rich land, though it may have been rich long ago. Romans get money out of it, because their tax-gatherers can get blood from a stone. If you rule it in Frankish fashion, taking harvest dues and hearth-silver, you won't have enough to live on. Look at Constantinople! The Roman Emperor who ruled it

96

was the richest lord in the world; Baldwin hasn't two pennies to rub together. When we get our fee it won't bring in half the money its Roman lord used to get out of it. Anyway, we won't get a fee, because our allies will cheat us out of it.'

'That doesn't worry me. They may try to cheat, but our swords are heavier than theirs. If they start anything we shall just take all Wallachia.'

'Prince William intends to take it anyway, whether his allies give him an excuse or not,' she answered calmly, as though such double-dealing were the most natural thing in the world. 'But I suppose King Manfred will get most of it in the end. Don't you see, my dear William, your fine allied army is after three different things. The Emperor Frederic used to write himself King of Albania, so Manfred will try to snatch what his father held. But old Angelus used to rule there so the Despot won't give it to him. The Despot wants Constantinople, and our Prince can't help him to take it from a Frankish Emperor. Prince William would be content with southern Wallachia; but he can't have it, because the Despot's favourite bastard is married to the daughter of the Wallach chieftain. You will be like three men in one boat, each steering for a different harbour. I'm sorry you must ride with the mesnie. Couldn't you break a leg and stay behind?'

'Now here's my wife willing me to break a leg. If tomorrow my horse rolls down the hillside I shall denounce you as a witch. Seriously, my dear, things are not so black as you see them. We don't trust Grifons and they don't trust us. Very well. We shan't get into a position where they can betray us. Remember, Frankish knights can ride through any army of Grifons. We may not be able to conquer the land, but at least we must come home safely.'

'What an unlucky boast,' exclaimed Melisande. 'Unsay it quickly. Tell St Theodore you didn't mean it, and put a silver cover on his shield to prove it.'

From the chest at the foot of our bed she rummaged out a little picture of St Theodore, the warrior-saint who is more popular in Romanie even than St George. It was a new picture, so far without silver covering; dear Melisande admitted that she had bought it in Andreville, to seek St Theodore's help while I was on the coming campaign. It must have been painted by a schismatic; but St Theodore is a genuine saint, honoured also in the Latin calendar. An ounce of silver on his shield would make a beginning for the complete covering which these little pictures expect from their devotees. I did what Melisande asked of me, which comforted her a little; though she still feared that my boasting must bring me bad luck.

On the other hand, every Frank in Romanie thought the campaign would be very lucky indeed. The most obvious and amazing example of this luck was that the knights of Satines came willingly to serve under Prince William. Last summer they had fought against him; but we were all a little ashamed of that stupid civil war which had weakened the Frankish cause, and the Megaskyr was absent in France. Once the St Omers had given a lead everyone hastened to muster under the banner of Villehardouin. Even the lords of La Bondonice and La Sole came with their mesnies, though no one had expected them to heed the oaths of homage they had sworn after the defeat at Mount Caride. Sanudo, Duke of the Archipelago, and Orsini, Count of Cephalonia, brought their meagre following; though they came as partners and allies, for no one has ever pretended that these Italian pirate-chiefs owe homage to Lamorie.

Another stroke of luck was that we did not have to invent a pretext for our invasion. In fact when we marched from the isthmus it was not to invade a hostile land. In Nice Michael Palaeologue had deposed and blinded the boy-Emperor, after the custom of the Grifons, and sought to impress his new subjects by extending his dominions. His brother had invaded Wallachia at the head of a great army of foreign mercenaries. Our ally the Despot Michael was hard-pressed by this John Palaeologue, and begged us to help him. Best of all, we heard that four hundred knights from Sicily had actually landed in

Wallachia. King Manfred was observing the terms of his treaty, a thing you can never count on in advance. These Ghibellines came from Sicily; but rumour said they were in fact Germans, equipped with the new-fangled German plate-armour. I hope I don't hurt anyone's feelings when I say that Germans have a higher repute on the battlefield than Sicilians; in their armour of plate they were said to be invincible.

Our army, as it entered southern Wallachia, was stronger than any force put into the field by the Franks of Romanie since the capture of Constantinople. We were nearly a thousand knights, with servants and grooms and spearmen about fifteen thousand men of all sorts. There were no ladies with us, unless you count a few of the kind of women who always follow armies.

Gossip from Lamorie said that the Princess Anna feared that the de la Roches would overthrow her husband in his absence, which is the kind of thing any Grifon would do in similar circumstances. She was supposed to have stormed at her lord, saying that while there was a single de la Roche in Satines she must stay in Lamorie to keep an eye on the foes of her unborn children. Which is likely enough in itself; but the men who told us of it would not have been allowed in the Villehardouin bedchamber to overhear a private conversation.

Once we had passed La Bondonice we were in the lands of the Wallachs, a race of foreigners strange to me. They adhere to the schismatic church, and in the old days they were subject to the Grifon Emperor; but they are not Grifons. One of the oddest things about them is their speech, which at a distance sounds like Italian though when you get close you find the words are different. Some of the Orsini's islanders claimed that they could understand it, but the Lombards of La Bondonice said that for their part they could not. On the other hand, there are many different dialects of Italian.

In their customs, as well as in their language, the Wallachs differ from their Grifon neighbours. They are herdsmen rather than farmers; they lead an unsettled life, moving with their flocks from one valley to another. But they go in for sheep more than horned cattle, and do their shepherding on foot; they are not so formidable as Turks or Pechenegs, who are all mounted herdsmen. Yet the Wallach warriors are not to be despised; tall shaggy men wrapped in long cloaks of sheepskin, very jealous of their honour and quick to take offence. They pasture their flocks wherever they find grazing, without bothering about the rights of the landlord.

At that time all the Wallachs in Romanie acknowledged a supreme lord, one Tarchonites; and his daughter was the wife of John Ducas, the bastard and favourite son of the Despot Michael. At the end of our first march over the frontier this Ducas met us at the head of his men, Wallachs with a sprinkling of Grifon nobles. They were mounted, but not on war-horses; their light ponies would be no use in the charge and the riders carried short curved sabres. That was a grave disappointment. Of course we had not expected to find foreigners capable of charging in line beside Frankish knights, but we had hoped for squadrons of horse-archers. The Nicene army we were to fight contained many counted archers, and we needed some of the same kind of people to keep them away from the main battle, where their interference can spoil a good joust.

It seemed that these light horses would be useless for anything except scouting, or ravaging the land of our enemies. We had no need of scouts, since we intended to march against the Nicenes and provoke them into meeting us; and as for ravaging, we could do that ourselves and did not want speedier and more agile competitors. We grumbled a bit, until Sir Geoffrey reminded us that with war in their land these savage warriors would not stand idle; unless they rode with us they would ride against us. It was better that they should be on our side, and we must make an effort to be pleasant to them.

While we passed through their land they were most hospitable. Old Tarchonites slaughtered a flock of sheep to feast the whole Frankish army. It was a barbaric and romantic repast, with rows of blazing bonfires stretching down the valley, while warriors squatted on the ground before joints of sizzling mutton. There was plenty to eat, always something to remember when you are on campaign; but not nearly enough to drink. These Wallachs make no wine of their own; and though they steal it from their neighbours, stolen wine seldom reaches headquarters, as any veteran will tell you. Where I sat, among the household knights, we were offered beer full of barley-husks. Some of the sergeants, I understand, had to be content with water.

But at the principal fire, corresponding to the high table, there was wine; which started a bit of trouble that had grave consequences later. Tarchonites sat there, with our ally John Ducas and his wife. I had already caught a glimpse of her, a tall plump woman with bold staring eyes; a real barbarian, but a fine animal of the kind that appeals especially to very civilised men.

She was the only lady at the feast. Of course some of our leaders made the usual courteous conversation, praising her beauty as though they were in a western hall; it was the only form of polite conversation they knew. That apparently is contrary to Wallach etiquette; but neither the lady Helen Ducaina nor her lord understood French, and no harm was done. Then, after the wine had gone round more than once, an Orsini discovered that he could make himself understood in Italian.

The rumour ran quickly from fire to fire that there had been trouble among the leaders. We could see that the Wallachs were annoyed with us, though we could not understand what they said. I think they were in two minds whether to attack us, though we were actually eating their food at their hearths, their guests in the strongest sense of the term. Perhaps that kept them from a breach of hospitality, perhaps it was the lucky chance that we had our swords with us. Anyway, the feasting ended early, and we went quietly back to our camp without a blow struck.

Next morning, when we took up the march again, Sir Geoffrey rode among his household to warn us against causing further ill feeling. He himself saw nothing very serious in it, but his uncle had commanded him to pass on the warning.

'Last night the only guest at the high table who had a good time was the lady Helen Ducaina,' he said with a mocking grin. 'If you can call a bare patch of ant-infested mud a high table. I mean the fire where the chief of these barbarians entertained the leaders. It was a sticky evening to start with; filthy wine, and everything spoken through interpreters, which takes the sparkle out of the wittiest crack. We each of us said something polite to the pop-eyed bitch – you know what one says on these occasions. How we would all fight the better knowing that she saw our prowess, and begging for a garter to wear in our helms. The interpreters made rather heavy weather of it, and I don't think half was passed on. Even so. John Ducas did not like it at all. Apparently at a Wallach feast you should look right through a married lady, or turn your back on her; at any rate, pretend she isn't there.'

My lord heaved a sigh, shrugging his shoulders.

'Then one of the Orsini boys found he could manage without the interpreter. His Italian is pretty debased anyhow, and he was reared in Rome where they are used to making themselves understood by foreign pilgrims. He jabbered his patois straight at the lady, and after a pause she began to answer him. Soon he was laying his hand on his heart, begging her to visit his island home. Mind you, I think he spread it on too thick. He was making fun of a she-barbarian who doesn't understand the convention of courteous love. If I had been her husband I wouldn't have liked it either. But John Ducas, boiling with rage, took quite the wrong line. Instead of complaining that a guest was being too familiar with the daughter of his host, which was the truth, he stood up and made a speech at uncle William. He pointed out that his father was the mighty Despot of Wallachia. His grandfather also had been Despot of Wallachia, and if you went back far enough his ancestors had reigned as Emperors of the Grifons in Constantinople, Equals of the Apostles and all the rest of the high-sounding titles. He spoke in Grifon, of course, so we could all understand him.'

My lord chuckled softly to himself.

'He went on much too long, though uncle William very civilly didn't interrupt him. All the time he was boasting of his lineage, saying how frightful it was that such a thing should be done to *him*; instead of complaining that a young man with too much drink taken had displayed a streak of ordinary Italian vulgarity. It was a good speech, of course, well turned and well constructed. Any educated Grifon can churn out the stuff at a moment's notice. He ended with a fine peroration: "You must apologise to my father, Despot and son of Despots, heir to the Empire of New Rome, guardian of our ancient culture and our true religion, the hero who will soon be enthroned in the seat of his mighty ancestors."'

Sir Geoffrey was shaking with laughter.

'Uncle William stood up to reply. He's a head taller than the angry little Grifon. For a minute he looked the little man up and down, to make sure we were all listening. I could see from the twinkle in his eye that there was a good answer coming; and he delivered it in Grifon, so that all his audience could take it in. He began very slowly and solemnly. "There has indeed been an insult to a noble line. I shall apologise to your father, the mighty Despot, son of all those eminent men you mentioned just now. But, my lord, I shall go further. I shall do even more than you have asked of me. I shall apologise also to your mother, as soon as I can find the washtub where she works in the castle of Arta. Thus full restitution shall be made to *both* sides of your noble family."'

'That broke up the party,' Sir Geoffrey went on after we had stopped laughing. 'It was naughty of uncle William. For one thing, the Despot did not leave his girl-friend at the castle wash-tub, though by all accounts that was where he found her. They say she is now set up in a snug little house in the town. All the same, John Ducas got what was coming to him. I have nothing against bastards as a class. The world is full of them, and we have all done our share in filling it. A bastard can be a gentleman of honour, as well all know. But a bastard who boasts of his ancestors – that's too much.

'So there's the whole story of last night's quarrel,' Sir Geoffrey continued quietly. 'I seem to have told it back to front, but that sometimes happens when I have got hold of a good tale. I was supposed to tell it as an awful warning against making advances to Wallach ladies. Don't do it, boys. Be faithful to your wives, if you can manage it. If not, no one will mind you chasing peasant girls. But Wallach ladies are out of bounds, remember.'

John Ducas and his men came with us to the muster. But they marched by themselves, and were not at all friendly.

CHAPTER SEVEN

Pelagonie

At the time I did not grasp the geography of Wallachia, the land we had ridden so far to defend; and I am still vague about it. But we could tell from the shape of the landscape that we were in a foreign country. It is as hilly as Lamorie, and in fact the mountains are higher; but everything is on a more spacious scale. The valleys are very wide, two or three miles as often as not; the great ranges sweep up gently, interrupted by flat shoulders on which are set small, poverty-stricken, strongly-walled towns. There is not much cultivation, and some of that impermanent; in summer the locals snatch a crop from the river beds, knowing that winter floods will sweep away their boundary-stones. Everywhere rock thrusts through the scanty soil. But in spring the rocky ground is covered with tall grass, very good pasture for cattle and sheep. From such a land the Despot drew a poor revenue, though all his subjects were warriors.

The little towns, studded with high-domed churches, were inhabited by Grifon burgesses; though most of them wore short swords in their sashes and moved with the swagger of free mountaineers. The herdsmen we saw in the open country were many of them Wallachs; but sometimes we came across little gangs of Arnauts, true savages who speak an incomprehensible language and live by stealing laden mules from one another. These Arnauts, said to be the fiercest warriors in Romanie, inhabit the region of Albania, which was claimed by both the Despot and King Manfred; but they acknowledge no lord and are constantly at war with their neighbours. Grifon merchants employ them to drive mule-trains, for they are skilful with mules and even the boldest robbers fear them. But they seldom arrive at their destination with exactly the goods entrusted to them; either they have stolen more on the way or other Arnauts have robbed them.

When at last we joined the great host of the Despot we found it made up of these motley races. It was the largest army I have ever seen, and every man in it was brave and active. All the same it was not really a formidable force; since the warriors were experienced cut-throats whose chief concern was to come out of battle alive rather than veterans who will stand in line and endure casualties. No Grifon trusts a Wallach, while both races fear and despise the Arnauts. Besides, these mountaineers wore light mail and preferred to fight on foot, though most of them had some kind of horse or mule to carry them on the march.

In a separate encampment lay the contingent sent by King Manfred, and we were very cheered to see them. At that time all the west was talking about the new plate armour devised in Germany, which made a knight invulnerable if he could find a destrier strong enough to carry it. Though these men had come from Sicily they were not Sicilians, but a draft from the German garrison of the island.

We joined the Despot in a wide valley, named Pelagonie after a little town at the head of it. The Despot's men were encamped on a spur of the western slope, behind a ditch and bank such as all Grifons dig for fear of night attacks. To the north lay the Germans, and we were directed to camp on the south. I think the Grifons would have liked us also to dig a ditch round our camp, as though we were afraid of our enemies. But apart from the disgrace of such a precaution we had no labourers to dig for us; Prince William had brought only knights and sergeants and their grooms. A good stream of clear water had been reserved for our use, and we found waiting for us in camp abundant pork, plenty of wine, and not quite enough bread. In these mountains forage is always a problem, but the local peasants had been set to cutting grass.

Before our arrival there had been no serious fighting, though much marching and counter-marching. The Nicene army, led by John Palaeologue, brother of the Nicene Emperor, had pushed far into Wallachia and taken many fortresses; but the Despot Michael had rallied his men, and on the arrival of Manfred's German contingent the Nicenes had retreated in haste. Now they were encamped on the eastern side of the valley, a few miles away but in touch with our outposts. We had come in time for the battle. If we won there would be unravaged country for us to plunder, and perhaps fees for all landless knights. It was the kind of campaign that suited us.

But nothing is ever quite so good as it seems at first glance. After a pleasant night in camp, passed in comfortable tents provided by the Despot, I strolled over in the morning to have a look at the Germans and their famous armour. They made no difficulty about admitting visitors; and since on that day there was no alarm the armour could be seen displayed on stands. There were back-and-breasts made each from a single piece of metal, joined by straps at shoulder and waist; there were knee-guards and elbow-guards, and curved greaves made all in one piece; commonplace nowadays, though at that time exciting novelties. But the man who showed me round was not quite of the type I had expected.

I cannot speak German, and few Germans speak French. But I had travelled through Italy and these warriors had held Sicily for King Manfred; so my guide and I could exchange information in elementary Italian, though neither of us was up to polite conversation. He was civil, and eager to be pleasant to an ally; but I could see that he was not a gentleman, and I took it for granted that he must be some kind of superior armourer or groom. Then he showed me a fine suit of armour, better made than most; and made me understand that it was what he would wear in the coming battle, for he was a man of mark in this German contingent.

I came away depressed. King Manfred had sent help to his father-in-law, as he had promised. His men were well armed and well mounted. But they were hired sergeants, without a knight among them. Mind you, I don't despise sergeants. For some operations, holding a tower or scouting in broken country, they are actually more useful than knights, since as a rule they can be trusted to obey orders; a second line of sergeants lends weight to the charge. But sergeants fight for pay, not for glory. No one expects them to hew a way to the enemy banner, or to dispute a lost field. In Romanie Franks are valued for their foolhardy courage, for charging against odds without thought of retreat. If Michael Angelus trusted these Germans to form the spearhead of his attack the spear would never strike home.

Back in our own camp my spirits rose. Perhaps the Germans were not so good as we had been led to believe, but none the less our army contained brave knights in plenty – the mesnies of Lamorie and Satines and the islands, the whole Frankish chivalry of Romanie. We could put into line more than eight hundred dubbed knights, gentlemen of honour. The great army of Nice, across the valley, containing no soldiers who could stand against us.

Meanwhile there was a lull in the campaign. For some reason, a sound reason for all I know to the contrary, each side waited to be attacked by the other; perhaps all these light-armed Arnauts and Wallachs are more useful in defending a rampart than in the charge. The idea was that if we waited there long enough John Palaeologue must attack us or lose prestige; he was the brother of the Nicene Emperor, who had honoured him with the high-sounding title of Sebastocrator. The Grifons would despise him if he clung to the defensive against a mere Despot.

But the Sebastocrator was not yet ready to launch his attack. He was gathering a very great army, and did not attempt to conceal the arrival of his reinforcements. We could see them marching in long columns over the skyline; though we could not see his tents, hidden below a fold of the mountain.

In the mesnie of Escorta we were quite content to wait. Our wine and pork were lasting out very well, and when there is wine enough no one minds a slight shortage of bread. Sir Geoffrey and the other great lords had brought their pavilions, gaily painted affairs with arms blazoned over the entrance and silken banners flying from the poles. The rest of us were very snug in canvas tents provided by the Despot. Their floors were deeply covered in heather, and cunning Grifon labourers had dug channels to carry off the rain-water. At that height in the mountains the nights were chilly, but by day the sun shone pleasantly from a blue sky. It was a comfortable, well-organised camp. Grifons are clever at that sort of thing.

Our leaders were always meeting in conference, as is the custom in every Grifon army. Since our plan was already decided, to await attack from the Sebastocrator, I wondered what they had to discuss so earnestly for long hours every day. But Sir Geoffrey was a most approachable, friendly lord, quite willing to talk over state secrets with any of his knights who took the trouble to ask him.

On the third morning I had a chat with him, as we strolled through the horse-lines after morning stables. Last night there had been a long council of war, interrupted soon after dark by an alarm that the enemy were forming for a night-attack on our camp. We had been called out to saddle up and stand to, and then sent back to our blankets. Naturally, I asked first about the reason for this false alarm.

'Don't grumble too much, cousin William,' he answered, 'though I know it can be maddening to haul out a good horse from the picket-line in the middle of the night and watch him cough. I hope your Tom took no harm? If he is coughing I can let you have some physic, but don't dose him unless you must. We may fight any day now, and a horse never does his best with physic in him.'

'That's kind of you, my lord. But why were we called out? Are these Grifon scouts any good at their job?'

'Very good indeed, and last night they did right to alarm us. They are clever at creeping close to an enemy camp. Soon after dark they saw movement among the troops of the Sebastocrator, which might have been the beginning of a night-attack. We would have looked very silly if Nicene foot had come scrambling among our tents while we lay in our blankets.'

'I see, my lord. So long as we were not ordered to saddle up for nothing. Good scouts get you out of bed too often, but at least you may sleep sound when they report nothing stirring. What was the Sebastocrator after, marching about in the dark?'

'Ah, now that's most interesting. I'm glad you asked.' Sir Geoffrey chuckled. 'There's no secret about what they did, anyone could see it. What it means is a different matter. In the council last night we had quite an argument about it. What do you think, William? Our scouts saw moving torches, and thought it was the Sebastocrator marching out to attack us. Then, after they had quite rightly given the alarm, they looked again and saw it was men marching into the enemy camp, not out of it. Can you make anything of that?'

'Reinforcements arriving after dark,' I answered at once. But Sir Geoffrey turned a quizzical eye on me, and I thought hard before continuing.

'Yes, well, reinforcements arriving after dark,' I muttered. 'But if you are on the march when the sun sets you can usually manage without a torch. Your eyes get accustomed to the growing darkness. Anyway, why should reinforcements press on after dark, to arrive exhausted? There isn't any desperate hurry. The Nicenes know we are waiting for them to move, and they need not attack until their army is complete. Perhaps they arranged for the reinforcements to come in after dark, so that we would not know their army had grown? But, in that case, why carry torches?' At last I understood. Very slowly, you may think; but war is a serious business and it is wise to be cautious with bright ideas.

'Our scouts were right both times?' I suggested. 'They saw the same men going out and coming in? The Sebastocrator is trying to frighten us, pretending to be stronger than he is?'

'That must be it, cousin William. Since the campaign opened the Nicenes have been trying to frighten our allies, boasting of the might of their invincible army for Asia. It's true they have hired a great many mercenaries. Turks and Hungarians and Pechenegs and perhaps a squadron of Germans in plate armour to cope with our Ghibellines. But the Sebastocrator has over-egged the pudding, as they say in Champagne. We know now that some of his reinforcements are bogus. Perhaps they all are. I wish I could convince the council on that point. It's too easy to frighten Grifons, if you give them long enough to look at the danger. They have such confounded vivid imaginations. The Despot's men are getting frightened. As for the Wallachs, they talk as though they had been tricked into joining the wrong side.'

'Is there a right side and a wrong?' I asked. 'I thought this was a straight struggle for lordship over a masterless fragment of the old Empire of Romanie.'

'Ah, but madam Melisande was reared in Constantinople. You have an unfair advantage over these simple provincials: you are beginning to understand Grifon politics. The Wallachs don't understand politics, but they don't like strangers. In particular they dislike Franks; and there are not so many Franks in the Sebastocrator's army.'

'Nobody likes strangers, my lord. I don't like them myself, and that goes for King Manfred's Germans. But you can't have much of a battle unless you allow strangers to join in. Anyway, in Wallach eyes Grifons must seem as strange as any Frank.'

'Not quite, you know.' My lord was serious, and a little worried. 'The Grifons have been here always, and they pray at the same altars as Wallachs. Above all, the great merit of Grifons is that they don't make improper advances to respect-able Wallach princesses.'

'Good Heavens, are they still brooding over that little affair?' I asked in surprise.

'They are indeed. I wish it had never happened. That Orsini boy was very foolish, but it was uncle William who really put the lid on it. I suppose I shouldn't blame him. A really effective insult came into his head, and though it might make him a troublesome enemy he couldn't bottle it up. Probably I would have done the same thing in his place. All the same, young John Ducas will never forgive his father for not taking it seriously. As for the Despot's other son, the one born in wedlock, Nicephorus, he's friendly enough to the allies of his father but he's just plain scared of the might of the Nicenes. Our leaders are as quarrelsome, and as distrustful of one another, as if – as if they were Crusaders.'

I laughed. The comparison was as true as it was unkind.

'Well, never mind,' Sir Geoffrey finished. 'We have eight hundred Frankish knights in this army, besides those German sergeants. We could beat the Nicenes and the Despot's men together, if they would stand to meet our charge. Now I must be off to another of those everlasting councils. See you later, cousin William.'

I sat down in my tent and wrote to Melisande, telling her that the campaign was not so straightforward as it had appeared in Lamorie, though Sir Geoffrey agreed that the mesnie of Escorta was in no danger. I did not know when I would be home, and I might not get a fee. But food was plentiful and I slept under cover.

A de la Roche courier promised to carry my letter to Estives. Afterwards someone going that way would drop it at Nicles or La Cremonie, and from there a draper or grocer would probably take it to Carytena. In Romanie everyone is always writing letters, and travellers are usually willing to carry them.

That evening, an hour after sunset, all the Wallachs deserted in a body, led by John Ducas. It was done very neatly and quietly, after our horses had been bedded down for the night; the scoundrels were out of reach before we could saddle up and ride after them. Arnaut light horse followed their tracks, even though it was dark; for at first we hoped that they had merely grown tired of the campaign and gone home to their valleys. Soon it was known that they had climbed the opposite hill and entered the camp of the Sebastocrator. At daybreak the remaining leaders met for another council.

We were worried and excited. Every Frank felt himself to be adrift in an unknown world where anything might happen. If a son could desert his father in the field and ride into the camp of his enemies, then the rocks on the mountain might pick up swords to attack us. More seriously, we could see that the battle would not long be delayed; this treachery must have been several days in the planning, which explained why the Sebastocrator had sat quiet on his hilltop. Now, unless he expected further desertions, he must be ready to attack us. Without waiting for orders, every knight armed himself and saw to the saddling of his horse.

It was past midday when the council broke up. Sir Geoffrey strode out, grim-faced and stony-eyed. I had never seen him so stern, even when he broke through the hostile line at Mount Caride. A group of us tried to speak to him, clamouring for news; but he pushed through in silence, white-lipped. Then he snapped: 'Go away. I can't tell you anything. I have been sworn to secrecy.'

This was so unlike his usual gay comradeship that we fell back feeling snubbed and miserable. I plucked up my courage to follow him to his tent, hoping that perhaps he would make an exception of his cousin. Again he turned and snapped: 'It's a secret, I tell you, a sworn secret. A secret even from my kinsmen. One of the foulest secrets that ever burdened the soul of a true knight. I wish I could tell someone, but I can't.'

Suddenly he stopped in his tracks, staring at me. His eyes wrinkled as though with a smile, though his mouth remained set.

'Don't go right away, cousin William,' he said thoughtfully. 'I have a secret I may not tell to a living soul. But I'm not a leper, you know, there's no need to keep away from my tent. In fact you might take a look at the tent-pegs. These Grifons have fastened the guy-ropes with a cunning knot I should like to see copied in Escorta. No, don't keep away from my tent, though at present I can't invite you inside.'

I walked slowly to the tent and bent down to examine its pegs, which were in fact very sloppily fastened. I could hear my lord's voice within.

He spoke slowly and distinctly, at the same time beating on a piece of wood; which can make quite a lot of noise – Grifon priests sometimes use a sounding-board of wood where Latins would ring a bell. I peeped under the tent-flap, and saw him banging at his tent-pole with the butt of a broken lance.

'Good old tent-pole,' he said loudly, 'on all my campaigns you have been with me, against Grifons and Esclavons and against my dear uncle William. Now I must leave you to fall into the hands of my enemies. And not only you, old tent-pole. I must also abandon my servants and my muleteers and indeed all my dismounted followers. For that matter some of the knights of my mesnie may be left behind. The leaders of the host have agreed to flee secretly in the middle of the night, from shameful fear and for no other reason. But the camp must be left standing, to deceive the Sebastocrator so that we get a good start. Therefore we may not warn our faithful followers, to whom we are bound by oaths of mutual fealty. The leaders will escape while their followers perish. O my tent-pole, what baseness, what ingratitude, what felony! A good knight should warn his followers of impending danger. But a good knight cannot break his pledged word. Before he revealed the hideous project the Despot bound me with an oath of secrecy. I swore by my hope of salvation never to reveal the decisions of the council to a living soul. But you, my dear tent-pole, have no soul; though you are more worthy of Heaven than the Despot or even my uncle William, who has consented to this foul treachery. Therefore to you I may open my heart, lamenting the shame to which I am bound by the oath I swore before the council.'

All this had been spoken in the high, clear, formal voice in which suitors take oath before a lawcourt. Now, without a break in the flow of words, Sir Geoffrey suddenly changed his tone.

'But if any living man should happen to overhear this lament,' he said in the normal friendly voice in which he addressed his knights, 'this lament which I speak only to my soulless tent-pole, let him tell his comrades. If all the knights of Romanie would go now, at once, to Prince William, they might be in time to avert the shameful flight.'

As I ran through the encampment I was lucky enough to come across the trumpeter of our mesnie. He was a well-trained sergeant, and I had to draw my sword before I could persuade him to blow the Assembly without orders from Sir Geoffrey. Once the call had been sounded dismounted knights came running from all quarters, mailed and bearing sword and shield. My news spread quickly. Within a few minutes we were all running in a disorderly mob to the pavilion of the Prince of Lamorie.

To give Prince William his due, I think he was glad to see us. He was not by nature a felon, and in previous campaigns he had risked his life gallantly enough at the head of his men. I don't know how he had been persuaded to agree to the cowardly plan; perhaps because he understood the Grifon tongue so well that he could be swayed by Grifon eloquence. That happens more often than you might suppose. A Frankish lord can appreciate good verse, but he is never trained to persuade; all Grifons learn rhetoric as one of their earliest lessons. A Grifon who is genuinely in earnest, as the Despot was earnestly set on saving his cowardly skin, can sometimes persuade a simple Frank against his better judgement. After the persuasion came that fearful oath of secrecy. There again the Despot had the advantage. Most Franks shrink from the mortal sin of perjury, no Grifon minds how often he forswears himself.

So far the Prince had not taken any steps to desert his men.

Perhaps when the time came he would have stayed with us anyway. Now that we had made up his mind for him there was no question of any lord fleeing without a blow struck. The Orsini and the de la Roches, and all the other great lords who had been bidden to the council, came to the Prince's pavilion and vowed to stay with us to the last. By this time it was the middle of the afternoon, but though we felt hungry we were too excited to go to dinner. We were crowding round the banner of Villehardouin, cheering and shouting and waving our swords, when a groom ran up to say that the Despot was striking camp.

At least we had spoiled his plan to sneak away in the dark and leave his men behind to get their throats cut. All the Despot's Grifons, and his Germans too, were getting out together without any attempt at concealment. But 'striking camp' was a polite name for what they were doing. The foot streamed away to the high peaks where pursuit could not catch them; the better sort were mounting, each with a bundle of valuables at his saddle-bow. They left their tents standing, except that servants helped themselves to any panels made of silk; they left their baggage, and their supplies, and great bundles of arrows that they were too cowardly to shoot at their enemies. A Grifon camp is always better stocked than a Frankish one. There were mounds of barley, sacks of flour, sides of bacon, piles of spare blankets, a pyramid of bulging wine-skins. All these were revealed as the cowards fled, and we looked forward to a great feast in the evening. Suddenly Sir Geoffrey pushed through the crowd to seize my arm, and I found myself one of the half-dozen knights he posted, on his own authority, to guard the wine.

The sight of armed sentries was enough to save the wine from pillage; we did not have to draw our swords. But standing there, looking across the wide and empty valley, we came to our senses sooner than our comrades in the crowd. On the opposite range of hills lay the army of the Sebastocrator, an army so dangerous that our allies had fled in panic without striking a blow; how did Prince William propose that we should escape the danger? The sun was setting. If we also retired in the dark we must abandon all our gear, and even then the light horsemen of the Nicenes might overtake us on the march.

Sir Geoffrey never forgot his followers, even those who had been posted on detachment. Just after sunset sergeants came to relieve us, and the cooks were keeping our dinners hot for us. We found all the eight hundred Frankish knights sitting round good fires, pleasantly full of pork and wine; while their leaders conferred in the midst of them, so that nothing could be decided without the knowledge of every warrior.

By now it was too late to escape the onslaught of the Nicenes next morning. We were in for a battle against heavy odds.

I was too exhausted, and too hungry, to pay attention to the council going on just out of easy hearing. But I realised that our leaders must be sensibly discussing practical business when a crier summoned any knights who had fought against Turkish horse-archers in Syria to come and give their advice. There were quite a number of them; for many knights who hold fees in Romanie pass a year or two at Acre doing their duty by the Holy Places.

Presently the council broke up, and by the light of flaring pine-torches my lord collected the mesnie of Escorta to hear his plans for the coming battle. That is how I see Sir Geoffrey today, when I shut my eyes to pray for his soul; rocking easily on his feet in the glare of the torches, the blazon of Bruyere on his surcoat, his mail coif thrown back on his shoulders and his fair hair cascading below his linen cap, his left hand on his sword and his right raised as he spoke; at ease in danger, mocking, happy, deadly to his enemies, the elder brother of his knights.

'Well, gentlemen, it's like this,' he began casually. 'What with public meetings and changes of plan and one thing and another we have loitered in this camp until we can't get away without a battle. Tomorrow the Sebastocrator of Nice will attack us in overwhelming force. If we try to run away his light horse will overtake us. Very well, we run away all the same; but we run away through the middle of his army. That is to say, we charge his line, break it, and keep going. To my mind that's much the safest plan.'

When the cheering had died away he continued easily.

'I suggested this plan, and the council agreed to it. So to you and me fall the honour of leading the charge. We gallop in a wedge, behind the banner of Bruyere. The others, Villehardouin, de la Roche, Pallavicini, Stromoncourt, Orsini, fit in wherever they may be most useful. So don't complain that I stint you of glory.

'Now all this won't be as dangerous as it sounds,' he went on. 'The Nicenes look like a very big army, but in fact they are a lot of little armies. The Sebastocrator leads his own men, the usual Grifon foot and light horse. They won't bother us. In addition he has masses of hired mercenaries, Turks, Magyars, Pechenegs, and the Wallachs of John Ducas if they haven't changed sides again. Mercenaries seldom die hard. We can ride through any of those if we hit them squarely. There's only one group of the enemy who may stand up to us; two or three hundred Germans in plate, like the Germans who fled this afternoon with the Despot and his men. Germans fight well, always, and they have this new armour. All the same, as I explained at the beginning, there are at most three hundred of them and we are eight hundred. So that you can say we are the largest army in the field. Eight hundred men who speak the same language and have been trained to fight in the same way. If you back me up properly I don't see how we can be beaten. You will back me up. I know.

'All the same, it won't be a walkover. We mustn't make any mistakes. The Sebastocrator has one great advantage, his horse-archers. Horse-archers can be deadly to mailed knights, as any veteran of the Turkish wars will tell you. That's why we consulted the veterans when we made our plan. If a mounted bowman gallops away, shooting behind him, there's nothing you can do to harm him; and sooner or later he will hit your horse. However, we have thought of a counter. It was my idea in the first place, so you will agree that it must be a good one. Here it is:

'We don't know how the Nicenes will draw up their line of battle, but we can be sure of one thing. The Sebastocrator will put in the forefront his mailed German horse, the most highly paid and highly esteemed of his mercenaries. Mind you, there will be good men and true knights among them, for all that they take wages to fight for schismatic Grifons against Crusaders. Their leader is the Duke of Carinthia, and some of them are genuine volunteers who came to fight the sergeants of King Manfred because in Germany they are sworn foes of Hohenstaufen. They couldn't know that Manfred's men would run away with the others. Well, those are our most dangerous opponents, and the Sebastocrator will be delighted if we charge straight against them. They will be placed where we can get at them easily. That's what we do, without any hesitation. We begin to gallop before we are within arrow-range and ride straight for the Germans. Follow me into their ranks, and out the other side. Then the horse-archers can't shoot at us, for fear of hitting their own allies. Is that clear? Any questions?'

There was a scattering of the usual silly questions, which people *will* ask at these conferences to show they have been listening. In which direction would we ride after we had broken through? How would we recognise the Germans in the line of battle? (These both got the same answer: follow the banner of Bruyere.) But no one could think of an improvement on the plan devised by Sir Geoffrey.

We ate and drank as much as we could hold, since tomorrow we must cut loose from our supplies. Then we went to bed early, in fine tents under a load of extra blankets, just for the pleasure of using the Despot's baggage. We were not particularly frightened. Our position was so hazardous that a famous Grifon warrior had chosen public disgrace rather than remain in it. But Sir Geoffrey had explained to us what we must do, and with him to lead us we could do it. I slept soundly and awoke feeling cheerful. As I strolled towards the breakfast fires an encounter with my lord brought me to my senses.

He was already armed, if indeed he had disarmed during the night; and on his way back from the horse-lines. He put his hand on my shoulder and led me aside to a dingle beside the latrines, where a powerful stink kept loiterers away.

'William,' he said with one of his engaging smiles, 'you may be my kinsman; and anyway I know you for a true knight. I want to give you a private message. If by some chance you should get back to Lamorie, tell the lady Isabel that she is under no obligation to live in Carytena. She hates the place, and it doesn't agree with her. But she may think it her duty to stay there until some cousin of mine comes out from Champagne to take over. It won't be necessary. Lamorie will be full of vacant fees, and there will be no danger of usurpation.'

I was still not fully awake. I answered mechanically: 'I will deliver your message, my lord.' Then I grasped the meaning behind it. 'If by some chance I should get back? So most of us will remain in the valley of Pelagonie? Last night you made it sound so easy.'

'Last night I was encouraging the troops, cousin. Today I am talking business. In an hour or so we shall charge against twenty times our numbers. It's the best end, now that we are in this trap. Our enemies are the schismatic enemies of God. We shall die like true knights, shield on neck, helm closed, sword out. That's the end that knights are dubbed for. It has been waiting for us all our lives. But, as I said, some of us may be lucky. If you are not among them, mind you take some Germans with you. Now what about breakfast? I can smell bacon frying.'

I pulled myself together enough to smile as I left him. There was a great crowd round our half-dozen priests, but I got myself shriven before I ate.

All the time I ran my fingers over Tom's girth and bridle, and checked once again the fastening of my mail, I felt myself to be in a queer waking dream. I kept on thinking: That was the last mouthful I shall ever eat, this is the last time I shall hear a lark singing – until we were mounted and forming into line, and I could say: This is the last time I shall fondle poor Tom's floppy ears. So that at least one of these doleful prophecies came true.

I had been silent and abstracted; but that is nothing unusual just before a charge, and my neighbours respected my privacy. When we were in line and ready to move off I forced myself to take an interest in my surroundings.

For the first time I saw the army of Nice, which by this time filled the floor of the valley. There must have been more than twenty thousand men, the greater part of them mounted. In the centre I could recognise the great battle-flag of the Sebastocrator; behind it was a square block of Grifon foot, who did not interest us. On the right of these foot rode the contingent of armoured Germans; there could be no mistaking the western heraldry of their shields among the regimented patterns of the Grifons. Close helms hid their heads, and their armour of plate made them look larger than life-size. At first I could not make out what else seemed strange about them; then I saw that they carried no lances. Their equipment was so ponderous that they could not charge at the gallop, and therefore they were armed only with heavy swords.

On the wings of the array, edging forward to give it the shape of a half-moon, rode the unarmoured horse-archers, insignificant men on common little nags – and our most dangerous foes.

Tom began to dance under me, and suddenly I was awake and living in the present. A length ahead of me rode Sir Geoffrey, with Sir John de Catabas carrying the banner of Bruyere just behind him. On my right were three other knights, with the rest of the mesnie of Escorta behind us; behind them jostled all the destriers of Frankish Romanie, bearing eight hundred of the most gallant knights in the world.

Behind the solid clump of ungainly Germans stretched the bruised grass of the farther slope. My eye followed it to the crest, sharp against the blue sky. Over that crest lay safety, Melisande and the soft comfort of Lamorie. We outnumbered the Germans by at least two to one. We were the Franks of

Romanie, who had conquered broad lands from the Grifons. We might be in a tight place, but only very good men could keep us there. All round me thundered the war-cry: Passavant – Get Forrard! Suddenly I felt confident.

When we charged the enemy were crossing the valley-floor. Four hundred yards of smooth ground stretched before us, the slope favouring us all the way. Tom had no turn of speed, but he was sure-footed; I held his neck straight and kept my place.

I was on the outside of the column; but on the left, the safe side, with my shield between my body and the foe. In fact I was safer than if I had ridden in the centre, where a fallen man must be trampled to pulp. As the distance narrowed I dug in my spurs, until Tom squealed with rage. When his blood was up he would not flinch from angry stallions, for all that he was a mere gelding. Then I was squeezing him for the final bound. My lance tore at the palm of my hand as it shivered on a German shield.

The Germans met us at a slow trot. As we galloped into them the shock was tremendous; but they were heavier men on heavier horses, and they held us. The man who had taken my lance on his shield remained firm in the saddle. His horse also kept its feet. But something had to give; his girth snapped. The saddle, with rider still erect, slid over the horse's tail. Then I drew my sword and crouched under my shield, and the air seemed full of heavy Nuremberg steel.

The banner of Bruyere forged steadily ahead. In the joust Sir Geoffrey had singled out the Duke of Carinthia, and had overthrown horse and man together. Sir John de Catabas kept station half a length behind him, his right hand busy with the banner and his sword still scabbarded. Behind us the other mesnies added their weight to the charge, and 'Passavant' sounded buoyantly.

I found it useless to bang with my sword against a German cuirass, forged from a solid plate of steel. Nowadays the young men use the point, and go for the joints in the harness; but most of us were new to plate-armour and we did not know how to cope with it. We plied our spurs more than our swords, urging our horses to break the hostile line.

I think we would have managed it, in time. We were still edging forward when disaster fell on us. Suddenly I was amazed to see the horse which blocked my way collapse on his side, and then I heard the unmistakable hiss of an arrow. They fell all round us, but chiefly on the Germans. For a moment I had a wild hope that some allies somewhere were helping us to win clear; though they were doing it in a very risky fashion, for several of their arrows had fallen on Frankish horses. Then I remembered that we had brought no archers into battle. Only our enemies carried bows.

Both sides were so astonished by the arrows that fighting ceased. I had time to look around, time to understand the amazing but characteristic perfidy of the Grifon commander. His Hungarian and Turkish horse-archers had surrounded the melley, in which his most valued mercenaries were closely engaged; they poured their arrows into friend and foe alike.

Only a Grifon would have ordered this shooting down of his own men. The ruse won him the battle, and I believe that modern Grifon experts on military affairs praise his resource most highly. If any of my readers should be tempted by the plump golden hyperpers of Constantinople to take service under the schismatic Emperor, let him remember how Grifons treat their mercenaries; in Grifon eyes the only good Frank is a dead Frank.

The Germans were falling fast, and there was still a chance that some of us would win clear. I heard a great shout of 'Passavant' as Sir Geoffrey charged again. Then his crest vanished as his horse was shot under him. Of course all his mesnie charged to his rescue. We were desperate to get out of this trap, but not frenzied by instant fear; for the little Turkish arrows could not penetrate sound mail. Our horses were vulnerable, but not their riders.

All the same, a knight caught under a dead horse might be trampled to death; Sir Geoffrey must be saved if we could do it.

As we pushed forward there was a stir on our right flank, and the Prince at the head of his mesnie charged to help us. It was the most gallant deed ever performed by Prince William, and I hope it was recorded in Heaven. Like every other Frank in Lamorie he loved his nephew, though sometimes he was exasperated by Sir Geoffrey's casual independence.

A great helm with its towering crest makes an attractive mark for arrows. The Prince was the next to disappear. His mesnie pulled up in a welter of floundering horses to keep off the Germans while he struggled to his feet. That was the last I saw of the battle. Two arrows lodged in Tom's quarters, penetrating to the guts; he reared up in pain, and fell backwards before I could slip my feet from the stirrups.

When I recovered consciousness a few moments later Tom was lying dead across my legs. I was unhurt, but I could not move. I pulled my shield over my head, and unfastened the chain which held my sword-hilt to my breast. Then I managed to unfasten the belt which held my dagger as well as the empty sword-scabbard, and pushed the whole thing to arm's length. A plunderer who finds a good sword on the field will go off with his booty; but if he takes it from the person of a helpless enemy he is tempted to use it before moving on.

The massacre of horses was quickly over. Soon the noise of fighting died away. Then a Grifon foot-sergeant was pulling at my shield and grinning into my face. He played with me a little, pricking at my mail with the knife in his hand. But from the way he looked at my feet I could see he knew about knightly spurs; calling some comrades to help him, he levered Tom's carcass off my legs. Half an hour later I was standing stripped to my shirt, my hands bound behind me, a prisoner of the Grifons.

CHAPTER EIGHT

The Grifons

O nce my hands were tied I knew I was reserved for ransom. I could look about me, no longer in fear of imminent death. After such a disastrous defeat it was comforting to see that very few of our Frankish knights had been killed; there were nearly as many prisoners as there had been horsemen in the charge. Even in that unfortunate situation I was amused to note that the Grifon soldiers, who are ruled by regulations in everything, had carried out what I suppose were standing orders in their army. A small group of prisoners had been left with hose as well as shirts; and they were all great lords who had worn crested helms. Everyone knows that a crested helm means a great lord, but only Grifons would decide that a helm-wearer deserved to keep his shanks decently covered; and having made that rule, carry it out punctiliously in practice.

Sir Geoffrey, thank Heaven, was on his feet and apparently unhurt. So were the Prince of Lamorie and the leaders from Satines and the islands. That does not mean, of course, that they had hung back in the onset. The mail of a rich baron is proof against arrows and swords, so that he is unlikely to be killed in a mellay unless someone deliberately cuts his throat while he lies helpless on the ground.

I may as well add now, what I learned soon after, that our terrible defeat at Pelagonie cost us few lives. All our horses were killed, but hardly any knights or sergeants; as to the foot, chiefly servants and grooms, the Nicenes just chased them away. They were too poor to pay ransom, and they worshipped after the

Grifon rite; which made them fellow-Christians whom no Grifon could bring himself to kill in cold blood. It was just the kind of battle a Grifon could be proud of: won by a dirty trick, with hardly any loss of life.

For their dead horses the German mercenaries received handsome compensation; but they went back at once to Carinthia, angry with their employers. Their leader, however, was buried on the field. Twice Sir Geoffrey had struck him before the Turkish arrows spoiled the mellay, and a man who had been struck by Sir Geoffrey, however strong his mail, seldom recovered from it.

We were kept hanging about, thirsty under a hot sun, while servants set up on the battlefield the great silken pavilion of the Sebastocrator. Of course the Grifons wanted to glory in their victory; they don't often beat Franks. The Sebastocrator seated himself on a folding chair in the entry of his tent, his guard formed up around him displaying all the captured banners, and our leaders were brought forward to kneel before him. That was humiliating and unpleasant, but we deserved it for allowing ourselves to be beaten. We lesser prisoners were too far off to hear what was said; but it seemed to me, from the gestures of the guards, that what had begun as a formal ceremony of triumph had degenerated into an angry debate. The Grifon lords were all talking at once, and Prince William got up from his knees to shout back at them.

I began to feel frightened again. It sometimes happens that an army grant quarter on the field, and afterwards the victorious leader loses his temper and orders a massacre; every Christian in the east remembers what happened at Hattin, where Saladin first offered quarter and then murdered all the knights of the Temple and the Hospital because he was angry. It was comforting to remember that Grifons, though sly, are usually merciful; and that the Sebastocrator was not their ruler, but answerable to an Emperor in Nice. No Emperor would thank a commander who threw away the ransom of all Lamorie and Satines.

Presently the ceremony of triumph was over, and things returned to normal; which was most depressing. While we stood on the field, among the dead horses, we still thought of ourselves as warriors who happened to have been beaten; when the Grifons had untied us, given us the coarse drawers worn by peasants, and let us drink some of their nasty watered wine, we became captives, perhaps slaves, who must get into the habit of doing as we were told. We were herded into a roped enclosure, and told to rest before marching on the morrow. Our enemies no longer feared us; we were just another gang of prisoners.

I worried about the prospect of my own ransom. I held no land, and I had spent most of my savings on horses and gear for this campaign. Melisande would do her best for me, begging from her kin and her friends. In normal times rich men contribute willingly to the ransom of a landless knight whom they know; but now there would be many ransoms to be paid, until every Frankish household in Romanie would be feeling the pinch. It might be years before my wife could raise the money; or she might give up in despair, and leave me to die in slavery. Half the prisoners were in the same plight; by discussing our prospects together we increased our misery.

Then the great lords were brought into the enclosure, and Sir Geoffrey called for the mesnie of Escorta to gather round and hear what he had to say. He put such a gallant face on our troubles that immediately we felt more cheerful.

'Gentlemen,' he began, 'we are all in this together. The Grifons have spared our lives, and now I suppose it is only a question of money. Since some of us have more money than others I suggests we form a common fund. I shall tell my steward to raise all he can, and I want all of you to send the same message to whoever controls your possessions at home. The mesnie of Escorta will be ransomed as a unit. None of us shall go home until all are free. Do you agree with me, gentlemen?'

It was to be expected from the best knight in all Romanie. It was comforting to hear it, all the same.

When we had finished crowding round to kiss his hand in gratitude someone called out: 'I suppose our lives *are* safe? What was all that argument before the tent of the Sebastocrator? Will they try to make us swear some oath that honour forbids?'

'We are safe for the present,' my lord answered with a shrug. 'No knight expects to live safe all his life. If that's what you want, my dear fellow, you must take off your spurs and get yourself tonsured. We are held for ransom, and that's honourable enough. It happens to the best of men. They may try to make us swear something, of course. They may ask us to do homage to the Nicene Emperor, or to repudiate our lawful superior the Pope.' There were chuckles from his Ghibelline audience. 'But if we stick together they can't get any promises out of us,' he went on. 'They would like us to swear never to bear arms against any Grifon ruler, but they like our ransoms even more. They won't give up all that lovely money, no matter what we swear or don't swear. So don't make any rash promises; they won't get you home any sooner. Take orders from me, and do as I do. Then we shall all be freed together, poorer and I hope wiser.'

'All the same, someone annoyed Prince William. I saw him answering back. What was it all about? An oath never to attack the Grifons?' I inquired, anxious to know the worst.

'Oh no,' my lord answered in a soothing voice, 'though I suppose that will come sooner or later. It was just a slanging match. The Grifons reproached us for our presumptuous invasion of the lands of the mighty Emperor of the Romans; and Prince William, who speaks the language perfectly but learned it rather from stable-boys than from clerks, answered him as he deserved. He said that there is only one Emperor of the Romans, Baldwin who rules in Constantinople; though many little chieftains among the Grifons had decorated themselves with the title. But even if Michael Palaeologue was one of these little chieftains we had not invaded his land. We had come to Wallachia by invitation of its rightful lord, Michael Angelus, father-in-law of Prince William and our ally. It was true that the Despot had deserted us in the field, but such behaviour is common among Grifons. The Sebastocrator, if he had any conscience or honour, should apologise for his unprovoked invasion of a Christian land, setting free without ransom the gallant warriors who had been captured while defending it from infidel Turks.'

There were murmurs of appreciation, and a little laughter. We all felt much better.

'It was a jolly good speech,' my lord continued, 'just the kind to get under the skin of a stuffy Grifon. There were two really nasty points in it: the bit about a Christian land and the invasion of heathen Turks. All these Grifon lords depend on the goodwill of their schismatic bishops, who teach that schismatics should never wage war on one another; and all Grifons loathe and fear Turks. Some of the Grifon nobles were as angry as the Sebastocrator, but half of them had a job to keep a straight face. They admire oratory, you know, and uncle William was getting home with every thrust.'

'It was dangerous to anger him so,' objected some knight or other. 'We are in the power of the Sebastocrator. He may kill us or spare us.'

'Ah, that's just where you're wrong, my boy,' Sir Geoffrey corrected him cheerfully. 'You know how these Grifon lords tyrannise over their followers. There's none of the healthy freedom enjoyed by great vassals in the west. The Sebastocrator is Michael's brother, but that makes it all the more important that he should obey orders; otherwise he will lose his eyes, if not his head. We are the prisoners of Michael of Nice, and the Sebastocrator must produce us unharmed before his sovereign. What will happen then is another thing, of course. I for one won't show off my mastery of the Grifon tongue by answering him back until he splutters.'

My lord was right, as might be expected of a great leader who could always see into the mind of the enemy. The Sebastocrator was very angry, but he dared not harm us. On the day of our capture we had nothing to eat, and to drink only a little sour wine; but supplies are always short just after a battle. Next morning we were given a coarse but sufficient breakfast, and then we set off on the long walk from Pelagonie to the Channel of St George.

None of us were accustomed to walking. But we were fit and strong; and they lent us litters for the wounded, though we ourselves must carry them. Grifons arrange these things very well; they shine as quartermasters, though not as warriors. Every night we found food waiting for us, and straw to sleep on under some sort of roof. Though our guards were mounted they did not drive us too hard. A few of our comrades died, but not more than you would expect in any army on the march. By the time we reached the coast our leg muscles had hardened and we had grown accustomed to our lot. Trudging through the prosperous towns by the shore I found myself staring about with interest, quite enjoying myself. Grifon towns are fascinating places; tiled roofs, paved streets, domed churches, until some little market with a couple of monasteries looks richer and grander than Paris.

When we reached the lord of Nice he would decide what was to be done with us, and that might not be so pleasant as long healthy walks through the countryside.

Every evening we talked about ransoms. Even knights with rich fees had very little ready money; Romanie has the reputation of a wealthy land, and that tempts everyone to live up to the limit of his purse. But a tallage for the ransom of the lord is one of the basic obligations recognised throughout Christendom; stewards and bailiffs could be trusted to sell timber and jewels wherever they might find them in Lamorie, without bothering too scrupulously over rights of ownership; every Latin bishop must contribute, for without knights to defend him he would quickly be chased back to Italy by the faithful of his diocese; with any luck our kin might be able to draw on various funds established throughout the west for the ransom of Crusaders taken prisoner by the infidel. If Palaeologue of Nice was willing to sell us our freedom we could find the money to buy it.

If he demanded oaths as well it might be more difficult. Some of our knights made the point that an oath taken under duress does not bind the conscience; but that argument has never appealed to me, for all that my famous Briwerr kinsman used it concerning King John's Great Charter. Every oath, except perhaps a baptismal vow, is taken under some kind of duress; you swear homage as the condition of enjoying your land peaceably; you swear truce so as to stop the fighting when you have been beaten. Sir Geoffrey agreed with me that since the Grifons had spared our lives we could not plead 'the mortal danger which makes afraid even a brave man', as the lawyers define it. If we bought our freedom with an oath, we must pay up like honest men.

Until we reached the Channel of St George I had not realised how little remained of the mighty Frankish Empire of Romanie. It is easy enough to speak of a city constantly menaced by enemies; the few castles which remain to us in Syria live always under threat of siege, as do many towns on the borders of Spain or Germany. The point is that Constantinople was completely hemmed in by the dominions of a single lord; all the Christian fringe of Asia obeyed Palaeologue, as did the European shore facing it. The great city was an island within the realm of Nice. To make matters worse, though we speak of Venice as ruling the eastern seas, the Channel of St George and much of the Marmora were controlled by the Grifon fleet; the Venetian squadron in Constantinople was barely strong enough to hold the harbour and its approaches. Our guards ferried us across the Channel of St George in perfect security, without bothering to keep watch for Venetian rescuers.

At that time Michael Palaeologue kept his court in the town of Lambasse, on the Asiatic shore; one of the finest Grifon cities I have seen, though empty and much decayed. All the idlers from miles round came to see the Frankish prisoners led through the streets, and as we walked to the palace we had to hold steady under a shower of rubbish and brickbats which was not much less trying than Turkish arrows. When we got there we did not see the Grifon ruler; we were paraded in a courtyard, only just aware that Grifon lords dressed in gorgeous silks were examining us through the iron grille of a window. It is very hard to keep your dignity when you are being stared at like a bear in a pit.

Then the great lords among us who had been summoned to the tent of the Sebastocrator were picked out for private speech with the lord Michael; it is typical of the clerkly Grifons that at Pelagonie they had made a list of our leaders, and checked it carefully at Lambasse to make sure it was still accurate. The rest of us continued to stand about in the courtyard.

Two hours later our leaders rejoined us; and Grifon soldiers, very angry, hustled us along to a large empty stone granary. They shut us all into one bare room; they then brought us a meagre dinner of musty salt meat and stale biscuit, with nothing to drink but water. They barred the doors and left us to talk things over among ourselves. The negotiations for our release had begun badly.

As usual, Sir Geoffrey gathered his followers round him to explain what had passed. His hair hung to his shoulders in a sweat-damp mop, and a bristly beard sprouted all over his cheek-bones. But his canvas shirt and drawers were clean and neatly mended, he had washed his face in some of his scanty allowance of water, and he held himself erect. He was still a good knight, though an unlucky one.

'If only these outlandish Grifons knew something of the customs of civilisation,' he began with an amused and exasperated smile. 'Palaeologue meant well, I'm sure of it. Probably he thought he was being generous. But he offered us impossible terms, terms that we couldn't accept even if we had wanted to; and then lost his temper when we refused them. I'm afraid you boys are in for rather a rough time. I must tell you everything that happened. Then you will see that we couldn't do other than we did.

'At the beginning I had such a shock that I nearly fainted,' he went on. 'Palaeologue didn't ask for money. On the contrary, he opened the discussion by offering *us* great sacks of hyperpers. That's a fact, he had them ready beside him to show there was no deception. He begged Prince William to take this gold and share it out among his followers as he thought fit. There was only one condition. We must spend it in France. At first we couldn't understand what he was getting at. Gradually it became clear that he proposed to *buy* Lamorie and Satines and Negripont and the islands, and that when we had taken the price he offered we were to *buy* other fees in the west. Then he would be Emperor of all Romanie as it was before the conquest, but we would be no worse off. He added that he was sure we would be happier among our own kind of people, with peasants ploughing for us who spoke our own language and worshipped by the same rite.

'Yes, that's what he was after. I can see you are as surprised as we were. He thought he could buy fees and lordships and castles as though they were horses. I won't say that no castle has ever been sold. Of recent years in Italy some gates have been opened to the surprise of all beholders. But I can lay it down definitely that no castle has ever been sold before witnesses, the vendor walking away afterwards with a sack of gold on his shoulder . . . . Well, uncle William volunteered to answer, since he speaks the language better than any of us.'

He paused, as we all murmured what we thought of this Grifon lord who tried to buy castles for cash down.

'Uncle William put it very clearly,' my lord went on. 'But Palaeologue remained unconvinced. You know how these Grifon realms are ruled. The Despot owns everything; his subjects have no rights against their lord. He may hang anyone, or blind anyone, or shut him up in a monastery, without a trial, merely at his own whim. I believe they have a written law somewhere, but it does not bind rulers. So when the Prince of Lamorie explained that he could not sell the castles of his vassals Palaeologue thought he was quibbling. He repeated his offer, and when it was refused again he lost his temper and withdrew it. The discussion ended with him stating new terms. We are to stay in prison – and it will be an uncomfortable prison – until every Frankish castle in Romanie has been handed over to the mercenaries of Nice. Then we shall be released, to make our own way back to France.'

Turning down the corners of his mouth, he shrugged his shoulders.

'Now let's look on the bright side. We don't have to worry about collecting a ransom. These Grifons are so rich that they don't want our money. And we must remember that these terms are not the last word. Palaeologue was in a temper when we left him. Presently he will calm down, and then he will want to negotiate. You know Grifons. They can't bear a final break, a struggle to the death with no quarter given. They believe that every dispute should end in compromise. Before we are very much older Palaeologue will be looking for some dignified way to climb down. But until he recovers his temper we shall be in for a hard time. Don't weaken. It will end.'

As my lord turned away I called after him: 'Would you, Sir Geoffrey, surrender Carytena to buy your freedom? Ought we to ask the Prince to do what the Grifons want of him?'

He threw back the answer casually over his shoulder. His mind was made up and he did not have to pick his words.

'Surrender Carytena? How could I? It isn't mine to give away. It belongs to the barony of Escorta, which came to me from my father. When I am gone some other baron will come after me. I suppose the castle *could* be yielded, if every free man in the barony were willing to see it go. But that's so unlikely that I shan't bother to ask them.'

Palaeologue put pressure on us by making our imprisonment as rigorous as he could. Our food was bread and water, for the wounded there were neither salves or bandages, and we were kept day and night in our prison so that our filth should accumulate round us. It was not in fact so bad as it sounds;

because even the great Emperor of Nice could not eradicate the deep-seated Grifon instinct for compromise. The soldiers of Nice suspected that even if we were to die in captivity other Franks might be victorious one day. Besides, to give them their due, Grifons are kindly by nature. There was no alleviation of the bread and water, because wine and meat would have cost someone ready money. But our guards removed the filth from our prison, dropped straw and an occasional blanket in dark corners, and allowed us out in batches for fresh air and a little exercise.

A dozen or so of the wounded died; probably they would have died if they had been attended by all the surgeons in Romanie, for the Turkish arrow leaves an ugly gash. The rest of us stayed healthy and cheerful and defiant. Our chief worry was lack of news from home; but we took it for granted that the old men we had left in garrison, and our ladies, would somehow keep the Grifons out of Lamorie.

The winter took some of the heart out of us. Luckily in those parts it never gets very cold; but the change of seasons brought home to us that we were in for a long imprisonment. I was twenty-six years old, and five years married. Perhaps my children would be grown when next I saw them. If we had been shut up in separate cells probably some of us would have been tempted to take service with the Grifons; but we were still kept in that large deserted granary, where we might talk to one another and encourage the despairing.

Prince William behaved very well. He never sought better treatment in virtue of his rank, and set the example that every fit man should take a turn in looking after the sick. Our guards were impressed by his solicitude for his men, which they ascribed to heroic Christian charity; Grifons never understand that among Franks all knights are at bottom equal, for they themselves make a very great distinction between the important and the less important. From time to time the Prince reminded us that by enduring our captivity without seeking mercy we were helping in the defence of Lamorie; so long as we stuck it out the Grifons would not get our castles. In prison we were holding their walls as truly as if we had been standing on the battlements.

But the man who did most to keep us to our duty was Sir Geoffrey. He was always cheerful, and it was amazing to see how neat and clean he kept himself in that cold bare prison. He spent the whole day going from group to group among the captives, getting us to tell stories in turn, to sing, or even to compose new songs. Best of all, he knew how to get on the right side of our Grifon guards. He could speak their language perfectly, including all the soldiers' words that an interpreter never explains to you. He knew their manners and customs, and what they thought about the duty of a warrior. He made them see that we were not just stubborn barbarians, refusing to make peace with the glorious culture of Nice; we were family men and Christians, suffering hardship so that our wives and children should keep the property that was rightly theirs. He could make jokes too, especially rather seditious jokes about the absurd claim of Michael Palaeologue, tyrant of the petty Despotate of Nice, to be considered Emperor of all the Romans. The guards talked to him in return, and from their chatter we learned something of what was passing in the outer world.

It was saddening to know that Michael Angelus, who had deserted us on the battlefield, still flourished like a green bay tree. But we were cheered, all the same, to learn that he had gathered his forces afresh and driven the Nicenes from his land. No enemy had dared to invade Lamorie. The great victory of Pelagonie had not increased the dominions of Nice by a single acre of land.

All the same, when my twenty-seventh birthday came round in the summer of 1260 I was feeling very low and miserable.

During this summer Palaeologue renewed his negotiations with our leaders. He could not be convinced that we were unable to yield the castles held by our wives and comrades in the name of Prince William; more than once he offered us great wealth if only we would return to the west and leave him the whole Empire of Romanie. He let us know that the Genoese were now backing him, so that Baldwin in Constantinople had no western allies save our old enemies the Venetians. Therefore we could expect no help from the west. But Prince William never weakened.

It was some consolation that Palaeologue did not despise us. The Grifons saw us as honourable but unlucky warriors, who must be bullied until we gave in; they did not treat us as malefactors. For these conferences with the Emperor our leaders were allowed to wash and comb their hair, and they were seated at a table to talk with him. Certain conferences lasted for many hours; and since neither side gave ground the participants must have passed the time in chatting about other matters.

At the beginning of autumn Sir Geoffrey came back from a conference very cheerful, and sought me out where I squatted loafing against the wall of our prison. By this time I was so bored and unhappy that I spent most of the day trying to sleep; for the night would be a time of misery whether I slept through it or not.

'Cousin William,' he said in a low voice, 'think over what I say to you, and give me your answer tomorrow. I can offer you comfort, but on conditions that you may think impugn your honour. I myself don't think it dishonourable. The thing is, the Emperor has taken a fancy to me. He has invited me to live at his court, provided I give my oath not to escape. I have given that oath. But I asked to have a Frankish attendant, what they call here a cupbearer, something between a servant and a squire. That also has been granted. So for one prisoner I can get decent food and limited freedom and perhaps a horse to ride in the hunt. I give you the first refusal because you are perhaps my kinsman and you seem to be taking imprisonment very hardly. Will you do it? You will have to pass as a servant. But I don't see anything wrong in assuming a disguise in the presence of our enemies.'

I answered at once, without reflection. 'If the best knight in all Romanie can live at the Emperor's court as a prisoner on parole it cannot be dishonourable. I will be your servant, my lord, and gladly. I have taken oath to serve you in the field, and our war against Nice is not yet finished. There's only one thing that worries me. Will it look as if we are deserting our comrades in affliction?'

'I have taken great care not to desert them. Every night we shall sleep here, and go out again in the morning. If you can steal anything useful, remember to bring it back. It's a pity we have no money. In every court all the leavings from the table are earmarked as someone's perquisite. But we may be able to get hold of a little wine and meat. The real trouble is, will you mind waiting on me as a servant?'

'On *you*, my lord? No.'

Perhaps I was too willing. Other Briwerrs may blame me for having lowered the dignity of our house. But there was very little I would not have done to get out of that gloomy granary.

It was a queer sort of life, standing behind my lord's seat at meals, and riding behind him when the court hunted. I had to remember that in public he could not treat me as an equal, for the Grifons might have been angry if they had known he had smuggled a knight out of the dungeon. In the west the most difficult part would have been mingling with the other servants. But here all my colleagues were Grifons, and I could not talk easily with them; though after six years in Romanie I had picked up a few oaths and names of things to eat. My lord, who was as fluent in Grifon as in French, chatted gaily with the courtiers, and even with Palaeologue when he was commanded to ride beside him.

Palaeologue was interested in the western way of life, though like other Grifons he could not understand it. He was himself a brave warrior and a successful ruler, but he could not grasp that a gentleman who owes allegiance to a superior is not in all things the slave of that superior. Again and again my lord had to describe his trial before his peers at Nicles, and the mild penalty which had purged his treason. Among Grifons treason is the unforgivable sin, though they are always committing it; an unsuccessful traitor loses at least his eyes, and usually his life. That does not make them faithful to their lords. Palaeologue himself had attained power by blinding the child of his dead lord, and when there were proper Emperors in the old days the throne was always passing from one dynasty to another.

The courtiers, as far as I could judge them through the fog of a strange language, were intelligent and brave and elegant. But not one of them would have stood by his lord in adversity. They had come to court to get power and place from the ruler of their land for the time being. If they clung too long to a losing faction they would find themselves blind monks; and their competitors, far from admiring their constancy, would despise them for having been too stupid to change sides in time. No Frank could like these faithless scoundrels, though when things were going well with them they were gay and courteous and interested in the arts.

Sir Geoffrey held his own among them. I myself would not have been so friendly to Prince William's captors as he was. But, as he said to me, the code of chivalry does not cover all cases, and a good knight must sometimes improvise his own rules of conduct.

He rode gallantly in the hunt, and quickly picked up an amusing game they play on horseback; a very good game called polo, as exciting as a tournament without the risk of broken bones. All the time he was hammering home the truth that Prince William could not yield up the fees and castles of his vassals without their consent, and doing what he could to lighten the captivity of his comrades; so his favour with the enemy did us good and was in no way blameworthy. But his main interest was the pursuit of various court ladies. I might easily have found out from the other servants, even through the barrier of language, whether he had caught any of them. I chose not to do so. One day I hoped to be back in Carytena, and I did not want any awkwardness when I was telling the lady Isabel our adventures. Sir Geoffrey might tell her if he wished; he could talk himself out of anything.

In June 1261 I was twenty-eight years old, and we had been nearly two years in captivity. For me life was not too hard, and in a sense we had all grown used to it; but release seemed no nearer.

One evening towards the end of July we were all as usual sleeping in our prison. By this time there were blankets and straw, and we had made friends with some of our guards; I cannot say that even my comrades who never left the prison were enduring great hardship. Suddenly we were roused by a great outcry in the town, shouts and cheers and the chant of monks walking in procession. Presently a group of guards unbarred our door. They were half-drunk already and rapidly getting drunker; and they could not bear that we should be ignorant of the great news. They shouted that Constantinople had fallen to Palaeologue, and actually gave us a skin of wine with which to celebrate the disaster. We drank it, of course; in that prison wine was too rare to be wasted.

Next day Palaeologue set off to make his state entry into his new capital. He took with him his most valued trophy, his Frankish prisoners. We were all mounted for the journey; and in general, since the Grifons were feeling very happy, the conditions of our captivity improved. On the way my lord found out from the courtiers exactly how the last remnant of our Empire had been lost.

By an absurd chain of accidents the city had been taken with its impregnable defences still intact. A small force of Nicene troops, less than a thousand mercenary light horse, were crossing from Asia into Thrace. To vex the Emperor Baldwin Palaeologue ordered them to ride close by the city. A Grifon from the suburbs sought out their commander, with news that the Venetian galleys had sailed from the harbour, taking most of the Frankish garrison for a raid on some island in the Black Sea. Furthermore, this man knew of an unguarded tunnel under the walls, an ancient sewer big enough for a man to crawl through.

The Grifon commander took a chance. He sent a few men through the tunnel, who got in safely and captured a gate from within. At sunrise the Emperor Baldwin awoke to find the streets full of Grifon soldiers and citizens, all marching on his palace. He sent orders to the Venetians to hurry back, and with his few courtiers held the palace until they returned. But when the Venetians reached harbour they flinched from an assault that would entail fighting through the populous city to the palace of Blachernae three miles from the anchorage. Baldwin and his Flemings were bolder than the Italian sailors; they cut their way down to the water-front and embarked. Then the Venetian fleet sailed for the Channel of St George, leaving Constantinople in the hands of the schismatic Grifons.

On the 4th of August 1261 Michael Palaeologue, the adventurer who had blinded his child-lord to steal the throne, rode in triumph through his great city as the new Emperor of all the Romans. I rode in his train, with the other Frankish prisoners. It was a painful experience, for the crowd pelted us with rubbish until we looked very silly. But at least I was granted an opportunity to see the greatest city in the world in all its glory. It is indeed a very fine place, though not improved by two sacks and numerous conflagrations within the last sixty years.

The Emperor Michael rode the whole length of the city, from the Golden Gate in the south-west to the cathedral, which his priests were busily reconsecrating for schismatic worship. In the great polo ground before the cathedral the procession dispersed, and we Franks were led off to a new prison by the harbour. Just as we were dismounting, while a throng of abusive citizens pressed round us, a Grifon of the lowest class pushed up to slap my face; as he did so he whispered: 'William Briwerr?'

A Frank who makes his home in Romanie must have his wits about him all the time. I shook my head, to indicate Yes after the eastern fashion, and pushed with my open hand as though to get rid of him. He slipped a paper into my palm, and vanished in the crowd.

That evening I examined the paper. As I had expected, it was a letter from my dear Melisande.

'I cannot send money; this will pass through too many hands. But my family has friends in every city of Romanie, and I can at least tell you the news. You have another fine son, named William. Your household is well and safe. The Franks hold their castles. But Prince William must come home soon, for Lamorie is in danger from a domestic foe. Guy de la Roche is returned from France, Duke of Satines by grant from King Louis. He has been chosen protector of the Franks, in the absence of our natural defenders. He rules well, and the few remaining vassals like him. The Princess Anna asks her lord to recall how the first Villehardouin acquired the Principality. Tell him to make any terms, even to the half of his land; or he will lose the whole of it. Do not try to answer this letter. The messenger would cheat you, or would himself be caught and hanged. Only a born Roman can intrigue with Romans. Written by your loving wife.'

You will note that neither my name nor Melisande's appear in the letter. If the Emperor's agents had intercepted it they would have known that someone was trying to warn the Prince, but no harm would have come to me.

As soon as I had the chance I showed the letter to my lord, and then tore it into small pieces which we buried in the latrine. It was not a thing to keep lying about. My lord went to warn Prince William.

For ten days or so Sir Geoffrey and I continued within the city our queer double life, feasting at court by day and returning at nightfall to our dungeon. In the great city I saw the markets, already filled with Genoese wares instead of Venetian, the palaces, and especially the remarkable hot baths. We agreed that it would be tactless for Franks to go near the walls, and we would not enter the schismatic churches; so I have never seen the most famous sights of Constantinople. Also it was unsafe for us to go anywhere without Grifon courtiers to guard us, since the citizens hate all westerners with blood-thirsty fanaticism;

they were so unpleasant that I took pleasure in looking at the acres of ruin left by the Frankish sack sixty years before. Constantinople is an evil city, and one day it will come to a bad end. But it is very beautiful; if it were ruled by a decent Frankish dynasty it might yet flourish.

Then Sir Geoffrey arranged another peace conference. The Emperor Michael was in a very good mood, having achieved the greatest of his ambitions; and Prince William had been frightened by my news from Lamorie. It was worth trying once again to find acceptable terms, in spite of the many previous failures. I like to suppose that my lord hit on the compromise which solved the problem, but more likely it was some Grifon clerk; they live by compromise.

After the conference had sat for most of the day all prisoners were assembled in the evening to hear a report from Prince William. We were very excited to know that at last things were moving, but also determined not to give in weakly, after we had stood out for our honour during more than two years.

'Gentlemen,' said the Prince, as we squatted at his feet, 'the Emperor will give us our freedom, without ransom, in return for certain castles. He is asking very much less than he demanded just after the battle two years ago, and in my opinion he is asking for what is mine to give him. But before we go any further I want to be sure you agree with me. We are to hand over to the Emperor's soldiers the castle of Mistra, which I built at my own cost, the town of Malvoisie, which I captured fifteen years ago, and the castle of La Grande Maigne, built by my father. When these are in his hands the Emperor will release us. In addition he will recognise our lordship over the remainder of Lamorie and the Frankish fees of Satines and the islands; and he will swear a perpetual peace with us. Shall I accept these terms?'

We all shouted encouragement. Prince William had been remarkably generous, more generous than one would expect from an artful, litigious Villehardouin. The castles were indeed his to surrender, built by himself or his father; and the only free feudatories who would be compelled to transfer their allegiance were the Grifon archons of Malvoisie, who would not suffer by becoming the subjects of a Grifon Emperor. No one would be the poorer save the Prince himself.

We were so excited that the Prince had to calm our enthusiasm.

'We don't get out of here tomorrow, you know, or even as soon as the treaty is sealed,' he called to us. 'There will be solemn ceremonies of ratification; and then someone must go to Lamorie, summon a parliament, and get the castles handed over. Not until his garrisons hold them will the Emperor release us; and I can't say I blame his caution.'

'What happens if your vassals in Lamorie refuse to carry out your orders?' someone shouted.

'Then the whole thing is called off and we stay here,' the Prince answered shortly. 'For more than two years I have been explaining to the Emperor the limits of a lord's power over his free vassals, and in the end he has learned his lesson. My sealed warrant to my castellans will not be enough. He must have the actual castles before he lets us go.'

'Then who carries your warrant?' came another question.

'Sir Geoffrey de Bruyere, of course,' the Prince answered without hesitation. 'He can persuade the parliament, if they are unwilling to do as I command. And he will come back honourably to prison if he fails, so that there will be no reprisals against those who stay behind. It's a task for a good knight. I shall send the best knight in all Romanie.'

I felt a hand on my shoulder. My lord stood just behind me.

'You come with me, cousin William,' he said in an undertone. 'But first you must swear a great oath to return if our mission fails. If you prefer to stay rather than swear I shall think none the worse of you. Coming back will be very hard after riding as free men through Frankish land. Don't try it if it will be too hard for you. Remember, it must never be said that a knight of Escorta gave his promise and failed to keep it.'

I tried to see the situation fairly. If the war continued it would indeed be hard to return. But suppose I were recreant? How could I speak to my children? I would have no chance to speak to Melisande, for she would leave me. To be alone and shunned in Lamorie would be worse than sharing the captivity of so many brave men.

I answered firmly. 'If need be I shall return with you, my lord. But if you recommend this treaty the parliament will accept it. The barons of Lamorie will follow your advice.'

'I'm not so sure that I do approve of this treaty,' he said with a shrug of his shoulders. 'Perhaps it would be better for the Franks of Lamorie if they hung on to all their castles and left us to die in prison. But if my uncle sends me I must support his plan, since I go as his advocate. It's settled, then. Through Nicene territory you ride as my groom, and when we reach the Frankish lands you become my household knight. We shall start as soon as the oaths have been exchanged.'

That took time. The Grifons are a ceremonious race, and their schismatic priests make every religious function into a long liturgy. The oaths were sworn on the high altar of their great cathedral, a huge building reaching to the sky, its walls covered with terrifying pictures of menacing, self-righteous angels and saints. But the relics which gave sanctity to the oaths had been fetched from Nice; for the unfortunate Emperor Baldwin had dispersed the halidom of Constantinople, selling holy bones to buy his daily bread.

In addition to the oath-swearing, Prince William stood sponsor to one of the Emperor's children at a great baptism in the cathedral. Among Grifons the tie between father and godfather is as strong as between brothers, and it is unthinkable that one should make war on the other. At the same time our Prince swore to a perpetual peace. I may add that he swore in good faith, intending to keep his oath. Of course the Emperor Michael attacked us as soon as he thought he had us at a disadvantage, just as among the Grifons brother often makes war on brother. They are a faithless people, though amusing companions to live with.

CHAPTER NINE

The Parliament of Ladies

In the early autumn Sir Geoffrey and I rode out from the Golden Gate of Constantinople. Before us stretched the paved road built by the mighty men of old, running straight as an arrow from Constantinople to Salonique, throughout its length within the dominions of the Emperor Michael. We carried an imperial pass which entitled us to impress post horses at every stage; in addition my lord carried a heavy bag of gold, for our travelling expenses when we reached the Frankish castles bordering on Satines.

We made good time, bearing in mind that our comrades must remain in prison until our return; but on that wonderful road it was easy to travel fast. There are fine stone bridges over every stream, comfortable inns in every village, and little forts garrisoned by Pecheneg mercenaries wherever the country is wild enough to shelter robbers. But few stretches are waste. For most of the way good farmland lies on either side, farmland as carefully cultivated as any garden; at this season they were ploughing after a fruitful harvest.

Every few miles we came to a little town, its ancient walls neatly repaired with gleaming freestone; the road led straight through, from one gate to another. The churches glowed with coloured mosaic inside and out, and the markets were thronged with orderly crowds. The whole land was most wonderfully peaceful and prosperous.

'This is Romanie without the Franks,' said Sir Geoffrey as we gazed about us. 'It seems a pity to spoil it. I suppose the Marquis of Montferrat came this way, when our fathers were setting up the Empire which has just vanished. But these Grifons have been quick to repair the damage. Would you like to end your days in a civilised land such as this?'

'No, my lord,' I answered, 'and neither would you. It's no place for a good knight, or indeed for any free man. These people have plenty to eat and some of them wear silk. But they are all slaves to an Emperor who won his throne by blinding a child. Even now their next Emperor may be scratching himself on a dunghill, or cutting throats on a mountain. They will obey him, whoever he may be. No self-respecting Frank could be happy among Grifons.'

'Very forcefully put, cousin William. I suppose there are two ways of living in the world, and we may choose between them. You can be safe and clean, with a fine church to worship in and a strong stone wall round you. But then you must pay taxes to some lord who has appointed himself your guardian, and he will fix the amount you pay to him. Or you can carry a sword and guard your own head night and day. Then you may choose your own lord and overthrow him if he breaks the ancient custom. But you can't have safety and freedom together. We have chosen the second way.'

We rode through Salonique, a great city almost as splendid as Constantinople, and soon afterwards passed the evening in a little village buying horses; for we had reached the limit of the Empire, and no postmaster lets out a horse to be ridden beyond the frontier. We climbed a steep pass, where the path was broken and overgrown since few travellers came that way; and saw on the next hilltop the castle of La Bondonice.

I cannot describe the sensation of freedom, release, and wellbeing which came over me as I answered the challenge of the sergeant by the gate. I was not in fact free, for if our mission failed we were both bound in honour to return to Constantinople; but I was once more among Franks, free men who upheld their own rights with their own swords and themselves decided in their lawcourts the penalties they must enforce with their own power. I had left behind that murderous palace where a tyrant gave wealth to one fawning courtier and removed the eyes of another, making new law at his whim.

At La Bondonice they lent me a sword, and a kind lady sat up all night sewing the blazon of Briwerr to the front of my surcoat. We were heroes, with the added attraction that we seemed to have returned from the grave. From La Bondonice to Estives, and then on to Satines, it was roses all the way and they rang the church bells to welcome us. Best of all, I was a knight once more; though my lord, with his usual kindness, had never given me any order which would make my pose as his servant irksome or dishonourable.

We rode fast, for everyone pressed fresh horses on us; but we could not ride fast enough to keep up with the news of our coming. At Satines they were ready for us. The Archbishop came down in procession from his great cathedral on the citadel, as we were led up the steep ascent we passed a fountain running with wine, and in the marble gateway at the summit we found the Duke of Satines waiting to greet us. As my lord dismounted the lady Isabel ran forward to fling herself into his arms.

That night Duke Guy gave a feast in the tall marble gatehouse, a feast which spread itself over the whole citadel and the town below. At La Bondonice and Estives we had been greeted by ladies and old men; but here there were gallant knights in plenty, for Guy de la Roche had taken a numerous mesnie to France. They inquired tenderly after various de la Roches and St Omers who had fought at Pelagonie, but once they knew that their kinsmen were either alive or dead, as the case might be, they seemed to lose interest in Sir Geoffrey's mission. All the talk was of the hawking, the Te Deums, and the tournaments which would be organised to celebrate his return from captivity. He kept on explaining that he must hasten on to Nicles, or wherever the parliament of Lamorie would meet, as quickly as possible; no one paid any attention.

His lady was obviously delighted to see him, and as much in love with him as ever. She sat beside him at the high table, danced with him afterwards, passed the whole evening at his side, in a manner most unusual between husband and wife. Good manners demanded that I leave them alone together, so I did not hear what they talked about. But the lady Isabel was evidently telling him a great deal; and it seemed that he did not like everything she told him.

I discovered from the ladies of her suite that my Melisande was at home in Carytena; our children were well, and the castellan had kindly given my household a proportion of my pay, on the assumption that wherever I might be I was still serving my lord. I gathered that on the whole Lamorie was quiet and peaceful, obedient to the Princess Anna in spite of her Grifon birth; though of course the land was very nearly defenceless if an enemy should invade it.

The lady Isabel had been in Satines for two years, ever since her father returned from France. She was quite open in her dislike of Carytena as a home, and displayed no interest in the governing of her barony. She seemed to take more pride in her new status as a Duke's daughter than in her position as chatelaine of a great fee. The Princess, knowing her dislike of Carytena, had invited her to join the court at Andreville; but she had refused, with contemptuous remarks about a court ruled by a Grifon lady, and invidious comparisons between the amenities of Lamorie and Satines. The vassals would not be pleased to see her when her husband brought her home again.

Rather late the next morning my lord sent for me. He was lounging in the sunshine, gazing casually at the carving outside the lovely cathedral. He greeted me pleasantly, as though there was nothing in particular on his mind.

'I never get tired of looking at this,' he said with a smile. 'Quite unlike the normal work of St Luke, such as you see in every good collection of relics. The subjects are as interesting as the exquisite carving. That lady-devil, for example, sitting her pony so gracefully while she whacks with an axe at that holy man. If there are others like her in Hell it can't be such a bad place after all. The holy man himself repays study. He handles his sword like a veteran, but his dress is really very curious. When you arm, do you first put on your helm? A job to get the hauberk over it. Yet that's what this fellow did, and he was interrupted while arming. Otherwise he wouldn't have gone into battle as St Luke saw him, with sword and helm and shield, and the rest of him stark naked.'

'Perhaps the carving does not represent a holy man overcoming a lady-devil?' I hazarded.

'What other subject could they choose to adorn the Church of Our Lady of Satines? Some secular legend? Perish the thought. Unless indeed this place was not built to be a church, but is some ancient idol-house taken over by the clergy. Don't say that where any de la Roche can hear you. They are all so proud of their beautiful and holy cathedral.'

'It is a very fine building, my lord. Are we going to stare at it much longer?'

He gave me a searching glance. 'Have a heart, cousin William. Last night I saw my wife for the first time for two years. Of course you have not yet met your Melisande, so you are still eager for travel. You are in a hurry to reach Lamorie?'

'The longer we delay, my lord, the longer do Prince William and our unfortunate comrades remain in prison. We ought to deliver our message as soon as possible. Though I agree that I am also eager to see my wife and children.'

'Exactly, cousin William. The parliament of Lamorie should be summoned without delay. But serious obligations may detain me here in Satines. That's why I want to speak with you in private. Come into the open, where we cannot be overheard.'

We stood looking over a sheer drop to the distant sea, with behind us an acre of blinding white marble floor where no eavesdropper could hide.

'You'd think, wouldn't you, that everyone would want peace with the Grifon Emperor?' my lord began in a low voice. 'Our best knights lie in a confounded uncomfortable prison, Lamorie is defenceless, and our gallant Prince William has offered to ransom all his followers by giving up castles which belong to him alone. Certainly no one in Satines should object to such a practical arrangement. Yet Duke Guy has made all sorts of engagements for me, and won't hear of me moving on just yet. My dear wife also wants to keep me by her. She fears that hard riding at this season might injure her health. You know how it is – difficult to get away from a pressing host without seeming rude to him.' He gave an eloquent shrug.

'So I want you, cousin William, to go on ahead and tell Princess Anna to summon the parliament of Lamorie. She'll do it as soon as she knows I bring terms from the Prince. A pity I can't give you credentials, but after two years in captivity no one has a ring or a seal. You will just have to persuade her to trust you. Once parliament has been summoned Duke Guy must attend it, as protector of Lamorie; and if he goes he must take me with him. But nothing will be done until the Princess has summoned parliament.'

'You want me to ride to Princess Anna? When do I start?'

'No time like the present. Here's a rope, curiously enough, coiled up behind this column. If I tie one end *here*, and throw over the other end, you could scramble down the wall and no one the wiser. The only difficulty is that I have no money, and I don't know where they have stabled our horses. So you may have to do more walking than riding. But you have your sword with you, I'm glad to see. In some lonely part of the road you might try asking a traveller to lend you his mount.'

With my heart in my mouth I scrambled down the sheer man-made cliff. It was not so high as the precipices which encircle Carytena, but it was high enough for a fall to break my skull. The rope held firm, and I reached the bottom safely. I looked back at the citadel before slithering down the rocky slope; any sentry who saw me escaping like a thief would raise the alarm. But Sir Geoffrey had an eye for castles and their limitations; he had chosen a projecting corner of the ramparts where no sentry could see me unless he leaned over to peer down.

It was not until I was dodging among the cottages at the foot of the slope that I realised the full implications of my flight. I was always slow to understand the politics of Romanie. Sir Geoffrey had done it all so smoothly and calmly, beginning with that flippant dissertation on sacred art, that it was hard to grasp that he was engineering my escape from his father-in-law's stronghold, where we were lodged as honoured guests; and that in his view my mission was so urgent that it justified highway robbery and horse-stealing.

Two miles along the western road I met a Grifon priest, titupping along on a tiny donkey. There was no one else in sight. I did not try to explain myself in his foreign language; I showed him my sword and he lent me his donkey. The beast carried me as far as the monastery of Dalphinet, then occupied by a community of French Cistercians.

The guest-master at Dalphinet believed my tale. He could judge from my speech that I was a Frankish knight, and he chose to take me for an honest one. He promised to return the donkey, and in exchange lent me one of the Prior's riding-mules. Next morning I passed close under the great rock of Chorinte, and knew I was home again in the principality of Lamorie.

I was hungry and cold by the time I reached Carytena, urging my mule over the tricky mountain road from the north. The sentry on the lower gate did not recognise me, but after I had sworn at him in French he weakened so far as to let me climb to the inner bailey. Soon I was lolling in a hot bath, with baby William gurgling in his cradle, Melisande listening to my adventures, and little Geoffrey Briwerr standing by with a dry towel.

Melisande saw at once why Sir Geoffrey had sent me to carry his message in secret. 'The castellan here will give you horse and arms, and a couple of sergeants to attend you. In your proper state as a household knight of Escorta you will easily get an audience with the Princess Anna. She will be very glad to hear your news. As soon as messengers can ride out the parliament will be summoned. After that even Duke Guy, though he's capable of anything, will not dare to detain the envoy who has come to arrange the release of Prince William from his long captivity. Don't you see, dear honest William? Duke Guy is the only lord of Frankish Romanie who escaped imprisonment. He is also the only lord with a strong mesnie, since most of his knights went with him to France. He is the obvious protector of Lamorie, in the absence of our natural defenders. Once he wanted to be independent of the Prince, and fought a bitter war to gain his freedom. In his wildest dreams he never thought that Lamorie would be subject to his lordship. Now it has happened, and he is reluctant to end his rule.'

'But his daughter is lady of Carytena,' I objected. 'Surely he would not dispossess the son-in-law who fought for him at Mount Caride?'

'Why should he dispossess Sir Geoffrey? If he is suzerain of Lamorie Sir Geoffrey can be lord of Carytena under him.'

'Sir Geoffrey would never hold Escorta from a traitor lord. He is loyal to Prince William, and will never desert him.'

'He deserted him not long ago,' Melisande reminded me, 'and for love of la Roche. That's where the Duke makes his mistake. He takes it for granted that Sir Geoffrey will fall in with his plan. He doesn't understand the mind of his son-in-law. Perhaps no one understands it. But perhaps I do, who also was born in Romanie and suckled by a Grifon nurse. In Sir Geoffrey the Frankish tie of homage has been weakened by his foreign upbringing. But that has not made him a Grifon. He sees himself as a paladin out of the old romances. He is a hero ruling by the sword in an unwarlike land. So naturally he is always tempted to help the weaker side.'

She ended with an elaborate Grifon wave of the hand, which was meant to explain everything though it left me no wiser.

'Eh, what's that? Help the weaker side? But it may not be the right side,' I said in bewilderment.

'The ordinary laws of fealty do not bind the great Sir Geoffrey de Bruyere of Escorta,' Melisande explained patiently. 'He is so great that he may follow his own conscience, and that naturally inclines to the weaker side. His alliance ought to make it the stronger, of course. Perhaps he may now have noticed that in both his great battles, Mount Caride and Pelagonie, his side was defeated despite his prowess. He may yet learn wisdom. For the sake of his future happiness I hope he does. But at present he cannot join his father-in-law to pillage his uncle, while his uncle lies defeated in prison. No hero could behave so.'

'This is all too subtle for me. Sir Geoffrey is a good and faithful knight.'

I may have been right, even though my mind is slow. Dear Melisande with her Grifon blood is apt to see subtlety in the plainest transactions.

'The Princess will see it as I do,' she went on. 'You must go to her without delay, and as soon as she hears your message she will summon the parliament.'

'Of course I shall hurry to her, my dear,' I said quietly. 'Those were my lord's commands, when he sent me climbing down a rope from the citadel of Satines. I will always obey the commands of my lord, unless he tells me to do something dishonourable. But I think you see more in this quite ordinary mission than really lies behind it.'

I don't know to this day which of us was right. In point of fact the Duke of Satines resigned his protectorate when the time came, without trying to oust Prince William from the land his father had acquired by trickery in the absence of the rightful heir; but perhaps if the Princess had not been informed until later of the suggested peace with the Emperor he might have hung on to it. A simple knight has only to be faithful to his lord and he can't go wrong; great men grapple with more complicated problems.

As soon as I reached Andreville the Princess received me. An interpreter stood beside her, but she had picked up a good deal of French though she did not care to speak it on formal occasions. As I described our captivity and the terms suggested for our release she swore vividly in her own tongue (I can recognise Grifon swear-words), throwing out her arms and stamping her feet to emphasise her distress.

The interpreter summarised her long reply in a few sentences which did not convey the emotion of the original.

'Palaeologue in Mistra will be a running sore in the body of Lamorie. But unless we give him what he asks Duke Guy will take all. As to the oath of perpetual peace between Villehardouin and Palaeologue, my lady would point out that she is an Angeline, by birth a hereditary foe to the Despots of Nice. She cannot keep a lasting peace with Michael the usurping blinder of little children. That does not matter, since Michael himself will quickly break his oath. My lady adds that you have done well, and that she is grateful to you. As soon as may be the parliament will be summoned to meet at Nicles, and you will be welcome to attend it.'

Those last words were specially worth remembering. In some countries such an individual summons would have made me a peer of parliament, and my heirs after me for ever; a remarkable distinction for a landless household knight. But the Princess Anna was a foreigner, unacquainted with the custom of the west. Probably she did not understand what she was doing. I have never claimed a seat among the peers of Lamorie.

It took ten days to send out the summonses and collect the barons in Nicles. During that time I was the social lion of Andreville, invited everywhere to tell the first eye-witness story of the disaster at Pelagonie and our subsequent captivity. But my importance vanished when Sir Geoffrey arrived in Nicles with the de la Roches, to propound the terms of peace recommended by our Prince.

Every fee in Lamorie was represented in that unusually full parliament, but most of the knights of Lamorie lay in prison;

therefore their ladies came to Nicles to represent them, and that famous gathering has been remembered ever since as the Parliament of Ladies. Except for Sir Geoffrey and myself, and the de la Roche knights, the only men present were two veterans who had been too old to ride to Pelagonie: Leonardo da Veroli the Chancellor of the principality, and the elderly and prudent Peter des Vaux.

For the convenience of the ladies we did not meet on horseback. Benches had been placed in the customary meadow, and we came to the meeting on foot. We began with the usual Mass of the Holy Ghost, celebrated in the Prince's hunting pavilion since Nicles lacks a Latin church. Then we all went in procession to our places. Princess Anna, representing the suzerain, sat in a chair of state beneath a canopy; the ladies from the Baronies of the Conquest had a special bench apart; and the wives of the other vassals sat close-packed on forms arranged in a horseshoe. In the midst was a tribune like the ambo in a church, from which a speaker might address the whole assembly.

First the Chancellor read the official Latin version of the proposed terms of peace. The Princess then gestured to Sir Geoffrey to come forward and explain the treaty in French. But Duke Guy bustled quickly to the tribunal and no one ventured to stop him, so that he had the first word.

The Duke wore his coronet and a mantle of state; he carried in his hand a silver-gilt ducal sceptre, and was girt with a tremendous ducal sword. He was an elderly man, his belly overflowing his girdle; but he was the only great lord in Nicles that day and he made a great impression. The rows of ladies whispered together, rustling their linen coifs or their tall Grifon headdresses.

Yet Duke Guy's impatience was a tactical blunder. There was a genuine case to be made against the treaty; but a continuance of the war would be so much to his personal advantage that he was not the man to make it. I suppose he knew he was a good speaker, and could not trust any of his followers to argue so convincingly.

He began skilfully enough by reminding his hearers, before they had time to think of it for themselves, that only a few years ago he had been in arms against Prince William. Now, he maintained, they were friends. He had sworn fealty, and the men of Satines had ridden loyally to Pelagonie. He was the loyal vassal and true friend of Prince William, but even more was he the friend of Lamorie. That was why he must recommend that the treaty be rejected.

Once the Emperor had a foothold in Lamorie, so ran his main argument, the Grifons would drive us out. It was more than fifty years since our peasants had been harried by imperial tax-gatherers; they had forgotten those pitiless exactions, and remembered only that Michael Palaeologue worshipped by the same schismatic ritual as they. His agents would stir up the villagers, until even our Grifon sergeants might betray us. It were better that the Prince and all the chivalry of Lamorie should die in prison, he said, rather than that the last surviving fragment of Latin Romanie should be lost to the west.

But that, he went on, was to take a very tragic view of things. The Emperor was a Christian and a gallant warrior; he did not murder his prisoners. Besides, when all was said and done he was a Grifon, and Grifons love money. He would like to hold our castles, of course, and he was trying very hard to get hold of them. But if we stood firm and refused to part with them he would eventually agree to take a ransom for Prince William. Say No, he concluded, and begin to collect a tempting ransom. Then we shall keep our castles and, probably, get back our Prince.

The ladies were impressed. The Duke had reasoned with them as though they were experienced statesmen, and their vanity was flattered. Besides, I have noticed that people who take no part in great affairs often consider politics an even dirtier business than in fact it is; they assume that in such matters dishonesty will always be the best policy. The Duke's advice was callous, ruthless, and dishonourable; like physic, it tasted so unpleasant that it must be good for you.

Now it was the turn of Sir Geoffrey to argue in favour of the treaty. He took his stand on the tribunal, slender and handsome and cheerful. He wore a plain tunic and surcoat, in the colours of Bruyere but without blazon; his fair hair shone through the little silk net which kept it in place; he carried no sword, since he was a prisoner on parole. In spite of his more than thirty years, he must have seemed to many of the ladies like a boy pleading for the indulgence of his elders.

He began without formality, in the tone of a knight chatting with the ladies in a rose-garden.

'The Duke of Satines is a gentleman of honour, who has given us good advice without thought of his own personal advantage. We all know that, ladies, don't we? I admire him because he is my father-in-law. You admire him because he is a gallant knight. What clinches it is that the holy and chivalrous King of France admires him, and has just shown it by rewarding him with a Dukedom as the fit penalty for treason.'

Everyone laughed except the de la Roches; and they fidgeted awkwardly, since they could not openly take offence.

'The Duke has given us good advice, I say, the advice of a prudent knight to prudent ladies. That is why I tell you not to listen to him. Prudence is a virtue, as any clerk will tell you. But it is not a virtue to which the Franks of Romanie should aspire. If our fathers had been prudent they would have stayed at home in France. If Prince William had been prudent, and the gallant knights who were captured with him at Pelagonie, they would have closed with the Emperor's first offer, and taken sacks of gold to leave Romanie for ever. Ladies, we are not prudent, Franks are never prudent. That's why we are here, ruling in an alien land.

'By God and His Sepulchre,' he cried suddenly, in a voice of thrilling fervour, 'we Franks have ridden from Portugal to Jerusalem, and we have conquered wherever we went. Was Godfrey prudent, who escaladed the wall of the Holy City? Or the blind old Duke of Venice who bade his squires lead him over the battlements of Constantinople? The holy King of France that now is, was he prudent when he leapt into the surf at Damietta, a King fighting on foot among the spearmen? Prudence – bah!

'Oh no,' he went on in a conversational tone, 'our Prince was honourably captured in fair fight, and we'll honourably buy him back from his captors. That's the civilised way of waging war. Remember, what the Prince has offered is his own to give. Rather than barter away the fees of his vassals he has endured two years of prison. All he asks is that you obey his commands, as vassals should, handing over the castles which he has ordered to be delivered to the Grifons. As soon as you do that you will get back your husbands, and the gallant unmarried knights who serve you in all courtesy. Fair and noble ladies do not look complete without them.

'By the way,' he continued, 'the Duke has forgotten one clause in the treaty. There is to be perpetual peace between Lamorie and Constantinople, a peace ratified when our Prince stood godfather to a son of the Emperor. You ladies who have been bred in Romanie know how binding is that tie among the Grifons. One of two things must follow. Either the peace will endure, and then we shall be in no danger from Grifon castles on our border. Or the Grifons will treacherously break the peace, which is what I expect and all of you expect also. But if this happens, noble ladies, the knights whom you have so sensibly freed from captivity will chase away the cowardly Grifons. So whatever happens the remnant of Frankish Romanie will be safe.'

He bowed to the Princess and stepped down from the tribunal. As some of the ladies began to cheer, the Duke hurried to address them again, and they fell silent to hear him.

Duke Guy was genuinely in earnest, genuinely thinking of the welfare of Romanie. 'We must do what we can to free Prince William,' he said, 'but we cannot yield these castles, the keys of the country. We'll try money once more. Perhaps the first time we did not offer enough. Do you collect all you can in Lamorie, and I will double it from the resources of Satines. That ought to tempt even an Emperor. Or perhaps he will accept a substitute, a hostage for Prince William. I myself am willing to go, if he will take me. Offer any amount of money, or any lord or lady among the Franks as hostage. But if the Emperor is obstinate Prince William must die in prison for the sake of his people. At Pelagonie he risked his life for you. A man of his birth will submit to the sacrifice, if he must. That will be sad, but better than introducing enemy garrisons into the very entrails of Lamorie.'

That made an impression. The Duke's offer to stand hostage showed that he was not after personal advantage. The surrender of castles is always a grievous business, leaving a scar on the pride which is slow to heal; whereas every day great lords are killed in battle or die in captivity, and their heirs succeed without disturbance. Even I saw how much better would be our condition if Prince William had died at Pelagonie instead of being captured.

Sir Geoffrey saw the unpopular corollary to that argument in time to sway opinion in his favour. 'If the Prince remains in prison,' he shouted, 'so do all your husbands. Until he has his castles the Emperor will not release a single Frankish knight.'

That turned the scale. Ladies who would have endured with fortitude the loss of their ruler longed for their husbands back again. Not that Lamorie was an earthly paradise in which every married couple remained faithful until death should part them, but because even the freedom of grass-widowhood is no fun if there are no gentlemen about. Until the Emperor chose to release his prisoners Lamorie would remain a land of women and old men.

By acclamation the Parliament of Ladies accepted all the terms proposed by the Emperor. There would be peace between Lamorie and Constantinople, and I would not be compelled in honour to return to prison. I have said nothing about my own feelings during this debate, but the fear of being compelled to keep the terms of my parole had been almost more than I could bear.

Sir Geoffrey and I must still return, bringing the assent of Lamorie to the treaty of peace. We rode in comfort, travelling slowly because we had with us two ladies, Jeanne de Chaudron the Prince's niece, and Margaret de Neuilly, daughter of the Marshal of Lamorie, whom the Princess had nominated as hostages for the Prince's good faith. But they would live in luxury at the imperial court of Constantinople, not lie in a stern prison; they looked forward to this glimpse of a novel and civilised world.

By the spring of 1262 the Prince and his knights were free, and the Emperor had his castles.

CHAPTER TEN

Jeanne de Catabas

℃

Even after all the prisoners had returned Lamorie was not what it had been before the defeat of Pelagonie. We were no longer the conquerors, the new race of warriors from the west who were taking over the guardianship of eastern Christendom. We were a rearguard, holding what we could for so long as we could; not planning for the distant future, not expecting our grandsons to tend our graves. By all accounts that is how it has been in Syria for the last eighty years, since King Richard of England did his best and accepted defeat; now the feeling of mingled despair and desperation had spread to Frankish Romanie. You could smell it in the air, you could see it in the way the knights held themselves; they hoped to cling to their castles until old age should finish them, they did not look to a future which would bring wider lordship and greater wealth.

Yet more good knights rode behind the anchored cross of Villehardouin than had ever ridden before. These recruits did not make us feel stronger, because the reason for their presence lowered our spirits. They were fugitives from the lost city of Constantinople, who had fought their way out with nothing but their mail and perhaps a bag of golden hyperpers. They had fought bravely against heavy odds, and they had been beaten; they expected to be beaten again, when the Grifons should pursue them to Lamorie. Refugees always depress their comrades; but refugees who stand on the borders of the enemy are the most depressing kind, always looking over their shoulders for a safer refuge.

The Emperor Baldwin had not lingered in the remaining corner of his lost Empire. He had put into Port Leone, and from there journeyed on to Italy, where gossip said he was trying to sell his crown to any lord who would pay cash for it – and finding no takers. I don't know why he did not return to his native Flanders; perhaps his kindred would not welcome him. His wanderings through Italy as a penniless pretender were a very bad advertisement for the Principality of Lamorie.

The most important of the refugees who remained in Lamorie was the lord Ancelin de Toucy, a nobleman of very high birth, grandson of the French Princess who had become the Empress Agnes. He was an honoured guest of Prince William, for he was the brother of the Prince's first wife who had died young and childless. He drew an income from lands near Andreville; but he held them during pleasure, not in fee. He was no longer young, but it was said that he was still a very good knight in the field.

With him came a great crowd of landless Franks and Grifons who had adhered to the Emperor Baldwin until there was no future for them in Constantinople ruled by Palaeologue. It was easy to find employment for the men in some mesnie; but the ladies, especially the young ladies, were difficult to fit in. They were too well born to marry Italian burgesses; there was not room for all of them as waiting ladies in great households. If they hung about our castles with nothing to do idle knights would presently seduce them and the resultant bastards would bring shame on Lamorie. In the end most of these helpless young ladies travelled on to Italy, where they found harbourage in brothels or convents according to inclination. In the meantime they were naturally eager to marry any landholding knights who would have them.

Among these penniless young ladies was a hanger-on of the lord Ancelin who called herself Jeanne de Toucy, though since both her parents were bastards she had little right to any particular name. But her father had been a knight, properly married to her mother; and she had been brought up as a Frankish lady. She was of pure Frankish blood, and incidentally very beautiful. But her mother was long dead and her father had been killed in the fighting round the Palace of Blachernae. She had no dowry, and no surviving kin to take an interest in her. During the feasts and tournaments which celebrated the return of Prince William her beauty made a stir; but Melisande told me she was sorry for poor Jeanne, who must end as a courtesan unless she was wise enough to seek refuge in an Italian convent. 'Our knights don't marry a pretty face, they look for a rich dowry,' she said with a sigh. 'But they will chase that girl, and she is too young to say No for ever. Mark my words, if she stays among us for a year she will leave with a baby, on her way to a brothel in Italy.'

Instead of which she made a very good marriage, and came to live in the castle of Carytena as an honourable wife.

Sir John de Catabas met her at a tournament, where he also was a spectator because of his rheumatism. When he learned her name he recalled that years ago her father had rescued him during a skirmish against the Bulgarians. He was a good knight, scrupulous in repaying obligations. He decided that the best thing he could do for the orphaned daughter of his benefactor was to marry her.

Sir John held land to the south of Carytena. But since the cession of the Prince's castles it was right on the borders of the Grifons, too exposed to raiders for a lady to live there; and his duties as constable kept him in attendance on Sir Geoffrey. When he was not on campaign he made his permanent home in Carytena, and it was there he intended to bring his bride. When he announced the impending wedding he gave a little talk to the household knights lounging in the hall, warning us how we must behave if we wished to keep his friendship.

'As you know, gentlemen, I'm not much of a hand at serving the ladies, singing and playing cat's-cradle and backgammon; all those antics in the bower that help a knight to seduce honourable wives.' He glared round at us, puffing out his grey moustache with a gusty sigh. 'Whores don't attract me either, I'm not like some of you young men. So in general I have had very little to do with females of either kind. Now I am going to marry a very young lady, of noble birth and surpassing beauty. I'm old enough to be her grandfather. Yes, I am. I've had this moustache a long time. Anyway, she is much younger than I am. It's not to be expected that she will love me. I suppose she will choose some younger and better-looking man to amuse her by the fire in the hall and hood her falcons for her when she rides in the country. That's the old custom of chivalrous courtesy, and I have nothing against it. *But* the lady Jeanne will be my wife, and her honour will be in my keeping. So don't any of you young men think you can do more than touch her fingers. Rheumatism won't keep me out of the lists if honour calls. The lady Jeanne de Toucy is poor and unfortunate, without kin to uphold her. The lady Jeanne de Catabas will be protected by my sword. Don't force me to draw it, any of you.'

He glared round again, looking very fierce.

But we were all on his side without any persuasion. We liked Sir John. We also admired his chivalry in offering marriage to the daughter of his old friend, as the most courteous way of providing for her. Mind you, if he had fallen in love with a pretty face we might have laughed at him; the jealous old man with a flighty young wife is a stock figure of fun. But he made it clear he was undertaking nothing more than a work of charity. He was marrying, not for love, but because it was the most honourable way to support a young lady. We knew that he would have lived happier unmarried, as he had lived for the past fifty years and more. As an injured husband he would be a formidable foe; but in addition no one wanted to give pain to good old Sir John.

Yet when I told Melisande of this encounter she had her doubts.

'If Sir John wants to look after the daughter of his old friend he would be wiser to give her a good dowry,' she said. 'Also that might come cheaper in the long run. A poor damsel who marries well is apt to make free with her husband's money. I don't see how she can be happy, when he doesn't even pretend to be in love with her. He will marry her from charity, and she will marry him out of gratitude. It's no foundation for a decent family life. Let's hope gratitude keeps her straight, and the prospect of one day being a wealthy widow. But the other ladies here may despise her, and she may take her revenge by stealing their men. Poor thing. She will be unhappy here. You and I must do our best to make her stay as pleasant as we can.'

To me this was a new idea, and I said so. 'No damsel of good birth expects to marry for love; it's against nature. If Jeanne's father were still alive he might have given her to Sir John, or indeed to someone older. What any sensible girl wants is a husband, and especially a husband who holds land. She doesn't expect to choose the man she will marry. Anyway, what's all this about happiness for wives? Wives make the best of it. They aren't supposed to be happy.'

'Is that how you felt when you married me?'

'But you can't argue from us, my darling. Ours was a most imprudent match. It happens to have turned out well, but it's not the kind of thing you can recommend for others.'

In answer Melisande first pulled my nose and then kissed me, so I never had the opportunity to develop my argument.

The wedding between good old Sir John and the maiden in distress captured the imagination of Carytena. The ceremony took place in the castle chapel on St John's Eve, midsummer night 1262, and practically the whole homage of the barony was there to see it. Sir Geoffrey in person gave away the bride, whose gown had been designed by the lady Isabel and sewn by her waiting ladies. Afterwards there was a great feast in the castle hall, with the happy couple in the place of honour. On bended knees Sir Geoffrey filled the bride's cup, and the lady Isabel poured water for Sir John to wash his hands. There was a great deal to drink for everyone; but at the end of the evening the usual ribald jokes were omitted, because Sir John was looking very stiff and proud and nobody wanted to make him angry. Bride and bridegroom were conducted to their bed-chamber with lighted torches, but we sang a fairly inoffensive Grifon nursery rhyme instead of the verses usual on these occasions.

Later we sang round the fire the songs specially composed in honour of the marriage, and very funny they were though unsuitable for a place in this memoir. It had been a great day, all the more important because my lady had come specially from Satines to honour it. Nowadays she spent most of her time in the beautiful and commodious castle of Satines; on the excuse that her sick father needed the company of his children.

A week later things were back to normal. The lady Isabel returned to her father's sickbed. Sir Geoffrey led out the mesnie after a party of raiding Esclavons, but as usual we did not catch them. On this foray the only unusual incident was a slight mishap to Sir John the bridegroom. On our return he took a short cut beside the winding track from the lower bailey; his horse missed its footing and turned over on him, so that he damaged his ankle and must rest it for a month before he rode again.

We laughed a little among ourselves at this accident. Sir John was normally a sound though prudent horseman, the kind of rider who gets there in good time without doing anything spectacular on the way; when he set his horse at that rocky slope he must have been showing off before his bride, watching from the donjon above. It was amusing to see that our blameless knight was not after all superior to every human weakness.

Melisande and I were still lodged in our comfortable tower room, almost as much a fixture in the castle as the weather-vane above us. In addition we had been given the room below for our younger children, while Geoffrey, aged seven, slept with the other pages in the hall. So we might be private together, a rare amenity in a castle on a permanent war footing.

If we had been living in England I would have sent my Geoffrey right away to be nourished in a strange castle; a page must learn to stand on his own feet, without running back to mother when things go hard with him. But at that time Lamorie was very disturbed, because of our loss of prestige at Pelagonie. To send a boy on a long journey would be hazardous. Besides, Melisande maintained that it was not the custom of Romanie to send away children to be nourished. She even suggested that he might be brought up by his own natural parents, a sure way to make a milksop out of the hardiest boy. So we compromised by making him a page in Carytena; though I suppose Melisande won the compromise, as usual, since her eldest son remained where she could see him every day.

All that summer Sir Geoffrey remained in Carytena. He was needed, with the Esclavons so troublesome; and he enjoyed the comforts of home after the hardship and disgrace of his long imprisonment. He had plenty of visitors, with all Lamorie full of fugitives from the lands farther east; and in the absence of his lady he made the castle a centre of gaiety and good hospitality. When we were not riding after the Esclavons we went hawking on every fine day, and in the evening we danced.

Sir Geoffrey was a fine dancer, and interested in dancing as a pastime. He had some excellent Grifon musicians, and enjoyed teaching them the tunes of the west. Sometimes he would devise new figures, or even complete new dances; and rehearse the knights and ladies of the household until they could perform them perfectly.

One great advantage of hawking over hunting as an amusement is that for much of the time you may ride gently beside a lady and talk with her. In those days I kept a hackney besides my destrier; and if I chose to put up with the bother of pottering about on a hot war-horse Melisande could come out with me on the hackney. It was a fine summer and we had some very pleasant days; though I am not patient enough, or neat enough with my fingers, to be a falconer of the first class. Usually my little tiercel rode hooded on Melisande's wrist, while we watched Sir Geoffrey fly his peregrines.

*

On the day after Sir John's mishap there was a great hawking expedition, with a picnic sent ahead on muleback. It was a glorious July day, strong sun without oppressive heat, the kind of weather that makes even a Frank see Romanie as a fairer land than the west. The short grass smelled of thyme; the farther mountains glowed purple. As we began the descent to the lower gate our horses whinnied, glad to be in the open and yet too happy to play up.

When he had gone a few yards Sir Geoffrey pulled up, as he often did, to gaze back at his beloved home. The usual group of servants watched us from the gate, and on the battlements above a lady stood alone. Sir Geoffrey screwed up his eyes to recognise her.

'Hello, madam Jeanne,' he called cheerfully. 'Why don't you come with us? It's too fine a day to hang about on a hot rampart-walk.'

'Thank you, my lord,' she answered in her clear young voice. 'But I have no knight to escort me, with Sir John bandaged to the knee. And anyway my hackney is waiting to be shod.'

'Nonsense. Of course you must come. In Carytena we never get enough sunshine. Here are dozens of brave knights to protect you. My own lady has deserted me for Satines, so I shall make it my business to ride with you. As for the hackney, take one of the lady Isabel's.'

He shouted in Grifon to the grooms, and we all pulled up to wait while young madam Jeanne got into her riding boots.

When at last we set off we went a long way over the central plain of Escorta, until presently we saw in the distance a building of white marble, a place where the wise men of old used to make magic and worship their demons; an uncanny spot, where Christians look over their shoulders.

In a nearby marsh Sir Geoffrey flew his falcon, and the rest of us loosed our lesser birds among the cloud of waterfowl. All the time madam Jeanne rode as close beside Sir Geoffrey as if she were a child on a leading-rein. Soon after midday the mules reached us with the picnic; we dismounted to eat cold tunnyfish and black olives, a very good repast that you get only in Romanie. Grooms led our horses about to cool off, while we lay on the grass staring lazily at the purple peaks in the distance. Romanie can be a very good land. Presently Sir Geoffrey and madam Jeanne strolled off to inspect the ancient ruin.

For a knight to walk any considerable distance is always odd; to walk over rough grass while a groom holds his hackney is very odd indeed. Yet Sir Geoffrey was a very good knight and a gentleman of honour. His followers stared with interest, but no one sniggered.

My eyes left the couple to glance questioningly at Melisande. 'No, I think not,' she said casually. 'With anyone else one would suspect the worst. But Jeanne is still a child and Sir Geoffrey likes old Sir John. I think they have quite genuinely gone to look at the old ruin. Sir Geoffrey makes a hobby of inspecting them. Remember what he said to you about the carvings outside Our Lady of Satines.'

After about an hour my lord rejoined the company, the lady still beside him and peering up into his face. He must have noticed our stares, but he kept his face expressionless. As far as I could see madam Jeanne was quite unchanged. 'Nothing doing,' Melisande murmured beside me. 'They have really been discussing the old devil-carvings.'

So it went on, day after day, for so long as Sir John was laid up. Sir Geoffrey rode out to hawk, madam Jeanne rode beside him, and at the midday halt they would wander off by themselves. But the most ferocious scandalmonger in the castle, which was full of ferocious scandalmongers, could never see them looking as though they had committed adultery. It really did seem that Sir Geoffrey had chosen his companion for the charm of her conversation; though little Jeanne knew no more about feats of arms, or horses, or hunting, or public affairs, the subjects that interest a knight, than any other girl-bride straight from the ladies' bower.

Then Sir John was well enough to come out, when we all went after a boar who had been damaging the crops. Ladies, of course, cannot help to take a boar; but they can ride near enough to watch from a distance. A young man can show off with a boar spear almost as well as with a lance in the lists. It is sad that there are no more wild boars alive in England.

Naturally, Sir Geoffrey dismounted to kill the boar single-handed, though there were huntsmen to back him up if anything went wrong. He walked straight up, took the boar's charge, and spitted him neatly on the spear. Sir Geoffrey stood there looking very splendid, with the hounds baying and the snarling angry beast bleeding on the end of his spear. He would have been more than human if he had not glanced back at the spectators for applause. We all cheered and blew the morte on our horns – except madam Jeanne who was so busy talking to her husband that she never even glanced down the glade to see the death-stroke.

All day she rode beside Sir John, and spoke to Sir Geoffrey only to exchange polite greetings. But in the evening, when we celebrated the successful hunt, she sat at the high table on the left of Sir Geoffrey and talked to him with animation, though she shared the dish of Sir John who sat on the other side of her. No one could object to this placing. While the lady Isabel was absent in Satines the constable's wife took precedence of all others. No one could object, but we all stared curiously.

As we were getting into bed Melisande confessed herself puzzled.

'There's an attraction there, all right,' she said, 'but with any luck no harm will come of it. The little girl is overwhelmed to find the great Sir Geoffrey de Bruyere so publicly her knight. But she's a good girl all the same; and even if she doesn't love Sir John she must be grateful to him. She has a head on her shoulders. Let's hope it keeps her straight.'

'It will be rather horrible if they go too far,' said I. 'Both married, and he her husband's lord. It's not the sort of thing good knights ought to do, though I dare say good knights have done it in the past. I wonder what Sir John is thinking? He's another good knight, of course, but he must be feeling puzzled.

No problem of conduct should ever puzzle a good knight; the code of chivalry has an answer to every question. Yet does loyalty to your chosen lord outweigh the duty of revenge on the scoundrel who seduces your wife? If he takes an unknightly line poor Sir John will feel miserable, much more miserable about that than about his wife betraying him with a better man.'

'That may be true, but it's unkind,' said Melisande sharply. 'Don't talk about it any more. What would *you* do if *I* betrayed you with Sir Geoffrey? I haven't, have I? One reason is that he has never asked me. He's the most charming and attractive man in all Romanie, and the best knight. Any woman might forsake home and children, not to mention her wretched husband, for the privilege of being his leman. But he will never love a lady. He has no love to spare, for he loves himself only. Or rather, not exactly himself, but the image of the best knight in all Romanie that walks about Carytena blazoned with his arms. So nothing will come of this fancy. Now get into bed and go to sleep, and don't harbour uncharitable thoughts about your lord and mine.'

Although Melisande had herself opened the topic I accepted her rebuke. We had been married for eight years.

In the autumn, before the weather grew bad enough to make travel unpleasant, the lady Isabel came back from Satines. I suppose kind friends had warned her to look to her own defences before she made further conquests among the vassals of her father, who was still far from well but not in any immediate danger of death. She brought with her a great train of ladies, and a few young unattached knights of the de la Roches and the St Omers. Carytena became a very gay and crowded castle.

She persuaded Sir Geoffrey to send out challenges for a tournament, though in these hard times it was a greater expense than the barony could properly afford. Furthermore, Carytena is not a good centre for tournaments, lying as it does off the main road and lacking level ground near the castle. The lists were marked out in a plain some miles to the north-east, and pavilions were set up for the feasting afterwards; though this was the beginning of November, when it can be cold under canvas even in Romanie. However, as Melisande said with a sniff, few visitors to a tournament plan to spend their nights alone.

Prince William did not come to his nephew's party. He was busy negotiating a comprehensive treaty with Venice, to wind up the war in Negripont which had never been properly settled. Since his current Princess was a Grifon she took no interest in Frankish feats of arms. But we had one most eminent visitor, the refugee nobleman Sir Ancelin de Toucy.

The unlucky Sir Ancelin had very little to do, and very little money to do it with. But he had brought his mail from Constantinople, for he had been wearing it when he fought his way from the Palace to the quay. He was a good jouster, who wandered over Lamorie from tournament to tournament, like the professional champions of the last century.

You can't have a real tournament without a mellay, which was indeed at one time the only item on the programme. But nowadays no one likes mellays, dangerous affairs which are no true test of skill. However, the host may lay down the rules for each tournament, and Sir Geoffrey decreed that the only weapons used in the mellay should be spears of light cane, such as the Saracens of Syria use in their jousting. Our mellay was in consequence a very half-hearted affair. Knights coming from the south, led by Sir Geoffrey, charged knights coming from the north, led by Sir Ancelin; but many keen jousters arrived a day late on purpose to miss it. The south won, but no one was seriously hurt; as had been intended when the rules were laid down.

I rode in this mellay, though I did not enjoy it. It was difficult for a household knight, living in the castle, to avoid following Sir Geoffrey. No one knocked me off my horse, and as far as I could see I did no damage. I was glad when it was over, and so were all the other participants. Last year at an encounter on

London Bridge there was jousting only, with no mellay on the plea of lack of space. I consider that a sensible innovation.

The second day was devoted to individual jousting after the latest French fashion; with lists to protect the spectators and a barrier lengthways down the middle to keep the destriers galloping straight. A well-run affair, where success should go to the better horseman and warrior.

I took a part, though an undistinguished one; because it was expected of me. A knight from Negripont, a Venetian who had taken up the sport in middle life, was looking for an opponent of about his own calibre. We ran two courses, and the result was a draw. In the first encounter both lances were broken but we kept our saddles. In the second I went backwards over my horse's tail, and so did he. There should have been a third course to decide but he cried off, claiming that his saddle was damaged past mending; so I suppose the draw was slightly in my favour, though no one suggested I had won his horse and arms.

Sir Geoffrey had chosen madam Jeanne to present the prize as Queen of Beauty. The lady Isabel behaved very well, taking the part of chief attendant on the Queen and advising her on points of blazonry and etiquette when the poor girl was unable to identify the combatants under their great helms. Of course there was a lot of ill-natured gossip. There was no need for Sir Geoffrey to make the lady Isabel Queen of Beauty; it can be rather dull when the host does the obvious in this way. It is better to pick out some unknown young lady; and so launch her on society. But if you do not choose your own wife it is foolish to choose her rival.

The principal jousters were trying too hard, which spoils the fun of any tournament. Obviously Sir Geoffrey had planned the whole affair on the assumption that little Jeanne would crown him; but Sir Ancelin was determined to bear off the prize, because he could not endure to be second in anything; and Sir John de Catabas suddenly decided that this was a good opportunity to dazzle his young wife with his veteran prowess. Young Guy de St Omer, a friend of the lady Isabel who had volunteered to make the fourth in the first-class Round Table, received harder knocks than he had expected.

Each of these four must encounter the three others. So poor St Omer was unhorsed, abruptly, three times in succession. He had never expected to come out higher than fourth; but afterwards he complained that jousting at Carytena was less courteous and more dangerous than most battles. Sir Geoffrey was adjudged the victor over Sir Ancelin, for though both kept their saddles Sir Ancelin's horse sat down on his tail when the shock hit him. But Sir Ancelin gained the advantage over Sir John de Catabas, who lost his stirrups and shifted in the saddle though he did not part company with his horse.

Thus everything depended on the last encounter, between Sir Geoffrey and Sir John. If Sir Geoffrey won he would gain the prize, if he were beaten the three of them would be level with two victories and one defeat for each. They rode at one another very fiercely, but I was one of the many who watched Jeanne's face instead of this collision between famous champions.

I am sorry to say that she displayed no emotion except boundless pleasure. She was little more than a child, and the knowledge that her husband was disputing with such a great lord for a crown she would bestow flattered her vanity without touching her heart. If they had killed one another before her eyes I think she would have clapped her hands and crowed with delight. I whispered to Melisande beside me: 'It's all right. She doesn't care a pin for either of them.'

'But supposing they both care for her?' my wife whispered back. 'That's where the trouble lies. Nobody minds if a lady breaks her heart with hopeless love. It was Lancelot who brought ruin to the Round Table, not Guinevere.'

There was an amazing crash, and I looked down at the lists. Both horses were back on their haunches, shocked to a standstill; both knights kept their saddles. Sir John's broken lance-head was embedded in Sir Geoffrey's shield; it was blunt, of course, but if it had been a candle the force of the thrust would have driven it into the painted leather. Sir Geoffrey's lance was unbroken, and his opponent's shield gleamed unscarred. Instead Sir John looked oddly smaller. I had to peer again before I saw that the whole of the white swan's head and neck which was his crest had been carried away, wreath, mantling, and all. A shining furrow glinted across the bare flat top of his helm.

As Sir Geoffrey pulled his horse round to salute the Queen of Beauty a roar of cheering greeted this feat of arms. The stroke at the helm is rarely attempted; partly because if it goes wrong you may break the neck of a good knight, which no one wants to do in a friendly joust; partly because it is almost impossible to achieve, since your opponent's lance will strike your shield and unsettle your aim before your lance reaches his helm. But Sir Geoffrey had aimed so true, even as the other lance hit him, that he had removed the whole crest without giving Sir John so much as a headache.

Little Jeanne simpered rather unattractively as she leaned down from the tribunal to place the crown, a wreath of beaten silver, on Sir Geoffrey's helm. We all felt sorry for Sir John, overcome by a better knight under his wife's eyes. Sir Geoffrey made the situation even more embarrassing by announcing that he would not take the prize he had given for his own tournament; it should go to the next most worthy knight, his old friend and loyal vassal Sir John de Catabas.

'Aren't men fools?' Melisande whispered. 'If he wasn't going to take the prize why the devil did he ride in the joust?'

'Never mind,' I whispered back. 'He has been gracious in public, and he must be feeling very pleased with his own chivalry. Perhaps that will make him more sympathetic to the unfortunate Sir John.'

Everyone was very sympathetic to the unfortunate Sir John, and at supper in the draughty pavilion the ladies cooed over him. That did not make matters any better, but you might argue that so far nothing had gone wrong. It was obvious that Sir Geoffrey liked the company of little Jeanne more than the company of any other lady, his wife included; but expert opinion agreed, and in Carytena opinion was very expert, that so far no adultery had been committed. This was a genuine chivalrous romance, such as the old poets used to sing of: a gallant knight and a fair lady sighing for hopeless love of one another, and doing nothing practical about it.

During the worst of the winter there could be no hunting or hawking, and we were more or less confined to the castle unless there were Esclavons to be chased through the snow. For the first time for some years the lady Isabel stayed at home and tried to make life cheerful for her lord. Some of her young friends and relations from Satines visited her, and it was really a gay and amusing season. But we all felt self-conscious in our amusements. At any moment half the company were peering into corners to make sure that Sir Geoffrey and madam Jeanne had not slipped away quietly together.

In a way this was the done thing. When I was a young page at Ludlow half the knights were sighing with hopeless love for half the ladies. We marry strangers, for money or for land. (I am an exception, and my marriage has been happy and successful, but that does not prove anything.) Yet unmarried knights, with strange brides waiting for them in some distant castle, are constantly in the company of young ladies also waiting for absent husbands. Courteous love is as good a way of getting through the winter as any other pastime; and its great advantage is that if properly conducted it does not lead anywhere. The knight sighs and composes verses; the lady sighs and embroiders favours. Presently they marry someone else and grow old, forgetting the fancies of their youth. What else is there to do in foul weather or after sunset? You can't always be playing backgammon.

But it isn't every day that the famous lord of a great fee, with his wife beside him, falls in love with the bride of an elderly husband who is also his vassal. Sir Geoffrey saw Jeanne for long hours every evening, normally in the presence of her husband; but she was not in any real sense his equal, except on the theory that all those of gentle birth are equal. Another lord in that position might have used his authority to send away the husband on some mission, or even offered him money or land to shut his eyes. I don't suppose such a base idea entered Sir Geoffrey's head; it was not the way he did things. All the same he made it quite clear that what he wanted to do, while winter kept him indoors, was to talk with madam Jeanne and with no one else. For hours he would sit opposite her in a window, and what they found to say to one another for so long I can't imagine.

The lady Isabel tried to do something about it. First she made a third in these long intimate discussions; and when she found that did not work she brought in a fourth. With rather heavy-handed cunning she made up to Sir John, who was puzzled but gratified. The odd quartette were always together, two Bruyeres and two Catabases; but linked to the wrong partners.

My lord's sense of mischief led him to compose a new dance, for four dancers only. It had a catchy tune, and the minstrels liked it. On Christmas night the two Bruyeres and the two Catabases danced it before all the company. The dance was named Lord Geoffrey's Fancy.

During our captivity among the Grifons I had been very close to Sir Geoffrey. Back in Carytena that intimacy did not continue, for landholding vassals must come before a mere household knight. Perhaps I felt slightly mortified, but Melisande was sensible enough to keep me from showing it. All the same, I owed a debt of gratitude to my lord, who had taken trouble to ease a captivity which was more than I could endure. After a certain amount of wrestling with my conscience I determined to risk his displeasure by tackling him about his private life.

It was difficult to catch him alone, without either little Jeanne or the lady Isabel at his side. My chance came during the twelve days of Christmas, when I took a night's duty in the guardroom. In normal times the sergeants of that well-run castle could be trusted to furnish a sober, alert, fully-dressed guard without supervision from a household knight. But at Christmas there is so much drink flowing that someone in authority must hang round the guardroom just to keep an eye on things. The Esclavons know our calendar, and like to put on a raid when they think we shall be drunk and incapable.

Late at night I was sitting over a brazier in a corner, so that by the fire the sergeants might throw dice without the constraint of a knight overhearing their oaths, when my lord put his head in the door.

'Everybody happy?' he asked. 'Plenty of wine, plenty of cakes, plenty of wood for the fire? Now then, Nicolas, if you dice away your Christmas livery you must go naked all next year. Oh, there you are, cousin William. Come up to the watch-tower and look at a light to the northwards. The Esclavons may be keeping their own Christmas, or it may be a burning rick.'

In inky dark we stood alone on the tower, agreeing that the distant spark of light did not come from burning thatch.

'It's like old times, cousin William, you and me alone together. Escorta is better than Constantinople, isn't it?'

'Yes, my lord,' I said respectfully but firmly. 'All the same, I sometimes worry about the future of your house.'

'You too, cousin William?' he answered in an easy voice, though I could not see the expression on his face. 'What nasty minds you have in my castle of Carytena. Do you suppose madam Jeanne is my leman? I assure you, on my honour as a knight, that she is not. Does that satisfy you?'

'It is very good news, my lord, though I am shocked to hear you suppose that your bare word might be doubted. But if madam Jeanne is not your leman, what is she? Something more than the lady of a respected vassal, that is evident to all the world.'

'She is my friend. I like talking to her. That she's pretty is of course an added attraction, but not the chief attraction. She is a lady bred in Constantinople, next to Paris the greatest centre of civilisation and courtesy. But the best thing about her is that she's young. I am midway between thirty and forty, with a crushing defeat and two years of imprisonment behind me. My youth is slipping away. Who knows, the next time I ride into battle I may actually feel cautious? Soon it will come to you, too, cousin William, and you will know what I feel now. When I talk with little Jeanne I am young and gay again. That's worth a little harmless gossip.'

'If you say so, my lord, but the gossip isn't harmless. It harms Sir John de Catabas, for example. He is a gallant knight and a most faithful defender of the barony of Escorta; yet you make him look foolish before a great company of his equals. If he wasn't such a loyal vassal he would leave your service. Even though you have not done anything for which your confessor can blame you, what you do is unfair to Sir John, and to the lady Isabel, and for that matter to madam Jeanne. Forgive my frankness, but we are alone and it is time someone told you these things.'

'Frank advice is a kinsman's duty, cousin William. You do right to say what you think. All the same, put yourself in my place for a minute, and consider whether I am greatly to blame. The lady Isabel can never be my companion; her heart remains in Satines. When I put the ring on her finger she didn't marry Bruyere of Escorta, she married a neighbour who would make it easy for her to visit her true home. I do her no wrong when I seek the company of another lady. Little Jeanne knows what I want of her and what I don't want. She understands me, and she accepts the position. I do her no wrong. As to Sir John, any wrong that comes to him stems from his own actions. He did wrong when he married a helpless young girl, without affection on either side, merely to tickle his conscience with a pleasant glow of well-doing. Perhaps he looks foolish. I can't help that. He looks foolish as the elderly husband of a pretty young wife who doesn't love him, not as a cuckold. He isn't a cuckold, as I told you. That's the position, and you must accept it. What I do isn't wrong, and I like doing it. Therefore I shall go on doing it, whatever well-meaning asses may advise me for my own good.'

'This well-meaning ass is silenced, my lord,' I answered.

Laughing, he slapped me on the shoulder. 'Frankness between kinsmen, as I said, cousin William. You were right to offer your advice. But there's nothing to worry about. I shan't steal the wife of my vassal. I am a knight. I know the rules and I shall keep them. All the same, there's no denying that the grass over the fence often looks greener.' He laughed again, moving to the head of the stairs.

'Come on, that's enough preaching, even for the Christmas holidays. Let's go down to that guardroom before the Esclavons steal the swords off my sergeants as they doze on the floor.' My lord had not bound me to silence. I was discreet, naturally. But I have no secrets from my wife; that would be impossible, even if I wanted to.

'I'm worried,' said Melisande when I had told her. 'Sir Geoffrey is a very good knight, and he knows the rules, as he said to you. But the best knight in all Romanie may be so chivalrous that rules do not bind him as they bind ordinary men. Suppose it amuses him to see Jeanne as a lady in distress, and himself as her rescuer? Chivalry has nothing to do with chastity. I would be happier if he had talked about the Ten Commandments, rather than the obligations of knighthood. He will never do anything that he himself considers dishonourable, but he isn't interested in the good opinion of his neighbours. William, what would you do if Sir Geoffrey should disgrace his knighthood?'

'He holds my fealty, he got me out of a Grifon prison. I have eaten his bread since I came to Romanie. If he were to deny his baptism and join the infidels perhaps I might leave him. Short of that, my dear, I shall stick to him.'

'Then we must just hope for a change, for things can't go on as they are. Lancelot was loyal to King Arthur for years, but in the end he was caught in Queen Guinevere's chamber. Perhaps Sir John will take his wife on a good long pilgrimage; St Patrick's Purgatory in Ireland would about do. Perhaps the Duke will persuade Sir Geoffrey to stay with him in Satines or Estives. Perhaps Jeanne will catch some sickness that will spoil her pretty face. Perhaps she will fall in love with some boy of her own age; she doesn't really love Sir Geoffrey, she's just flattered by his devotion. That would be the best solution, though it's almost too much to hope for. Failing that, Sir Geoffrey is headed for trouble; and my dear loyal husband is determined to jump into the trouble with both feet if his lord leads the way.'

Melisande was never one to allow herself to be carried along by the tide of events; if things were going wrong she would try to alter them, after the fashion of a lady reared among the intrigues of Grifon Romanie. Perhaps it was at her suggestion that several ladies and knights began to talk about the spiritual benefits of pilgrimage, and the pleasure to be got from visiting crowded and popular shrines; they talked of these things especially in the hearing of madam Jeanne de Catabas.

Little Jeanne had never before considered going on pilgrimage. She had been reared in Constantinople, whose citizens think no shrine can be holier than their own lofty cathedral, save perhaps the Holy Sepulchre. And though it is possible to visit the Holy Sepulchre, if you don't mind cringing before infidel guards, in those days no one of gentle birth would do it. We still nourished the dream that one day we would fight our way into it.

So when Jeanne talks of pilgrimage she meant a pilgrimage westward. There are the tombs of the Apostles in Rome, and every Frank born in Romanie is anxious to see Italy; I even heard her mention wistfully the Sainte Chapelle which the holy King Louis was building in Paris. It houses Our Lord's Crown of Thorns, and is conveniently situated among the best dressmakers and goldsmiths in the world. She pointed out to her husband that a pilgrimage to Rome, and perhaps on to Paris if they could afford it, would bring her soul to great spiritual enrichment.

We all entered into the spirit of the intrigue, bringing it up in casual conversation. We pointed out that it was a good time to visit Rome, for King Manfred had chased out the Pope and a

Ghibelline garrison held the holy city. To visit Rome while it was under papal control might be awkward, since although we were Crusaders we were also under the ban as Ghibelline partisans.

Sir John answered firmly that a pilgrimage was out of the question. It would cost more than he could afford; and anyway this was no time for a knight to leave Lamorie, while the Grifons threatened invasion from their castles in the south. These reasons were valid so far as they went; but I believe he had a stronger reason, which he would not openly avow.

He had taken it into his head that to remove his wife from Carytena would be to doubt the honour of Sir Geoffrey, his lord. A good knight should not doubt his lord.

So all four of them remained in Carytena, Sir Geoffrey, the lady Isabel, madam Jeanne, and Sir John; each of them increasing the burden on honour and chivalry, like masons who build a church tower higher and higher, to see how far they can go before it falls down.

CHAPTER ELEVEN

A Pilgrimage to Rome

℘

Before the twelve days of Christmas were ended we had heard grave news of approaching war. As we had expected from the moment the treaty was sealed, the Grifon Emperor planned to violate his oath of perpetual peace. The pretext he chose was absurd. Prince William had bought his freedom by yielding up four strong castles, but no one had bothered to delimit the open country that went with them. In particular no mention had been made of La Cremonie, the undefended town which the Prince had greatly embellished. Prince William kept Christmas there, as had been his custom for many years. La Cremonie lies almost at the foot of the great new castle of Mistra, which the Prince had lately handed over to a Grifon garrison; but the Prince put his trust in the treaty of peace and rode there without an army; though of course his knights rode with him to keep Christmas at the table of their lord according to the usual custom of the west.

You might suppose that the Emperor Michael would appreciate the compliment. Franks trusted his honour, and rode unarmed to feast below his strong castle. But the Grifon commander at Mistra chose to call it an armed invasion of his territory. He sent a messenger, a Gasmule of low birth, to complain that hundreds of Frankish knights were frightening his peaceful peasantry; he added, for good measure, that the town of La Cremonie lay in the banlieu of Mistra, and that the Prince of Lamorie had no business there even if he should visit it without an army.

Prince William, of course, refused to leave the hall which he had built at his own cost for his own feasting. There were high words on both sides before the messenger withdrew in anger. There had been no formal defiance, no open declaration of war; but it was known that the commander of Mistra had written to Constantinople for reinforcements, and that in the summer a great army would invade Lamorie.

In Carytena we saw news of war as good news. On campaign Sir Geoffrey might forget his infatuation; and anyway a brisk war ought to get us back the four castles we had yielded to the Grifons.

But in the meantime we had our worries. In January 1263 the lady Isabel was summoned once more to Satines, where her father was gravely ill. Melisande was sorry to see her go. Sir Geoffrey, still passing most of his leisure with madam Jeanne, might forget that he was a married man unless he saw his wife constantly.

The other worry ought to have been more serious, but in fact we surmounted it without trouble. Now that they had abandoned the pretence of honest friendship the Grifon authorities in the south began to intrigue with our peasants.

All Grifons are intriguing with somebody all the time; it comes to them as naturally as breathing. Even if they had been willing to observe the terms of the treaty it was hard for them to leave our peasants undisturbed because of the way their tyrannous state is intertwined with their schismatic church. All Grifons everywhere obey the Patriarch of Constantinople, even those Grifons who are subject in temporal affairs to an infidel or Frankish master. But the Patriarch is not the direct vassal of God; he also has a temporal master, the Emperor, who has appointed him and may dismiss him. So that our Grifon peasants, in so far as they were subject to their clergy, were also subject to the Patriarch, who is subject to the Emperor. They must serve two masters, and two lay masters. The Emperor's commander in Mistra could give orders to Grifon priests, even if he were not intriguing with the laity.

It has been pointed out to me that the relationship between Emperor and Patriarch is very like the relationship Ghibellines advocate between Emperor and Pope; a straight condition of master and servant. Therefore we, Ghibelline allies of King Manfred, had no grounds for complaint. But the Franks of Romanie were not Ghibelline by conviction; on the contrary, we saw ourselves as Crusaders and devout servants of the See of St Peter. It was just that we had to maintain our communications with Italy and the west; and if that entailed making war on the Pope and suffering his excommunication it was a great pity but better than being driven from Lamorie.

Grifons endure excommunication with as much fortitude as Franks; but ultimate loyalty to their schismatic church takes precedence of any duty they owe to their temporal lords. Agents from Mistra moved about among our peasants, preaching that it was their duty to aid the Emperor in his holy war against the Latins; by the way, this Emperor has never fought a holy war against the infidel, nor indeed has any other Grifon. There was a rumour that these agents had made contact with the Esclavons of the mountains, who adhere to the schismatic church in so far as they are Christians at all. I did not credit the rumour. It was impossible to believe that civilised men would call in Esclavon allies; on the other hand, in matters of state Grifons are capable of any wickedness.

Whatever may have been their evil designs, I am glad to say that in Escorta the Grifons of Mistra failed completely. Sir Geoffrey had proved himself a very good lord of all his dependants, courteous and just and merciful, understanding the customs of the people and generous to relieve distress. He kept his petty officials under stern control, so that maidens went unravished and orphans received their inheritance in full.

With the result that one day in February a group of shock-headed peasants appeared at the lower bailey, bringing with them two seedy Grifon agents, their hands bound behind them. In the great hall, before all the homage, a spokesman declared that these agents had promised that in the spring a great army would appear to free the Grifons from slavery; in the meantime they were to take note of the defences of Carytena and the numbers of the garrison, and to murder any stray Franks whom they might find alone. The peasants had consulted their elders, who could remember the tyranny and high taxation of imperial rule. After long discussion they had decided that they preferred Sir Geoffrey, his foreign knights and his foreign church, to the expensive glories of their native Empire.

It was a most amazing expression of confidence, unparalleled in any other province of Frankish Romanie. As a rule Grifons will desert any lord to advance the interests of their church, which to them is the badge of their race. In their eyes any spiritual subject of the Patriarch of Constantinople is a Grifon and a brother, even if he happens to speak Esclavon and run naked on the mountains.

The agents were hanged, of course; but mercifully, without torture, because Sir Geoffrey pointed out that they had been serving their lord at the risk of their lives. To encourage our peasants we all went out on a foray against the Esclavons, but the weather was so bad that we did not catch any.

Then we settled down to prepare for the approaching war. I got our armourer to make me two small steel plates to protect my knees. They were smooth rounded metal caps with a strap behind the knee, such as every knight wears nowadays; but in 1263 they were a novelty, and I was the first household knight of Escorta to wear them. I would have liked to buy a new destrier, but prices were very high. So I made do with the local-bred mare I had already. A mare won't use her forefeet in battle like a stallion, and some say that it is unfitting for a knight to ride a female animal; but in Romanie some of the greatest lords ride mares, as do the infidel Saracens. Sylvia was a very handsome little chestnut, swift and gallant and a comfortable ride; I had bought her cheap because she was past her prime, and not really up to the weight of a mailed knight. But her gallant heart made up for her small size.

About this time Prince William wound up the War of

Negripont by a final concord with Venice. The war had ended in a draw, and the treaty recognised facts. Venice acknowledged the Prince as suzerain over the whole island, and agreed not to support rebels against his authority; but the Prince did not get the fees which had been held by the late Princess Carintana, and must be content with suzerainty only. It was a comfort to know that the Venetian fleet would not join our enemies, but so long as Palaeologue held Constantinople the Venetians would not help us either. Those merchants are careful to keep on good terms with whoever controls the eastern trade, whether schismatic or infidel.

At the beginning of Lent there died, after a long illness, Guy de la Roche, Megaskyr and first Duke of Satines. All the great lords of Frankish Romanie attended his funeral. But Sir Geoffrey could not take the whole of his mesnie, for fear of the Grifons in Mistra; I was one of those who stayed behind, and madam Jeanne was another. Luckily, in those troubled times, there was no dispute about the succession; Guy's elder son, John de la Roche, was universally acknowledged as the second Duke of Satines. He willingly did homage to the Prince of Lamorie, so that the Franks seemed stronger and more united than before. Duke John was a good knight, well able to defend his people, though troubled by gout in the feet which hampered him as a horseman.

But for the time being the Franks were weakened by the death of a veteran ruler. Duke John must receive the oaths of his vassals, and go round his Duchy claiming his rights, before he could bring his mesnie to join his overlord. We would have to begin the war with the knights of Lamorie only, though there was no doubt that Duke John would come when he was free to do so.

While Sir Geoffrey was at the funeral Sir John de Catabas, his constable, commanded in Carytena; which made little madam Jeanne the chatelaine. They had been married for only a year, and above the salt she was still the most recent bride. But she kept the servants in order, and took the chief seat at the high table, without a trace of discomposure. She might have been born to rule a great castle, instead of being the child of unimportant hangers-on at the tottering court of the Latin Emperor.

Nothing could discompose little Jeanne, neither the gossip of other ladies nor the occasional surliness of the cooks, who resented the rule of such a young and inexperienced mistress. She always took it for granted that everyone would be anxious to help; and her smiling self-confident approach made it almost impossible to snub her. When you consider that the world at large took her to be Sir Geoffrey's leman, the placid way in which she greeted censorious visitors was amazing. Some stranger knights thought that a lady who had once broken her vows must be fair game for every pursuer, and chased her very openly; until a frown from old Sir John frightened them into more courteous behaviour.

Melisande and I, and the other permanent residents of the castle, were certain that she had not yielded to Sir Geoffrey; in fact that he had not yet summoned her to yield. She seemed to take her position as a matter of course: that she should spend all day in company with the knight who served her in courtesy (and who was also her lord), and at night retire to the bed of her elderly husband. It was even stranger that she did not seem to mind the absence of Sir Geoffrey. At the high table she sat smiling, serene and self-possessed and as pleased with the luxury that surrounded her as a cat lying on a warm hearth.

'She would still sit there smiling if the Grifons were breaking in at the far door,' I said angrily to Melisande as we prepared for bed one night. 'She doesn't mind the prospect of a bitter war, she doesn't mind the absence of Sir Geoffrey, she doesn't mind the presence of her husband. Could any disaster bring a furrow to that placid brow? Do you think she cares a pin for either of her good knights?'

'She cares for no one outside herself,' Melisande answered calmly, 'and so far that has been the salvation of Carytena. She doesn't mind if Sir Geoffrey is unhappy, she doesn't mind if Sir John is unhappy. The present state of affairs suits her very well, and she will make no move to change it. She has all the luxury of a leman, and none of the guilt. I suppose it's like that for someone who has been born really beautiful. She takes it for granted that any knight will lay down his life for her, and will also take No for an answer when she wants to be rid of him. I wonder if she felt frightened when Constantinople fell? That's the only time in her life when she has been in danger. Now she is safe, and she will stay safe. She knows that if only one knight was left alive of all the Franks, that one would look after her. No wonder she is serene.'

'Will she be so serene when the lady Isabel has returned? Now that the old Duke is dead there is nothing to keep her in Satines, and she ought to be here to take charge of the castle when the mesnie rides out to war.'

'That won't worry little Jeanne,' said Melisande with a smile. 'Sir Geoffrey with his lady beside him will be easier to control than Sir Geoffrey alone. She will keep out of trouble, she would have kept her feet dry in Noah's flood. She is completely selfish; and a good thing too, when you consider the havoc she could wreak if she were to fall in love. She likes Carytena as it is. She doesn't want anything altered.'

I thought of this conversation when Sir Geoffrey returned, bringing three gowns of the heavy silk of Estives as a present for his constable's lady. The lady Isabel, who returned with her lord, had evidently decided her future tactics. She brought a belt of enamelled gold as a present for the lady who had assumed the heavy responsibility of chatelaine during her absence. Once more the four of them were inseparable; though there was no more hawking, as the knights of Escorta prepared for war.

It would be a dangerous campaign. Of course we had agents in Constantinople; you can buy agents wherever Grifons are gathered together. These warned us that the Emperor Michael had taken into his service a powerful band of Turkish mercenaries; these would be shipped to Malvoisie, under the command of the Sebastocrator Constantine Palaeologue. Another army would march into Wallachia, so that we could not expect help from the dubious allies who had left us in the lurch at Pelagonie. The Grifon fleet would menace the islands, to occupy the Orsini and the other Frankish vassals. This was not a mere border-foray, to win a castle and a few valleys; it would be a serious attempt to add the whole of Lamorie to the Grifon Empire.

Prince William called his knights to a muster at Andreville, since Nicles was now too near the enemy border. But Duke John of Satines explained that he could not come until after he had visited his outlying fees; so the place of muster was changed to Chorinte, where we would wait for the arrival of the mesnie of Estives. That left undefended the south of Lamorie, but there was no help for it; our strong castles must hold by their own strength until the knights rode down from the north to relieve them.

The only good news was that the Pope was on our side, in spite of our alliance with King Manfred. Pope Urban, a Frenchman, was the friend of all Franks who tried to spread true religion in the east. He sent money to Prince William, and an absolution from the oath of perpetual peace he had sworn to the faithless Grifon Emperor. I take it that he also lifted our excommunication, if indeed we had been excommunicated as Ghibellines. But in those days no one knew whether he was really excommunicate or not, and the only thing was to hope for the best.

In three days we were due to leave for the muster at Chorinte; all over the castle they were packing biscuit and shoeing mules. With the enemy so near we must leave a garrison in Carytena; a few invalid knights had been chosen to stay behind with a force of Grifon sergeants. Sir John de Catabas would be castellan; his right hand was now so crippled with rheumatism that he could not hold a sword, though the gallant old boy insisted that he could still manage a horse with the reins held in his left. While he was in command the castle would be safe, though perhaps the Grifons of Mistra would ravage the open country.

It seemed that the queer scandalous Carytena way of life would jog along without disaster for another year. Sir Geoffrey would be removed from all feminine society, Jeanne would be left to share the castle with her husband, the lady Isabel would visit her old home in Satines. By next winter Sir Geoffrey might have grown tired of Jeanne, or, better still, he might pick up on campaign some vulgar concubine who would console him in bed without taking place beside him on formal occasions.

Then, one evening, when I came to our tower room after checking the loading of supplies, Melisande was waiting for me in a great state of agitation.

'Little Jeanne wants to run away to Italy,' she burst out before I had time to sit down. 'Something has shaken her at last, and it's fear, fear for her precious skin. This afternoon she came to me privately and asked my help as one Poulaine to another. Those were her exact words. I don't know where she picks up her horrible language. If a *man* were to call me a Poulaine I would expect you to cut off his head.'

I should explain that Poulaine, chicken, is an opprobrious name given to Franks born in the east. Sometimes you hear it from the lips of supercilious Crusaders fresh from France, the kind of man who denounces all truce with the infidel and can't understand why the knights of Acre don't march straight against Damascus. In Lamorie no decent man would use it, since it could be applied to Prince William and indeed to most of his baronage.

'I suppose she didn't know any other way of describing a Frank born in Constantinople,' I replied soothingly. 'She is still very young. Since she called herself one she didn't mean it as an insult. You ought to make allowances for her ignorance.'

'You mean I ought to make allowances for a pretty girl,' my wife answered. 'Jeanne has only got to flash her eyes at you and she will be forgiven anything. If an ugly old woman called your wife a Poulaine you would challenge her husband.'

'Well, she *is* a pretty girl, as well as a silly one. But go on. What help did she want from a lady born in the same city? You see? There isn't a graceful way of putting it.'

'Money, of course,' snapped Melisande. 'She must have asked every other lady in the castle before she came to me. Do I look as though I had money to lend, in this disgraceful old gown and tattered coif?'

'Money? How curious. I've been poor all my life, and I don't think I have ever asked anyone for money. One doesn't often need it. I have asked for a destrier, and for mail, and for a place in the mesnie. I want land as badly as you do, but it's no use asking for it. But money, no. What will she do with this money? Buy herself a fee, as Palaeologue suggested we should do after Pelagonie?'

'Don't tease, William. This is serious. Jeanne wants money to buy a passage to Italy, and she wants to go to Italy because otherwise when the Grifons capture Carytena they will rape her and cut her throat.'

'Good Heavens, what a thing to say! What a thing to be said by a Toucy, even one sprung from a long line of bastards. Hasn't the girl any shame at all?'

'I thought so. Men will forgive a pretty girl almost anything, and make excuses even if she does something unforgivable. But cowardice is never forgiven, the prettiest face can't excuse it.'

'Well, you know, Melisande, it *is* the unforgivable sin, for Franks living in Romanie. We can stay here only so long as the Grifons are afraid of us. Once we run away there will be no coming back. Why is Jeanne so frightened, anyway? This is one of the strongest castles I have ever seen, and Sir John, who commands it, won't forget to look after his own wife.'

'Yes, but remember she has seen only one fight, and that was the fall of Constantinople. She told me that she was with the party who fought their way on foot from Blachernae to the harbour, through three miles of yelling Grifons. Her father was killed before her eyes, and his body mutilated as it lay in the street.'

'That explains why she thinks of Grifons as dangerous, but it doesn't excuse it. Her father was killed, and it's bad luck she saw it. But the other knights got her away safely. It's the duty of a knight to protect ladies, and if necessary get killed doing so. There are knights in Carytena who will protect her. What did you say to calm her fears?'

'I didn't waste time trying to calm them. I just told her I couldn't help her. I said that if she wanted money she must ask her husband, but she mustn't let him know that she is afraid. I told her to say that she wanted to go to Rome for the welfare of her soul.'

'Sir John will be interested when he hears it. He will wonder what his wife has done that only St Peter can forgive. Of course he has no money to spare, with the war just beginning. So that's that. But I'm glad you told me. Now I know what to think of madam Jeanne, and I don't care what becomes of her. Frightened, indeed, and of Grifons!'

On the next day a most maddening accident befell me. I was riding Sylvia at the quintain from odd angles, to make her handy, when she crossed her legs as she turned at speed. We rolled over together, and because my shield hit the ground awkwardly I broke a bone in my left arm. It was only one of the bones between wrist and elbow, but for some weeks I would be unable to control a horse. It was garrison duty for me, while the mesnie of Escorta rode to Chorinte.

'Are you sure you didn't put a spell on me?' I said to Melisande while she made a sling for my bandaged arm. 'Long ago you wanted me to break a leg before battle. If this had been a leg instead of an arm I would know it was your doing.'

'Keep still, or this will hurt. As though I would want my husband here in the castle, when all the other ladies have a holiday! Don't get too proud if the damsels hang round you. Remember, with Sir Geoffrey away there will be no competition. You aren't really the most attractive knight in Carytena.'

'Who knows? I shall be next week, anyway. I might try my luck with little Jeanne.'

Standing in the gate with Sir John de Catabas I watched the mesnie ride off to the muster. The whole barony of Escorta was left under the protection of five knights and about thirty Grifon sergeants.

At midnight a flustered page awoke me, to say I was wanted urgently at the outer gate. I grumbled, and so did Melisande, for the outer gate was down by the river and rain was falling. I would have to put on a tunic and cloak unless I were to shiver, and with my arm in a sling that was a tiresome business. But when I told the page to go away and say he couldn't find me (which Melisande pointed out would mean that I was sleeping in the wrong bed) he showed me a token. It was a little shield-shaped jingler from a spur-chain, blazoned with the arms of Bruyere; Sir Geoffrey had been wearing those spurs when he rode out in the morning.

'Private business for my lord,' I said to Melisande. 'It must be something urgent, or he would have told me before he started. I must go, of course. Help me with these blasted points. If ever I lose a hand in battle I shall have to become a friar; their frocks are the only thing you can put on with one arm. Now this is bound to be frightfully confidential. When I come back don't press me to tell you what I must not.'

Melisande pinched me. 'Have I ever done that? If it's anything interesting I can find out by myself.'

I was puzzled to imagine what my lord could want of me. In his place some great men would arrange a fatal accident for Sir John and another for the lady Isabel. That would simplify things, but it was not how Sir Geoffrey would behave. Besides, I flatter myself that anyone in need of an unscrupulous assassin would not come to me.

The sentry on the upper gate managed to restrain his curiosity as he let me out. I asked whether he had obtained the castellan's permission before opening the gate, as laid down in standing orders. He answered No, since standing orders also laid down that a direct command from the baron of Escorta must be obeyed without question.

At the lower gate I found Sir Geoffrey himself, sheltering under the arch as he chatted with the sentry. When I arrived he motioned me out on to the bridge, where no one could overhear us through the driving windy rain. What astonished me most of all was to see that he wore tunic and surcoat under his long cloak. That morning he had ridden to war in his mail. It was strange that he should take it off to ride back again, even if there was something urgent to be done in Carytena.

'Cousin William,' he began, as we squatted for shelter behind the windward parapet of the bridge, 'you have been faithful ever since you took oath to me, and I think I have repaid your fidelity. When I could get one man out of that Grifon prison you were the man I chose. So now I give you a most unpleasant task, just to make things even.'

He laughed. It was a nervous titter, such as I had never heard from him. In great astonishment I realised that he was afraid of me. What on earth was the matter?

'Of course I shall do anything you command, my lord, even though it should be unpleasant or dangerous. That is, I shall do anything a knight may do with honour.' I was so confused that I put in this warning, though it was hard to suppose that Sir Geoffrey would want me to do anything dishonourable.

'I don't want *you* to do anything you shouldn't,' he said with a rush, as though anxious to get it over. 'All *you* have to do is to tell the others what *I* have done. It's bound to be said that I have dishonoured my knighthood, and that's why I want to explain everything to you; so that you can put it fairly before the world. It's like this. One of the first duties of a knight is to help ladies in distress. That's so, isn't it?'

'"To protect the Church of God, to foster the widow and the orphan, to help ladies in distress." That's what I swore at my knighting. A lady in distress is not the first obligation. She comes third.'

I spoke firmly, for already I feared what was coming.

'The third duty, then, if you want to be accurate. But in Lamorie widows and orphans receive their due inheritance, and the Church of God stands secure. So I may rightly put everything aside when a lady in distress appeals to my knighthood. That's what I have done, cousin William, and that's my reason for doing it. Make that clear to everyone. The lady Jeanne de Catabas is in distress, driven to distraction by fear of invading Grifons. In addition her spiritual life is in a bad way, and she needs to pray at the tomb of St Peter. She is already under vow to visit Rome, and feels overwhelmed with guilt because the vow has been neglected. She has appealed to me to help her.'

'But the lady Jeanne has a husband,' I broke in. 'Her duty to Sir John takes precedence of any vow. Anyway, I never heard it was the duty of a knight to help cowards run away when they are frightened. How did she appeal to you? She is here in the castle and you rode with the mesnie.'

'She rode after the mesnie and caught up. Now she is on her way to Clarence where I shall join her tomorrow. As soon as we can find a ship we shall cross to Italy, and I shall escort her to Rome. There it is. That's what you've got to tell them in Carytena.'

'My lord, you have been summoned to the muster,' was all I could answer at first. When I had thought it over I tried to find out how much bad news I would have to break. 'What does Sir John know of this?' I inquired.

'Nothing at all. You must explain it to him. That's why I called you out of bed in the middle of the night. I can't tell him face to face. If you like you can say that I am afraid to tell him.'

'It doesn't matter what *I* say, my lord, here on this bridge where no one can hear us. It will be said that you were afraid to face an injured husband, whether I say it or not. Sir Geoffrey, can't you give up this frivolous distraction? You owe a duty to your peasants, who look to you for protection. You owe a duty to your uncle the Prince, who holds your fealty. You owe a duty to Sir John de Catabas, who has grown old and crippled in the service of Escorta. Most of all you owe a duty to your own honour, to your knighthood, to your self-respect. Get little Jeanne to creep back to her husband's lodging. He's a kind man, he may pretend to notice nothing. Then ride to your mesnie, and fulfil the essential duty of a Baron of the Conquest; lead your men against their enemies. I shall say nothing about this evening, and there will be no stain on your repute. There is still time to put everything right.'

I could not see my lord's face. I suppose that was one reason why he chose midnight for this interview. I must judge his state of mind from the tone of his voice; now this changed to a discourteous and unknightly mixture of joviality and bluster.

'Cousin William, I am Sir Geoffrey de Bruyere of Carytena, your lord; and incidentally by universal consent the best knight in all Romanie. I know the rules of chivalry, because they were made by knights no better than I am; and I have the prowess and the authority to alter those rules if I feel like it. You can say, if you like, that I am running away with another man's wife when I ought to be defending my people. What of it? That is my fancy. That is what I choose to do. This won't be the first time a pretty young woman has left an old husband for a rich and handsome protector. There won't be an earthquake or an eclipse, or any other striking sign of Heaven's wrath. I'm not ashamed of what I do. It may be contrary to the rules of the Church, but those rules were not made to bind heroes. I do not break a marriage. This marriage was already broken. I bring happiness and safety to a lady in distress. And, damn it all, why shouldn't I do as I choose? Is there anyone in Lamorie who can stop me? Now will you deliver my news to Sir John, or must I climb up to the castle and tell him personally? Can't you see that I want to slip away quietly, without forcing him to fight me?'

I was trying to think of an answer when he went on, unable to bear my silence.

'Get down from your chivalrous horse for a moment, cousin William. I am taking away another man's wife, but surely that's an old knightly custom? I'm not asking you to help me, only to break the news after it's all over. I am being quite straight-forward with you. And little Jeanne is really in genuine distress.'

'I'm sorry, my lord, that I did not answer sooner. There is no need for further explanation. I understand what you propose to do. I was silent because I was thinking over what you said just now, about her running off with a rich and handsome protector. You are handsome, I agree, though you are now on the verge of middle age. But you will not be rich after the Prince has heard of your misdeeds.'

'Personal abuse won't stop me. I came without my sword, on purpose so that no one could provoke me into fighting. I want you to deliver a message, not to improve my morals. Will you deliver it?'

'That's a direct order from the lord who holds my homage, and it's my duty to obey it. I shall deliver the message, which you need not repeat. To whom shall I deliver it? To Sir John only, or to the whole castle?'

'I have made a mess of this interview, haven't I? I wanted to part friends. But you didn't make it easy for me, you know. I want you to tell Sir John first of all, and then to see that the whole castle knows of it. That will spare Sir John the embarrassment of explaining what has become of his wife. I am telling the truth when I say that I don't want to hurt him.'

'And your mesnie, Sir Geoffrey? Do your knights still take part in this war?'

'They have orders to join the Prince and follow him. Escorta will be weakened only by a single lance. At the tomb of St Peter I shall pray for victory, and that ought to do nearly as much good.'

I could tell from his tone that he was laughing again, that horrible mocking laughter of a man who is ashamed of his conduct and strives to palliate it by making out that he is no worse than others. My appeal to knightly duty had not moved him. There was no more to be said.

I turned to the gate, which the sentry held ajar. Then I

looked back at the muffled figure shapeless in the murk, and in my mind's eye saw the smiling gallant Geoffrey de Bruyere I remembered.

'Come back safe, my lord, and come back soon,' I called into the darkness.

'Thank you, cousin,' came the answer, 'I shall come back to answer for my deeds.' Then the sentry shut the gate, and I began the steep trudge to the inner bailey.

Sir John de Catabas looked rather silly, sitting up alone in the big curtained marriage-bed. I had not realised that in the day-time he wore a wig. But his eyes were not silly, as he glared at me from under bushy brows.

'Thank you for telling me in private,' he said quietly when I had finished. 'No use crying over spilt milk. An injured husband always looks ridiculous; but an injured husband who cannot revenge himself and still ramps about will feel ridiculous also. I shall be as calm as I can.'

'Shall I send to Prince William for another castellan?' I asked, amazed at his self-control.

'Of course not, and it's an unworthy suggestion,' he snapped, with the first hint of anger. 'You don't suppose I will change sides just because my wife has left me? I hold the fee of Catabas by knight-service from the barony of Escorta, and I shall do my duty even if my lord chooses to neglect his. I stay here, I stay in command, and I shall exact obedience from the knights who are under my orders. No sniggers, no waggling fingers at the temples. Is that understood? Then pass it on. With this castle to defend against the Grifons we haven't time for private quarrels. That's all.'

Melisande had cakes and mulled wine waiting for me, for it was nearly dawn by the time I reached our room. 'There's nothing private in this, in fact the sooner everyone knows it the better,' I began, and told her all that had passed. She did not interrupt.

'So Jeanne has got away to safety after all,' she said when I had finished. 'For Sir Geoffrey it's just an amusing escapade.

Presently he will grow bored with Italy, and return to Carytena which he loves better than any lady in distress. I wonder what his uncle will do to him?'

'If he hangs him he will be within his rights, and the mesnie of Escorta will look on with approval. Desertion in the face of the enemy, stealing the wife of a vassal, a sacrilegious pilgrimage undertaken in mortal sin. He has offended against all the laws of God and man. Do you think I should have taken back my homage then and there, at the outer gate? Then I could ride off to seek a better lord.'

'Perhaps I might not come with you,' said Melisande with a smile. 'He hasn't done *us* any harm, and he befriended us when we were penniless. Besides, he's Sir Geoffrey. You are angry with him now because you can't see him. When he comes back and tells us all about his adventures the old charm will come over us. We shall roar with laughter, and pray for a happy outcome to his trial.'

'He will need our prayers. He has no defence. But, as you say, I can't really hate Sir Geoffrey. This has been coming for a long time, and now that it's here it's not so bad as I feared it might be. The really astounding thing is the composure of Sir John.'

'The injured husband? His horns are the least important thing about him. Sir John married Jeanne out of duty, and except for the disgrace he won't mind losing her. He is in love with the barony of Escorta, and always has been. Besides, he is an old man – he can almost remember the conquest. To him it is still wonderful and strange that Franks should bear rule in Romanie. He has only to see armed Grifons and at once he reaches for his sword.'

'Not today. With that crippled hand he can't hold a sword. But I agree that he's the last man to leave a castle when the Grifons are about to besiege it.'

By midday the whole barony of Escorta knew of their lord's elopement. The lady Isabel seemed less affected than anyone else in the castle. During the last year she had grown accustomed to the idea that her lord no longer loved her, and it seemed to all of us that she thought of herself as a de la Roche of Satines rather than as the lady of Escorta. Sir John, inspecting grim-faced the stock of arrows and biscuit, made no comment. No one dared to refer to it in his presence. While we sat at dinner we saw beacons flaring on the outer watch-towers. Sir John ordered the gates to be closed and extra sentries posted. Cut off from the world, the castle of Carytena awaited attack. From the highest turret fluttered the banner of its absent lord, his constable scanning the valley as he leaned against the pole.

CHAPTER TWELVE

The Grifon Invasion

Next morning the Sebastocrator who had vanquished us at Pelagonie rode down the valley of the Charbon at the head of three thousand horse. Though Carytena had been built to block this gorge our tiny garrison could do nothing to hinder the Grifons; we could not spare men for a sortie and they kept beyond arrow range. At least we could deny them the bridge Sir Geoffrey had built close under the lower gate; but not far away they found a ford and struggled through it. They were riding to the sack of almost undefended Andreville, as they shouted joyfully to our sentries; and while Prince William lingered at Chorinte, waiting for the mesnie of Estives, there were no Franks in the field to restrain their ravages.

Three thousand horse sounds an enormous army, more than could be put into the field by the Emperor or the King of France. But that is to judge by western standards. These men were not mailed knights. Most of them were skirmishing light horse from Asia, scarcely better armed than their Turkish enemies; with in addition a few local Grifons from Malvoisie and La Grande Maigne, forsworn vassals of Prince William who had joined their schismatic fellows in hopes of driving the Franks from their holding in Romanie. These were even less formidable than the Asiatics, though they were valuable guides to the best plunder. The knights of Lamorie and Satines could have scattered them in one fair charge; but the knights of Lamorie were at Chorinte, and the knights of Satines busy settling the private affairs of their new Duke.

Some of our peasants who loved Sir Geoffrey told us the news, though of course we could not expect them to stand by us openly; we were the weaker side, and no Grifon will openly support the weaker side. What they told us was very grave; it seemed that we had seen only half the might the Emperor Michael was bringing against Lamorie. Besides a fleet of experienced pirates, who would pounce on the islands if they were left undefended, that un-Christian Emperor had sent into our Christian land a great host of infidel Turks. Another three thousand of these horse-bowmen had struck north into the central plateau, pillaging as they rode to lay siege to La Grite.

For ten days we sat in Carytena, listening to news of disaster. There was only one ray of light; the local peasants, for what they were worth, now fervently supported our side. If you introduce Turkish horsemen into a prosperous country you cannot expect even your co-religionists to like you. Fugitive peasants would sometimes bring to the castle the head of a Turkish straggler, and receive in exchange a few silver pieces; but usually it was the other way round. Turks cannot plunder a country without killing every man they meet; populous hamlets had been wiped out to the last baby.

It was disconcerting that we had no news of the Prince. The whole force of Lamorie was concentrated on the isthmus, not more than three days' ride from La Grite. If Prince William did not march to relieve de Tournay's castle, the head of one of the twelve Baronies of the Conquest, he must believe himself too weak to meet the Grifons in the open field. Meanwhile in Carytena we could do nothing, except keep our gates shut and look as menacing as we could on the battlements. I myself was almost fit to ride again, for the bone in my forearm knitted rapidly; but Sir John would not allow me to carry a call for help to the Prince. He said that our plight must be known, or guessed, and that Prince William was an experienced leader who must have good reason for all he did. I think that at bottom Sir John was ashamed to call attention to the danger of

Carytena, deserted by its lord in the stress of invasion; but of course he was too proud to say so.

In this time of terror Melisande's calm fortitude was a great consolation to me.

'I never supposed I was immortal,' she said with a shrug as we discussed the situation on a windy corner of the battlements. 'I shall take my turn at throwing down stones when the assault comes. As a last resort I have heard you can melt lead from the roof and drop it on the scaling ladders.'

'That would be the end of Carytena as a habitable building,' I interrupted.

She shrugged and went on. 'What happens after that depends on who captures the castle. If it's Grifons I can talk to them in their own language, and anyway they usually spare women and children unless they are sadly out of temper. If it's Turks I must not fall into their hands alive. That's not difficult to manage. If I brandish a knife some Turk will cut me down. I shall look after the younger children. Sophie and little William can help me to throw stones; they'll enjoy it. Then if it's Turks I shall see that they fall off the battlements at the last minute; if it's Grifons they can ask for mercy and perhaps get it. But Geoffrey is old enough to decide his own future. He will be eight next birthday – if he has another birthday.'

'He can manage his crossbow,' I said proudly. 'The Wallach dirks in the armoury are not too heavy for him. He will make a good end, I am sure. I may not be here to see it, unfortunately. I'm sorry it's come to this, my dear. Perhaps I should have sent you all off to Italy while there was time.'

'Don't be sorry for us. The children and I were born in Romanie, and it is right that we should die in the land of our birth. We may even qualify for the Crusading pardon, especially if it's Turks who break in. It won't last long, and then we shall be very well.'

But the little group of horse and foot who approached Carytena next morning were not the vanguard of the besiegers, as at first we feared. They were the scanty invalid garrison of La

Grite, who had yielded their unbreached castle in return for a promise that they might retire in safety. We thought it a shameful bargain, though the middle of a war was no time for saying so; but they had an excuse of sorts. They explained that the foolish Sir Geoffrey de Tournay had left his castle unprovisioned; it lay so far from Mistra that he never expected the enemy to reach it, and the muster at Chorinte needed his bacon and biscuit. Now a garrison of Grifons had been installed in La Grite (and indeed the Grifons hold it to this day), but the main body of Turkish raiders had turned southward to join up with the Sebastocrator near Andreville.

Sir John called a meeting of all the Franks in the castle. He had to call it in two shifts, or the walls would have been left unguarded; but I believe he made exactly the same speech twice. Melisande and I heard the first version.

'Gentlemen,' he began, 'it is our duty to uphold the Frankish cause here in Romanie, and I have a plan for it. But since the plan is very desperate I shall first explain it to you, and carry it out only if you agree. This is what I propose: We can't let the Sebastocrator capture Andreville and the Princess Anna. If he does all the Grifons of the land will forsake us, seeing us helpless against the great army of the Emperor. So I shall take every horseman from the garrisons, young or old, sick or crippled, and charge the Grifon host before Andreville. It means that our castles will be left unguarded, it means staking everything on one throw. But if it fails we shall be no worse off than if we sit in our castles waiting for the Grifons to capture them one by one, as they have already captured La Grite. Will you follow me?'

'How many men can you gather?' asked a fugitive from La Grite.

'Does it matter? A hundred? Two hundred? I shall collect every Frank from the garrison, but still the Grifons will out-number us.' Sir John shrugged his shoulders.

'May I go?' I whispered to Melisande beside me.

'Of course. Volunteer at once, to persuade the laggards. If the worst comes to the worst you will die in hot blood, and the undefended women and children will perhaps get mercy from the Grifons.' Melisande was the best kind of wife for a household knight.

Next day we rode out from Carytena, a column of seventy mounted men and boys. I was surprised at our numbers as we clattered over the bridge, but the fugitives from La Grite had been added to the knights, sergeants and pages of Carytena. Even young Geoffrey Briwerr rode in the rear, astride a quiet hackney; he wore a leather jacket and a light steel cap, for in the armoury there was no mail small enough to fit him. But his short boar-spear could kill a Grifon if he shut his eyes and galloped into him.

Among these seventy there were only a dozen mailed knights mounted on trained destriers; and all of us were disabled in some way, by age or wounds or infirmity. I was one of the fittest, though my left arm was still weak and painful. I rode immediately behind Sir John; who sat straight in his saddle and looked most warlike, though he could not hold a weapon in his rheumatic right hand.

We rode first south-east and then north and then west, making a wide circle before we returned to the valley of the lower Charbon. The enemy had passed on westward and the country seemed deserted, but it was astonishing how many Franks we picked up from Bucelet and the other castles or from isolated watch-towers where they had taken refuge from the invasion. There was something the matter with every one of them, too old or too young or too sick for active service; that was why they had not joined the Prince's muster at the isthmus. But they were willing to ride with us for one last charge in the open rather than wait under a roof for their throats to be cut; and even a sick Frank is worth a good many sound Grifons.

The enemy were encamped not far from Andreville, in the plain where the River Charbon issues from the mountains. As the crow flies they were not more than a long day's ride from Carytena, though we had ridden for five days to catch up with them. The country had been so ravaged that we were short of food, and without grooms or footmen we were tired by the unaccustomed work of looking after our own horses. But our numbers had grown remarkably. When Sir John counted heads he found we were 312 horsemen strong, and 42 of these were genuine dubbed knights in complete mail.

On the other hand friendly peasants informed us that the combined force of the enemy, Grifons and Turks encamped side by side, was at least six thousand men. These peasants were full of the latest Turkish atrocity; the infidels had sacked and burned the Benedictine monastery of Our Lady of Isova. Turks enjoy sacking a Christian shrine, but as a rule their Grifon paymasters restrain them. The Sebastocrator had not attempted to save Isova, holding, like many Grifons, that Latin monks are more hateful than infidels.

That was not how the local peasants saw it. Unfitted by lack of education to understand the niceties of schism, they had a genuine reverence for Our Lady and a dislike of infidels who sack her shrines. Some of them came to our camp armed with bows and ox-goads; and though we could not put them in our line of battle they were helpful in looking after our horses. Above all they raised our spirits, prophesying that Turks who had insulted Our Lady would come to a bad end.

We passed the night only two miles away from the great Grifon army, whose camp we could see spread before us in the plain below. They seemed unaware of our presence; I suppose because their Turkish light horse would not patrol to the rear, where the villages had already been plundered and there was nothing to be taken. In any case, we were so few that we did not look like an army; the hills were dotted with the camp-fires of unarmed fugitives.

A sound night's rest would have helped us to fight; but no one has the strength of mind to pass what may be his last night on earth in deep unconsciousness. Even a warrior who is not worried about the Judgement wants to look at the stars for what may be the last time. There was a good supper for us, and peasants to see to our horses; so we were better off than we had been for the last three days. But no one slept. After I had made my confession I went over to the fire where the pages were gathered, to see how my son was facing his first battle. But except for the usual good wishes I could find nothing to say to him. There was nothing to be said. A boy in his eighth year should not be sent into battle; but if Franks wish to rule in Romanie that is how they must conduct their lives. Geoffrey was frightened, of course; but no more frightened than I was, and pride would keep him in the ranks when the time came. After I had left him I found his little hackney in the horse-lines, and gave it a loaf of barley saved from my supper. It was a well-made little gelding, which looked as though it could gallop; a good feed might give it the bottom to get away if we were put to flight.

By first light the field-masses were finished, and as the east began to glow we formed up; a front rank of mailed knights, then the sergeants, with the half-armed volunteers in the rear. But every man was mounted, and we could charge in one body.

Sir John de Catabas took post three lengths in front of the first rank. While he spoke to us a peasant carried his great helm and held the bridle of his destrier. He made a very good speech. Later I was amused to hear it reproduced in verse as rhetorical and rhythmic as a bishop's Easter sermon. That was not how it sounded at the time. Sir John took a romantic view of the glory of knighthood, but he had little formal education.

'Well, you cripples,' he began, 'the real warriors of Lamorie have gone off with Prince William to the isthmus, leaving us to look after their homes for them. If we were fit for battle we wouldn't be here at all. That's something to be proud of, and by tonight we shall feel very proud. We are going to scatter that Grifon army. They have a lot of men in camp over there, but what sort of men? Hired soldiers, infidels, heathen, schismatics, renegades, outcasts from their own people, speaking different tongues, serving the Sebastocrator only because he pays them money. He hasn't paid them to die for him, and they won't.

'But we are the Franks of Romanie, children of the heroes who conquered this land. We speak one language, we fight in the same way, we know one another, we serve the same lord. The Prince left us at home, thinking us unfit for war. Let's show him his mistake. Let's do a famous deed of arms, something that will be remembered for as long – as long – as long as Noah's Ark rests on Ararat.'

Evidently Sir John had been trying to think of some famous battle of the past, and could not name one.

'Now then,' he went on, 'I ride in front. That's my privilege. The bother is that I can't hold a weapon. So I shall carry the banner of Villehardouin, and it must be strapped to my wrist. I shall bear it straight to the tent of the Sebastocrator, and then someone must unfasten it and plant it in the ground. Wait a minute while I get ready, and then follow me.'

That is the right sort of speech to make before battle, much more inspiring than formal rhetoric.

After the banner had been strapped to his hand a mounted page fastened his helm for him (I wish it had been my Geoffrey, but it was not). Under the great swan-neck crest Sir John looked nearer eight than seven feet high. As he wheeled his destrier to face the foe he gave a great cry of Passavant, Get Forra'd, and we all took it up, digging in our spurs.

As we settled down into a steady canter the sun rose through a nick in the hills behind us; it shone on our leader's white surcoat with its red Crusading cross. Our Grifon sergeants called on Our Lady in the high nasal tone they use for religious invocations, and that reminder that we were avenging the desecration of her shrine lent us courage; but the shouts of Passavant were louder. The army of the Sebastocrator would know that Frankish knights were charging down on them almost before they could see the dust of our destriers.

The invaders were still folding their blankets and lighting their breakfast fires. Their horses stood unsaddled in the picket-lines, or grazed under guard near the camp. But Grifons always take precautions against surprise, much more thoroughly than do Franks. There was a standing guard of about a thousand men, mounted and armed and ready for immediate action. When we were five hundred yards from the camp this guard rode to encounter us.

Luckily they were Grifon light horse, carrying lance and sword; not Turks, whose arrows might have been dangerous in the open plain. They rode against us pluckily enough, but what can a thousand Grifons do against three hundred Franks? Sir John galloped right through them without a scratch. He sat erect, the banner of Villehardouin streaming above and the angry red beak of his swan-crest reaching nearly as high as the banner-staff. Not one of them would break a lance on the shield of that grim figure; at the last moment they opened their ranks to let him through.

With the rest of us they were more obstinate. The first to come at me was a gentleman, as I could see from the steel-headed mace he carried instead of a lance. My little mare was too light to bowl him over, horse and man, in true Frankish fashion. But she was very easy to guide. At the last moment I swerved, to meet him nearside to nearside; as he raised his mace my lance caught him under the arm, where all mail must be weak.

Then other horses were ridden against me and Sylvia came to a stand. I dropped my lance to draw my sword. By swinging it in a circle I cleared a space. It is dangerous to let Grifons get too close, for they have an unchivalrous habit of stabbing at the horse rather than the man. For light horse these people were very stubborn. They halted the whole column, though we had charged into them at speed.

But at close quarters our heavier swords and mail of proof gave us the advantage. A hundred of them must have been on the ground by the time their centre broke and the two wings galloped clear. A furlong of trampled earth stood empty between us and the enemy camp, empty save for the tall erect figure of Sir John, cantering alone towards the great multi-coloured pavilion of the Sebastocrator.

That was the end of the battle; though there was still a good deal of galloping and jostling, and killing of fleeing foes who showed us only their unguarded backs. Nobody likes to cut down unresisting fugitives, or at least I personally don't like it. But often it is the only way to get full value out of a victory; and these were the men who had murdered our peasants and pillaged the shrine of Our Lady of Isova.

The dismounted Grifons in the camp never attempted a stand. Each man grabbed what he could pick up and ran off towards the horses. As we blundered among the tents we found the embers of their cooking fires a greater obstacle than all those thousands of hired soldiers. Grifons do not always fight badly, as I know better than most men. But we had taken them by surprise, and panic is often infectious. They ran like sheep, crying that St George was leading angels against them.

We had none of us expected to win. I suppose Sir John had made up his mind to perish gloriously in the midst of the foe. When he realised that we had won after all he pulled up; among the tents we caught up with him, and in a body we all surged towards the great eagle-banner which marked imperial headquarters.

We very nearly caught the Sebastocrator in his nightgown. As a rule Grifon commanders are hard-working men, who get up early; but Constantine Palaeologue was the Emperor's brother, and could I suppose take liberties. His pavilion was pitched in the middle of the camp, so that it took us some minutes to reach it. When we got there the opening was crammed with unarmed servants, who fell on their knees to kiss the legs of our horses in an abject desire for mercy. They got it, too, I am glad to say; such creatures are not normally worth robbing and a knight gains no glory by killing them.

Sir John halted. A sergeant unfastened the banner of Villehardouin and fixed it in the earth beside the Double Eagle. We waited eagerly. We knew that the camp would be full of valuable plunder, but it seemed discourteous to begin the sack before our leader had taken possession of the captured headquarters. With the entry crowded with servants, we none of us supposed that there would be anyone in the back of the tent.

Behind the luxurious silken walls there was a sudden scurry, and a small bay hackney whizzed through the opening as though a lighted torch were fastened to its tail. He was one of those beautiful little racehorses that Saracen princes sometimes give away as presents; though they give only stallions, so that without mares we cannot breed them for ourselves. This delightful little horse was unsaddled; on his bare back sat the Sebastocrator, naked except for a nightgown of green silk trimmed with purple.

He was through and away before anyone could make a move to stop him. We gazed after him, chiefly from envious longing to possess such a beautiful little horse. But no one tried to pursue, for no destrier could overtake that little whirlwind.

We later heard that the Saracen hackney carried the Sebastocrator without stopping from the plain of Andreville to the castle of Mistra; where he arrived, still clad in his nightgown, so swiftly that he bore the first news of his own defeat. As a prisoner he would have been worth a fat ransom, but perhaps it was better so. Nothing so demoralises a garrison as the sudden arrival of a frightened commander-in-chief, well ahead of his troops.

Sir John dropped his reins to tug at his helm with his one useful hand. The sergeant who had taken his banner helped him to remove it. When his head was free he stared at his followers, still with the unmoved face of a warrior; even in this supreme moment of victory he did not smile.

'Well, gentlemen, that's that,' he said. 'The banner of Villehardouin is where I said I would plant it. *Ville Gagnée*, one might say, except that this isn't a town. Dismiss. Stand down. Go off and get rich. Don't sit there cheering. Don't shout my name. The banner of Villehardouin led you to battle and the banner of Villehardouin gained the victory.'

'But I shall climb Ararat to tell them in Noah's Ark that Sir John de Catabas bore the banner,' someone shouted. We sat our horses in line, cheering again and again; until we saw that the servants of the Sebastocrator were slipping away to plunder on their own account, and we must move off to forestall them.

Henceforth no one ever thought of Sir John as a cuckold. He was known throughout Lamorie and Italy as the victor of Brenice, the name of the little hamlet where the Grifons had pitched their camp. For the rest of his life he basked in glory and ease and honour. Perhaps he was happy; I hope so. But it was impossible to fathom the mind of such a devoted and inarticulate knight.

After we had been dismissed my first action was to seek out my son. Geoffrey was unhurt, proud and delighted and almost mad with excitement. On his little round buckler was a scratch, to prove that a foeman had struck at him; though I myself think he had damaged it by bumping into a rider beside him. He admitted honestly that so far as he knew he had not killed anyone. But he had faced death, and ridden in a glorious victory, all before his eighth birthday. I knew that when he grew up the honour of the Briwerrs would be safe in his keeping. I have been as fortunate in my children as in my wife.

We took a very rich plunder: food and wine, silk and cloth of gold, arrows and flimsy but decorative eastern mail. We found very little gold or silver, for the Turks who had ravaged our villages carry their valuables in their belts day and night. But in the pavilion of the Sebastocrator there were a golden chalice and paten stolen from Our Lady of Isova, and a number of holy books bound in silver. These did not make us any richer, since we must return them to the shrine; but to recover them gave us the pleasant feeling that we were avenged on the sacrilegious plunderers. My share was a length of silk dyed the deep scarlet reserved for princes of the imperial house; there was enough of it to make a gown for Melisande. Little Geoffrey got an enamelled belt, with a figure of St Theodore on the clasp; a thing of no intrinsic value, but a pleasant memento of his first battle. It would give him an opening to boast of his adventures in the company of other pages.

Best of all, we took more than a thousand horses, chiefly

Grifon hackneys. The others were ugly, long-haired Turkish ponies, too shaggy and bad-tempered to carry a knight in battle but gallant and sure-footed on a journey. There were no destriers, and few heavy horses of any kind; in the east they don't breed them.

The common soldiers of the Grifon army just vanished into the landscape; on foot they slipped into the dense woods which covered the foothills. Some got back to Mistra, some were killed by our peasants; but a great many of them disappeared for ever. Either they died in the forest, being townsmen who could not fend for themselves; or they joined up with the Esclavon bandits in the mountains. The Grifon commanders at Mistra had to fetch reinforcements from Asia.

The hired Turks rejoined their paymaster in a body, unharmed. These nomads never stray far from their horses, even in camp; they never scatter, either, even if they must flee. A few minutes after we broke into the camp they were mounted; but their leaders had a look at the battle and decided that there was no point in helping Grifons who were already beaten. The Turks rode back to Mistra, very ready to defend themselves if anyone should bar their way. So the wicked infidel mercenaries escaped unhurt, while the civilised Grifons lost heavily. But then the Grifons were more to be blamed, for introducing Turkish savages into a Christian land.

After dividing the plunder we marched a little way to the south-east, to make sure that no enemy could get near Andreville. If we had followed up resolutely we might have frightened the Emperor's men clear out of Mistra, though if they had closed the gates of that strong castle we had neither foot nor engines for a siege. But Sir John refused to lead a band of three hundred cripples to the invasion of a well-defended province; he said that at Brenice God had granted us an unexpected victory, but that it would be unmilitary to base a plan of campaign on expectation of a string of further miracles.

So we remained halted in the barony of La Glisere. Perhaps

we missed a great chance of freeing our land from invaders; certainly the chance has never come again, and the Emperor still holds Mistra. But I myself was very glad to wait until Prince William had joined us with the knight-service of Lamorie, and so were most of our band; so we cannot complain.

Within a few days the Prince brought up his men, though the knights of Satines still lingered at home. There was a great feast in honour of Sir John, and a solemn Te Deum among the ruins of Our Lady of Isova. But the Prince did not think himself strong enough to advance against Mistra so late in the season, and after clearing up a few bands of Grifon stragglers we were dismissed to our homes for the winter.

At Carytena we had a great welcome; Christmas began in the middle of Advent, when we should have been fasting but for our Crusading privilege. But though we tried to be merry we could not forget the absence of Sir Geoffrey. The lady Isabel presided at the high table; it was generally known that in future she would spend more time in Carytena. But we all felt a bit ashamed of ourselves because the lord who held our allegiance was behaving shamefully.

We had heard nothing from him, and now that winter had closed the sea no news could be expected before the spring. At the height of the panic caused by the Grifon invasion he had sailed with madam Jeanne from the harbour of Clarence; they had slipped across unnoticed in the throng of fugitives, and there had been no open scandal. But later his absence when every knight was desperately needed had made his desertion notorious throughout Romanie. We dreaded the coming of spring, when the army would muster and we would have to answer awkward questions from the knights of other baronies.

The legal position was also in a tangle, which did not affect landholding vassals but might cause trouble for household knights. Sir Geoffrey was guilty of a felony, default of military service. If the Prince chose to bring an action in the High Court the barony of Escorta must escheat to its overlord. In the meantime, pending legal action, Sir Geoffrey remained enfeof-fed of his land – provided he was still alive. But he had vanished without trace, and one day he must die. There would be endless rumours about his whereabouts, and a clear field for every kind of impostor and bogus claimant. A fee always suffers when its lord is absent; but when the lord is not only absent but missing things are very much worse.

A few days before Christmas I talked over our future plans with Melisande. Ought we to leave Carytena of our own accord, before the new lord began to cut down expenses by dismissing household knights? I wanted to try my luck elsewhere, without waiting to be moved on; but that was chiefly because my pride would suffer if I were dismissed. In France and Italy I had always left my employers of my own free will, and some of them had begged me to stay longer.

'Whatever happens we won't starve,' said Melisande cheer-fully. 'In Romanie there is always room for another good knight from the west. If no Frank will hire you any ruler of the Grifons would be glad of your sword among his mercenaries. But service as a mercenary is no life for a family man. You live from month to month, or at most from one Christmas livery to the next. In the end you will be too old to ride, or perhaps disabled by wounds or disease. Then you draw no more pay, and what becomes of your wife and children? Whereas if you stay here Sir Geoffrey will give you a fee when he comes back.'

'When he comes back . . . . Have you any reason to suppose he will come back, or that if he does he will continue as baron of Escorta? Besides, I'm not sure I want to serve a felon knight. It would look like condoning his disgraceful conduct. For years I have enjoyed the privilege of a Crusader, and it seems only decent that I should use my sword in the real Holy Land. Over there things are looking up. At any moment the barons of Acre may push inland, and then there will be fees to distribute. Or if you don't want to leave these parts, where you know the language and the people, I might ask Prince William to take me into his household, or try my luck among the islands. The

Venetians pay well, though they never give you a fee; and I could sit in a boat, urging on the rowers, long after I am too old to ride a destrier.'

'There is more to sea-fighting than urging on the rowers. It's a skilled craft, and you are too old to learn it. As to seeking your fortune in the Holy Land, that's plain ridiculous. I don't mind if you go there for a single campaign, to do your duty and avoid some of your time in Purgatory; though your family will have to live very simply while you are on pilgrimage. But you know as well as I do that the barons of Acre are very near final defeat. If the King of France with all his power couldn't regain Jerusalem the single lance of Sir William Briwerr won't do it. No, if you want to leave Escorta you must go to Prince William. Why not stay here? One day things will come right again.'

'Why do you say that? Sir Geoffrey is a disgraced felon. We don't know where he is, or whether he wants to come back again.'

'We know Sir Geoffrey, that's why. When you see him again you will be eager to follow him, and every Frank in Romanie will help him to get out of his scrape. If he should die in mortal sin, which God forbid, there will be a fault in the scales when St Michael comes to weigh his soul. He can get out of any trouble, just because he's Sir Geoffrey. Even the Grifons, who hate us, treated him well when he was their prisoner. Besides, what has he done that was so very terrible? He ran away with another man's wife, and as a faithful wife myself I must deplore it. But it's a thing that has been done before. Come now, if you had caught him in bed with madam Jeanne here in the castle, would you have felt it your duty to leave the service of such a recreant?'

'That's different,' I said in exasperation. A husband must always think carefully before he expounds the male view of chastity to his wife. 'When we marry we promise fidelity, and a good knight should never break a promise. But there are promises and promises. I am not in charge of Sir Geoffrey's morals – though someone is and he will have to answer for them in the next world. All the same, adultery is not an unforgivable sin. I wouldn't mind if Sir Geoffrey had seduced every lady in Carytena – except one, of course. He could keep ten lemans in his solar, and his knights would make allowances. Jeanne may be the wife of his vassal, but he did not use his lordship to get her. All that part of it is wrong, but not so wrong as to disgrace him. But he was needed to defend his people, and he wasn't there. That's what I can't stomach.'

Since Melisande seemed to be agreeing with me so far, after a pause I added: 'What makes you so certain he will come back?'

'Because he never loved little Jeanne, and if he has to choose between them he will choose Carytena, which he does love. Poor Sir Geoffrey! It's all part of this silly business of being the best knight in all Romanie. That's a whole-time job, and he can never sit back and enjoy his happy life. He must be gallant and gay and a terror with the ladies, when all the time he would rather be chatting with his falconers or persuading his peasants to keep their goats away from his saplings. Jeanne made all the running, you know. She caught him, he didn't catch her. But she never got into his bed, which made her all the more desirable. Now he's got her; for the last half-year he has had her and nothing else, if he is really travelling under a false name. No tournaments, no jolly boasting in hall as the wine goes round, no hawking, no audience of experts when he dances. Just Jeanne, who has heard all his stories and is too young to know any stories of her own. I expect he is looking out for an honourable excuse to come back, with or without her. That's why I say he will return.'

'He will return? And I shall forgive him? You are sure? Then I suppose we ought to stay here.'

'Of course we must stay. I have just thought of the clinching reason. A knight should have thought of it first, instead of leaving it to his lady. Next spring the war will begin again, and you are still a knight of Escorta. For you to leave now would be as bad as anything you impute to Sir Geoffrey. If the lady Isabel keeps us through the winter your sword must serve her in the next campaign. Now are you satisfied?'

On hearing such a definite expression of opinion any prudent husband must concur.

CHAPTER THIRTEEN

Turks and Grifons

In Carytena we were not actually hungry, but it was a poor Christmas. Outside, on the high plain and in the deep valleys, our peasants starved. Raiding Turks had driven off the stock and spoiled the crops; the villagers had saved the vintage, which came about the time of the glorious battle of Brenice, but otherwise they had nothing to show for a year's hard work. The Esclavons were bolder than ever, with Sir Geoffrey absent. Throughout Lamorie our grip was weakening; it seemed that Frankish rule over any part of Romanie was on the way out.

From her high chair on the dais the lady Isabel still ruled the little world of her castle. But her position was insecure; a childless wife could not hold her husband's fee indefinitely, still less could a childless widow hold it in dower. As soon as the war left Prince William leisure to attend to civil affairs he would presumably grant Escorta to some vassal better able to render due service. In addition, we all knew that the lady Isabel disliked Carytena and would feel happier in Satines, where her brother would make her very welcome. Nevertheless she sat in her high chair, looking very stately and worshipful, from the early winter dusk until the late Christmas bedtime, keeping in her hands the direction of all the barony's affairs, civil and military.

Since she so gallantly did her duty we all backed her up and made things easy for her. She was spared one tiresome difficulty that sometimes bothers lady regents; there was no criticism of the constable who commanded her knights in the absence of her lord. Sir John de Catabas was the hero of the day; there was talk that Prince William might give him command of the whole knight-service of Lamorie. The Prince was in poor health and growing old, so that he was reluctant to lead his knights in person. But such an appointment, though it might have turned out very well, would have appeared ridiculous. A great lord cannot retire, for reasons of age and infirmity, in favour of a vassal even older than himself and disabled by rheumatism. Instead it was made known that Sir Ancelin de Toucy would lead all Lamorie to battle. No one could object to him. He was descended from the royal house of France, and so fitted to command great lords; and he was experienced in warfare against the Grifons. The only thing against him was that he was landless, and that would soon be put right.

Meanwhile the utmost decorum reigned in our threadbare and underfed castle. Sir John never spoke of his missing wife, or took any steps to win another lady in her place. I think he had almost forgotten his marriage, in his new-found glory as hero of an almost miraculous victory. The lady Isabel had apparently no favourites; she took pains never to be left alone with a man, which is easy enough in a castle crowded with its winter garrison. It was a very dull Christmas, with everyone setting to the right partner. Even courteous love, songs and sighs and attentions that mean nothing and are intended to be meaningless, were frowned on from the dais.

In early spring came orders for the mesnie of Escorta to join the muster at Nicles. It was known that the Grifons of Mistra were preparing another great army of invasion. Their Turkish mercenaries had remained in Lamorie throughout the winter; and their agents had been busy among our Grifon subjects, so that many decent sergeants forswore their allegiance to join the banner of their race and religion. I say 'decent' sergeants because Grifons break an oath without holding themselves dishonoured, since vassalage and fealty mean little to them; but they believe the defence of their schismatic church to be the first duty of a warrior. I had lived long enough in Romanie to see that these men were acting honourably by their own lights.

The Grifons also took into pay bands of Esclavons, half-armed scoundrels who are useless on a genuine field of battle. But they knew the country and they were ruthless plunderers, so that it would be hard for us to protect our peasants. Even those village elders who last year had delivered up the Grifon spies sent word to Sir John that their young men would join the invaders. In Escorta the peasants liked the house of Bruyere, but affection never kept a Grifon from joining what he believes to be the stronger side.

The most ominous news was that at last the Emperor Michael had been persuaded that his brother the Sebastocrator was not a very good captain. At Pelagonie he had beaten us by shooting down his own mercenaries; but that is not a trick which can be repeated, and at Brenice his flight had been disgraceful. The rumour ran that the Turks had refused to serve under him, insisting on a braver leader. But the Emperor's brother could not be deprived of his command. So the Emperor adjusted matters by keeping the Sebastocrator in supreme command, and sending as his military adviser a nobleman of great energy and personal courage, one Cantacuzene. This Cantacuzene would charge in front while the Sebastocrator gave good advice from the rear. It looked as though this time the Grifons would perhaps fight with greater determination.

During the winter the strong walls of Nicles had been strengthened, so that the Italian trader settled in the place could hold it against anything less than a formal siege with stone-throwers and Greek fire. Everyone said this was an improvement, but it did not seem so to me. The Franks of Romanie were now on the defensive, clinging to their remaining towns as the Crusaders cling to Acre; when first I came to these parts everyone was discussing the approaching conquest of Salonique.

When the Grifons marched out from Mistra we did not even stand to meet them. The Prince rode out to take a look at their army, and gave orders that we must retire. But the burgesses manned their wall and the Grifons marched by without stopping to besiege it, so Nicles remained Frankish.

For three weeks we retreated before the invaders, a most depressing and miserable opening to a campaign. We were eager to charge the foe, whatever the odds; at Brenice that had worked, and this year it might work again. But the Prince was determined; he said the Grifons were too strong to be beaten, and that the loss of a pitched battle would be the end of Lamorie. Help might come from the west, where both Pope Urban and King Manfred were friendly to us; help might come from Satines, though the Duke was plagued by raids from Wallachia and from the sea. If no help came we must grin and bear it; for if a Grifon army should chase us we could not stop running this side of Italy.

Perhaps the enemy feared ambush in country which no Grifon soldier had penetrated for more than fifty years. They had maps, of course, because Grifons always use maps; but these would not show the castles and bridges built by the Franks. For whatever reason, they repeated exactly the invasion of last year, as though there were only one road into Lamorie. From the upper Charbon they marched past Carytena and so down the gorge to their old camp at Brenice. This time they did not scatter to plunder the villages, where there was very little left worth stealing; and I had no fears for the safety of Melisande and the children, guarded in Carytena by Sir John de Catabas and a strong garrison of veterans.

From Brenice the enemy pressed on northward towards Andreville, as far as a desolate nameless upland where stood a little chapel dedicated to St Nicholas. All this time we had kept in touch with them, marching as a rule a few miles to the eastward. There had been a few pointless skirmishes, and our presence made it difficult for small parties of Turks to plunder off the line of march; but the Prince would not permit us to attack.

That kind of patrolling without fighting is very trying to the temper. Our knights disliked it intensely, and some of them threatened to charge without orders; until the Prince was driven to explain to all his followers his reasons for hanging back. He put up Sir Ancelin de Toucy to do the talking, since he was well known to be an expert on Turkish warfare. Sir Ancelin explained that the Grifons were trying to lure us into a trap, tempting us to charge against mounted bowmen. If we attacked, the Grifon foot would hold us up long enough for our horses to be shot by Turks lurking in the background. Therefore we must keep our distance. It all sounded most logical and convincing, but at the same time depressing. If the Grifons could ride through our land secure from attack then we ought to call off the war and offer tribute to the Emperor; unless we gave up altogether and went home to the west.

However, when the invaders reached the little chapel of St Nicholas they were getting very near Andreville, and it was agreed that we must do *something*. Then it became clear that though the Prince wanted to do something he did not know what to do. There is really no answer to Turks, except to sit behind a stone wall and wait for them to go away. If the Turks live so near that they can easily come back, presently the open country goes out of cultivation and the castle-dwellers must retire for lack of food; that is why the frontier of the Grifons in Asia retreats year by year. If the Turks were to settle in Mistra the whole of Lamorie would become desert, growing no harvests to support western knights.

All Prince William could suggest was that we should ride in full battle array right up to the Grifon army, and then halt just out of arrow range. While we were so close they would not dare to detach foragers, or batter the walls of Andreville; eventually they would eat up their supplies and go back to Mistra for more.

It was impressed on us most earnestly that we must obey the trumpet, not charging unless the Prince gave the signal. This was a new venture, not very promising and deadly if it should go wrong. But it was our only hope of persuading the invaders to leave the fields of Lamorie. As I mounted Sylvia I felt very gloomy. But at least we would have a close look at the enemy, instead of inspecting burned farms and murdered peasants after they had passed; it was not very encouraging, but it would break the monotony.

Then God helped us when least we expected it; as sometimes He will help single-minded Crusaders who march stoutly against infidels and schismatics.

In line we rode over a low ridge, lances couched and our leaders faceless under their great helms. Less than three hundred yards away the Grifons awaited us; in front a dense mass of foot, the light horse in the rear, on the flanks Turkish horse-bowmen. Even I could see the trap. It looked so dangerous that when the trumpet sounded for us to halt we obeyed willingly.

When the Grifons saw us they waved their weapons, cheering and shouting what I suppose were insults. Then their foot moved about restlessly, going through the motions of an advance without actually getting any nearer. On the wings the Turks withdrew slightly; but Turkish ponies are swift and handy, and we knew that if we came forward they could close the range in an instant.

It was an undignified exchange: two angry armies shouting insults and defiance at one another like small boys who want to be able to tell mother afterwards that the other fellow began it. Suddenly Sir Ancelin saw the ridiculous side of it, and began to laugh boomingly through his helm.

He was in the centre of the line, some way to my right. But I recognised the sound, unusual on a battlefield. Soon the laughter spread; for really it was very absurd that grown men should come armed and in mail to such a childish slanging match. Presently some hundreds of Frankish knights were sitting their horses in line, laughing their heads off at a crowd of angry Grifons.

The Grifons could not see the funny side of it. Although they had ravaged our land, bringing infidel Turks to help them plunder the Christian peasants, they saw themselves as gallant defenders of their schismatic church, venturing nobly to thrust back an enemy who had occupied the birthright of their

Emperor. They were heroes, and proud of it. Their foot shouted more rudely than before, but they were still forbidden to advance. Their leader was the first man on the field to lose his self-control.

A single horseman spurred out from their array, as sometimes in the west a champion will challenge an army. His horse was a magnificent strawberry roan, with the neat head, flowing tail, and clean legs of a Saracen racer. The rider wore an open helm, gilded under a tall crest of horsehair and ostrich feathers; his corselet was of overlapping scales, burnished until they flashed in the sun; on his thighs were hose of scarlet silk, but from knee to toe his legs were protected by gilded greaves, each fashioned from a single plate of steel; his rectangular shield bore only the double-headed eagle, for Grifons seldom display personal arms; a long sword in a scabbard of scarlet leather hung from his saddle-bow, and in his hands he carried a massive steel mace. He was evidently an officer of high rank, and the whisper ran down our line that this was Cantacuzene, the fighting commander of the hostile army. On that day I never saw the Sebastocrator, and I suppose he was posted well to the rear.

Cantacuzene knew a little bad French, including the obscenities which are the first words a foreigner picks up in any language. He shouted that we were cowards who dared not defend the ill-gotten gains won by our brigand fathers; and other insults less relevant to the situation, referring rather to our behaviour in bed than on the battlefield. At the same time he made his horse curvet and prance on his hind legs, while he himself brandished his mace.

If he had really been challenging to single combat any champion of Lamorie we would have respected him, even though his challenge was phrased in unknightly terms. But we knew that any knight who charged him would have his destrier shot full of Turkish arrows before he could break his lance on that unscarred double eagle. Cantacuzene was acting as bait for his own trap, and losing his dignity as he did it. We laughed all the more, as at a tumbler after dinner. When he shouted out a catch-phrase in French whose double meaning was surely unknown to him someone threw a copper coin towards him.

Cantacuzene could understand that insult, even if our French repartee was going over his head. Standing in his stirrups, he waved his mace over his head; at the same time he dug in his spurs. Then – it was really glorious and I still smile as I write it – his horse gave a great buck and the gallant champion of Constantinople shot clean over its head.

Half a dozen Frankish trumpets pealed the Halt, but our whole line trotted towards the fallen hero. The Grifon foot also advanced in a disorderly mob, while the Turks drew their bows; but they dared not shoot, for fear of hitting their own ridiculous leader. It looked as though the Grifons would reach him first, until the Prince sent forward at full gallop a knight of his own mesnie, Sir Robert de Brienne. His lance pierced the fallen man just before the foot came up; then he turned his destrier very neatly and got back safely to our own line.

For a few minutes we skirmished with Grifon spearmen; since we had advanced at a slow trot we could not bowl them over. But the real danger was that we had now entered the trap prepared for us; the Sebastocrator would not hesitate to order the Turks to shoot at his own foot, as once he had ordered other Turks to shoot at his German mercenaries. It seemed absurd that by falling off his horse Cantacuzene might bring victory to his followers. I felt very frightened, waiting for the first Turkish arrow. But Prince William also recognised our danger, and soon his trumpets were sounding the Retreat. We were very glad to fall back out of range.

So there we were, back again where we had started; a line of Frankish knights facing a line of Grifon foot, and both sides too cautious to come to close quarters. Cantacuzene was dead, but the Grifons had recovered his body; so far as it went the skirmish might be considered a draw.

But the Sebastocrator had lost his trusted captain, and if he renewed the battle he might have to lead his men in person. After half an hour of silent glaring, for both sides were now too angry to shout facetious insults, we heard a great to-do of trumpet calls and shouted orders. The Grifon foot marched off in good order, their light horse interposed to act as rearguard. The Turks, straggled away in their usual sloppy fashion, which by seeming to invite a sudden charge has been fatal to many Frankish armies. After all no battle was fought beside the hilltop chapel of St Nicholas. We watched the Grifons retire, and presently became aware that they were striking camp.

Next day they set off south and then east, retracing their march up the valley of the Charbon. A great invasion had ended in shameful fiasco just because the invaders had lost one famous warrior. Yet perhaps the Sebastocrator acted with prudence; perhaps Cantacuzene was the only man in his army willing to fight.

Some of my readers may think there is something unknightly in treating as a joke the death of a brave man, killed honourably in his mail by the lance of a foe. All I can say in rejoinder is that the whole Frankish army thought it funny. Cantacuzene died a hero, and his descendants should honour his memory; but before that he had been bucked off his horse, and that is funny wherever it happens.

Without his hero the Sebastocrator was at a loss. His great army of invasion marched right back to the frontier; and then sat down before the walls of Nicles only because that was the nearest of all the Frankish fortresses in Lamorie. The trouble was that even now, when our enemies were so obviously disheartened, Prince William dared not lead us against Turkish arrows. It seemed that we must sit on the hills, within sight of the siege, until the walls were breached and the Italian burgesses slaughtered.

Then after a few days a change came over our camp. Suddenly everyone knew, without any public announcement, that secret negotiations had begun. Many of our knights had been bred in Romanie; and there were Grifon sergeants in our ranks, though more of them had deserted to serve with the enemy. Romanians, whether Grifon or Frank, can smell an intrigue in the wind, especially a treacherous intrigue. Something was up. That incompetent and cowardly Sebastocrator had lost the confidence of his men. The most popular form of the rumour suggested that the Grifons of Lamorie who had joined the imperial army were about to change sides in a body.

That proved too good to be true. Instead, while Nicles still held out most gallantly, the army of the Sebastocrator divided; the Turks left the main body and rode off to Carytena. Melisande was there, and Turks never show mercy to women and children; but Turks are also notoriously incompetent at siege-craft, so I was not unduly worried. The enemy had split, and we ought to be strong enough to take on one half of them.

I expected immediate battle, either before Carytena or before Nicles. But you must remember that a simple Norman of English birth can never keep up with the devious politics of Romanie. Prince William gave strict orders that the Turks must not be attacked.

A few days later we were summoned to parade mounted and armed; but for a parliament, not for battle. I wore my best surcoat; with the blazon of Briwerr worked in silk. It was as smart as anything in Lamorie, and I would never wear it where it might be cut about by enemy weapons.

When we were assembled the Prince informed us that we were to receive envoys, and must greet them courteously even if we were surprised to see them. Sir Ancelin de Toucy would accompany the envoys and explain the proposed treaty, which was so important for the future of Lamorie that it must be ratified by the full homage.

Sir Ancelin, unarmed, then rode into the midst of the assembly; on either side of him rode a Turk with drawn sword.

A stir ran down our ranks, as knights wondered whether to attempt a rescue; Sir Ancelin seemed to be a prisoner. But the Turks could kill him before anyone could ride them down, and we quickly saw that this was a sensible business arrangement.

Two Turks had ridden into a crowd of enemies, with Sir Ancelin as their hostage.

When the Turks grinned cheerfully a few knights smiled back. Then Sir Ancelin addressed us.

'Gentlemen, may I present to you two eminent noblemen, Malik and Salik. They are of high birth in their own land, and they command the Turkish band in the Grifon army. Now they want to try another paymaster. It isn't that they have any preference as between Frank and Grifon, but the Sebastocrator hasn't paid them since the opening of this campaign. So until the end of the season they will fight for us without pay, on condition we grant them the plunder of the Grifon camp. Next year either we pay them, or they go home unmolested. It seems to me a sensible arrangement, and Prince William approves. But it won't work unless the knights of Lamorie are willing to receive these Turks as comrades, and therefore I need your agreement also.'

'Are these people infidels, or merely heathen? Will they accept baptism?' called the constable of Patras, who led the Archbishop's mesnie and so felt himself to be the guardian of religion in our army.

Sir Ancelin glanced at the Turks, speaking in a foreign tongue. He was his own interpreter; later I learned that in the old days when the Franks still ruled Constantinople he had commanded the Emperor's Turkish mercenaries.

'These two lords are infidels,' he reported, 'and so are most of their followers. As you know, the servants of Mahound very seldom forsake their devil, and those who do are not to be trusted. No honourable infidel ever seeks baptism. But they have in their band some simple heathen, savages new come from the distant east; and these will gladly become Christian. What they want is a civilised religion, and they don't much mind which it is. Will that do?'

'Then by employing this band we shall be winning souls for Christ,' said the constable of Patras in a satisfied tone. 'That gets round the religious difficulty. We are not leading infidels to war against Christians, we are converting the heathen. There can be no objection.'

'But what pay do they demand? Have we the money? Will it mean an aid from all fees, in this year when we can hardly make ends meet? If we can't pay them what will they do? Will they desert us as they have deserted the Sebastocrator?' That was the Chancellor, old Sir Leonardo di Veroli.

'They have lost their wages for this campaign, and they have resigned themselves to the loss,' answered Sir Ancelin. 'All they want from us is the plunder of the Grifon camp. They have promised that next year they will leave Lamorie for ever, except for those who agree to become Christian. They want to fight the Grifons because they dislike them, and because fighting is their trade. They don't expect to be paid for it this time.'

After that generous offer the parliament made no more objections. It was agreed unanimously that Malik and Salik should ride with us against the Grifons as trusted allies, not as mercenaries.

As soon as they learned that the Turks had joined us the diminished Grifon army raised the siege of Nicles and retired towards Mistra. As they passed through La Cremonie they removed all the Grifon burgesses to a new town which was building below the great castle. That was the end of La Cremonie, which still lies desolate; a pity, for it had been a pleasant place, the first place where I felt myself to be at home in Romanie. But from the military point of view this step was encouraging, as showing that the Grifons were now on the defensive.

The rest of the news was also encouraging, though it did not improve the military situation. The Sebastocrator had sailed from Malvoisie for Constantinople, ostensibly because the Emperor needed his services in the capital. He was still a great man among the Grifons, but I suppose they saw at last that he was unfit to command troops in the field. The army of Mistra was now to be led by two noblemen from Asia: Philes, who held the high rank of Grand Domestic, and one Macrinus. It was likely that it would be better led than in the past.

With the Turks on our side and the Grifons back among their own fortresses our castles need not be strongly garrisoned. Sir John de Catabas joined us to take command of the mesnie of Escorta. His hand was still too stiff to hold a sword, but he sat his horse like a young man. He knew us and would make us do our utmost. It was beginning to look as though we might win this war.

Among Sir John's pages was my young Geoffrey, already a veteran and making sure that the others knew it. I did not see too much of him, for the whole point of sending out a boy to be nourished as a page is to get him away from the shelter of his family; but he assured me that all was well with Melisande and the younger children, and that the castle of Carytena was in no danger even though the Esclavons of Escorta were raiding once again.

Our strengthened army marched south for Mistra, hoping to drive the Grifons clear out of our land. But on the way we heard that the Grand Domestic had moved westward to lay siege to the de la Roche castle of Veligoute. Since there was still a strong garrison in Mistra the Grifon army was now divided, and we rode swiftly to interpose between its two parts.

Unfortunately, just as we always heard of every movement of the Emperor's men, so did the Domestic know what we were doing. In Romanie it is impossible to keep anything secret. Between Veligoute and Mistra lies a steep range of mountains, a northward continuation of the chain of La Grande Maigne. I never learned the French name of these hills; but in the Grifon tongue either the range or the pass through it, I am not sure which, is known as Makryplagi. In this strong position the Domestic awaited us, having raised the siege of Veligoute.

Everything promised a good straightforward battle, the kind of fight in which Franks should always beat Grifons. The other side had no horse-bowmen to complicate our tactics. Frankish knights were to storm a strong position held by Grifon horse and foot; that it was a strong position only made it easier for us, since it is only difficult to beat Grifons when they keep retiring out of reach.

Our vanguard was placed under the command of Sir John de Catabas, which meant that as at Pelagonie the mesnie of Escorta would charge first before the whole host. Our main battle was made up of Turks, under their own leaders but advised by Sir Ancelin de Toucy, who could speak to them without an interpreter. The rearguard, the mesnies of Villehardouin and de la Roche, would be led by the Prince in person. Prince William excused his post in the rear by saying that he was feeling his age; it never occurred to anyone to note that Sir John de Catabas was considerably older, and with a useless right hand in addition. In those days the Franks of Lamorie divided warriors into two classes: good knights who fought bravely while taking care of their own lives, and Sir John de Catabas who was capable of anything.

As a matter of fact the Grifons put up a very good fight; or at least the first line of them. At the top of the pass there was a stretch of flat ground. The Grifons had built a wall of loose stones at the edge of the ascent. Their foot held this wall, and on the flat ground in rear there was room for their horse. But the real trouble was that until we reached the crest we could not see the enemy, and they then were very close to us. That can be unnerving.

We plodded up a steep slope, the mesnie of Escorta in the van with Sir John de Catabas at the head of it. The going was so steep that my saddle began to slip; I had to lie forward on Sylvia's withers and take my feet out of the stirrups, for she was herring-gutted, with no bulge in her ribs to hold the girth in place. But years of campaigning among the crags of Escorta had accustomed me to riding in any posture.

As our faces came level with the wall the Grifons loosed a shower of arrows, and we had to scramble at them without the impetus of a proper charge. Over the heads of the foot we could see in a line of horse in the background, the usual light-armed sergeants in flimsy mail; but even light-armed sergeants can do damage if they charge full tilt into knights who have been brought to a halt. It all looked most unpleasant. After a little ineffectual poking we retired down the slope to avoid the arrow-shower.

Sir John stormed at us, of course, and as soon as we were reformed led us to a second attack. It was most humiliating to be stuck there in plain sight of all the other mesnies. But it was also most dangerous to charge home against the Grifon wall. Before the second attack I managed to tighten my girths, though it meant riding into the assault with my mail gloves dangling from my wrists for lack of time to wriggle into them again. But now I could sit properly in the saddle.

Again we were driven back, though this time I got so close to the wall that Sylvia's feet and my lance dislodged some loose stones. But it was a position that must be captured quickly or not at all; once we were brought to a stand the arrows thudded at close range into our mail. Perhaps it was a pity that safety lay so near; fifty yards down the slope and no arrow could reach us. It was a strong temptation, to which we yielded.

A third time we tried, again with no success; though we did for a few minutes get in among the enemy. We drove their foot back from the wall, by this time a mere heap of scattered stones; we were pushing them hard when their horses charged and got us on the run. Once over the brink there was no stopping us until we were safe from the arrows, but luckily the Grifons were too cautious to pursue.

It seemed that Sir John was going to throw a fit before all his followers. He trembled with rage; as we formed up again he shouted a speech at us, a really well-balanced speech considering that it must have been composed extempore; but it did not strike home to our hearts.

He told us that the men of Escorta were shamed before all their comrades, that our knightly spurs ought to be hacked from our heels, that if we counted on the Crusading pardon to free us from the penalty for the disgusting sins in which we wallowed we were very much mistaken; that pardon was granted to knights who fought infidels or schismatics, not to knights who run away from them; religion apart, it was unseemly that knights should retire before miserable infantry. Then he went on to speak of honour, and chivalry, and the ladies who were waiting to hear of our gallant deeds. Those were not things we had thought about during this war; you don't, if you welcome Turks as allies. But suddenly I saw that Sir John himself was a true knight out of the old romances. He had been cuckolded by his lord, and still he served the fee he was sworn to protect; at Brenice he had charged so gallantly that he had been reasonably mistaken for St George; when he said that next time he would go on alone, to plant the banner of Villehardouin in the Grifon camp, I knew he meant it; even though the malicious little demon who points out the ridiculous side of solemn occasions reminded me that Sir John could not plant a banner anywhere, unless he got a servant to help him.

Sir John meant everything he said, even to the flourish at the end about death before dishonour. But none of his hearers were stirred by his devotion. We would attack again if we must; because a trained fighting man obeys orders even when he knows them to be futile. But we were resigned to defeat, and anxious chiefly to survive it. You cannot live long in Romanie and continue to believe that western knights are always invincible.

The next assault would have been a very nasty affair, unwillingly delivered and bloodily repulsed; luckily another leader came up to send us spurring against that ruined wall. Sir Ancelin de Toucy pushed past to address us as we formed in rank, and his approach was more in keeping with our private sentiments.

'What's this, boys?' he said with a grin. 'My beastly savages sent me to find out whether you are still on their side. Are you? You ought to be, you know, if you can recognise what is good for you. Malik and Salik have given up the promise of six months' pay for a chance to plunder the camp of the Grand

Domestic; and they ought to know what it's worth, since they were inside it a few weeks ago. There will be enough for us as well. These Turks have a very high standard of living, though you might not think it to look at them. As I said, they sent me to ask whether you are still fighting. But I watched as I climbed this damned steep hill and I can see you are not. Instead you are playing hide and seek with a gang of rascally Grifon foot-soldiers. That's enough of that. What will your ladies say when they hear of it? Now go and clear those people out of the way, and while you rob the dead my Turks can have a go at the horse in the second line.'

I don't say that is the only way to talk to wavering knights; sometimes an invocation of glory and chivalry will spur them on to heroism. But it was the way to talk to the mesnie of Escorta on the hillside of Makryplagi. Our fourth assault was delivered as fiercely as if we had never been repulsed.

I suppose the Grifon foot were as tired as we were. Every time they pushed us back they must have expected their own horse to come in and complete the business; and three times their horse had left them still holding the forefront of the battle. That is a lot to ask of infantry, who consider that since they are socially inferior to horse they may also give place to them on the battlefield.

Suddenly we were over the wall and advancing across the level summit, driving before us those unhappy archers and spearmen. There were still the Grifon horse to be dealt with, and we were exhausted; Sylvia could hardly lift her feet off the ground. But just at the right moment Sir Ancelin led up his Turks, and behind them rode the Prince and his rearguard of fresh knights.

The first squadron of Grifon sergeants made a fight of it, though of course they were quickly overthrown. But the supports who were drawn up behind them, far down the reverse slope of the pass, rode off the field in panic without waiting to draw their swords. Among Grifons that happens much too often. They take pride in the fact that their armies are commanded from the rear; they say it is a mark of civilisation, and that a general in the rear can seize chances and order manoeuvres that would never be seen by a hero in the thick of the fray. It may be a good way to get full advantage from a victory; but when things are going wrong a commander behind his men can do nothing but lead them in flight.

The mesnie of Escorta took no part in the pursuit. We had got to the bottom of our horses; we dismounted on the hillside to plunder the dead by the wall, as Sir Ancelin had foretold. But it was by all accounts a most bloody and remunerative pursuit.

The Grifons were pressed so hard that soon their squadrons dissolved into a cloud of fugitives. The Prince's men were after good ransoms, and did not trouble themselves to kill humble sergeants; but Turks enjoy killing for its own sake and they rode, with bloody swords and empty quivers, until their ponies could go no farther. It was ironical that these blood-seeking Turks should after all take the greatest haul of ransoms. The Grifon leaders had in cold blood deserted their men to seek shelter in a deep cave among the mountains. The Turks found them in this blind alley, to the number of more than three hundred and fifty; practically all the officers of the army of Mistra, from the Grand Domestic down. It was such a mighty catch that Malik and Salik could not keep it all for themselves. After some argument the leading captives were delivered to the Prince.

For the time being there was a pause in the War of Mistra, though of course it will not really end until one side or the other has been driven right out of Lamorie; after various truces and treaties it still smoulders at the present day. Prince William ravaged the open country as far as the walls of Malvoisie, but there was such unrest among our own Grifon subjects that he had not the leisure to besiege any strong place. The frontier remained as before; save that La Cremonie, the disputed town, was now empty and desolate.

Malik and Salik were loosed on the rebels of Escorta and

central Lamorie. They harried them so savagely that the local village chiefs soon begged for peace. Then, to our great relief, the infidel Turks honestly began their long journey home by riding north into Great Wallachia; many were killed by Wallachs or Grifons, but it is said that the others got safely back to Asia. May they remain there.

Some heathen Turks accepted baptism, on the condition that they should be given land as well as eternal salvation. Oddly enough, they made useful settlers. The lesser men among them are excellent shepherds and horse-breeders; their gentry, for Turks value good birth, undertook the obligations of knighthood and in some cases married Frankish heiresses. Though a horde of Turks is an unmitigated evil, a single Turk can be taught decent behaviour. They are brave, and they keep their promises. If they were not unfortunately dedicated to Mahound it might be possible to make civilised men out of the whole race.

The ransoms of the Grifon leaders brought needed money into our ravaged country, though by bad luck the Grand Domestic died a natural death while we were still haggling over his price. With great forethought Sir Ancelin had sought and obtained the ransom of Macrinus as the reward of victory. He did not exchange him for money, but bought the freedom of his brother Sir Philip, who had been captured at the fall of Constantinople and held in a Grifon prison ever since. Many other Frankish captives were freed at the same time, for the Emperor was willing to pay very high for Macrinus. We supposed that one of the few fighting captains of the Grifons was needed at any cost. But it turned out that Palaeologue wanted his eyes rather than his sword. There was a rumour that at Makryplagi Macrinus had deliberately betrayed his lord, in the interest of some rival claimant to the Empire. As soon as the prisoners reached Constantinople he was blinded, and then cast into a dungeon where he died. That is how Grifons reward their leaders.

CHAPTER FOURTEEN

The Return of Sir Geoffrey

℃

By autumn the mesnie of Escorta were back in Carytena, preparing to keep Christmas in a land ravaged but at peace. The Turks had reduced our peasants to obedience, in the usual Turkish manner. But there were still enough of them alive to plough the fields, and by next harvest there would be bread for all. The spoil we had taken in the Grifon camp, and the first trickle of Grifon ransom-money, enabled us to buy grain in Sicily. The prospect of freedom from invasion meant that after two or three good harvests the barony of Escorta would be as prosperous as before the war.

My dear Melisande was well, and as beautiful as ever; our three children were growing up to be French-speaking castle-dwelling gentry, with courteous manners and the prospect of a sound education. I still held no fee, and when I died they would I have no inheritance; but Romanie is a land of opportunity. They had a much better chance of success than if I had stayed on the March of Wales as younger brother and hanger-on to a poor rustic knight.

The lady Isabel ruled the barony well, and kept such good order in the castle that it was an excellent place for young children to grow up in. Her military affairs were managed by her constable, Sir John de Catabas, so famous as the hero of Brenice that no one recalled his cuckoldry. He was a dull old stick, who frowned on tournaments as likely to damage mail and destriers; but in one way that was a good thing, for it meant that the lady Isabel did not like him as a person. Her de la Roche cousins were always in and out of the castle, and they saw to it that we were kept amused; but Sir John and his liege-lady, both lacking their married partners, could rule the fee jointly and be constantly together without raising the slightest breath of scandal. Sir John was a good knight, who would never surprise his comrades. You could trust him to manage the fee of another without scheming to take it for himself, and leave him alone with the most attractive lady. Not the best company for a jolly Christmas, but a useful man to have in command.

Then, on the morrow of Epiphany 1265, very early on a dark winter morning, I was roused from sleep by Melisande climbing back into bed. Even the most courteous husband is entitled to ask for information in these circumstances, especially as Melisande seemed to be trying not to wake me. 'Good morning, my dear. Where have you been?' I asked, I hope without any tremor of alarm in my voice.

'Outside, where just now it's very cold,' said Melisande with a shiver. 'If you want details, I have been down to the lower gate. The sentry there can vouch for my good behaviour.'

'Very well, my dear, but you should have told me you were going. You know it's against standing orders, after the castle has been shut for the night. Everyone does it, of course, but it annoys Sir John. Now I shall know what he's talking about when he tells me to keep better order in my household. I won't ask who it was you met. One of those devious Grifon intrigues, I suppose. One day I shall hear all about it, when you are ready to tell me.'

I turned over as though for more sleep. It was unkind; but I was genuinely curious, and I knew that the quickest way to get the news out of Melisande was to pretend it did not interest me.

Sure enough, she prodded me fiercely in the ribs and told all.

'I went down because of something a kitchen-maid whispered yesterday. You will never guess whom I met there, not if you go on guessing for a thousand years. So I must tell you. I have been talking with madam Jeanne de Catabas, if that is still her right name.'

That made me sit up. I climbed out of bed and worked my tinder-box until a torch was burning in the wall-ring. There would be no more sleep before morning Mass.

'Yes, little Jeanne is back from Italy, and anxious to know how the land lies. Will Sir John kill her at sight, or lock her up in a dungeon for life? I said he wouldn't harm her, and that at worst he would turn her out again. I hope you agree with me? It will be terrible if I have enticed her to her death.'

'You were quite right,' I answered soothingly. 'Sir John would never harm a lady. He would think it unknightly. In fact he thinks it unknightly to lay a finger on a lady, either to please her or to hurt her. Perhaps that's why his wife left him.'

'That's more or less what I told Jeanne. There's a chance he may take her back, and if he doesn't she will be no worse off than she is now. She plans to enter the great hall at dinner-time. She will publicly admit her wrongdoing and beg for mercy. Perhaps he will forgive her, and if not she will be allowed to leave the castle. Poor little Jeanne, I don't know what will become of her.'

'She ought to have thought of that before she ran away with Sir Geoffrey. But has he cast her off, to beg her way back to her husband? It's not like him to desert a lady, even after he has ruined her. Surely he has not been so rash as to come back with her to Carytena? That would be too much. Sir John must fight him, and it will be a miserable joust. Sir Geoffrey will gain no glory by knocking down a cripple old enough to be his father; but if Sir John is in earnest the only way to stop him will be to bowl him over. Whatever the outcome, a good knight will be hurt and shamed.'

'Don't fuss,' said Melisande sharply, 'though I'm glad you recognise that every problem in life can't be solved by a good joust. Sir Geoffrey brought back Jeanne to Lamorie, but he was too sensible to come here and hand her over to an angry husband. He is waiting in Andreville to make his peace with Prince William. After all, he can't be sure that he is still lord of

Carytena. His uncle could hang him, though I don't suppose he will. Jeanne told me all about it, but it's a long story.'

'Never mind. Tell me while I dress. If I know all about it I can inform Sir John quietly, which I suppose is what you want. Otherwise *you* will have to see him in private, and rumour will be buzzing all over the castle. Besides, I should look silly if I have to admit that my wife knows something important and I don't.'

I began to pull on my hose. It was nearly dawn, not worth while trying to sleep again.

'You want to know because you are curious. The other reasons aren't very convincing,' said Melisande. 'Very well. I shall tell you what Jeanne told me. I am repeating what she said, I don't vouch for it. You may doubt her word without doubting mine.'

She sat up in bed, smiling under her red silk nightcap. I wrapped a cloak round her bare shoulders.

'Well, the two of them found a ship to take them to some port in Apulia, Sir Geoffrey carried a draft on a Venetian merchant, and in Naples of Italy they cashed it without trouble. They lived in comfort at the best inns, giving out that they were pilgrims returning from the Holy Land. Sir Geoffrey used his own name, but without any mention of Lamorie or Escorta. Champagne is full of Bruyeres, and everyone assumed he was one of them. But, and this is important, Jeanne passed as his widowed sister and they never shared a bed. They behaved like pilgrims, too, hearing Mass every day and visiting all the more important shrines. Though Jeanne says she never dared to take Communion, and as far as she knows Sir Geoffrey did not either. So there was no sacrilege.

'From Naples they crossed Apulia again, and made the pilgrimage to St Michael at Monte Gargano. Then they wandered about the Kingdom for the best part of a year, living quietly because their money would not last for ever but living in comfort all the same. To Jeanne it was a foretaste of Heaven, at least that's how she put it. She had never before been out of

Romanie. To live in a land where there were no Turks or other infidels, where all the peasants spoke a western language and prayed in Latin churches, where the craftsmen made every day the luxuries we import at great expense, was exactly what she wanted. It's true, you know, that she was afraid of being captured by angry Grifons in Lamorie, as she had so nearly been captured in Constantinople. Now all her enemies were on the far side of the Adriatic, and for the first time in her life she might sleep unafraid. What that child must have gone through in Constantinople, with Frank-hating Grifons all round her! But of course she never dared to tell her father of her terror.

'Jeanne told me they had one great disappointment. They could not visit the tombs of the Apostles. It seems King Manfred lost control of Rome just about the time they landed, and it wasn't safe for Ghibellines to go there from the Kingdom of Naples.

'That reminds me. By all accounts there is a great war brewing in Italy. The Guelfs have a new leader, the Count of Anjou, the brother of King Louis. He has been proclaimed Senator of Rome; his men hold the city, though he has not yet arrived.'

'Yes, yes, I know,' I interrupted quickly. Though I am all for talking scandal at any hour, a chilly dawn is no time for a discussion of international politics. 'There will be a war soon, and quite likely the Guelfs will win it. We out here will be just as well off, in fact better. The Guelfs are a more suitable party for dedicated Crusaders.'

'Very well, I shall continue with Jeanne's adventures,' said Melisande placidly. 'For a whole year she and Sir Geoffrey lived very happily in Italy, lodging in inns, or as guests in great castles. But Sir Geoffrey always took the precedence of a simple knight. He could not ask for a seat at the high table for fear of being recognised. I expect he enjoyed his lowly rank; if you are really grand you can afford to despise grandeur. Of course he could not ride in a tournament; experts would have recognised his style even if he had borne false arms. Anyway, he had no mail with him. But except for tournaments he enjoyed all his normal amusements. He and Jeanne were very happy.'

Melisande sat up straighter, and took a deep breath.

'Now comes the difficult bit,' she went on. 'Remember, I am passing on what Jeanne told me. You may believe it or not without calling me a liar. But I must add that I believe Jeanne, though her story is most unlikely. She assured me again and again, with great emotion, that all the time they have been absent from Carytena Sir Geoffrey has in truth treated her as a sister. They never made love, they never committed adultery, Sir John is not a cuckold. Jeanne ran away without his permission. If you like, she deserted him. But in the sense in which ordinary people use the words she has not been an unfaithful wife. That's what she says, and I believe her. You may do as you please.'

Silence fell while I weighed this remarkable information. Its oddity almost made it carry conviction. It was not the kind of story an erring wife would invent. For one thing, if true it reflected on her attraction as much as the more normal explanation of her flight reflected on her morals.

'Well,' I said after a pause, 'I suppose it's just possible. Jeanne ran away because she was afraid of the Turks, not because she was in love with Sir Geoffrey. Even I can see that. When he had taken her safely over the Adriatic he had done all she wanted of him, and she need not go on to tempt him to become her lover. I don't think she cares very much about love anyway. If she did, she would not have endured so cheerfully the embraces of old Sir John. I can believe it of Jeanne, quite easily. Sir Geoffrey is the stumbling-block. Probably he has lost his barony, he may lose his head, he has certainly spent a great sum of money; and all for the company of a rather stupid young girl, and for the pleasure of showing her the sights of Italy. That's not my idea of Sir Geoffrey. And if she was holding him off while permitting him to hope she couldn't have kept it up for a whole year.'

'There you are wrong,' Melisande answered me. 'It's exactly how Sir Geoffrey might be expected to behave. He is the best knight in all Romanie, and he makes up his own rules of conduct as he goes along. He doesn't mind what others think of him, so long as his own conscience does not reproach him. Like many other good knights, he thinks of all women as nothing but cuddly little dolls. So long as he did not possess little Jeanne, in his own eyes he has done her husband no wrong. The fact that he had taken her away for more than a year, that Sir John didn't know where she was, that the whole world saw him as a horned cuckold, wouldn't weigh with Sir Geoffrey a bit. He would be innocent, for all that his neighbours thought him guilty. A true knight, conscious of his own uprightness, does not deign to refute slander. Yes, I can see Sir Geoffrey behaving like that. My own opinion is that Jeanne is telling the truth, though I wouldn't grasp a hot ploughshare to prove my faith in her.'

'I don't know what to believe,' I answered doubtfully. 'I suppose it does not concern us. For the time being we can both take the line that we believe anything told us by a knight or lady of honourable birth. So that's that. Sir Geoffrey and little Jeanne toured Italy as brother and sister, visiting holy shrines for the good of their souls. An innocent pastime, if there hadn't been a war on here in Lamorie. Why did they interrupt their spiritual exercises? Why have they come back, to what must be a frosty welcome? Did Jeanne bother to tell you that, after stuffing you with these unlikely stories?'

'Oh yes, she explained it most convincingly. They didn't come back of their own accord. It was all because Sir Geoffrey ran out of money. He knew that any Italian merchant would let him draw another bill; the credit of Escorta is good from Venice to Palermo. But of course that meant going to the merchant and proving his identity. He had brought his signet, and after a bit of argument he got his money. But the merchant talked, and soon everyone knew who they were; until at last the story reached King Manfred. He sent sergeants to arrest Sir Geoffrey, and it seems gave him a frightful dressing-down at a private interview; though of course Jeanne wasn't there, and all this is just what she thinks happened. In the end Sir Geoffrey left the King's court a free man, but with seven days to get out of Italy and return to his duty. If he disobeyed the command he would be outlaw. So they came here, and Sir Geoffrey surrendered himself to his uncle in Andreville.'

'That was courageous,' I admitted. 'He might have ridden north to join the Guelfs. But then we all know he is brave. What will happen to him? I don't see that he has any defence. If I were in the parliament I should have to pronounce him a felon, though afterwards I would petition the Prince to show mercy. Is Jeanne afraid for him, or doesn't she care?'

'I think she cares. You know, William, she is silly, but she isn't entirely base. Remember, she came back to take her own punishment. But she says Sir Geoffrey is convinced that no harm will come to him. He has a trick up his sleeve that will induce his uncle to pardon him, though she doesn't know what it is.'

'It had better be a good one. If he wasn't Sir Geoffrey I would say he deserved to hang on the common gallows. But it's nearly time for morning Mass. What happens immediately? Is there anything you want me to do this very day?'

'Today, after dinner when we hope everyone will be in a good temper, poor Jeanne will appear and throw herself on her husband's mercy. If Sir John cuts her down then and there no one can do anything. If he locks her in a dungeon I hope you will help her to escape after a month or so, when she has been punished enough. That's the most I ask of you. But it will help her to know that you will be at least half on her side for love of Sir Geoffrey. You *are* on her side, aren't you?'

'I won't withstand Sir John to his face, because he is in the right. But I'll be there, with my sword and a purse full of money, just by the door. If she has to flee in a hurry I can lend her the money and get her past the sentry on the gate. It all depends on the mercy of Sir John. He'll be within his rights if he kills her. I suppose she won't start explaining, as soon as she arrives, that she has never been more than a sister to Sir Geoffrey?'

Then I went off to the washplace, very excited at coming events. It was always exciting being married to Melisande, who knows everything before it happens.

By dinner-time everyone in the castle knew there was something in the wind; everyone, that is, except Sir John. Melisande had decided, in the end, that it was better to allow his wife's arrival to take him by surprise. Perhaps the rumour from the lower gate had not reached the lady Isabel either, since she held herself very aloof from the general company. It was natural that the two people most closely concerned should be the last to hear the news.

It was a fish day, but in Romanie you dine well on fish. We had fresh tunny, and mussels, and octopus, and wine unstinted. Sir John did himself very well. His teeth troubled him, as they trouble most men of his age; and he dined better on fish than on beef. He drank as heartily as he ate, never noticing that all eyes were on him. As he finished up with figs in syrup he seemed serene and content; Jeanne would find him in better temper than usual.

Suddenly she stood before the dais, looking very pitiable. She wore a plain green surcoat, without fur; and her saucy little coif was hidden by a deep hood. She bent her head and hid her hands in her sleeves, like a penitent waiting outside the confessional. The lady Isabel recognised her, and caught Sir John by the arm. He stared without a word, then set his jaw and rose from his seat. Suddenly he noticed that everyone was watching him, and didn't like it. He came down from the dais and took his wife's finger most courteously, as though to lead her out in the dance; then he stalked with her back across the dais into what by rights was Sir Geoffrey's own private solar at the end of the hall.

My hand came away from my swordhilt. Of course he might be going to strangle her in private; but that was not in his character, and if he did I could not interfere. It looked rather as though he wanted to talk with her. Once Jeanne got talking she would be safe; that young woman could talk herself out of any predicament.

The rest of us emptied our cups from sheer excitement; but then the lady Isabel withdrew by the far door, a signal that dinner was over. The butlers passed no more drink, and there was nothing for us to do but go into the courtyard. I hurried straight to my tower room, and waited for Melisande to come and tell me the inside story.

It was some time before she came, and then it was only to turn me out. 'Jeanne needs somewhere to be private, and Isabel won't allow her in the bower. You can't have a loose woman in the same room with respectable damsels, that's what she says. But this is *my* room, so much mine that I can tell my husband to leave it. Jeanne may rest here, in spite of the lady Isabel.'

'Jeanne stole my lady's husband,' I pointed out. 'If I had been stolen you might take offence.'

'Perhaps, perhaps not. We need not go into it. Now run away and look at the pretty horses in the stable. Whenever I need you you are always fussing about in the stable, so now you may as well go there to please me.'

'Is it a happy ending?' I asked as I went out.

'The best. I shall tell you later. I don't want Jeanne to find a man in this room.'

Shortly before sunset I looked down from the upper bailey to see figures crossing the bridge below the castle; Jeanne, mounted on a good mule, and behind her a sergeant leading a pack-pony. So I knew the coast was clear, and came back to my tower to hear all the news from Melisande.

'It turned out most fortunately,' she said with a sign of satisfaction. 'Sir John has behaved like a courteous knight, and I shall never listen to another hard word against him. When he got Jeanne alone he just asked her why she had come back, and she answered that King Manfred had commanded her to beg forgiveness from the husband she had wronged. That was sensible of the girl. She didn't try to convince him that she had never committed adultery. He wouldn't have believed her anyway.'

'Even if he chose to believe her he couldn't say so in public,' I pointed out. 'Unless all the world believes in Jeanne's chastity, and that's impossible, he would just gain the reputation of a cuckold who is easily deceived. He must treat her as guilty, whatever he thinks in his own heart.'

'She didn't place that strain on his good nature. Later on I may perhaps let him know that his wife remained physically faithful, if that will comfort him. Today he followed his conscience, and it's a good one. He told Jeanne, of course, that she could not come back. He offered her a little manor up in the mountains, if she had nowhere else to go. But if she could manage by herself he would be happier if she left Romanie. That's what she wants, of course. So she will go to Apulia, and live as a lay boarder in some convent of nuns. She must call herself Jeanne de Toucy so as not to bring shame on the house of Catabas. The nuns will know privately that she is married, to stop her committing bigamy. But to the world in general she will be an orphan refugee from Constantinople.'

'That's all very well, but a corrody in a good convent costs money. Will Sir Geoffrey pay?'

'Oh no, that would be shocking, to get rid of a discarded mistress by turning her out to pasture among nuns. Jeanne is a Toucy, remember, and since Makryplagi the Toucys have golden hyperpers by the sackful. Her own kin will make all the arrangements. A corrody is a lump sum. Once it's paid Jeanne will have a home for life.'

'It seems to me that someone arranged this in advance. The Toucys are ready to pay up, and there is a convent waiting for Jeanne. I wonder who fixed it? But if it's a secret don't tell me.'

Melisande smiled happily to herself. A lady bred in Constantinople is never overtaken by events.

'I suppose Jeanne was willing?' I added as an afterthought. 'It will be tiresome if she gives scandal in a respectable religious house.'

'Of course she is willing, and she will behave herself. In Italy, where the Turks can't get at her, she will be happy. She won't run off with a man, either. She is incapable of real love for anything except her own beautiful body. That's what made her such a dangerous coquette. She will go down well with the nuns. They will be charmed by her beauty, and the holy ladies have a soft spot for a girl with a dashing past provided she lives respectably in the present. Think of the stories Jeanne can tell them at recreation. She will live happy ever after.'

As far as I know she did. I never heard of her again.

Sir Geoffrey was said to be living quietly in a friary at Andreville, awaiting his trial before the parliament of Lamorie. I wanted to see him, to let him know that he still had friends and supporters among the knights of his mesnie; but I thought it unfair to ask permission for such an errand from Sir John, who was still our constable. To my surprise, the old man raised the subject of his own accord. He was a good knight; and Sir Geoffrey was his lord until sentence had been pronounced on him. It was given out to all the homage that our absent lord had returned to Romanie, and was now awaiting audience with the Prince his uncle. If any of his vassals wished to pay their respects to him in Andreville they had only to give in their names and ask for leave of absence.

When I had been granted leave I slipped off on my own, without taking even Melisande. I avoided the party of knights and servants who were bringing money and clothes and horses on the instructions of the lady Isabel. Sir Geoffrey had rescued me, me alone, from a most unpleasant Grifon prison, and in gratitude I owed him more than the ordinary fealty due to a lord. If I saw him alone I could find out how to be most useful to him. I scarcely admitted, even to myself, that I must see him alone, and talk with him, before I could be sure that I was still on his side.

The parliament had been summoned to meet as soon as possible; but that would be the first Sunday in Lent, for you cannot hold a parliament in winter. I had plenty of time to find out where Sir Geoffrey stood, and where I stood. If, after I had seen him, I still wanted to help him I could perhaps be of use in planning his defence. I had no influence among the barons who would judge him, but at least I knew how the ordinary bachelor knights of Lamorie regarded his desertion. Sir Geoffrey would be out of touch with local opinion, which he frequently misjudged even when he was living in the country; and I was afraid he might trust too much to that mysterious something up his sleeve which he thought would win him a pardon. He always looked on the bright side. He might not grasp that even a papal bull, counter-sealed by the King of France, would not alter the fact that he had deserted his lord in a time of grave danger to wander about Italy with a pretty woman.

The porter of the friary in the suburbs of Andreville made no difficulty when I asked to see Sir Geoffrey. Evidently my lord was not under close arrest, nor taking sanctuary by clinging to the horns of the altar. I was not invited in, but then that often happens when a layman visits a religious house on purely secular business; good friars reserve their hospitality for the needy. Instead I was told that Sir Geoffrey would come out to me, and in the meantime the porter gave me wine and little cakes on a tray.

Then my lord strolled out on foot and unattended, pleased to see me but not at all surprised that I had come. In face he looked actually younger than I remembered him; for I was the older by two bitter campaigns while he had passed his time in the peace and comfort of Italy. There were no lines round his mouth, no grey in his hair, no wrinkles at the corners of his eyes. He smiled pleasantly, without a trace of embarrassment. His fashionable wisps of moustache and beard sprouted from freshly shaved cheeks, and his chestnut hair hung rippling to his shoulders.

He was dressed as a penitent who was also a culprit awaiting trial. Tunic, hose and surcoat were all made of plain grey cloth, without blazon or badge. He wore no jewels, save for a thin gold chain round his neck. His coif was a net of black cords.

But the general effect was not that of a knight fallen into poverty and misfortune. His hose clung to his legs without a wrinkle, his tunic had been tailored to fit him, everything he wore was of the finest broadcloth except where a shirt of very white lawn peeped out with careful negligence at neck and wrists. The simple coif was knotted from pure silk, and his plain black shoes were of soft Cordoba leather. He carried neither sword nor dagger, since he was under arrest; but from his black leather belt hung a wallet of grey doeskin which any lady would have been proud to carry at a great feast. He held his head high, walking with a gay dancer's step.

I thought at first: 'He is dressed to win sympathy. But he will fail, since he is too proud to make himself look humble.' Then I saw, more worthily, that Sir Geoffrey did not dress to make an impression on others but only to please himself. His clothing was appropriate to the best knight in Romanie, fallen under the temporary displeasure of his Prince.

He embraced me as an equal, calling me cousin; then he helped me to hitch my horse to a ring in the wall and walked with me in the street, his hand on my shoulder. After ten years in Romanie I should have been accustomed to walking in a town, but it still seemed to me odd every time I did it. We sauntered on the cobbles between white walls, with a hot sun blazing from a blue sky; the well-dressed burgesses pattered about their business without staring at the most notorious felon in Lamorie, for Grifons have very good manners. Suddenly I was reminded of our first meeting, long ago in La Cremonie. Romanie is a fair land, and I had been very happy in the service of Sir Geoffrey.

'My lord,' I said without thinking, 'the knights of Escorta are bringing money and horses for your use. Why don't you take the next ship for Acre? I will come with you, and together we shall fight the infidel until we recover the Holy Sepulchre.'

'A very good life, cousin William,' he answered gravely, as

though he were genuinely considering it. 'But I am too old to begin again, and we both have duties nearer home. What would become of my Isabel and your Melisande? No, I shall continue in Lamorie. I like it here.'

'What will become of the lady Isabel when the Prince has escheated Escorta? My lord, you must face facts. The old life is over. The best you can hope for is forfeiture, probably imprisonment as well, perhaps even the axe or the rope. Get away while there is time. Your uncle will not pursue you, but if you stand trial you must be found guilty.'

'What? Run away, as though I were ashamed of myself? I have done no wrong, except to default on a service to my overlord. That's nothing worse than getting into debt; though of course the debt must be paid sooner or later. I gather you had a talk with Jeanne, so you must know that I didn't wrong even Sir John de Catabas. I shan't say so in public, of course. As I see it, chivalry demands that I put a slur on my own honour rather than insult the charms of a beautiful lady. My friends will know the truth, because they will accept my denials in private. Otherwise there is only this default of service. The high court must find me guilty, but it's not an offence that calls for serious punishment.'

'We were in grave danger from the Grifons, my lord, and we looked for your lance to help us.'

'Nonsense. From Grifons no one is ever in grave danger. Wave a sword at them and they run away. For a time you were in grave danger from Turks, which is quite another thing. You and I, who were at Pelagonie, know how dangerous they can be. But in the first campaign my loyal Sir John led you better than I could have done it myself; you won quite easily without any help from my lance. And in the second campaign Sir Ancelin de Toucy turned the tables on those pompous Grifon nobles; again a matter in which I could not have helped, since I cannot speak a word of Turkish. My absence made no difference. No, the court will find me guilty, and perhaps threaten all sorts of penalties. Then I shall produce a letter which I have here in my wallet, and they will be so pleased at my news that they would forgive me worse crimes than a pilgrimage to Italy.'

Sir Geoffrey twirled his moustache and tossed his head, already seeing himself the central figure in a crowded parliament.

Agitation made me forget my manners. Hooking a finger into his girdle, I faced him so that he must listen until I had finished.

'My lord, you have a mesnie of loyal knights. We can rescue you from captivity, and get you out of the dominions of Prince William. I at least will fight for you, for so long as you are my lord. But after parliament has given judgement your fees will escheat to the Prince, and you will have no vassals. Then my loyalty must revert to your overlord, Prince William, and if I were to help his enemy I should be recreant. So you must make up your mind. Flee now, with the help of your knights; or face condemnation and punishment. After you have been condemned you will have no knights.'

'Cousin William, you haven't been listening. I shall stand trial, and I suppose I shall be found guilty. But what with my eloquent plea in mitigation, and the letter I shall read to the court at the end of the proceedings, no harm will come to me. I shall leave Andreville a free man, and lord of Escorta. That's what will happen, mark my words. Come to the parliament and see for yourself.'

He led me into a tavern. When the landlord came running to serve him he pressed me to share a flagon of costly Italian wine. But I realised that he had no money, for his wallet was fastened and sealed securely; so I said I preferred the local Malvoisie and paid for it before he could interfere. Like every other Grifon in Lamorie, the landlord valued the promise to pay of Sir Geoffrey de Bruyere as better than mint-fresh hyperpers. I did not want his faith to be shattered, when Sir Geoffrey was outlaw and penniless.

We talked for a while of Italy, and the prospects of the coming war between King Manfred and the Guelfs; when I took my leave Sir Geoffrey bade me carry his duty to the lady Isabel and say that he would soon wait on her. But I carefully did not promise to deliver his message, which I thought went too far even coming from the best knight in all Romanie.

As you will have seen, I had no chance to demand an explanation of my lord's conduct. Evidently he was not ashamed of himself, and confident that the parliament would not blame him though he must be found guilty of a technical default. When I got back to my lodging I decided that I was still bound by my oath of homage, at least until the trial. I would attend the parliament, and decide where my duty lay after hearing Sir Geoffrey's defence.

The high court met in the old round church of Santa Sophia; not on horseback in the open, as was the custom at Nicles. For Andreville is the seat of the law courts, a city of peace; and it is unusual for knights and barons to ride to it in arms.

Of course the church was crowded. The lords of parliament filled the circle under the dome, the necessary clerks and officials sat on the steps before the altar-screen, eager spectators crowded the doorways. But by this time Melisande had joined me, and she persuaded the Grifon sacristan to find places for us at the front of a steep narrow gallery. We looked down on coifed heads crowding below, shifting and turning and mingling; for all the lords must stand save for Prince William, who sat in a highbacked chair of state.

In a little cleared space before the altar-screen stood Sir Geoffrey, dressed in his neat and sober clothes of grey. It gave me a pang to see him in that splendid assembly, the only knight without a weapon. I don't hold with the Italian fashion of carrying swords in church, so as to make it easy to murder your enemies at the high altar; but on formal public occasions every knight should carry a sword or at least a dagger, to show his quality. Sir Geoffrey was alone, as well as unarmed. He looked so isolated and helpless that we must all feel sorry for him.

The trial began with endless time-wasting legal rigmarole. Andreville is a warren of lawyers, and they wanted to show the gentry how these things should be done. A parliament on horseback gets to business more quickly, since no lawyer can keep his horse quiet long enough to prove the obvious. Now someone must swear on the Gospels that there had been a Grifon invasion, and someone else that Sir Geoffrey had been summoned to the muster, and someone else that he did not come, and someone else that he later returned from oversea and surrendered to the Prince's justice, and the last one of all that the man in the grey surcoat over there was that Sir Geoffrey they had all been talking about. Everyone in court knew it already, but it had to be gone through at tedious length before the serious business of the parliament might begin.

At last the culprit was asked what he had to say. Sir Geoffrey tossed his hair, pointed a toe, put a hand on his hip, and launched out into a prepared oration.

At his opening sentence the audience rustled with surprise, and in her excitement Melisande pinched my thigh until I had to push her hand away. He was speaking, like any old-fashioned minstrel, of the over-mastering power of Love.

Love, he explained, conquers all. Then he said it again in Latin to make it sound more impressive. Love has misguided some of the noblest knights in the world, bringing them to sin and even to shameful death. Long ago Sir Achilles withdrew from the battle for love of the damsel Briseis; Sir Antony lost the empire of the world for love of Queen Cleopatra; even Sir Lancelot, the doughtiest champion of the Round Table, betrayed his lord for love of Queen Guinevere. The Duchess Eleanor of Aquitaine, the fairest lady of her day and Queen successively of France and England, had wrecked a mighty Crusade by her fatal beauty. (At this there was a stir, for the indiscretions of Queen Eleanor were still well remembered. She was the grandmother of the King of England then reigning.) Love is a devouring force. The nobler the spirit, the more easily does Love overcome it. He asked his hearers to note that all the stories of disastrous Love dealt with noble knights. The grosser souls of burgesses and peasants were not so easily infected;

while the clergy, by the special Grace of God, were notoriously immune. (Here he stared fixedly at the leman of the Archbishop of Patras, a grocer's wife and dressed beyond her station, who sat in one of the galleries.)

He himself was a knight, who had devoted his life to feats of arms as earnestly as anyone who sat in judgement on him. Just as once his horse had been pierced by Turkish arrows, when he had been chosen by universal acclaim to lead all the chivalry of Romanie in a desperate charge, so now Cupid's arrow had pierced his heart. (His cultured audience could follow the reference.) For love of a fair lady he had abandoned his duty. For more than a year he had been blinded by love. Yet this madness, though all-conquering, might sometimes be cured. The cure was, naturally, the example of a more noble knight.

So it had been with him, Sir Geoffrey concluded. He had been summoned before King Manfred, that stainless paladin. The King had reasoned with him, but the example of royal devotion to duty had been even more impressive. The King of Sicily was a worthy son of his famous father, the mighty Emperor, who had never been turned from his course by feminine charms. Sir Geoffrey had acknowledged his fault. Thanks to the virtues of King Manfred he had come home to submit to the judgement of his peers.

'What is he getting at?' Melisande murmured in the pause that followed. 'It wasn't like that at all. He wasn't in love with Jeanne, and he never touched her. Most of the barons know the truth, or have heard rumours of it. Besides, his chosen examples prove that he isn't speaking seriously. King Manfred notoriously neglects his duty; though his dissipation is hunting, not love-making. As for the Emperor Frederick, he was never influenced by love; but he kept infidel dancing-girls by the score and fathered bastards all over Italy. Is Sir Geoffrey quite deliberately making fun of the court? The barons would like to acquit him, if he gives them an excuse. But they will harden their hearts if he makes them look foolish.'

Sir Geoffrey was speaking again:

'One last point, my lords. In strict law it has nothing to do with the accusation you are judging, but perhaps you ought to bear it in mind when you decide my sentence. I have here a letter from King Manfred. I shall ask a clerk to read it aloud, but I know what it contains. The King of Sicily sends help to his friends in Lamorie, three hundred sergeants and their pay for three years. They are even now on the sea. They will be at the disposal of the Prince of Lamorie to serve him as though they were his own vassals. The King makes only one condition. I am to command them, or they will go home again.'

He ripped open the fastenings of his wallet, and with a bow handed a parchment to a clerk.

Sir Geoffrey led his rejoicing mesnie back to Carytena. He rode fully armed, himself bearing the banner of Escorta; for Sir John de Catabas had very sensibly announced that age and infirmity compelled him to retire to end his days in peace on his remote manor. Peasants came out to greet their returning lord, led by Grifon priests. Bonfires flared on the hills, and everyone was gay.

I turned to Melisande, riding beside me.

'There he goes, once more the best knight in all Romanie, not a whit older or wiser than when I was presented to him at La Cremonie, in the good old days when there were no Grifons in Mistra. With a destrier between his legs and mail on his shoulders he can't go wrong. The trouble comes when he sits in his hall in peacetime. Then he follows where his fancy leads him, and there's no telling what he will do next.'

'None the less, the best knight in all Romanie,' she answered. 'You should be proud to serve him. But I wish I could have seen the guilty pair in Italy. Sir Geoffrey in love with his own prowess, thinking only of his superb strength and hardihood. And little Jeanne in love with her own beauty, thinking only of her well-shaped little body, which must not be marred by angry Grifons. What a couple they made! Each lost in self-contemplation, each utterly satisfied with his own person. Yet all the time they were together. What did they find to talk about? The wonder is that they didn't part in sheer absence of mind, not noticing that the other was no longer there. He never talks about her, have you noticed? Soon he will be describing the shrines he visited in Italy, quite forgetting that he did not visit them alone.'

'The best knight of this degenerate age,' said I, 'and it's an honour to ride in his mesnie. But I wish he would sometimes listen to good advice. I can't see our little Geoffrey ever getting a fee from his glorious and chivalrous godfather. Hallo, we must pull up for another address of welcome.'

CHAPTER FIFTEEN

Conclusion

Sir Geoffrey went home to serve in the continual war against the Grifons of Mistra and to defend his people from the rebellious Esclavons of the mountains. For Carytena was now a border castle, not nearly so pleasant to live in as when I first knew it. The Ghibelline sergeants whose arrival had won his pardon did not stay for the full three years of the treaty. King Manfred withdrew them after a few months, when he needed all his power to face the Count of Anjou. But the Guelfs won all the same, King Manfred was killed, and the Count of Anjou became King Charles of Sicily. So Lamorie joined the Guelfs and we all found ourselves faithful soldiers of Holy Church.

Prince William, nettled by the sneers of stout Ghibellines who reproached him as a turncoat, led his knights to Italy where they gained great glory fighting for King Charles at Tagliacozzo. But Sir Geoffrey and the mesnie of Escorta stayed at home, for now that the Grifons held Mistra raiding never ceased. It was not a bit like the Lamorie I had known in the old days; now it was a harried, hungry land, where peasants hid in caves and the cattle limped from being galloped into hiding to escape plunderers.

In the spring of 1271, more than sixteen years after I had first come to Romanie, Sir Geoffrey rode with some of the senior knights of his household to his other castle of Bucelet, down the valley. News had reached Carytena that the castellan was gravely ill, but when we reached the outer gate we saw the banner furled in sign of mourning, and the shield of Sir Thomas the old castellan hanging wreathed in myrtle over the main gate.

'God rest his soul, he was a loyal knight,' said Sir Geoffrey, drawing rein. 'I must call to condole with the widow, but we had better camp in the fields outside until after the funeral, which I suppose will be tomorrow. There are other affairs to be considered, for the welfare of the barony. Cousin William, come aside with me a moment.'

We dismounted together, and stood looking up at the bare grey stone of the castle, grim and forbidding against the blue sky. The castle of Bucelet was built for war; it shows little ornament and seems to smell of blood.

'Not a cheerful place,' said Sir Geoffrey, 'for all that I was born in it and feel at home in it. Carytena is more comfortable. All the same, the knight who commands in this castle is very much his own master. It must be someone I can trust. Cousin William, would you like to hold Bucelet for me?'

'In fee, my lord?' I asked; rather ungraciously, but I was too surprised to remember my manners.

'You forget, cousin William,' my lord answered with a rueful smile. 'How can I give land in fee when Escorta is mine only for my life? No, you would hold it as my castellan, during pleasure. But even that is promotion for a landless household knight.'

He saw the disappointment in my face. Suddenly he sat down on a large stone, forgetting the dead castellan and the errand for which he had dismounted.

'It's time we settled your future, cousin William. Your children are growing up with no home but Carytena, and though they are welcome while I am lord of Escorta my successor may want that tower for his own cousins. That's the trouble. I can't make any plans. For myself it doesn't matter. I am the best knight in all Romanie, and if my uncle turned me out tomorrow I would be welcome in any mesnie. With any luck I shall be dead before I am too old to ride in mail. But you mustn't squander your life serving me for wages, just because we happen to hit it off together. Is there any other lord whom you would like to serve?'

'Indeed not, my lord. How could I serve a de la Roche or a

Tournay after so many years in the mesnie of Bruyere, the best mesnie in all Romanie? I should miss you every hour of the day.'

'Very well. I thought that would be your answer. I have news for you. A Venetian has reached Clarence, saying that the lord Edward, son of your King Henry, is leading a great power to the Holy Land. You could join him in Cyprus. It's only right that you should visit Syria, since for so many years you have been a Crusader. Take your family with you. If the lord Edward gives you a place in his mesnie you may go back with him to the west. If all else fails Carytena will be waiting for you. But in Lamorie the sun is setting. When I am gone, and my uncle, this country will be a bad home for western knights. Go, while you are still young enough to begin again in your own country. Go, and take my affection with you.'

In the autumn of 1272 I returned to England in the mesnie of Prince Edward, to find that King Henry was dead and my new lord King of England. Then my eldest brother died without children, and since my other brother was a clerk our little ancestral fee came to me. I live quietly on my manor, and my mail hangs on a peg; though when the young men muster against the Welsh they value the advice of a far-travelled Crusader who has seen battles greater even than Lewes or Evesham. My William is in religion, a Crusading knight of St John of the Hospital. But both Geoffrey and Sophie have married; their children, always in and out of my solar, have been the occasion of my writing and the chief hindrance to it. The little patch of land that came to me from my father will descend to my grandson; no man can see further than that. Mine has been a good life, with adventure when I was young and the home of my childhood waiting for my old age. But the best thing of all was that I saw Lamorie in its glory, a land from out of the old romances, where good knights defended splendid castles against savages and infidels, a fairy-land whose like will never come again.

Even now Melisande gets letters from her Grifon friends, who think nothing of sitting down to cover a big sheet of paper. We know the main lines of what has been happening in Lamorie.

In 1275 Sir Geoffrey died, by an absurd mischance. After a raid on an Esclavon village on a hot day he was imprudent enough to drink from the village fountain. When he was younger he would never allow his followers to taste Esclavon water; in England you cannot imagine how Esclavons live in their villages. The barony of Escorta escheated to the overlord, Prince William.

It is said that even the birds in their nests mourned for the best knight in all Romanie. In Lamorie both Franks and Grifons wept for him; and here on the remote March of Wales the family whom he fostered see the world as poorer and more grey without him.

Soon afterwards the lady Isabel married Sir Hugh de Brienne, Count of Lecce in the Kingdom of Sicily. She has borne children to her second husband, so there may have been something in her complaints about the climate of Carytena.

Prince William died in 1278 and King Charles of Sicily took over the Principality. An Angevin governor rules in Andreville, and the high court of Lamorie has lost its independence. The whole land is a mere outlying province of Sicily, ruled and defended by Italians who go there for a few years and never regard it as their home. French knights of good blood no longer ride over the thyme of the hillsides; 'Frank' now means an Italian mercenary, thinking only of the next payday. The old courteous life has vanished.

But I have seen it: the colours of western blazonry burning under the bright sun, castles of shimmering white marble, the Latin chant in the Cathedral of Our Lady of Satines, columns erected by the wise men of old and the soaring domes of the cunning Grifons. That life will never come again. It ought to be remembered.

And I knew the best knight in the world, a knight so gallant that he did not hold himself bound by the rules which bind ordinary men. But even the best knight in the world can be too reckless of consequences.

AUTHOR'S NOTE

This is in outline a true story, even to Sir Geoffrey's address to his tent-pole before the battle of Pelagonie. See Rennell Rodd, *The Princes of Achaia*, Edwin Arnold, 1907, and William Miller, *The Latins in the Levant*, John Murray, 1908. The only entirely imaginary characters are the narrator and his wife, though there was a genuine Briwerr family in England. Public events happened as I have described them, though I have used my imagination in supplying motives and explanations, especially for love affairs.

The narrator's opinion of Greeks, Turks, and other foreigners is his own, and not necessarily that of the author.